Candy was feelin

It was so long sinc
wifery that she had
it felt like, and the
infant, after so much trauma, tore at her
heart-strings.

Kirk looked at her searchingly. She smiled up
into his eyes, and he gave her arm a little
pat. Quite suddenly she was conscious of a
sense of communication between them, and
a strange little thrill crept over her.

Dear Reader

Nature gets its own back this month! Stella Whitelaw's DELUGE takes us to the dangerous waters of the North Sea, and Meredith Webber's WHISPER IN THE HEART includes a terrifying bush fire! There's water in HEARTS AT SEA by Clare Lavenham, following a cruise ship, but STILL WATERS—despite the title!—by Kathleen Farrell brings us to earth in Edinburgh. All good stuff for you to enjoy.

The Editor

!!!STOP PRESS!!! If you enjoy reading these medical books, have you ever thought of writing one? We are always looking for new writers for LOVE ON CALL, and want to hear from you. Send for the guidelines, and start writing!

Clare Lavenham was a Londoner, but has lived mostly in Suffolk. She is widowed with two grown-up children. She has written articles, short stories and one-act plays, but her work as a hospital librarian led to her writing Medical Romances. She gets her backgrounds from her library work, and consults various medical friends when necessary. Her favourite occupations, apart from writing, are walking in the country and gardening.

Recent titles by the same author:

LOVE IN A MIST
SISTER AT HILLSIDE

HEARTS
AT SEA

BY

CLARE LAVENHAM

MILLS & BOON

MILLS & BOON LIMITED
ETON HOUSE, 18-24 PARADISE ROAD
RICHMOND, SURREY TW9 1SR

*First published in Great Britain 1994
by Mills & Boon Limited*

© Clare Lavenham 1994

*Australian copyright 1994   Philippine copyright 1994
This edition 1994*

ISBN 0 263 78758 3

Set in Times 11 on 12 pt.

03-9409-42087

Made and printed in Great Britain

CHAPTER ONE

CANDY BRYANT stood on the dock at Southampton and stared up at the beautiful white ship towering over her. It was so big and grand that she could scarcely believe it was to be her home for an indefinite period, yet the name *Bergsen* in huge letters on the side assured her that it was. This ship looked like a liner, about to sail across the Atlantic; she had expected something much smaller for a trip up the Baltic.

Right at the top she could see strings of brightly coloured bunting fluttering in the breeze—presumably put there to welcome the passengers who would arrive later—and further down there were rows of windows, clean and sparkling in the May sunshine. Below these, hundreds of portholes continued right down to the waterline. It was impossible not to wonder which of them would be hers.

The bulging holdall was slipping off her shoulder, and on the other side her suitcase was weighing her down. Taking a deep breath, Candy began to struggle up the gangway. An uncomfortable swaying motion accompanied each step but at last she reached the gaping hole in the ship's side where she found a crew-member on duty.

His appearance was Scandinavian but he seemed to understand English and nodded when Candy told him she was the new nurse. By following the signs she found her way to Reception, where a fair girl in a smart navy uniform with epaulettes on her shoulders gave her two keys—one for her cabin and one for the hospital.

'There are other keys you should have,' she said, 'but the doctor has those. I don't think he has come on board yet so you will have plenty of time to unpack.'

The reception area was large, with a thick maroon carpet and silver-grey panelled walls hung with oil paintings. There was a profusion of flowering plants, and two very grand staircases leading up and down like in a hotel. Candy had never been in the Savoy but she fancied that it must be something like this. As she looked vaguely round, wondering in which direction to go, the girl called out to her.

'Your cabin is two decks down and there's a lift round the corner.'

She found it without difficulty but was momentarily disappointed to find she had an 'inside' cabin with neither window nor porthole. This meant permanent electric light but it was astonishing how quickly she got used to it. The air-conditioning was excellent and it was nicely furnished. She had her own toilet apartment and plenty of storage space, and she would never have to do any domestic chores. Lovely!

She had shared her mother's house for the last two years, ever since her parents' divorce. Many times she had regretted the impulsive gesture which had made her give up her flatlet at the hospital, losing at the same time her cherished independence.

It was another—and much crazier—impulse which had made her throw up her staff nurse's job and go off to be a ship's nurse. But that was something she preferred not to think about.

She changed into her white uniform dress and looked at herself critically in the long mirror. Her red hair, hanging straight from a centre parting, curved inwards at the level of her small, firm chin. The colour was much admired by some people, but Candy would have liked it better if she had had the green eyes which went with it instead of blue-grey.

Now to explore the hospital. She already knew where it was—right next door! What could be handier? It had already been made plain to her that she would be on call at night and her door was clearly marked 'Nurse'.

Her hand shook a little as she fitted the key into the lock and she was very conscious of her total ignorance of shipboard life, and in particular the medical side of it. The only hospital she had known so far had been huge. What would this one be like?

Even more important—how would she get on with the doctor?

The door opened directly into the consulting-room, which resembled that of a prosperous GP, with a mahogany desk, several comfortable chairs and an examination couch with its own curtains. Everything seemed to be of the best possible quality. An annexe was lined with cupboards, all locked with their contents invisible, but the drugs cupboard was the usual glass-fronted type and Candy studied it with interest. It was extremely well-stocked, with all the drugs in regular use and, in addition, several which she recognised, from her hospital experience, as being newly on the market.

She was so absorbed that she did not realise that the outer door had opened again. An indignant male voice alerted her and she swung round in dismay.

'I was blaming the cleaner for leaving that door unlocked, but I suppose it was you?'

A very tall man filled the doorway into the annexe. Candy, only five feet three inches, was so startled by his appearance that she was momentarily silent. He only needed a horned helmet and leather clothing and he could have been a Viking, stepped straight out of the pages of her school history book. His fawn trousers and navy shirt were normal enough but his hair was a burnished gold, cut so that it closely fitted his head, and his eyes were a particularly vivid blue.

He evidently got tired of waiting for a reply for he went on severely, 'That door is *never* left unlocked—unless, of course, the surgery is in use. As far as I know there isn't a drug problem on the *Bergsen* but you can't be too careful.'

Candy said breathlessly, 'I'm terribly sorry—I didn't realise I had left it unlocked.'

Surprisingly, he smiled, transforming his whole face. 'I don't think you'll forget again, so let's put it behind us and get on with a proper introduction, shall we? I imagine you're my new nurse?'

'Yes, I'm Candida Bryant, but most people call me Candy.'

'Nice to meet you, Candy.' He enveloped her

small hand in his big one and treated her to another smile. 'I'm Kirk Nielsen.'

Candy smiled weakly back and wondered how much longer he was going to hold her hand. His firm grip was doing odd things to her equilibrium, which was ridiculous when she'd only just met the man.

Suddenly businesslike, he released her abruptly, went over to the desk and produced a large bunch of keys from his pocket. Dumping them on the bare surface, he began to sort them through.

'There are several keys here you ought to have.' He handed her half a dozen. 'Those are for the cupboards. In addition, you must be able to unlock the operating theatre and the small ward attached to it.'

'I don't expect you have many serious cases,' Candy ventured.

'No, but one must be prepared for absolutely anything. Normally I wouldn't operate on board unless it was absolutely necessary—to save a life, for instance—but it can happen. Have you done any theatre work recently?'

There was nothing weak about Candy's smile this time. It was positively triumphant. 'I was a theatre staff nurse, Dr Nielsen.'

'Splendid! Then you won't mind being anaesthetist, assistant and theatre sister all rolled into one?'

'I shall do my best,' she said demurely, and they both laughed.

As she followed her boss on a tour of inspection, Candy noticed that he limped slightly.

Perhaps he had been in an accident? There had to be some good reason for a doctor of his age—apparently about thirty—taking the comparatively easy job of medical officer on board ship.

'I've been on two cruises on the *Bergsen*.' He was standing in the middle of a small ward containing two beds as he spoke. 'On the first a man slipped and dislocated his elbow. He was elderly and suffered badly from shock, so I thought it advisable to keep him in here for the night. The only other time when this ward was used was when a passenger had a bad heart attack.' He gave her a wicked grin. 'It's handy having the nurse so near.'

'I suppose *your* cabin is at a safe distance?' Candy came back at him smartly.

'Quite right. I've got a very nice outside cabin among the staff quarters on the boat deck. I'll show it to you some time.' He unlocked another door and displayed a small operating theatre with some pride. 'This is very well-appointed. You name it and we've got it.'

Candy didn't attempt to do anything of the sort but she duly admired the claustrophobic little room, hoping she would never have to become more intimately acquainted with it. Back at the hospital she had been an experienced and confident theatre nurse, knowing exactly what was required of her. It would be different here, with all those other jobs to do in addition to normal duties.

'I suppose they've told you you'll be expected to act as courier when you're not busy with medical matters?' Kirk led the way back to the surgery. 'There are five full-time couriers but there's a great deal to do on the social side on a ship this size, so the nurse gets roped in as well. You'll probably find it interesting but you do have to remember that you're always on call medically, just as I am myself.'

It didn't sound as though she would be bored for lack of something to do!

They left the hospital together and walked along the apparently endless corridor leading to the stairs. Candy was intrigued to notice that there were bars fixed to the wall on both sides, between the cabin doors, and she wondered what their purpose could be. Suddenly it occurred to her that they might be for use in rough weather.

Kirk confirmed it when she asked him. 'I hope you're a good sailor?' he enquired, looking down at her with one eyebrow raised.

'I—I don't really know. I've crossed the Channel several times but the sea's been fairly calm.'

'There are some excellent seasickness tablets in the drugs cupboard. Just let me know if you have a problem.'

They parted at the top of the stairs and Candy set out to do some exploring and try to learn her way about the ship. Fifteen minutes later, she was out on the sports deck, staring at odd, white-painted markings, and trying to sort out her impressions, when a loudspeaker just above her head burst into life, startling her considerably.

'Calling Dr Nielsen—will Dr Nielsen come immediately to the purser's office, please?'

Candy hesitated, uncertain whether she should also answer the summons. It had sounded like an emergency but might be nothing more than some formality concerning the doctor alone.

Better to go and find out rather than ignore it.

Hurrying down the companionway leading to the promenade deck, she realised that she didn't know where the purser's office was situated, but it must be near Reception and she thought she could find that. The maroon-carpeted area was empty but there were voices coming from an open door and she went immediately to look in.

A bearded man in uniform and the fair girl she had seen before were standing rather helplessly beside a chair on which there sat a white-faced young man with thin dark hair, also in uniform. He was holding up his left hand with a handkerchief wrapped round it, and blood was rapidly seeping through and trickling down his wrist.

'Can I help?' Candy went up to the chair and, seeing her white nurse's dress, the others stood back with an air of relief. 'What's happened?'

It was the girl who answered her. 'Poor Steve—he has cut his hand very bad.'

Candy could see that. Very gently she unwound the handkerchief and revealed a nasty gash on the ball of the thumb. It was bleeding very freely and she guessed that it would need stitching. In the meantime, she would have to return to the hospital and find what was needed for bandaging.

At that moment the patient added to the drama by fainting. He would have fallen to the floor had not the bearded officer caught him. Holding him upright, he looked helplessly at Candy.

She was beginning, 'It would be better to lay him——' when Kirk came hurrying in and immediately took charge.

He was now wearing the same uniform as the others except that he was minus a tie and she guessed the summons had caught him in the middle of changing.

'This bleeding has got to be stopped.' He was on his knees beside the patient, now carefully laid out on the floor. Glancing up at Candy, he went on, 'I shall need something to make a proper pad and a bandage to keep it in place. Be as quick as you can.'

She sped back to the lower deck, but it took a few minutes to locate what she needed, and when she eventually returned she found that Steve had come round and Kirk was talking to him quietly. The others had vanished.

'Thanks.' Kirk held out his hand and then let it drop. 'You might as well do the bandaging, Candy. I hope your first aid's OK?'

'It used to be.' She started work, very much aware of his critical blue eyes, and aimed at nothing less than perfection.

Steve was explaining how it happened. 'It was the stupidest thing. I was only trying to undo a knot with the point of my penknife when it slipped. I keep it pretty sharp and it went straight into my hand.'

'Very neat,' Kirk murmured when Candy had finished. He turned to his patient. 'The nurse will see you to your cabin and you'd better take a short rest after passing out like that.'

It seemed a long way and Candy tried to

memorise it. Sitting on the bed, Steve looked at her ruefully.

'I feel such a fool, fainting just because I'd cut myself.'

'It was an extremely bad cut and that fleshy part of the thumb always bleeds freely.'

'So what? I'm supposed to be a tough guy, not the heroine of a Victorian novel.'

'Some people faint much more easily than others. It's nothing to do with toughness.'

'I never used to do that sort of thing,' he muttered, lying down with a sigh.

'Have you been feeling particularly tired lately?' she probed gently.

But he only shrugged and avoided her gaze. Wondering for a moment if he was anaemic, Candy remembered the quantity and redness of the blood and decided against it. The fact remained that he was far too pale for a young man working on a ship, even one doing an office job.

Noting that it was lunchtime, she moved towards the door, but the patient halted her by asking when the stitching was likely to take place.

'I simply can't be out of action for long,' he said anxiously. 'I shall be terribly busy—we all will—when the passengers start arriving around three o'clock.'

'I can't tell you exactly but I'll come and fetch you as soon as the doctor gives the word.' Candy paused with her hand on the doorknob. 'You will keep as still as possible, won't you? It's important that the bleeding should stop. Would you like me to organise some lunch for you?'

Steve made a grimace of disgust. 'No, thanks. I still feel a bit sick.'

She gave him a sympathetic smile and began to make her way slowly down two decks to the dining-room. It seemed strange to be on a ship with no passengers. A member of the crew was cleaning windows, and a little group of men was examining a mysterious piece of machinery on part of the promenade deck not open to the public. Otherwise it was quiet.

A few yards away on the quay vans were still unloading stores through a vast hole in the *Bergsen*'s side much lower down, but the Southampton customs buildings in the background looked deserted. Leaning on the rail, Candy studied the scene for a few minutes and then left the warm May sunshine to plunge into the cool, air-conditioned interior, where empty bars and lounges awaited the arrival of the passengers who were to take temporary possession of them.

She found the big dining-room and entered hesitantly, looking about her. Most of the tables had not yet been laid but a few in the far corner were occupied by a varied collection of people, the men in uniform and most of the girls in informal gear. Near by a long table was set out with an assortment of buffet food.

Everybody seemed to be talking animatedly and no one took the slightest notice of her approach, but as she paused she caught sight of Kirk's golden head. He was leaning forward to talk to a girl with a mass of long dark hair hanging all round her face. There was an empty chair next to him and, suddenly finding her courage, Candy made for it with determination.

'May I join you?' she asked.

Kirk glanced up and looked at her blankly for a moment, his mind obviously still on what his companion had been saying. Then he rose to his feet, bestowed on her another of his charming smiles, and pulled out the empty chair.

'Sure! Go and get yourself some food and then I'll introduce you.'

As Candy loaded her plate, a small part of her mind remained with the man she had just left. He was certainly incredibly good-looking but there was something slightly odd about that smile. After thinking about it, she realised that it never seemed to reach his eyes. Behind that vivid blueness, there was something troubling him.

'This is Dawn,' Kirk said when she returned. 'She's one of the full-time couriers. And this is Candy, my new nurse.'

The dark girl nodded in an offhand sort of way. She was extremely attractive, with a clear, tanned skin and huge dark eyes, and though she was sitting down it wasn't hard to guess that she would be tall, with the long legs of a model.

'The others are all scattered around,' he went on, 'and you'll soon get to know them. They're a friendly bunch.'

Candy didn't think that Dawn looked particularly friendly. Very likely she resented having her conversation with the doctor interrupted. At that moment the girl leaned forward and read Candy's name-tag, on which she had written 'Nurse Candida Bryant', which was what she was accustomed to wearing on her bosom at the hospital.

'That's much too formal. You should have put Candy in large letters, and Nurse underneath. Get yourself a new tag from the office after lunch.'

'OK.' Candy smiled to hide her resentment, and then asked Kirk when he intended to suture Steve's cut.

'Some time before the passengers get here. He'll be needed back at his job by then.' He looked at his watch. 'Say in an hour's time. Bring him down to the surgery and I'll be there.'

Dawn was doing her best to recapture his attention and Candy made no attempt at further conversation. The food was delicious and she thoroughly enjoyed it, at the same time absorbing snatches of conversation which reached her from various directions.

There was a courier at the next table who caught her eye and smiled. She had leaf-brown hair worn in a long plait over her shoulder, and a round, cheerful-looking face, Afterwards they walked out of the dining-room together, and the girl introduced herself as Emma Forbes, the keep-fit leader and teacher of ballroom dancing.

'I wouldn't have thought people'd want to do keep-fit on a cruise,' Candy said.

'You'd be surprised! Actually, it's a necessity with some. I take a class every morning after breakfast in the big lounge—except Sundays when there's a short service. Why don't you come along and try it? Several of the couriers do.'

'I can't. That's the time when the doctor and I have to be at the hospital in case any patients turn up.'

'What do you think of him?' Emma asked
curiously.

'Kirk? I—well, I hardly know him. He's a bit
overwhelming, don't you think?'

'Those macho types don't appeal to me, but
some people certainly find his Swedish good looks
rather devastating——'

'Is he Swedish?' Candy interrupted.

'I believe he has some Swedish blood. Anyway,
your predecessor found him a bit too glamorous
for safety and it ended with her leaving the ship.
There were all sorts of rumours but I don't know
if any of them were true.'

Candy made no comment. Familiar with the
way rumours spread around a hospital, she knew
that it was possible that such stories could easily
have no foundation in fact at all. Or, of course,
they might be at least partly true.

There was one certainty, though. The glamorous Dr Nielsen wasn't going to sweep his new
nurse off her feet. Past experience—still painfully
recent—had definitely put her on her guard
against any fresh emotional entanglement. In
future she would assume that no man could be
trusted and act accordingly.

Stifling a tiny, rebellious hope that she might
one day be proved wrong, Candy went off to
continue her exploration of the *Bergsen*.

Twelve hours later, she stood leaning on the
rail of the observation deck right at the top
of the ship. It had been a strenuous day and
she was tired both mentally and physically.
The sensible thing would be to go straight to

bed but she needed to unwind first.

It had been interesting watching the passengers arrive. There seemed to be a wide variation in age but all had looked well-heeled—the women immaculate in expensive clothes, the men wearing the latest in sportswear. They were of various nationalities but mostly English or American, with Swedish coming next, due, Candy supposed, to it being a Swedish ship.

Kirk had instructed her to unlock the surgery during the early evening, just in case anyone needed medical attention, but had only put in a brief appearance himself. Everyone had been busy unpacking and they had no patients.

'It'll be different in the morning,' he'd warned her with a smile.

Later, changing for dinner, Candy had chosen a plain black skirt teamed up with a white silk top, cut low at the back and front. To her relief, it had turned out to be just right, since few people had dressed up much tonight. There was dancing, though, and she'd found her partners a bit overwhelming, so that she'd felt she simply must get some reviving fresh air for a short while before going to bed.

The night was deliciously cool and she drew in deep breaths of ozone-laden air. On her right the lights of the Isle of Wight were sliding slowly past, and on the port-side the south coast of England was gradually receding. The cruise, which was to take them as far as St Petersburg, had begun and she ought to be feeling excited and happy.

Instead of that she was suddenly overwhelmed by such a sense of loneliness that a sob rose in her throat and threatened to choke her. Back in Canterbury her mother would already be in bed and asleep, and at the hospital the patients would all have been settled for the night long ago. She could so easily still have been part of that familiar scene, if only. . .

'A beautiful night,' Kirk said softly from behind her. 'May I share it with you?'

Candy swallowed convulsively and somehow found her voice. 'It's a free country.'

'That was not exactly the most enthusiastic welcome I've ever received,' he observed thoughtfully, joining her at the rail. 'If you really want to be alone, I'll go and stand on a different part of the deck.'

The suggestion was so absurd that Candy laughed but made no attempt to reply. Far below the sea slapped gently at the sides of the ship, and overhead the dark, moonless sky was sprinkled all over with stars. The lights of England were fainter now and soon they would be out in the Channel. A freshening wind was causing the temperature to drop rapidly and Candy felt a shiver beginning to travel all over her. Since their folded arms were touching on the rail, she knew there was no hope of hiding it from Kirk.

'You're cold!' he exclaimed at once. 'Why didn't you bring a wrap? It's daft to get hot dancing and then come up here.'

Candy accepted the rebuke with unusual meekness, knowing it to be deserved. 'It was so hot downstairs——' she began.

'Below.'

'What? Oh, I see. I suppose I've got to remem-

ber to say forward instead of front and aft when
I mean back. Anyway, it was so hot below that
I felt I must get outside for a short time.' She
paused and then added, 'It's lovely up here.' And
to her annoyance her voice shook slightly.

'It's my guess,' Kirk said, 'that you were not
only feeling hot but also a bit depressed. A big
ship full of total strangers can be a trifle unnerv-
ing.' He paused, and when she said nothing added
quietly, 'Has it brought on an attack of home-
sickness?'

'No!' The word burst from her with such force
that she felt it needed qualifying. 'It was to
get away from home that I came on this cruise
ship.'

'Would you care to enlarge on that?'

'I would not!'

'OK, OK, I only asked. Maybe you'll tell me
one day, when we know each other a bit better.'

'I might,' she said cautiously, horribly aware
that if she stayed here much longer, alone with
this man on a desert island of uninhabited deck,
he'd probably have the whole humiliating story
out of her. 'I really must go in, Kirk. It must be
one o'clock and I'm very tired.'

As they moved away from the rail another
shiver seized her and he slipped his arm round
her shoulders and drew her close. The warmth of
his body enfolded her comfortingly and she felt an
odd reluctance to leave the shelter of his embrace
when they reached the top of the companionway.

He descended the steep steps carefully and she
again noticed that slight limp as they walked along
the next deck. After the way he'd been quizzing

her, she had no hesitation in asking him if he'd
been in an accident.

They were halfway across the sports deck when
Kirk answered her.

'Yes. I'll tell you about it some time, but not
now. I'm too damn tired and so are you.'

Another companionway brought them to the
boat deck—where the lifeboats which everybody
hoped would never be needed were strung up on
both sides—and here Kirk halted.

'My cabin is here so I'll say goodnight.' His
lips brushed her forehead with the lightness of a
butterfly's wing. 'See you tomorrow, Sugar
Candy.' With a nonchalant wave, he disappeared
down a narrow passage.

In her own cabin, several decks below, Candy
found sleep elusive. Thoughts, impressions, memories tossed and turned in the maelstrom of her
mind, but eventually there emerged one which
made her smile.

Whoever had allocated the staff cabins on the
Bergsen had made it pretty certain that there
wouldn't be any night-time intimacy between doctor and nurse!

CHAPTER TWO

CANDY was early at the hospital in the morning but she found Kirk there before her. As she entered the phone began to ring and he answered it. A high-pitched female voice said something at great length and, when the flow ceased at last, he assured the lady politely that he would send the nurse up at once.

'What was all that about?' Candy asked.

'Lady Wickham wishes you to visit her in her stateroom on the veranda deck and take with you a supply of sleeping pills. She's forgotten to bring her own and hasn't slept a wink.'

Candy found the pills without difficulty and set off at once. She knew little about the veranda deck but managed to locate it. As she walked down the comparatively wide corridor, looking for stateroom number five, her feet sank into the carpet without a sound, and all the normal ship noises, such as the throbbing of engines, were inaudible. More than ever the *Bergsen* reminded her of a hotel.

The illusion was continued when she got inside, where her ladyship was awaiting her. The luxury cabin was panelled in cream picked out with gold, and the twin beds had padded cream headboards and quilts in soft rose-pink. Through an open door, Candy glimpsed an *en-suite* sitting-room with comfortable chairs and big vases of roses and freesias.

One bed was empty but the other was occupied by a very thin elderly lady with beautiful white hair. She might not have had a wink of sleep but she had felt up to putting her make-up on.

'Come in, Nurse,' she said graciously. 'I hope you've brought me some reliable tablets with no unpleasant side-effects?'

'The doctor recommends these,' Candy assured her. 'I'm so sorry your first night on board was so wretched.'

'My dear, I'm a martyr to insomnia, and my husband always sleeps like a log. So unfair. He was up at seven o'clock and off to get some exercise tramping round the promenade deck. He woke me just as I'd managed to get off.'

'That really was a shame,' Candy sympathised. 'Are you going to try and get a nap now?'

'Oh, no, I shall get up and take a stroll along the deck you can see outside the windows.' She broke into a tinkling laugh. 'I notice you're puzzled as to why none of the passers-by seems to stare in. They can't, you know; these are one-way windows and they can only see a reflection of themselves. So clever.'

It had been interesting to discover how the rich lived when on a cruise, Candy reflected as she returned to the surgery. She didn't envy them their luxury, and she said so to Kirk.

'Nor I,' he agreed, 'and certainly not this particular couple.'

She looked at him enquiringly, conscious of an

underlying seriousness, and after a moment he explained.

'Sir George Wickham cornered me after dinner last night. He told me that his wife is suffering from cancer at the pyloric end of the stomach and has been given only three months to live. Their doctor agreed to this cruise, since both of them were keen to have a last holiday together. It's not generally known, of course, but I thought you should be told.'

Candy was appalled. She had quite liked Lady Wickham, but had written her off as a very light-weight personality.

'I wish you'd said something before I went to see her.'

Kirk shook his head. 'Better that you shouldn't know then. That way you could be entirely natural.' They were both silent for a moment and then he continued briskly, 'I was quite busy while you were away, and I think we've got another patient coming now.'

There was a tap on the half-open door and a man entered, his arm in a sling made out of a patterned scarf.

'I slipped getting out of the shower and sprained my wrist. The wife fixed this sling for me but I think I'd be more comfortable with a proper one—if you wouldn't mind.'

'It's what we're here for,' Kirk said courteously. 'Let me have a look at it to make sure you've done no real damage.'

He examined the swollen wrist and then passed the patient on to Candy for bandaging. She did it carefully, trying not to hurt him, and was impressed by the man's cheerful acceptance of an unfortunate accident.

'Any time it feels uncomfortable,' she said, tying the sling, 'just look out for me on deck or in the big lounge, and I'll adjust it for you.'

He looked surprised. 'I thought you were only on duty when the surgery is open, and that's twice a day, isn't it?'

Candy laughed. 'My hours are from nine to midnight, so feel free to consult me at any time.'

'Good God! Don't you think you ought to join a trade union?'

They closed the surgery soon after that and Candy went next door to change into white cotton trousers and a sweatshirt. It hardly seemed possible that her medical duties for the day were probably over and she had, so far, not been allotted any other regular jobs. There seemed no reason why she shouldn't enjoy herself on deck, just being lazy.

It was a sunny morning, with only an occasional white cloud drifting across the sky, and a lot of passengers were on deck in the vicinity of the swimming-pool. Not that anyone was using it; most of the younger ones were on the sports deck.

Someone had just vacated a cushioned chair and Candy took possession of it. As she sat down she noticed a girl with long dark hair tied up in a ponytail who was sunbathing in a sheltered spot near the edge of the pool. She wore a scarlet swimsuit cut away in every possible direction, displaying a lean, tanned body.

It was Dawn.

It hadn't been part of Candy's plan to watch

the courier displaying her long legs, so she leant back and closed her eyes, soaking up the sun and hoping her crop of freckles wouldn't increase too catastrophically.

When she opened them again Kirk was poised on the edge a yard from Dawn's head. She lay unaware, almost asleep, as he bent and scooped up a handful of water. Swiftly he tipped it over her face and then dived into the pool. Her shriek made all the nearby passengers turn their heads, and they watched with smiling interest as she hurled herself into the water and set off in pursuit of her tormentor. Both strong swimmers, they ducked each other unmercifully until Dawn called a halt and climbed out again to resume her sun-bathing.

'It's lovely to see the young folks enjoying themselves,' an elderly woman next to Candy said, smiling. 'Makes me wish I was a bit younger so I could join in.'

Candy smiled too and made a suitable reply. Her eyes were on Kirk, who had now scrambled out and was drying his face and head preparatory to doing some sunbathing himself.

She didn't think she had ever seen such a magnificent specimen of manhood. But for a pair of tiny bright blue trunks he was naked, his powerful shoulders leading the eye down to a flat stomach and narrow hips. His hair gleamed like gold in the sunlight, and tiny matching curls grew profusely all over the upper part of his body. More than ever he reminded Candy of a Viking.

Mesmerised by his male gorgeousness, she couldn't take her eyes off him, but as they reached

his legs she remembered the limp and his explanation for it. Her searching gaze soon discovered
two long white operation scars showing up plainly
among the fuzz.

Her thoughts switched again as Dawn slipped
her arms into a white terry-towelling robe. For a
moment they stood side by side, the girl so dark,
and the man golden like a god.

'Make a lovely pair, don't they?' commented
Candy's neighbour.

Candy's enthusiastic agreement was overdone,
but the woman didn't seem to notice.

Averting her eyes from Kirk's sunbathing
figure, Candy struggled to keep her attention on
a guide to Stockholm that Emma had lent her.
She was reading a paragraph for the third time
and trying to absorb it when he suddenly appeared
before her.

'I hope you've put on plenty of sun-cream,' he
said severely.

He, too, had donned a towelling robe but it
was unfastened. Seen close to, he was even more
devastating than at a distance, and Candy's gaze,
travelling rapidly upwards, fastened with relief on
his face.

'I haven't got any on,' she admitted. 'And,
what's more, I don't possess any. I didn't think
I'd need it in May.'

'You must be out of your mind! With your
colouring you can't be too careful. Don't you
know there have been a lot of warnings recently
about the dangers of exposing yourself to the sun
without proper protection?'

'Because of the ozone layer?'

'Partly, but too much sun has always had a tendency to cause skin cancer.'

Accepting the scolding, Candy looked at her watch. 'The shop will be shut now, won't it? I'll go and get some cream when it opens this evening.'

'Good girl.' Kirk gave the top of her head an approving pat and went off, presumably to dress.

Dreamily, Candy watched him striding away, and then returned to her battle with the guide-book. When she looked up, the pool was again occupied. A youngish couple were cautiously descending the steps with little squeaks and shudders as the water crept up their bodies.

Candy watched them lazily, noting that the man had knobbly knees and skinny legs, and the girl far too many curves in the wrong places. But they were enjoying themselves, bouncing about and splashing each other. Neither seemed able to swim very much.

Before long the man climbed out, followed by his companion. She sat down at the top of the steps with her back to him and her feet still in the water. They seemed to be arguing about something—whether it was warm enough to sun-bathe?—and suddenly he gave her a playful push just as she was beginning to stand up.

With a shriek she lost her balance and fell forwards into the water.

Afterwards, Candy realised that the girl must have hit her head hard on the edge of the pool—one of those freak accidents which rarely happened. At the time, all she knew was that she had disappeared under the water and failed to re-appear. Acting entirely instinctively, she leapt to

her feet, raced the few steps which separated her
from the pool, and jumped in.

Instantly her trousers were saturated with water
and clung unpleasantly to her legs but she managed to swim. Lessons in life-saving learnt at
school surged back into her mind but there was
no need to try and put them into practice. All
she had to do was hold the unconscious girl's head
above water until her husband and two stewards
from the nearby bar could lift her up the steps.

As soon as she had been placed in the recovery
position, Candy seized one of the stewards. 'I
want the doctor sent for. Do you know how to
get a message broadcast over the Tannoy?'

He was Portuguese and his English was poor,
but he understood. 'I fix it.' He was off in a flash.

In an astonishingly short time Candy heard the
voice of one of the couriers ringing out from somewhere above her head, and a moment later Kirk
arrived at speed.

'What happened?'

Candy described the accident as best she could.
'She can't possibly have swallowed much water,'
she concluded. 'I was watching, so I was able to
get there almost as soon as she went under.'

His fingers were on the girl's pulse. 'No cause
for alarm here. She should come round quite
quickly.'

The distraught husband, on his knees, was rub-
bing the limp hands in a frantic sort of way.
Behind him the passengers were crowding the
poolside and Candy persuaded them to stand
back. When she turned round again, the girl's
eyelids were fluttering. She gave a slight moan

and a little water ran out of her mouth.

Kirk was examining her head beneath the tangled fair hair. He pushed it back from her forehead and disclosed a large bump already showing just above her temple.

'How did she manage to knock herself out in a ship's pool?' he asked quietly.

The man gave a garbled explanation. 'I never meant to hurt her. We'd been playing like kids and I thought it would be fun to shove her back in the water. It sounds daft now, but that's how it was.'

Candy confirmed his statement and Kirk listened without comment. Their patient had now come round completely but seemed bewildered. Both she and her rescuer were beginning to shiver and Kirk hastily organised the two stewards into carrying her back to her cabin. Both were strong and stocky, and they easily conveyed her between them.

The couple's cabin was not far from Candy's and she thought longingly of a hot shower as she helped to dry her patient and get her settled in bed. That done, she was able to escape and attend to her wet clothing.

When she returned, Kirk was sitting on the edge of the bed and apparently giving a lecture on concussion.

'You can't be too careful after a severe knock on the head. You must stay in bed at least for today, and longer if it proves necessary. I hope for your sake that it won't.'

'You can't hope it more than I do.' The husband turned to Candy. 'I haven't thanked you for what you did. You were there incredibly quickly, almost before I'd had time to realise what had happened.'

Candy smiled and repeated the explanation that she'd already given Kirk.

'I reckon you thought we were a couple of idiots,' he said bitterly, 'and, what's more, you'd be right.'

'It wasn't anybody's fault, Jim,' the patient put in. 'It was just one of those things.'

Kirk stood up and went over to the door. 'I want the nurse to look in at intervals throughout the day, but I don't think you'll need any medical attention apart from that.'

Outside in the corridor he turned to Candy. 'You seem to have covered yourself with glory.'

'Anyone could have done it,' she said hastily.

'The fact remains that you were the one who did.' He looked at his watch. 'We seem to have missed our mid-morning coffee but we can get some from one of the bars. I expect you could do with it.'

When they were perched on stools, sipping the hot drink, Kirk said suddenly, 'You mustn't expect such an exciting morning as this has been every day.'

'I certainly wouldn't want any more accidents at the pool.' She hesitated and then went on, 'You're a very good swimmer. Does your leg give you any trouble in the water?'

'Not really. In fact, swimming is supposed to be good for it. Did you know there's another pool, much larger than that one, down in the depths of the ship? I go in there every morning before breakfast.'

Apart from the limp, Candy reflected, he seemed very fit, and more than ever she felt curious about the accident which had caused him to work as a ship's doctor. They were alone at the bar and the two Portuguese stewards were chatting together at the other end, enjoying their leisure before the pre-lunch drinks rush began.

Suddenly Kirk turned his head and looked straight at her. 'I promised to tell you about the accident.' He hesitated, and then continued, 'I expect you've been imagining that it was a car crash but actually we were skiing, high up in the Italian Alps, and I was damn fool enough to suggest leaving the *piste* and taking a different route back. I won't inflict the details on you but it ended in disaster. It wasn't only my leg that was shattered.' He paused, pushing a dish of olives absently about on the counter. 'I was advised to take it easy for a while, but eventually, of course, I intend to return to my own field—neurology.'

Candy felt sure she hadn't been given the whole story, but it was obviously all she was going to get. She murmured a few words of commiseration, knowing them to be inadequate, and decided it was time to change the subject.

'Stockholm's our first port, isn't it? When do we get there?'

'If all goes well and we don't get delayed in the Kiel Canal, you'll wake up on Wednesday morning to find the ship about to dock. I expect you'll have to go ashore with one of the tours. You probably won't be given any choice, but, if you are, please pick the morning one rather than the whole day.'

'Yes, of course. Is it because you don't want me to be away from the ship all day?'

'It's certainly better if you're not but it's bound to happen occasionally.' Kirk steered the olives in her direction and, when she shook her head, took one himself. 'Actually,' he went on when he had finished chewing, 'I want to visit my grandmother in the afternoon. She's a dear old lady and I happen to be very fond of her.'

'Somebody told me you had Swedish blood.'

'That's right, but it's only a quarter. My grandmother is English but she's lived in Sweden for sixty years. As my parents live in Canada, she hardly ever sees them, so I like to visit her when I can.'

It was nice of him to keep in touch, Candy reflected. She refused his offer of more coffee, and they separated.

On Wednesday, Candy woke early and went eagerly on deck. It was only half-past six, and sea and sky had a milky look. The ship had reduced speed, and on both sides there stretched out strings of small islands, mostly wooded and many with a solitary house peeping out from among the trees, or perched on tiny headlands overlooking the water.

Early-rising passengers were staring at the scenery instead of exercising, and moving from one side of the ship to the other in fear of missing a particularly beautiful island.

If she went right up to the observation deck,

Candy reasoned, she would be able to see both sides at once. Climbing the last companionway, she was reminded of her first evening on board, when she had been joined up here by Kirk. He wasn't likely to be here this morning since the approach to Stockholm must be very familiar to him.

But he was.

'Did you know there are thirty thousand islands around here?' was his greeting.

Candy smiled. 'I suppose you've counted them personally?'

'Of course.'

He had given her only a cursory glance and his eyes were fixed on the multitude of miniature paradises strung out before them. Suddenly he startled her by seizing her arm so tightly that she winced.

'There it is!' He pointed towards a patch of trees and rocks just off the shipping lane, a tiny part of the symphony of green and blue but clearly very special to him. 'You can just glimpse the house if you're quick. There—see the pointed roof? That place was my idea of heaven when I was a boy.'

'Did you spend your holidays there?'

'Most of the summer holidays. It belonged to my grandfather and a whole army of Swedish cousins used to camp there, with the adults just managing to squeeze into the house. We used to swim and sail all day long and it never seemed to rain. God, we were happy! Then we all grew up and my grandfather died and the island was sold.' He sighed.

They had passed the island and his eyes had an
inward look, as though he were reliving those
halcyon days. Candy made no attempt to intrude
into his memories of the past but, not for the first
time, she wondered about her boss. After nearly
four days at sea, she still knew practically nothing
about the man behind the glamorous façade. He
had given her a few facts—such as how he had
damaged his leg—but his thoughts and feelings
were still hidden from her.

Come to think of it, though, she hadn't told
him much either!

Suddenly Kirk came back to the present and
asked whether she'd fixed up to go on the
morning tour.

'Good,' he said when she assured him it was
all arranged. 'I'll order my taxi for two-thirty.
You don't mind being left in charge of the ship,
medically speaking?'

Put like that, it certainly sounded alarming, but
Candy smiled and insisted she felt fully capable.

'I shall only be gone about two hours, so I don't
expect you'll have any problems.'

Stockholm could now be seen—a city built on
islands linked by bridges. The half-day tour was
due to start at ten-thirty and Candy got ready
before going to the hospital for morning surgery.
It was a shock to discover that she was apparently
the cruise company's only representative for the
tour of Stockholm, in charge of the comfort and
well-being of fifty passengers.

She had to check the tickets and make sure no
one was left behind at the various stops *en route*.
At first she was over-anxious, counting everybody

at least twice, but none of the tourists went missing and gradually she was able to relax somewhat and enjoy the drive round Sweden's capital city.

Churches, palaces, narrow cobbled streets in the old town, all were interesting in their different ways, and always there were gardens just round the corner. It was too early for flowers, since the cold northern winter had ended only a short time ago, but the grass was fresh and green, and the trees decked with new leaves.

Safely back on the ship, her courier responsibilities over, Candy lunched lightly from the buffet in the small dining-room—a three-course meal at midday didn't appeal to her—and went out on deck. She was leaning on the rail, lazily watching the activity on the deck below, when she saw a taxi draw up, and almost immediately Kirk came down the gangway.

He was followed by Dawn, and they went straight across to the waiting vehicle and got in the back together.

Although Candy liked the other couriers—and Emma in particular—she had never managed to get friendly with Dawn. She had to admit that she hadn't tried very hard for she sensed in the tall dark girl an undercurrent of hostility towards herself.

'She's fancied Kirk ever since he joined the ship,' Emma had said. 'So naturally she's jealous of you.'

'That's ridiculous! Kirk and I work together, that's all. Dawn has absolutely no need for jealousy.'

Emma laughed and tossed back her long plait.

'I expect she's afraid you'll fall for him like the last nurse did, and that that might cause him to reciprocate.'

At the time, Candy had found the idea absurd. Now, to her astonishment, she discovered her feelings had altered slightly. It really was rather strange that Kirk should apparently be taking Dawn to visit his grandmother. It suggested an intimacy that she hadn't realised existed.

So what? Her own relationship with him was entirely professional, so there was no reason for her to feel put out because he'd gone out with Dawn. Absolutely *none*.

Shrugging off the unexpected mood of slight depression, Candy went in search of a comfortable chair in a perfect position, and settled down with a book. Around her the big ship was quiet, more than half of her passengers ashore on the whole-day trip, and many of the others indulging in an afternoon nap. Before long, Candy's own eyelids drooped.

She was half awake and half asleep, her book disregarded on her lap, when an urgent and quite unfamiliar voice cut into her dream state with shattering effect.

'Nurse!' And then, with sudden doubt, 'You *are* the nurse, aren't you?'

Candy was wearing the cord trousers and thin sweater she had had on that morning, but she still had her name-tag. Struggling upright, she jerked herself wide awake and gave her full attention to a blonde girl in a black leotard whom she recognised as one of the dancers.

There were four of them on the *Bergsen* and,

in addition to the couriers, they were responsible
for the nightly entertainment in the large lounge.
Their performance was of a very high standard
and their costumes must have cost the earth.
Candy had watched them each evening before
general dancing began, and had marvelled at their
excellence.

'Certainly I'm the nurse.' She smiled at the
anxious-looking girl. 'Can I help you?'

'I wanted the doctor but they said at Reception
that he'd gone ashore. It's Marie—we were
rehearsing a new number for tonight and she suddenly collapsed on the floor. She says she's got a
terrible pain in her inside——'

'I'll come at once.' Candy stood up, considerably concerned. 'Will you lead the way? I expect
you know the shortest route.'

They soon reached the main lounge. Resplendent with sparkling chandeliers, it provided
comfortable seating for all those passengers who
did not wish to spend the evening in the cinema,
or watching TV, or quietly reading in one of the
many small, quiet lounges. There was a stage at the
far end and a small group of people was standing
round gazing helplessly at a dancer in a bright
green leotard who was lying curled up on the
floor and moaning softly. The vivid colour was
exaggerating the pallor of her face and her eyes
were screwed up with pain.

Candy went down on her knees and put a gentle
hand on the girl's bowed head, but without
response.

'I'm the nurse, Marie,' she said gently. 'I've
come to see if I can help you. Can you tell me

where it hurts and when you first felt it?'

'It's all over my tummy and I've had it slightly all day but I didn't take any notice. Then when we started dancing it got worse and worse, and suddenly I—I couldn't bear it.'

'If you would just uncurl a little so I can feel your abdomen——' She broke off as her patient shuddered. 'I'll be very careful.'

Marie obeyed to the best of her ability and Candy palpated the distended stomach as much as she dared. She felt fairly sure she was dealing with a case of appendicitis and that Kirk would have diagnosed the trouble immediately. She counted the pulse, which was fast, and felt the girl's forehead. She certainly had some fever.

'I'd like the doctor to see you as soon as he comes back,' she said. 'In the meantime, we can't leave you lying here, so do you think you can make it to your cabin with help?'

Marie agreed to try, and as she was hauled to her feet it occurred to Candy that she seemed to be reviving a little. That sometimes happened when someone with authority came along and took charge, causing panic to subside. Perhaps it wasn't appendicitis after all?

She sent another dancer off to Reception to make sure that Kirk got a message as soon as he returned, and then accompanied her patient into the bowels of the ship, where she shared a double cabin.

There was nothing to do now but wait.

CHAPTER THREE

IT WAS very quiet in the crowded little cabin, untidy with clothes, make-up, magazines. Marie lay very still and almost seemed as though she might drift off to sleep.

Suddenly Candy remembered that no one, except the dancers, knew where she was. Certainly not Reception. Supposing another emergency cropped up and she couldn't be found? She looked round for a phone and saw none. She and Kirk had them, of course, and all the more expensive cabins, but they weren't considered necessary for dancers.

She leaned forward and touched her patient lightly on the shoulder, and Marie's eyes flew open.

'I'm sorry, love, but I'll have to leave you for a few minutes.' She explained the difficulty. 'You'll be OK?'

'Oh, yes, thanks. Actually, I feel a bit better now.'

'I expect that's because you're resting instead of trying to dance.' Candy smiled. 'I'll be back in a few minutes.'

She went along to the lift and was soon on the same level as Reception, where she quickly explained what had happened. A glance at her watch told her Kirk was about due back, and on an impulse she went outside to find out if anything could be seen of him.

Obviously intuition had been at work. Looking down on the dock, she saw a tall man with hair like gold paying a taxi driver. Near by, Dawn was running up the swaying gangway with practised ease. By timing it with care, Candy managed to meet him when he entered the ship and, at the same time, allow Dawn to disappear first.

Kirk was looking relaxed and cheerful and she asked him if he'd enjoyed the afternoon.

'Very much. I found the old lady in great form and time passed all too quickly. How have things been with you?'

She told him about Marie and he frowned. 'Severe abdominal pain? I don't like the sound of that. Lead on and I'll come to the cabin and take a look at her.'

Marie was lying as Candy had left her. She raised her head slightly as they entered and produced a faint smile. 'I'm so sorry to bother you, Doctor.'

'It's what I'm here for!' He sat down on the edge of the bed. 'Do you mind if I take a look?'

Candy expertly folded down the bedclothes and pulled up Marie's nightdress. Kirk spent some time palpating the exposed area, giving particular attention to the right side.

Eventually he asked, 'Have you had this pain before?'

Marie hesitated. 'Not like this, but—well, I did have a slight attack a couple of months ago. It soon stopped and I was fine.' She looked straight at the doctor. 'You don't think it's anything

serious, do you? I can't have anything that's
going to stop me dancing.'

'My dear girl!' Kirk raised his eyebrows and
gave her a rueful smile. 'If you *have* got something
that's going to make dancing out of the question,
you'll just have to put up with it until you're
better. But that may not be the case. I'm pretty
sure you've got what people call a grumbling
appendix. It will certainly have to be operated on
one day but maybe we can hold it at bay for a
time. It's a pity you're a dancer instead of working
on a computer. You could hardly have anything
more energetic.'

'What about tonight?' Marie asked eagerly.
'Couldn't you give me a pain-killer?'

'No, I couldn't! It might be highly dangerous.
And there's certainly no question of your dancing
tonight. Tomorrow we'll see how you are, and in
the meantime you must rest quietly here and let
the others manage without you.'

Marie looked on the verge of tears, and Candy
asked, 'Is there anyone who could take
your place?'

'One of the couriers—Rose—has had some
experience. She might be able to help, but they'll
have to do something easy.'

They left her to come to terms with what had
happened, and walked along the narrow corridor
one behind the other. Suddenly Candy
remembered Steve's stitches and asked when Kirk
wanted to take them out.

'Six days should be enough, so you'd better ask
him to come along on Friday.'

'That's the day we're in St Petersburg, and

everybody will be going ashore. It'll be hectic.'

He agreed to make it Saturday and Candy resolved to look out for Steve that evening in order to warn him. The ship's officers were erratic in their attendance at meals, but today she was fortunate in meeting him when they both emerged from the dining-room at the end of the usual elaborate five-course meal. To her astonishment he was wearing a piece of plaster over the stitches.

'Why on earth did you put this on?' she demanded.

'People kept asking me what I'd done and I got fed up.' He scowled at the neat line of sutures as Candy indignantly whipped off the plaster.

'It's much healthier to let the air get to a wound. Come along to the surgery and I'll clean it up for you.'

He made no protest and she cleaned the whole area thoroughly, removing the stickiness left by the plaster, and told him the stitches were to come out on Saturday. When she had finished, she looked at him keenly.

Sitting on the edge of the couch, his shoulders drooping, he appeared just as tired and anaemic-looking as he had done the previous Saturday. His dark hair was lank and there were shadows under his eyes.

'Have you been feeling extra tired lately?' Candy asked diffidently.

To her consternation, Steve's pale face was suddenly suffused with angry colour. 'You're wondering if I've got AIDS, aren't you? Well, I haven't. I had myself tested last time I was at home and I'm in the clear.'

'There could be lots of reasons for feeling the way you do,' she said calmly, 'and I'm very glad we can cross AIDS off the list. Have you had any illnesses during the last few months?'

Steve frowned and Candy thought that he was going to shrug off the question, but eventually he said, 'I did pick up a very unpleasant virus about six weeks ago. It seemed to clear up but it's since then that I've felt so ridiculously under the weather.'

'There could be a connection. I'll have a talk with the doctor and see what he thinks.'

Steve looked dubious but raised no objection. As he slid off the couch, he put his hand lightly on Candy's shoulder and looked into her face. 'Thanks for listening to me. I haven't been able to talk about my problems to anyone else. The other officers probably think I'm a wimp.'

He kissed her lightly on the cheek. It was an entirely sexless salute and she accepted it with a smile. Before they could separate, a voice spoke from behind them.

'I hope I'm not interrupting anything. I didn't know anyone was here.'

Kirk stood in the doorway, looking from one to the other, his eyebrows slightly raised. Steve muttered something and shot past him.

Half amused and half irritated at being caught in such a misleading situation, Candy said quickly, 'I've just been cleaning up his thumb. The silly man had put plaster over your stitches.'

'He went past at such a rate I hardly had a chance to look at him.' Kirk went into the annexe and unlocked the drugs cupboard. 'How did he seem?'

'Just as tired and generally below par.' She sighed, her brow wrinkled in thought. 'I do wish we knew what's wrong with him. I asked him outright whether he'd had any illnesses recently and he mentioned a virus.'

'How long ago?'

'About six weeks.'

Kirk turned round with a strip of foil-wrapped capsules in his hand. 'He may have picked something up in a foreign port. We'd better ask him to come along here for a check-up.' He grinned suddenly, with a slightly wicked glint in his eyes. 'On second thoughts, *you* can ask him. He seems to have taken a fancy to you.'

Candy was annoyed to find herself blushing, but her attention was quickly switched from her own embarrassment as she noticed a difference in the way Kirk was limping as he crossed to the washbasin. It was much more pronounced than usual.

'Is anything wrong?' she asked.

'A spot of trouble with my leg. I was stupid enough to stumble over the step into my cabin and twist it slightly. A couple of Co-proximals will soon make me forget all about it.' He filled a plastic mug with water and drank deeply. 'I'm glad it happened *after* the visit to my grandmother. As it was, I was able to persuade her that I'd completely got over the accident.'

Candy never knew what made her say what she did then. Somehow the words seemed to slip out of her mouth of their own volition.

'Did Dawn enjoy the afternoon too?'

Kirk stared at her and then shrugged. 'I presume she did. If you really want to know, why don't you ask her?'

'I don't want to know all that badly!' Furious with herself for asking the question, Candy tried to laugh it off.

'The shops in Stockholm are extremely good, though horribly expensive.' Kirk lowered himself rather carefully into the chair by the desk. 'I expect Dawn had a good time looking round but I doubt if she bought much.'

'Oh!' Candy tried to meet his blue stare and failed. 'I—I thought——'

'You thought that I took her with me to see the old lady? Why ever should I do that? Dawn's good fun to be with but this was a family visit. She simply cadged a lift into the city centre and back, that's all. It's a heck of a long walk from here.'

'I'm sorry—I suppose it was rather a stupid mistake.' Candy made a move towards the door but Kirk put out a hand to stop her.

'Sit down a minute.'

She started to protest. 'I ought to be on my way to the main lounge——'

'I won't delay you more than a moment, but I think I ought to tell you the full story of my skiing accident. It might stop you jumping to such absurd conclusions.' He paused, and his eyes had an inward look. They were full of pain, as though he was reliving that disastrous day on the mountain.

'I think I mentioned that I wasn't alone,' he went on in a flat, expressionless voice. 'The other person was the girl I was expecting to marry, and we were high up on the ski-slopes. As we were both experienced skiers, I suggested we came down another way. Nicola liked a challenge and she raised no objection, so we set off. It was steeper than I'd realised, but we got on OK at first.'

He stopped and swallowed, and Candy waited quietly, sharing his distress but not daring to show it.

'Suddenly I saw an outcrop of rock and I knew we weren't going to miss it.' Kirk stopped again and then continued jerkily, 'There was an accident, of course. I broke my leg in two places—it was a compound fracture and a right mess. I also had broken ribs and a lot of minor injuries. But Nicola was—was killed.'

'Oh, Kirk—how terrible!' Candy stretched out her hand and he clutched it so tightly that she had to stifle a cry of pain. 'I can quite understand why you don't want to talk about it.'

'I killed her,' he burst out harshly, his face ravaged. 'I shall feel guilty about it for the rest of my life.'

'She went with you willingly—you didn't have to persuade her——'

'It was still my fault.'

Candy longed to take him in her arms and hold him close, to remind him gently of the healing power of time, but she knew she must do neither of these things. They had known each other less than a week and she did not dare to intrude on his privacy.

Maybe one day—but not yet.

He was still holding her hand and she did not

want to be the first to move. Suddenly he hurled a question at her.

'Have you got a boyfriend, Candy?'

Startled, she found the abrupt change of subject difficult to cope with. After the tragic story that had been unfolded, her own experience seemed trivial, yet Kirk was waiting for an answer and she floundered into speech.

'I've had a few boyfriends—what girl hasn't?'

'I'm not asking you about your past,' he reminded her gently. 'I asked if there's anyone special in your life *now*.'

'In that case, the answer's no.'

He looked at her thoughtfully, and she felt guilty because she knew she was stalling. It wasn't that she hadn't suffered either, but it hadn't really been heartbreak, even though it had seemed like it at the time.

'You're a bit of mystery to me,' he told her. 'I don't know you much better now than I did the day we met, and if we're going to work together for weeks I think the situation should be remedied.' He paused and raised one eyebrow. 'Don't you agree?'

'Well, yes, if you put it like that.' Candy recaptured her hand and united it with the other one in her lap. As she did so, she noticed the time. It was nearly nine o'clock.

'You'll get me into terrible trouble with the social director if you keep me here another minute!' She made a dive for the door. 'I'll tell you all about my problems some time—I promise! In the meantime, I must go and take another look at Marie before I appear in the lounge——'

'I'll do that.' Kirk got up. 'You get off to the entertainment. See you!'

The dancers were in the middle of their performance when Candy slipped in unobtrusively. Rose, wearing a lot of feathers but very little else, appeared to her untrained eye to be performing very well indeed. They were followed by a brilliant conjuror, who Candy knew to be Steve's fellow clerk in the purser's office, and then there was general dancing.

Kirk did not appear and she guessed he was resting his leg. She was tired herself after the eventful day and went off to bed before midnight for the first time. As she entered her cabin she found the phone ringing.

'I hope I haven't disturbed you,' came Kirk's voice. 'I just wanted to tell you that Marie seems a lot better. If there's no set-back, I may let her return to normal life the day after tomorrow, but she'll need careful watching. Did you get a scolding for being late?'

'Nobody seemed to notice.'

'So you could just as well have stayed to finish your story. Never mind; I shall look forward to hearing it at the first opportunity. Goodnight, love.'

It was the first time he had used any kind of endearment. It was one which she herself employed quite frequently when talking to patients and she knew it meant nothing.

Nevertheless, it pleased her.

The following day Candy went ashore at Helsinki, again in charge of a coachload of passengers.

Enchanted with the wide, clean streets, she enthused with the others over the Church in the Rock and the memorial to Sibelius, the great Finnish composer.

Back on the ship, she was given the job of selling tickets for a charity raffle, every one of which she had to dispose of by the end of the cruise. The passengers bought generously, but those with the most money—the occupants of the staterooms—were less easy to corner because they spent a lot of time in their private quarters.

Greatly daring, she visited Lady Wickham and met Sir George for the first time. Her ladyship was looking more frail than ever but she seemed pleased to see Candy, and her husband bought twenty pounds' worth of tickets.

It was such a busy day that she saw nothing of Kirk except during surgery, and the only personal conversation they had was on the subject of his leg, which he said was improving.

The next day they were at St Petersburg, for most people their first visit to what had been the USSR. It was a strange mixture of grandeur and shabbiness; beautiful golden domes glistening in the sunshine, huge empty squares, and distressingly badly paved streets. Candy spent the whole day ashore, her imagination gripped by the wonder and majesty of the city, its shabbiness forgotten. With the other passengers, she stood staring at the magnificent statue of Peter the Great on a leaping horse, and marvelled that one man could have conceived the notion of building a fabulous city on a useless marsh.

'How was it?' Kirk asked on her return to the ship, meeting her in the embarkation area. 'You look tired.'

'Don't you know you should never tell a girl that?' Candy tossed back at him, trying to hide the distinctly odd effect his sudden appearance was having on her. 'Actually, St Petersburg *was* very tiring. For some reason I'd expected it to be cold and the atmosphere was quite hot and sticky. We did more walking than usual, too. How have things been on board?'

'No problems.' He slipped his arm into hers. 'Come and have a reviving drink. No doubt you could do with it.'

'I sure could!' She smiled up into his face. 'But I simply must have a shower first. See you in twenty minutes!'

In her cabin she pulled off the clothes she had worn all day and plunged under the cool, refreshing spray. In a few minutes it had removed all her weariness and she was searching through her wardrobe for the dress she had planned to wear that night.

A short time later, clad in apple-green silk jersey, she joined Kirk in the Fiord bar. As she settled on her stool a great wave of contentment swept over her. It had been a fascinating day and the evening was making a good start. Life on a cruise ship was really great!

Many hours later Candy was awakened by a tapping on her door. Slipping her arms into an Indian-cotton wrap, she went to investigate.

Outside she found a middle-aged man in an

old-fashioned silk dressing-gown. He was looking frightened and he greeted her with considerable relief.

'I'm very sorry to disturb you, Nurse. It's the doctor I really want but I don't know how to get in touch with him.'

'What's the trouble, Mr—er——?' Candy asked.

'Watson's the name.' His worried eyes fastened on her face. 'I'm dreadfully anxious about my wife—I think she's having a heart attack.'

'I'll come at once.' Candy joined him in the corridor and locked the door behind her. 'Where's your cabin?'

Mr Watson hesitated. 'I really think the doctor——'

'I'll certainly contact him if I think it's necessary, but he wouldn't thank me for telephoning him if your wife is only suffering from indigestion. Is she complaining of pains in the chest?'

The question seemed to surprise him. 'Well, no, not exactly—but it's her breathing; it's terrible to listen to.'

'I see.' Candy was non-committal. 'Well, we'd better not waste any more time, so please lead the way to your cabin, Mr Watson.'

It turned out to be an inside one similar to Candy's but on the next deck up. As soon as they entered, Candy knew exactly why the husband had been so worried. Mrs Watson was lying propped up against her pillows and apparently fighting for breath. She had her mouth wide open and her loud gasping filled the cabin.

It was very distressing to listen to, but Candy

didn't think it was a heart attack.

She went over to the bed and laid her fingers on the patient's wrist. The pulse was fast but not irregular. She took both the trembling hands in her own and held them firmly.

'Have you got any pain, Mrs Watson?' she asked. 'In your chest, for instance?'

The only answer was a shake of the head, and the awful gasping continued.

Candy tightened her grip of the hands. 'You've been getting into rather a panic about something, haven't you?' she said gently. 'Try and breathe more slowly while your husband finds me a paper bag, or a polythene one will do——'

'Have you gone crazy, Nurse?' he demanded angrily.

'Not at all. Your wife is suffering from too much oxygen. I'm going to ask her to breathe into the bag and keep it up for a few minutes, so she inhales plenty of carbon dioxide to counteract the oxygen. It's a sure cure for the effects of hyper-ventilation.'

He started to protest but Mrs Watson gasped, 'Please, Robert, do as the nurse suggests. We can at least try it.'

Muttering to himself, Mr Watson soon produced the bag and Candy held it while his wife did as she had been told. It seemed like a miracle when the awful gasping ceased and she relaxed against her pillows, but it was impossible to feel any real satisfaction until the cause of the attack had been discovered.

When questioned, Mrs Watson hesitated. 'Well, I can't be sure, but I think I woke up with

the sheet over my face. I've always been subject
to claustrophobia and I don't like this inside cabin
anyway. I know the air-conditioning is excellent,
but having no window——' she shuddered '—it's
horrible!'

Candy would have liked to suggest a change of
cabin but she knew it would be pointless to mention it. All the outside cabins were already
occupied on the *Bergsen*. She was trying to think
of some helpful ideas when she became aware
that Mr Watson was getting more and more
worked up.

'I'm sorry, Nurse,' he exploded, 'but I really
can't accept your opinion without a doctor to confirm it. It just won't do, and I consider you are
failing in your duty even though you might be
right about the panic attack, but to me it seems
most unlikely. My wife is a sensible woman, and
I refuse to believe she would let herself get so
upset by claustrophobia.' He drew himself up to
his full height. 'I insist that you call the doctor.'

'Very well, Mr Watson,' she said coolly. 'I'll
go back to my cabin and ring him. It will take a
few minutes but I don't think your wife is likely
to have a recurrence.'

She sped down the stairs to her own cabin and
quickly dialled the number she'd been given for
contacting Kirk at night. He would be most
annoyed at being disturbed but there was no help
for it. In her own mind she was quite sure that
her diagnosis was correct, but Mr Watson was
entitled to ask for the doctor.

A sleepy grunt sounded in her ear and she
rapidly explained the situation. 'I'm quite sure she

was hyperventilating but her husband still thinks it was a heart attack. Do you mind coming along to look at her and—I hope—confirm my opinion?'

'What do you think? I'd only just managed to get to sleep properly, but I suppose there's no help for it.'

Why had he apparently been lying awake? Candy wondered as she hurried back. Was it anything to do with their conversation in the surgery? Had he been thinking about Nicola and grieving for her afresh?

This time there was no sound at all in the Watsons' cabin. The patient was breathing normally and her colour was good. Making no comment, Candy sat down on the end of the bed and joined in the silent waiting.

Before long, a tousle-headed Kirk, wearing a dark blue terry-towelling robe, appeared in the doorway. He had brought his stethoscope with him and also a sphygmomanometer. After greeting Mrs Watson courteously, he listened with great care to her chest, counted her pulse, and finally he took her blood-pressure—all with considerable gravity.

Candy watched with interest and marvelled that he should take so much trouble to reassure his patient and her husband.

When he had finished he smiled at her. 'Well, Mrs Watson, your heart is behaving itself extremely well considering the way you were treating it a little while ago. I agree with Nurse that you were suffering from an attack of panic which caused you to hyperventilate. It's very important to call a halt to such attacks as, if allowed to continue, they can lead to dizziness and nausea.'

'Oh, thank you, Doctor—what a relief!' She beamed at him and then turned to her husband. 'You needn't have got so worked up after all, Robert.'

He was looking, Candy reflected, like a man who didn't much care for being proved wrong, but he pulled himself together and apologised.

'I'm sorry to have troubled you, Doctor—and the nurse, too—but I'm sure you can understand my anxiety.'

They both assured him that they could, and said goodnight. As they walked down the corridor, Kirk put his arm round Candy's waist and squeezed her gently.

'Clever little diagnostician, aren't you?'

'It was pretty obvious even before I knew she suffered from claustrophobia.'

'Only psychiatric treatment can cure her of that,' Kirk said thoughtfully, 'but she seems a sensible woman. I don't think she'll let herself get in such a state again.'

The intimacy of the situation—three a.m. and both of them in their night-clothes—was causing Candy's pulses to misbehave nearly as much as Mrs Watson's had done. Her imagination travelled wildly in all sorts of unwise directions, like accepting his offer of an escort back to her cabin—should he make such an offer.

He didn't. When she halted at the top of the stairs leading down to the lower deck, Kirk stopped too.

Around them the whole ship appeared to be asleep, though Candy knew there must be men on watch, checking instruments, doing all the mysterious things that needed to be done during a voyage. The fact remained that she and Kirk were wrapped about in a total silence. Perhaps that was why they could hear their own hearts beating so loudly.

Kirk put his arms round her and slid them down her back, his fingers kneading the flesh beneath her thin wrap.

Unconsciously, she leaned towards him, her face lifted up to his, and his mouth came down on hers with a bruising fierceness. She closed her eyes and surrendered to the foolish ecstasy of the moment.

Kirk's arms suddenly dropped to his sides. Left off balance, Candy swayed and might have fallen if he hadn't steadied her with one hand. He was breathing hard and she could see the sweat on his forehead, but he managed a smile.

'What an opportunity wasted! I'm not sure whether we've both been extremely sensible or incredibly daft. Goodnight.'

CHAPTER FOUR

NOT another emergency! Candy forced her eyes open and stared into the darkness. One of the disadvantages of an inside cabin was that you couldn't tell whether it was day or night outside.

The noise which had awakened her suddenly became familiar and quite ordinary. Her alarm clock was telling her it was time to get up. Reluctantly she struggled out of bed, but it wasn't until she had had her shower that she felt she could face the world.

There was no sign of Kirk at breakfast, nor when Candy unlocked the surgery. He came in three minutes late and appeared to be in a silent mood. Perhaps he was regretting the confidences of yesterday?

'I suppose you reminded Steve to come and have his stitches out?' he asked eventually.

Candy confirmed it and a moment later the assistant purser arrived.

Kirk inspected the neat line on his thumb. 'You've healed very well, but please do be more careful in future when you're handling a lethal weapon like a sharp knife.'

He went over to the washbasin and scrubbed his hands, and Candy fetched a kidney dish to receive the sutures. As Kirk snipped them one by one, she glanced at Steve's face—some people hated having stitches out—but he was watching intently and showed no sign of nervousness.

When the job was done, he thanked them politely and then hesitated in the doorway, looking at Candy. 'Are you going ashore when we reach Bornholm tomorrow?'

The following day was Sunday and they were to have what the tour company described as a 'lazy day', visiting the Danish island of Bornholm. Candy had been told she would have to escort the afternoon tour, and after the long day in St Petersburg she was looking forward to a relaxing and enjoyable drive round the island.

'I have a free half-day,' Steve said when she had explained the situation to him. 'I thought I might go ashore with one of the tours if there's room. Perhaps I shall see you?'

'Perhaps.' Candy gave him a friendly smile, and stood back to allow three people to enter the surgery in a bunch.

They were in search of seasickness pills, though none of them appeared to be feeling unwell.

'It's just in case,' one woman said, gesticulating with a long, elegant hand sparkling with rings. She bestowed a brilliant but mechanical smile on Kirk who had risen politely to his feet. 'There's a little more movement this morning, don't you think? It's been so superbly calm so far that none of us has had a chance to acquire sea legs.'

'You certainly won't need pills if it gets no worse than this,' he said with a smile.

After that there was a pause in the stream of patients requiring medical advice, and Kirk suddenly reverted to the subject of Steve.

'I've begun to feel concerned about that fellow.

When we were attending to his cut, I thought he'd probably been living it up ashore and given himself a bad hangover, but after a week he's no better at all.' He looked thoughtfully at Candy, who was checking the drugs cupboard. 'If you do meet him on the tour tomorrow, could you try and do a little probing? He seems to fancy you so he might be more forthcoming than with me.'

'I don't think he's feeling well enough to fancy anybody at the moment,' she protested. 'But I'll certainly do my best if I get a chance.'

She re-locked the cupboard and glanced at her watch. There was another half-hour before she had to turn herself into a courier and help Emma organise bingo. If Kirk wanted to go on talking about Steve she had time to listen.

But he had changed the subject and was now telling her about the island they were to visit tomorrow.

'You'll like Bornholm. It's a pretty place with wonderful sandy beaches and toytown villages and farms, and everything looking freshly painted. I spent a long summer holiday there when I was a teenager——'

'With hordes of Swedish cousins?'

He grinned. 'How did you guess?'

Candy gave him an answering smile and offered no explanation, though she could remember vividly the conversation she had had with him as the ship made its way up the fiord to Stockholm. There were a lot of other things she could remember, too, like the way she had felt when she thought he was taking Dawn with him to visit his grandmother.

It would have been natural to view it as slightly strange. It was *not* natural to have been jealous. Or was it?

Shying away from the implications of that, Candy broke the silence which had fallen between them by asking Kirk if he felt tired after the broken night.

'Meaning that I look haggard and hollow-eyed?' he asked, giving her a challenging look, and then spoiling it with an immense yawn.

'Meaning nothing of the sort, but I don't expect you got much sleep.'

'You can say that again!' He sighed, leaning on the desk with folded arms, not looking at her. 'I'm afraid I was indulging in useless regrets about all sorts of things.'

Candy wanted to ask him if he'd been thinking about Nicola but did not dare. She understood how bitterly he blamed himself for the death of his fiancée and longed to find a way of helping him to view it differently. Unfortunately there seemed little chance of that.

'Regrets are nearly always completely pointless,' Kirk went on pensively. 'It's strange, isn't it? You can hold thoughts of that kind at bay for most of the twenty-four hours, but at night you're defenceless.'

'You've got nothing else to do at night,' Candy pointed out sensibly.

To her dismay he burst out laughing. 'How right you are, but somehow I'd never thought of it that way. Next time I lie awake at night with my mind a maelstrom of unprofitable thoughts, I'll get out of bed and find something useful to do.' He paused for a moment. 'Can't think what, though, in the middle of the night. Any suggestions?'

His mocking tone had been hurtful, and Candy was distressed because she had minded quite a lot. She was relieved when a tap on the door heralded the arrival of someone who had nearly left it too late.

It was Mr Watson.

'I just thought I'd pop along and tell you my wife is quite all right this morning,' he said breezily. 'Save you the bother of checking up on her.'

Was he being sarcastic? Candy didn't think so.

She said quickly, 'I looked out for you at breakfast but I expect I was too early. I'm so glad she's got over her attack.'

'I hope she won't have another. I don't mind telling you, I was frightened to death.'

'You'll know how to deal with it another time,' Kirk put in, 'and if you can't remember how Nurse coped with it you'd better get her to give you a lesson.' He passed them on his way to the door, addressing Candy as he did so. 'I'll leave you to lock up.'

'I should have thought a young chap like that would have found a more worthwhile job than being a ship's doctor,' Mr Watson observed disapprovingly.

'You'd have thought it was worthwhile if your wife really had been having a heart attack,' Candy flashed, rushing to Kirk's defence without stopping to think. 'He was in an accident. Haven't you noticed he limps?'

'Can't say I have.' Mr Watson was quite unsympathetic. 'Driving too fast, I suppose. Well, all I hope is it didn't involve anyone else.'

Candy bit her lip. She wanted to say, It wasn't a road traffic accident, but she reminded herself just in time that she had been told the unhappy story in confidence. Perhaps she ought not to have mentioned it at all.

Luckily, Mr Watson, having made his comment, had apparently dismissed the matter from his mind. He said casually, 'Well, Nurse, I'll be on my way to the main lounge. We thought we'd stay inside this morning as it's a bit chilly on deck.'

'I'm organising bingo when the keep-fit is over,' Candy told him. 'Does that interest you?'

'I'm afraid not, and thanks for the warning.' For the first time she saw him smile. 'We'll settle down somewhere else.'

Candy made sure the drugs cupboard was secure and then locked the outer door. As she went to her cabin to change out of uniform, her mind reverted to Kirk's strange mood. It could be due to an almost sleepless night, but she was beginning to feel fairly certain that he was having second thoughts about the wisdom of letting her into the secret places of his mind and heart.

Saturday seemed a long day and was certainly busy for the staff. In addition to running the bingo, Candy continued the sale of raffle tickets and, with the other couriers, rehearsed a song and dance act for the special entertainment on the last night. She didn't feel her attempt to turn herself into a cabaret girl was very successful but fortunately she was put in the back row.

She saw Kirk only at meals and then they didn't sit near each other. They had no conversation together until the evening, apart from the half-hour when the surgery was open, and on that occasion their conversation was confined entirely to medical matters.

When they did get to talking to each other as man to woman and not merely doctor to nurse, it began disastrously. . .

Candy was wearing a particularly pretty dress that evening. It was long and clinging—everyone wore proper evening dress on the *Bergsen*—and made of thin silk in an intricate pattern of pale green, cream and white. Looking at herself in the mirror, she felt reasonably satisfied, though, in her opinion, the sophisticated effect was spoilt by her increasing crop of freckles.

She hoped Kirk would like it.

But when they actually met, briefly, during the dancing, he looked only at her face and there was no admiration in those wonderful sapphire eyes, only a blue iciness which made her think of the frozen north of his father's country.

Candy's dawning smile faded and her features felt strangely stiff. She was about to turn away when Kirk spoke.

'I'd like a word with you later on, when you can spare the time.'

He had never spoken to her like that before and her temper flared. 'It depends on what you want to say!' she flung back at him.

But all he said was. 'I'll be on the observation deck. Please join me if you can.'

She was tempted to refuse flatly but curiosity stifled the wish, so she said nothing. Instead she greeted with a brilliant—and entirely false—smile a young man named Tim Harris who had frequently asked her to dance. His wife was pregnant and quite content to watch. They were a devoted couple and clearly found each other's company sufficient during the daylight hours.

It must be lovely to be so happily married, Candy thought wistfully.

The evening seemed long. Her mind wandered off constantly to the coming talk with Kirk. She couldn't even begin to guess at the reason for it. He was obviously annoyed about something but, as far as she was aware, she had done nothing likely to put him in a black mood.

At eleven-thirty he appeared suddenly at her side and announced that it was raining.

So far the cruise had been amazingly fine and somehow Candy had expected the weather to stay that way. The observation deck would be out of the question now, but it was the only place where they could be reasonably sure of being undisturbed.

'Maybe we'd better call off this mysterious conversation,' she said lightly.

'I'd rather not, if you don't mind.' He hesitated. 'There's my cabin, of course. How about that?'

Candy studied him thoughtfully, aware that such an invitation frequently had strings attached. Somehow she didn't think it was likely on this occasion!

'Very well,' she agreed. 'Just give me time to go and change. I don't want to trail this dress up and down wet companionways.'

She was still looking at him as she spoke and she noticed a flicker of emotion cross his face.

'It seems a pity. . .' he began, and then the blind came down again and he finished, 'As you wish. I'll wait here for you.'

She was back in a few minutes, wearing jeans and an anorak to keep off the rain. In silence she followed Kirk to his cabin on the boat deck. It was an outside one but the view was spoilt by the nearest lifeboat hanging in its davits, all ready for an emergency which didn't bear thinking about.

The cabin was small and untidy in an intimate sort of way, with a pair of cream trousers on the back of a chair and a discarded shirt on the floor. The bed looked rumpled and an open book lay on the shelf.

Kirk thrust the shirt into a drawer and his trousers into the cupboard. 'Sorry about the mess. Where would you like to sit? The bed's the most comfortable.'

'I didn't come here to be comfortable.' She sat down gingerly on the edge. 'I want to know what all this is about. You spoke to me earlier as though I'd committed some awful crime and I've been seething ever since. For your information, my conscience is entirely clear.'

'You surprise me,' he said bitterly. 'I wouldn't have thought it possible after what I learned from Mrs Watson just after dinner.'

Candy stared at him blankly, but before she could demand an explanation he went on to give her one.

'I nearly collided with her at the top of the stairs, and naturally I stopped to ask how she was. She assured me she was OK and then——' he paused a moment '—she said she was sorry to hear about my accident, and asked if my leg hurt very much.' Again he halted, his accusing eyes on Candy's face. 'How the hell did she know about it if you didn't tell her?'

She said quickly, 'Actually, I didn't, but——' only to be interrupted.

'Hardly anyone except the staff captain knows the cause of my limp, and now I suppose the entire ship will hear about it.'

The gross exaggeration gave Candy the courage to rush to her own defence. 'I'll tell you exactly what happened. Mr Watson was wondering why you had chosen to be a ship's doctor and I said you'd been in an accident——'

'I suppose it didn't occur to you that I'd told you the story in confidence? I didn't think it was necessary to *ask* you to be good enough to keep it to yourself?'

Candy leapt to her feet and glared down at him where he sat astride a chair. 'I did *not* betray your confidence! I said nothing about skiing or—or anyone else being involved. Mr Watson thinks you were in a car crash, and if he had been reasonably observant he'd have worked out for himself that you'd had some sort of accident. Either that or you'd got some congenital defect which caused a limp. Maybe you'd prefer people to think that?'

Kirk was silent for a moment but he held her gaze, and she saw the anger and hurt in his eyes change to a gleam of amusement. 'You haven't got red hair for nothing, have you?' he asked softly.

The air in the cabin was suddenly charged with emotion. Kirk stood up abruptly, nearly knocking

the chair over, and put his arms round her. Very
gently, he kissed the tip of her nose, and then
his lips nuzzled her cheek, sending tremors all
over her.

They reached her ear and he murmured a plea
for forgiveness. 'I should have trusted you and I
didn't—I'm so very sorry——'

Candy reached up and put her arms round his
neck. 'It's forgotten already.'

He captured her mouth and they clung
together, both swept by the same urgent need,
and for a short while they were aware of nothing
but the feel of each other's bodies in intimate
contact. It was wonderful and it was also dangerous, and Candy was the first to call a halt.

'I'd better go.' She disengaged herself gently
but firmly. 'I'm so glad we're friends again.'

'Me too.' Kirk released her reluctantly. He hesitated and then added, 'But you're still keeping
your secrets, aren't you, Candy? Might this just
possibly be a good moment to come clean? You
know a lot about me and I know absolutely nothing about you except that you were a theatre staff
nurse. There has to be more to you than that.'

'I told you I'd had a few boyfriends,' she said
defensively.

'You also added "What girl hasn't?" which I
accepted as normal. But I have a strong feeling
that something—or someone—in your recent past
has made you unhappy. Am I right?'

His eyes were searching her face and Candy
found it impossible to meet that penetrating gaze.
She turned away and went to stare out of the
window.

The ship was surging steadily towards Bornholm and distant lights showed they were not far from land. There was nothing else to be seen except a strip of wet deck and darkness beyond—not that she would have noticed if there had been. Her eyes were looking inward, back into the past. Slowly, she turned round again and then, quite suddenly, she found she actually wanted to tell Kirk about Barry.

'You're quite right that I was unhappy before I came away.' She sat down on the bed, folding her hands in her lap. 'Last December a new surgical registrar came to the hospital where I worked. He was divorced, like my mother, and he dated me fairly frequently. We got on very well, even though he was twelve years older than me. He said he was looking for a consultant's job. What I didn't know was that he was also looking for a suitable wife.'

'So what happened?'

'For a few weeks I really thought Barry was the man I wanted to marry and I'd never felt that way about anybody before. I took him home, of course, and Mum took to him at once. She's very pretty and lively, and looks much younger than her age, which is only forty-five, anyway.' She glanced up at Kirk. 'You'll probably have realised that they were closer in age than Barry and I.'

He nodded and Candy rushed on with her story, going so fast now that the words tripped over her tongue.

'To cut a long story short, as they say, they're now going to get married. My mother will make

a splendid consultant's wife, and she'll love organising dinner parties.'

'He's still got to land a consultant's post,' Kirk
pointed out. He paused and then added quietly,
'How much did you mind?'

'A lot, at first. That's why I threw up my job at
the local hospital and took this one. I felt bruised
emotionally and—and terribly humiliated.' She
hesitated, desperately anxious to get it right, not
to give a false impression. 'To be honest, I don't
think I was broken-hearted. The humiliation was
the worst part. I couldn't bear the thought of
people laughing at me because my mother had
stolen my boyfriend.'

'Your friends wouldn't have laughed.'

'No. I knew that really, but I still felt wretched.'

'It was a good idea to come away,' Kirk said
thoughtfully. 'I suppose it's too soon to ask
whether you're feeling any happier?'

The question found Candy unprepared. She
hadn't yet asked herself that and she had to think
before she could find an answer for Kirk.

Eventually she said, 'If I let myself dwell on
what happened, I'm angry and humiliated all over
again, but being on a beautiful ship like the
Bergsen is so exciting and different, and the
people are all different too, so that I can't help
feeling I'm at least over the first hurdle.'

'I'm glad,' he said simply, and smiled at her.

Suddenly aware of racing pulses, Candy jumped
to her feet. 'It's terribly late—I really must go.
Thank you for listening to me, Kirk.' She was at
the door, still babbling. 'I do hope this rain will
stop before tomorrow.'

Kirk caught her before she made her escape and put his arms round her tightly. 'You can't go without saying goodnight.' He kissed her forcefully. 'Take care on those wet companionways, love. See you in the morning.'

Candy got her wish and the sun shone again. She was standing by the coach, collecting tickets, when Steve appeared. She had never seen him out of the navy uniform before, and he looked much more attractive in jeans and one of the bright blue sweatshirts with BERGSEN across the chest which matched Candy's own.

Candy greeted him cheerfully and then turned to the pretty, fair-haired girl who was the local guide. As usual she found herself addressed in perfect English and it made her feel ashamed that she didn't know a single word of Danish.

Steve was not a talkative companion but he appeared to be taking an interest in the drive. Eventually they came to an area of forest and small lakes, and on the fringe of it a town which looked bigger than some. The coach stopped in the market square and the guide announced that they would spend a short time there.

It was Sunday and the shops were closed, but the window displays were attractive and Candy enjoyed looking at them—until she noticed Steve's lack of enthusiasm.

'Are you all right?' She looked at him anxiously.

'Just a bit tired, that's all. Shall we find somewhere to sit down?'

There was a public garden near by and they

soon found a seat. Longing to stretch her legs properly and do some exploring, Candy nevertheless felt impelled to stay with Steve, and suddenly she remembered that Kirk had asked her to try and find out more about him.

'You're looking better than you did a week ago,' she began encouragingly. 'I hope that means you're feeling better?'

He seemed surprised at the comment and muttered something which sounded like, 'Not really.'

'Does this tiredness hit you at any particular part of the day?'

That question seemed to require thought, but finally he told her that it was always worse after physical effort. 'That's why I'm tired now—we've walked the length of the main street.' He grinned ruefully. 'Daft, isn't it?'

'Not if there's a good reason for it. That virus you mentioned—can you remember any details of it?'

'It was just like a bad case of flu—sore throat, swollen glands, temperature. I was in bed for three days.' He turned to Candy with a gesture of impatience. 'Do we *have* to talk about my health? I'd much rather learn a bit more about you.'

'OK.' She gave him a rapid and quite unrevealing history of her career to date, leaving out everything personal, and then announced that it was time to return to the coach.

They could see it in the distance as they walked slowly up the street, with passengers converging on it from all directions. If they didn't hurry, they would be the last to arrive—which would look bad when she was supposed to be the courier in charge.

She seized Steve by the arm. 'Can you walk a little faster if I help you?'

He responded valiantly, leaning heavily on her arm, and she wondered what the passengers watching from the windows were making of it. Not that it mattered.

As they reached the market square, another coach from the *Bergsen* arrived and the first person to jump off was Alex, the official ship's photographer. He started snapping the descending passengers, and then suddenly swung his camera in the direction of Steve and Candy. Ignoring it, she pushed her companion towards the steps with a sigh of relief, and a moment later they were sitting side by side behind the driver.

Back at the ship, she could scarcely believe her luck when she found Kirk reclining in a comfortable chair on the promenade deck.

'Had a good trip?' He pulled another chair forward and she dropped into it.

'I enjoyed Bornholm.' She leaned back and half closed her eyes.

'What didn't you enjoy?'

Candy was on the verge of saying, The company of Steve, but it sounded so unkind that she altered it into, 'Steve was a bit of a problem. He seemed reasonably well at first but it didn't last, and as soon as we did any walking he was just as tired as he's been all week.'

'There has to be a reason for it,' Kirk said thoughtfully. 'Looking back, I remember noticing it before you joined the ship, but I'm afraid I wrote him off as rather a wimp. Our paths hardly crossed at all until he gave himself that rather spectacular cut.' He turned his head and gave her a keen look. 'Did you manage to find out any more about him?'

'Not a lot, but he's definitely been under the weather ever since he got that virus, which was like a bad dose of flu.'

A seagull alighted on the rail and squawked at them hopefully. Down below on the dock another coach was unloading its passengers. It would soon be time to unlock the surgery for a short period before people had to dress for dinner.

'There are so many things that might be wrong with Steve,' Kirk was saying, 'all of them causing intense exhaustion—leukaemia, myloma, lymphoma, for instance.' He frowned. 'But from my point of view it's rather a tricky situation.'

'What do you mean?' Candy asked.

'I'm not his family doctor. In spite of his state of health obviously requiring investigation, he's in no immediate need of my services.'

Candy had never had much patience with medical etiquette. In her opinion the only criterion was whatever was best for the patient.

She said indignantly, 'Surely there's *something* you can do?'

'I can write to his doctor and ask him to try and see him as soon as possible, but I don't even know if Steve gets a day off at the end of a cruise the way you and I do.'

'If he doesn't get one automatically,' Candy declared, 'then he should ask for special leave.

He'll need blood tests and all sorts of things, and
that all takes time.'

Kirk's fingers touched hers between their chairs
and then curled round them. 'You've certainly
taken his cause to heart.' He gave her hand a
gentle squeeze. 'He's a lucky guy to have you
rooting for him the way you've done ever since
you came on board. Is it because that hangdog
look appeals to your maternal instinct?'

'Don't be silly!' She extracted her hand from
his grasp, though she would rather have left it
where it was, and began to struggle out of the
low chair. 'It's time to get ready for surgery.'

Kirk stood up, towering over her. 'You haven't
asked me whether I've had any medical problems
during your absence.'

Candy paused briefly. 'Have you?'

'Marie has been somewhat obstreperous. She
insists the pain's quite gone and she's going to
dance tonight.' He sighed. 'I gave my permission,
but it was against my better judgement. I hope I
shan't regret it.'

CHAPTER FIVE

CANDY always enjoyed the dancers' nightly performance, but tonight she gave her full attention to Marie. Dressed in a skin-tight sea-green costume shimmering with sequins, she appeared just as radiant as the others and her elaborate make-up hid any defects which might have been visible before. Certainly she appeared to have no difficulty in contorting her body into all sorts of unnatural positions. The passengers, who did not even know she had been missing for a short time, applauded enthusiastically.

'She seems OK,' Kirk said, pausing briefly at Candy's side when the area was being cleared for general dancing. 'But I can't believe her abdomen isn't pretty sore. That was a very real pain she had.'

'Dancers are tough. I expect they have to be. They can't always be feeling on top of the world yet they never fail to look it.'

He nodded and moved on, and Candy did not see him again that evening.

In a funny sort of way, she was glad. Their relationship had moved on a stage last night in his cabin, and she wasn't sure she was ready for it. The speed at which friendships developed on board ship took a bit of getting used to. She had known that it occurred between passengers, but she hadn't realised that it also applied to the staff.

She had a lot to think about when she went to bed that night, but she was so tired that she fell asleep almost immediately and remained unconscious until the alarm woke her.

Out on deck, she found the ship about to dock at Copenhagen and she spared a few minutes for watching manoeuvres. She was about to turn away and go below for breakfast when she was surprised to find Dawn at her side.

'You seem to have enjoyed your visit to Bornholm, Candy,' the dark girl remarked with a slightly acid smile.

Dawn usually ignored her and Candy stared at her in surprise. Sometimes she wondered if the courier resented her close association with Kirk.

'You haven't seen the photographs yet? You should stop and look on your way into breakfast.' With a nonchalant wave of her hand, she drifted away.

Alex's gesture with his camera had seemed so unimportant that Candy had forgotten it. Now she remembered only too well, and she made a point of visiting the area where hundreds of photographs were displayed daily on huge screens. As she reached it, she met Emma coming away.

'Dawn told me there was an interesting one of you here and I was sufficiently curious to come and look for it,' she explained. 'I'll show you where it is and then you won't have to spend ages searching. Over here.'

Candy stared in dismay at the glossy photo-graph. The two bright blue sweatshirts stood out vividly—herself and Steve—arm in arm and apparently gazing into each other's eyes.

'He's caught you just at the right moment.' Emma burst out laughing. 'I never knew you and Steve had anything going for each other. You've kept it very dark.'

'Because it doesn't exist. He—er—wasn't feeling very well and I was helping him. That's all.'

'Well, that snap could certainly have fooled me! Not that it matters,' Emma added hastily, apparently realising that her comments weren't welcome.

Candy let the matter drop, conscious that she'd over-reacted. She might get a bit of teasing from some of the male passengers but it wasn't important.

With an effort, she dismissed the matter from her mind and went into breakfast. She ate hastily, conscious that it was going to be a very full day. After surgery she had to go off on an all-day tour which would take them as far as the castle where Hamlet was supposed to have lived.

Kirk had already unlocked when she reached the surgery and he greeted her with a surprisingly cool, 'Good morning.' Assuming that he was in a quiet mood, she got busy with changing the cover on the examination couch.

Suddenly it seemed to her that the silence was unusually prolonged. 'There's nothing wrong, is there?' she asked diffidently.

'Wrong?' He put down the medical magazine he had been toying with and turned his head to give her a long, puzzling stare. 'Depends on your point of view, I suppose.'

Candy gave the cover a final smooth with her

hand and came over to the desk. 'What's that supposed to mean?'

'You don't know?' His eyebrows shot up.

'I wouldn't be asking if I did!'

'Perhaps you haven't seen the photograph,' Kirk suggested frostily.

That *bloody* photograph! Candy bit her lip to restrain herself from saying it aloud. 'Of course I've seen it,' she snapped. 'So what?'

Kirk ignored the question and went on to tell her he had had his attention drawn to it by Dawn. 'She seemed to find it funny but the humorous side of it escaped me. I hadn't realised——' He stopped abruptly and then flung her a nonchalant, 'Never mind. It doesn't matter what I thought.'

'But it does!' It mattered an enormous amount but she wasn't about to tell him that, not when he was in this mood. 'If you'll only listen for a moment,' she went on more calmly, 'I'll tell you exactly what happened, and then perhaps you'll give Steve credit for trying to do a bit of easy sightseeing.'

Kirk listened to her explanation with an impassive face and was silent for a moment after she had finished. Candy waited impatiently, and when he did speak she couldn't pretend she found his comment entirely satisfactory.

'I agree that it was courageous of him but it would have been more sensible to stay on board and have a lazy afternoon. If he'd done that you wouldn't have had to put yourself into what appears to have been a very misleading situation.'

'*Appears* to have been?' she demanded incredulously, staring at him with accusing eyes.

Kirk waved a nonchalant hand. 'A figure of speech.'

'It didn't sound in the least like that to me. I got the distinct impression that you didn't believe me.'

He stood up and moved towards her but she backed away from him. 'You can't blame me for being a bit dubious. You've always had a soft spot for Steve and I'm sure he's attracted to you, and in the photograph you really did look as though you were very absorbed in each other.'

'I was absorbed in getting him safely on the coach, that's all.' An idea shot into her head. 'You said it was Dawn who showed you the picture. I suppose it was she who said we looked like lovers?' His expression confirmed it before he could speak and Candy went rushing on. 'I might have guessed that she wouldn't let an opportunity like that slip past her.'

Kirk's astonishment was obviously genuine. 'Don't you two girls get on?'

'Our paths don't cross very much but I don't think she's liked me from the beginning.'

'I've always thought her rather a nice girl, but there was certainly nothing friendly in her attitude towards you when she drew my attention to the photograph. She seemed to be suggesting that it just wasn't done for members of the staff to parade their relations with each other in public.'

'I never heard such rubbish in my life!' Candy was scornful. 'Who put Dawn in charge of the morals of the rest of us?'

There was a patient hovering in the doorway and Kirk's answer was only a smile and a shrug. As she greeted the stout man with a high colour,

Candy's thoughts were busy. How extraordinarily innocent men were sometimes! Kirk appeared to have no idea that Dawn would be jealous of any reasonably attractive girl who was constantly in his company.

As for her own reaction, she was in two minds about it. Her initial anger had gone, though she still felt irritated by the silliness of the incident. On the other hand, it was gratifying to realise that her relationship with Kirk seemed to be annoying Dawn!

Counting out indigestion pills for the patient, she put the whole thing out of her mind. He was followed by several people with minor troubles, and by the time the flow came to an end she had begun to worry about being late for the tour.

'I didn't like the look of that first chap,' Kirk said as she whisked round the surgery, putting things away. 'I hope he's seen his doctor about his blood-pressure.'

'I suppose you can't exactly ask him?'

'Not without an opening.' He looked at her with a quizzical smile. 'Do you have to buzz around like an infuriated bee?'

''Fraid so.' Candy locked the last cupboard. 'But I've finished now. See you this evening.'

'Have a nice day,' he called after her.

In her cabin, changing out of uniform, she was pleasantly conscious of a warm glow because they were friends again.

Candy enjoyed Copenhagen. She was no longer nervous at being in charge of a coachload of people, and today she had a particularly cheerful and friendly crowd who gave her no trouble at all. Apart from its rather annoying beginning, the day turned out to be one of the best so far.

Back on board, and transformed into a nurse again, she joined Kirk in the surgery. He had news for her concerning Steve.

'I had a word with the staff captain this afternoon, who, as you can imagine, wasn't at all pleased to be told that his assistant purser might be seriously ill. It was a difficult conversation because of having nothing concrete to tell him. At the beginning, in fact, he told me as politely as he could manage that I was making a mountain out of a molehill.' He gave her a rueful grin. 'I have to admit I nearly lost my temper.'

Candy could understand how he had felt. In her experience ordinary people quite often thought they knew better than the professionals and it was always annoying.

'And?' she asked.

'Eventually he agreed to give Steve ten days' leave, starting from the date we reach Southampton, but he'll have to apply for it himself.' He paused and then added, 'We now have to break it to the person most concerned.'

Candy hesitated and then said diffidently, 'I would have thought it might have been a good idea to do that right away. With nearly everybody ashore, Steve wouldn't be busy.'

'True.' Kirk's eyes met hers and held her gaze. 'I thought you'd want to be present. You've been very much involved.'

There was something in his voice she didn't

quite like. Surely he wasn't still thinking about
that wretched photograph?

'During the entertainment would be a good
time,' Kirk went on. 'You're not involved in that
tonight?'

'Oh, no—only on the last evening.' She quailed
at the thought. 'Shall I go to the office and fix it?'

'Would you mind?' He gave her a disarming
smile. 'You'll do it much better than I would.'

'Flatterer!'

They had been standing throughout the conver-
ation and Kirk suddenly took an impulsive step
towards her. He put his hands on her shoulders
and slid them down her back. She had nothing
on except bra and pants under the thin cotton
dress and she could feel his warmth. It had the
strange effect of making her shiver.

Quite unconsciously she leaned forward, lifting
her face slightly, and their lips met in a long kiss
which held so much sweetness and tenderness that
her emotions threatened to overwhelm her.

It was very quiet in the surgery and Candy could
hear the pounding of her heart. As Kirk released
her slowly she drew a long, quivering breath. They
stood looking at each other and suddenly she
found it impossible to meet his eyes.

Had that kiss been as disturbing to him as it
had to her? She longed to know the answer but
dared not even begin to guess what it might be.
With a stifled sigh, she went off to find Steve.

Later on, during the entertainment, she
returned to the surgery and found Steve just
ahead of her. He had been busy when she'd made
the arrangement, and had asked no questions.

Now he looked apprehensive.

'Sit down, Steve.' Kirk waved his hand towards the chair on the other side of the desk. 'Did the nurse tell you why I wanted to see you?'

'Only that you wanted to discuss my health—and I could have guessed that anyway.'

'I've been thinking about this extraordinary tiredness and I feel that it really must be investigated. If you had a shore job it would be no problem. Your doctor could arrange an appointment for you with a haematologist at the nearest big hospital, and you'd only have to take a half-day or so off work. On a ship it's quite different.'

Steve, lounging in a chair, looked at him blankly. 'So?'

'I'm going to write a letter to your own doctor—where do you live, by the way?'

'London—Wandsworth, actually.'

'Splendid! You'll have all sorts of famous hospitals practically on your doorstep.'

'That's all very fine.' Steve shifted uneasily. 'But what about my job on the *Bergsen*?'

'You mustn't worry about that. All you have to do is to ask for sick-leave. It means you'll have to miss a whole cruise——'

'Couldn't Steve fly to join the ship somewhere when his tests are finished?' Candy put in.

Kirk looked dubious. 'That's for the staff captain to decide, but I should think it would be simpler for him to get a temporary substitute for the cruise. Steve will probably have to wait a week for the results of the tests to come through.'

'You keep talking about tests,' Steve burst out, 'but what are they *for*? It's me you're talking about so I reckon I've got a right to know.'

There was an infinitesimal pause and then Kirk said gently, 'There are a number of possibilities, all of which can be treated, but I would prefer not to enumerate them. There's seems no point when it's all guesswork. Much better to wait until you have been tested.'

'That chap you mentioned—haema—something. . .?'

'He's a blood specialist. A great many illnesses can be diagnosed by testing a patient's blood.'

'Oh, God——' Steve's voice broke. He leaned forward and bowed his head on his folded arms on the desk.

Candy jumped to her feet and crossed to stand beside him. She put her hand on his shoulder and pressed gently. 'This has all been a horrible shock to you, I know, but I'm sure you'd like it cleared up so you can begin to feel better. It's wretched to feel tired all the time.'

'Every day is something I've got to get through somehow,' came Steve's muffled voice. 'I never used to feel like that.'

She wanted to assure him that this was a temporary bad patch which would soon be over, but she didn't dare. The treatment might take a long time and be unpleasant, and maybe he would never return to the *Bergsen*.

In the meantime it was important for him to think positively.

'When you've got accustomed to the idea of seeing specialists and getting treatment, you'll be glad something is being done. You couldn't have gone on much longer as you were, and I wouldn't be surprised if you'll start feeling psychologically better almost at once, just because the problem is being tackled.'

Steve raised his head and she saw that his eyes were damp. 'You really think so?'

'Yes, I do—honestly!'

He sighed and hauled himself to his feet, making an attempt to stand up straight. 'Thanks for all you've done,' he said to Kirk. 'I'm not as grateful as I ought to be right now, but I shall be working on it.'

They all smiled and Kirk reminded him to see the staff captain at the first opportunity.

'I've paved the way,' he said, 'so it shouldn't be too difficult.'

When Steve had gone, Candy expected Kirk to make an immediate move, but instead of that he lingered.

'Have you decided what you're going to do when the ship reaches Southampton?' he asked. 'Will you go and see your mother?'

Candy shook her head. 'Canterbury would be an awkward journey by train. Besides, I'm not sure I want to—not just yet. I haven't made any plans but I suppose I might go up to London and visit a nursing friend who recently transferred to St Mary's.' She hesitated and then said casually, 'What about you?'

'I haven't got a home to go to because—as I think I told you—my parents live in Canada. I've got various friends and relations in England but nobody I particularly want to visit. Last time I stayed in the neighbourhood and explored the New Forest. I wasn't feeling at all sociable.' He, too, hesitated. 'How about if we both did that?'

For a moment Candy was too startled to reply. What exactly was he suggesting?

Her face must have given her away for Kirk said briskly, 'Single rooms at a comfortable hotel. What do you say?'

She asked a question of her own. 'Are you feeling more sociable this time?'

'You could say so. I'd certainly appreciate a short break—with the right person. Something tells me you might do very nicely.'

'Thanks very much!' Her heartbeat had quickened but she managed to sound gently teasing. 'Supposing I think you're not the right person for *me*?'

'That hadn't even occurred to me,' he said solemnly, and they both burst out laughing.

After a brief visit to Oslo, the ship surged on towards Southampton. On the morning of their arrival, Candy woke early and lay thinking. She hadn't needed much persuasion to agree to Kirk's suggestion, and now she was happily looking forward to the short break. Another cruise would start tomorrow, but the time in between belonged to her—and to Kirk.

Arrangements had been made for the passengers to go ashore at nine-thirty, and there would be no surgery hour that morning. No need, therefore, for her to put on her uniform. . .

She was wrong about that.

Just as she switched off the shower, there was a loud knock on her door. Dripping, she struggled into a towelling robe and went to see who it was.

To her surprise, she found Tim Harris standing there. He was fully dressed but had forgotten to brush his hair, which stood up all over his head like a chestnut-coloured mop.

'Oh, Nurse, I'm so sorry to bother you but it's Laura, my wife—I think she's going to have the baby!'

For a moment Candy was speechless. Perhaps Tim read the appalled look in her eyes for he went on apologising.

'I'm afraid it being the last morning must make it very difficult for you——'

'Not necessarily. It shouldn't be a problem to organise her removal to hospital. Have you timed the pains?'

'We tried to, but they seemed almost continuous.'

'Oh, God——' Candy swallowed the exclamation. 'Is the baby due?' she asked instead.

'Not for a month. We thought it was safe to come on the cruise. They say first babies are usually late.'

'Often but not always. I do wish you'd called me earlier, Tim. When did the pains start?'

'About four o'clock but Laura didn't wake me for quite a while. She didn't realise it was all going to be so quick.'

'You'd better get back to her.' Candy tried to conceal her growing alarm. 'I'll phone the doctor and then get dressed. Where's your cabin?'

It turned out to be one of the best ones on the promenade deck. Candy made a mental note of the number and dispatched the distraught husband back to his wife. Then she phoned Kirk.

For a moment he seemed as shocked as she had been, but he quickly rallied.

'I don't suppose it's as urgent as they imagine, so we'll probably be able to pack her off to hospital. It would certainly be a great deal better for both mother and child, and I'm sure the staff on board wouldn't be at all pleased to have someone giving birth on this particularly busy day. See you at the cabin in a few minutes.'

'Anything you want me to bring, apart from surgical gloves and a stethoscope?'

'That'll do to be going on with, thanks.'

They met outside the Harrises' door. Kirk was well turned out in shore-going clothes— grey trousers and a navy shirt with his hospital tie—but Candy was in her usual white dress. They exchanged slightly rueful smiles and then gave their full attention to this unexpected problem.

'How's your midwifery?' Kirk asked quietly.

'I—I'm not sure. I did the usual course after I passed state finals but I haven't had any practical experience since.'

'We'll manage.' He gave her a quick pat on the shoulder.

The door was flung open by Tim who looked, if possible, even more agitated than when Candy had seen him earlier.

'Thank God you've come! I was getting really scared the baby might be here first.'

Laura was lying on her back, her dark brown hair spread out over the pillow and beads of sweat on her forehead. Candy went straight to her and took one of her hands in a firm grip.

'You can stop worrying, love, and just leave it to us,' she said with an encouraging smile. She waited for a moment while the mother-to-be dealt with a contraction, gasping and moaning, and trying hard not to, and then continued calmly, 'The doctor wants to examine you to see how far this impatient infant has progressed. Can you turn on your side if I help you?'

Kirk, his sleeves rolled up, was now gloved and ready. He said quietly, 'I'm going to examine you from the back, Laura. Just try to relax.'

'Relax!' she gasped. 'You must be out of your mind, Doctor!'

He smiled. 'It makes it easier for you as well as me if you try. Have you been going to any prenatal classes?'

Another pain seized her and it was her husband who answered. 'We live at the back of beyond in Cumbria. There weren't any classes within a twenty-mile radius.' He gave a nervous laugh. 'Is—is the baby just going to be born?'

'It's not quite as imminent as you thought, but certainly there's no time to waste. I'll check the foetal heart—though I don't think we need have any worries on that score. The child seems very strong and healthy.'

When he had done so, he straightened up and looked from one to the other. 'As I thought, everything's fine, and now we must discuss the best course of action. I'm afraid there's no question of getting Laura transferred to hospital, but we do have a small hospital on the ship. It will be much better for everyone if the baby is born there rather than in your cabin.'

Tim looked shocked. 'But how is she to be got there? She can't walk.'

'No problem,' Kirk said calmly. 'The medical department on the *Bergsen* is very well-equipped, and one of the items supplied by a thoughtful management is a wheelchair.' He turned to Candy. 'Will you fetch it for us, please?'

She sped off, trying to hurry without actually looking as though she was dealing with an emergency. It was still only seven forty-five and normally there would not have been many people about, but today, because the passengers were going ashore soon, the corridors and stairs were swarming with people. One or two glanced at her curiously, but on the whole they were immersed in their own affairs.

It was different when she came back with the wheelchair, but she escaped catching anyone's eye and so avoided being delayed. After that, with Laura installed, there was no hope of dodging attention, but the two men proved so dextrous in manoeuvring the chair that they reached the lift within seconds.

Candy went ahead of them down the long corridor and unlocked the hospital. The little ward had a slightly shut-up smell and she turned up the air-conditioning. The beds were kept permanently ready for occupation and Laura was settled in one of them without delay. She looked at the end of her tether and lay back with a sigh of relief.

Now to find the maternity kit. This sterile pack containing what would be needed for the actual birth was a vital piece of equipment, and Candy hadn't seen it since her first day. Luckily she quickly located it.

'Not long now,' Kirk said cheerfully. 'Would you like something to help you through the final stage?'

Laura shook her tangled head. 'No, thank you. I've managed so far and I'll stick it out to the end.' She closed her eyes, bracing herself for the next onslaught of pain.

It came within a few seconds and Candy clasped one of her hands while Tim held the other. Kirk, now clad in a green operation gown and cap, was scrubbing up at the basin. The other two wore masks and Candy had on a disposable apron over her dress. Everything was ready and there was nothing to do now except await the birth.

Candy had an odd sensation of existing in a vacuum. There was no sound in the room except the humming of the air-conditioning and the small noise of the patient's breathing. After a while even this got quieter and it almost seemed as though Laura had slipped into a doze. If she had been awake since four o'clock, and suffered a good deal of pain, she was probably very tired. All the same, she shouldn't feel in the least like sleeping at this stage.

Candy suddenly became aware that Kirk was looking very hard at her over his mask. He was trying to convey something and, with a flash of inspiration, she consulted her watch. Eight minutes since the last contraction.

With outward calm, she got up casually and bent to check the foetal heart.

She did it very carefully, taking a long time

over it. Laura seemed unaware, lying very still
with her chest rising and falling quietly, but Tim
turned his head and looked from nurse to doctor
in a questioning sort of way. He was not alarmed,
just slightly puzzled.

When Candy was quite sure, she straightened
up and stood back. Without a word being spoken.
Kirk moved to the bedside and did his own check.

At that moment Laura opened her eyes and
asked eagerly, 'Is the baby nearly here? The pains
aren't nearly so bad now.'

Kirk's eyes were serious but he managed to put
a smile into his voice as he replied, 'This energetic
youngster of yours has battled so vigorously to
get born that he has tired himself out.'

'Sexist!' Candy murmured, keeping it light.

'If you like, but until we get a pronoun that
covers both sexes "he" will have to do. I'm sure
Laura wouldn't want her baby to be referred to
as "it".' He began to undo a sterilised pack.

Tim asked sharply, 'What's that? What are you
going to do?'

'Give the baby a little help.' Kirk took out some
forceps and addressed Laura. 'When you feel the
urge to push, however slight, please do exactly
that. It will help me a great deal, and the
baby, too.'

It was all so calm and casual that only Candy
knew the seriousness of the situation. For some
reason—and she didn't think it was anything to
do with struggling down the birth canal—the child
was showing signs of distress. The sooner he—or
she—was born, the better.

She fetched a towel and laid it across Laura's

drawn-up knees so that she wouldn't be able to see exactly what was going on. Then she took up her position on the opposite side of the bed to Kirk. Tim remained close to his wife, holding her hand tightly. Sitting awkwardly on the edge of the bed, Kirk manoeuvred the forceps into position with the utmost care.

For a while nothing much seemed to happen and then he gave a sudden exclamation and announced, 'Won't be long now.'

Candy leaned forward to have a look and distinctly saw a little head covered with wet chestnut hair just visible on the perineum. Her instinct was to call out to Tim to come and look, too, but something seemed to restrain her.

A few minutes later she was glad.

CHAPTER SIX

EVEN now the birth seemed to be going slowly, but Candy told herself that that was a good thing. It could make all the difference between having stitches and not needing them. Nevertheless, she felt an odd sort of foreboding which seemed to be reaching her from Kirk. Although he appeared cool and very much in charge of the situation, she sensed that something was worrying him.

Suddenly he barked out the one word, 'Scissors!'

Candy had them in his hand within a split-second. As she looked down she saw to her horror that the umbilical cord was round the baby's neck.

No wonder there had been foetal distress. The child was being slowly strangled. Already the little face had a blue tinge.

Kirk acted swiftly. One snip and the cord was free. Carefully and steadily, he drew the baby out into the world. Neither of the parents realised at first that labour was over, though Candy knew that it was usual for someone to hold the infant up so that they could see it.

She was all ready to clear away any mucus which had collected in the mouth and she did so rapidly, noting that the child was a boy. She held her breath as Kirk picked him up by the ankles and administered a hearty slap in the time-honoured tradition.

Take 4 Love on Call

Mills & Boon Love on Call romances capture all the excitement and emotion of a busy medical world... A world, however, where love and romance are never far away.

We will send you four LOVE ON CALL ROMANCES absolutely FREE plus a cuddly teddy bear and a mystery gift, as your introduction to this superb series.

At the same time we'll reserve a subscription for you to our Reader Service.

Every month you could receive the four latest Love on Call romances delivered direct to your door postage and packing FREE, plus a free Newsletter packed with competitions, author news and much more.

And remember there's no obligation, you may cancel or suspend your subscription at any time. So you've nothing to lose and a world of romance to gain!

Your Free Gifts!

Return this card, and we'll send you a lovely little soft brown bear together with a mystery gift... So don't delay!

FREE BOOKS COUPON

YES Please send me four FREE Love on Call romances together with my teddy bear and mystery gift. Please also reserve a special Reader Service subscription for me. If I decide to subscribe, I will receive four brand new books for just £7.20 each month, postage and packing free. If however, I decide not to subscribe, I shall write to you within 10 days. The free books and gifts will be mine to keep in anycase. I understand that I am under no obligation - I may cancel or suspend my subscription at any time simply by writing to you. I am over 18 years of age.

9A4D

EXTRA BONUS

We all love mysteries, so as well as the FREE books and Teddy, here's an intriguing gift especially for you. No clues - send off today!

Ms/Mrs/Miss/Mr _____

Address _____

_____

_____

Postcode _____ Signature _____

Mills & Boon Reader Service
FREEPOST
P.O. Box 236
Croydon
CR9 9EL

NO
STAMP
NEEDED

SEND NO MONEY NOW

ARE YOU A FAN
OF MILLS & BOON
LOVE ON CALL ROMANCES?

IF YOU are a regular United Kingdom buyer of Mills & Boon Love on Call Romances you might like to tell us your opinion of the books we publish to help us in publishing the books you like.

Mills & Boon have a Reader Panel of Love on Call Romance readers. Each person on the panel receives a questionnaire every third month asking her for *her* opinion of the past twelve Love on Call Romances. All people who send in their replies have a chance of winning a FREE year's supply of Love on Call Romances.

IF YOU would like to be considered for inclusion on the Panel please give us details about yourself below. We can't guarantee that everyone will be on the panel but first come will be first considered. All postage will be free. Younger readers are particularly welcome.

Year of birth . . . . Month . . . .

Age at completion of full-time education . . . .

Single ☐ Married ☐ Widowed ☐ Divorced ☐

If any children at home, their ages please . . . .

Your name (print please) . . . .

Address . . . .

. . . .

. . . . Postcode . . . .

THANK YOU! PLEASE TEAR OUT AND POST
NO STAMP NEEDED IN THE U.K.

DR/0994/RD

Do not affix Postage Stamps if posted in
Gt. Britain, Channel Islands or N. Ireland

2

BUSINESS REPLY SERVICE
Licence No. SF195

MILLS & BOON READER PANEL
P.O. BOX 152,
SHEFFIELD S11 8TE

Postage
will be
paid by
Mills & Boon
Limited

It was all that was needed. A loud, indignant yell followed and both parents exclaimed excitedly, though Tim—who had behaved so well—was white-faced and looked as though he might faint now that it was all over.

Laura, on the other hand, was flushed and radiant, and already sitting up and holding out her arms. Candy wrapped the baby in a towel and handed him to her, and then both she and Kirk withdrew a little and looked at each other.

'Whew!' He wiped his brow with his sleeve and added, below his breath, 'That was a near thing.'

Candy was feeling absurdly emotional. It was so long since she had done any midwifery that she had completely forgotten what it felt like, and the safe arrival of the Harris infant, after so much trauma, tore at her heart-strings.

Having temporarily lost her voice, she merely nodded, and Kirk looked at her searchingly. She smiled up into his eyes and, still wearing his blood-stained gloves, he gave her arm a little pat. Quite suddenly she was conscious of a sense of communication between them, and a strange little thrill crept over her.

There was still work to be done—the placenta to be checked and the mother made comfortable. Candy helped to make sure everything had come away safely, and dispatched Tim to find a clean nightdress for his wife.

Meanwhile, Kirk had gone into the surgery to ring the nearest hospital and arrange for Laura and her baby to be transferred there.

'I've asked for an incubator,' he said when he

returned, 'since the baby is a month premature.'
He smiled at Laura. 'But I'm pretty sure it's not
needed.'

Candy's heart sank as she contemplated all
that had to be done before she and Kirk could
escape for their brief holiday. She couldn't
leave the ship's staff to clear up in here and
get it ready for a new cruise to the Western
Mediterranean, though they would presumably
do the final cleaning. Then there was her own
cabin next door, still in a muddle because she
hadn't planned to leap straight out of bed and
get down to work. She hadn't even packed her
overnight bag.

Kirk was telling Tim that he'd better go and
prepare to vacate the cabin, getting the job done
as quickly as possible. 'Would you like any help?
I'm sure Candy won't mind.'

'Of course not,' she said gallantly. 'Come
on, Tim.'

They went up in the lift together, and it wasn't
long before she realised that his state of euphoria
had rendered him almost useless at dealing with
ordinary problems—like packing his wife's overnight possessions separately from his own, and
similar practical matters.

Somehow they got it all done in time, and the
cabin ready for the steward with his cleaning
materials. Going below, they found that the
ambulance had arrived.

Escorted by doctor and nurse, the little pro-
cession moved off. Descending the gangway was
a difficult manoeuvre but the men accomplished it
without incident. Standing at the top of it, Candy

looked for the last time at the little family with whom she had briefly been so closely connected, and then turned away with a heart full of thankfulness.

'Without any doubt,' Kirk said, 'this has been the most traumatic experience I've had since I became a ship's doctor. I definitely don't want a repetition.'

'I shouldn't think an emergency birth happens very often—especially one like this.' She glanced up at him as they re-entered the embarkation area. 'I'm a bit surprised that Laura was allowed to come on the cruise when she was eight months pregnant.'

'The company requires a certificate from the family doctor. If he thought she'd be OK, there'd be no problem.'

They reached the hospital and surveyed the chaotic scene.

'Will the cleaners see to this?' Kirk asked with a note of doubt in his voice.

Candy shook her head. 'Shouldn't think so—they aren't like the cleaners in a hospital on shore.' She heaved an unconscious sigh. 'I'd better make a start.'

He put his arm round her shoulders. 'Cheer up! It won't take long if I give you a hand.'

Candy looked at him in astonishment. 'Doctors don't usually volunteer for this sort of job.'

'This one is going to have a bash at it,' Kirk said firmly.

His efficiency amazed her. Within fifteen minutes the hospital was tidy and ready for the official cleaners with their mops and polish, and

all that was left to do was to get ready to leave
the ship.

Southampton was busy with office workers shopping in their lunch-hour. Kirk drove his white
BMW carefully through the mêlée, and Candy
was glad to sit quietly and look forward to what
was to come.

At last they were clear of the town and speeding
towards the New Forest.

'Will a pub lunch be OK?' Kirk asked.

'Great!' Candy suddenly remembered she'd
had no breakfast. 'I'd even settle for a wayside
café.'

'There should be plenty of pubs in this area.
We'll stop at the first one which looks promising
and see what it can provide.'

It looked very promising indeed, with a
thatched roof and rows of hanging-baskets filled
with geraniums. There was a garden blazing with
colour, and a swimming-pool surrounded by
white-painted tables and chairs. Candy would
have liked to eat out there but was far too hungry
to argue about it.

They settled happily in the cool, dark interior,
and both chose a ploughman's—pâté for Candy
and Stilton for Kirk. The lager was cool and
refreshing, and a delicious sense of well-being
crept over Candy as she relaxed properly for the
first time that day.

'I wonder how long they'll keep Laura in hospital?' she said when her appetite had become less
demanding.

'A couple of nights, perhaps. Do you have to

talk about this morning? Personally I'd like to forget it.'

'Because it nearly ended in tragedy?'

'Exactly. It could so easily have turned into a nightmare, with two heart-broken parents and a dead baby to cope with.'

'It's because of your skill that it didn't,' Candy said warmly, smiling at him across the table.

'Skill be damned! I've been shuddering—mentally—ever since because I might so easily have left it a bit too long before using the forceps. I'm a neurologist, after all, not an obstetrician. Having to be jack-of-all-trades on a cruise ship is a bit scary now and then.'

'I expect all doctors are scared at times, whether they're on a ship or not.' Candy balanced a piece of pâté on a wedge of French stick but, instead of putting it in her mouth, she laid it down again. 'Was it because you were thinking on those lines that you were so quiet all the way here?'

'Was I quiet?' He looked at her in surprise.

'You hardly said a word.'

Kirk reached across the table and touched her hand. 'I'm sorry—that must have been very boring for you.'

'Not really. I thought you were concentrating on the traffic.'

'I was to a certain extent—in Southampton, anyway. After that I started brooding about things that could have gone wrong this morning, as I've just been telling you. A most unprofitable exercise, I assure you.'

They were silent for a few minutes and then Candy said tentatively, 'How about making a pact not to mention this morning again until we get back to the ship?'

'Now, that's a really sensible suggestion! By then it should have slipped to the back of our minds and we shouldn't want to mention it at all.' He paused and then added, 'With any luck, we shall have quite a lot more to think about by then. Where would you like us to book in for the night?'

The question sounded so suggestive that her heart missed a beat but she managed to reply in a normal voice. 'Somewhere in or near the forest would be great.'

They found just what they were looking for not far from Lyndhurst. It had once been a manor house, but was now a hotel which still looked as though it was in private ownership. Beyond the grounds, the trees of the New Forest could be seen, and two ponies with their foals were nibbling the grass near the main entrance.

The entrance hall had been left as it was, with the addition of a reception desk. There was a wide fireplace with logs laid ready for a cool evening, a bowl of red peonies on an antique table, and a general air of welcome.

'Yes, we have two single rooms on the second floor, overlooking the garden.' The receptionist, young enough to be interested, glanced from one to the other, her expression friendly but otherwise blank. 'Adjoining rooms, actually. If you'll sign the register, I'll get the keys.'

It was the first time that Candy had stayed in a hotel with a man and she was annoyed to feel herself turning slightly pink. Kirk seemed quite unperturbed and she guessed that he and Nicola had often holidayed together.

Why on earth did she have to think about the girl who had died so tragically? Candy wrote her name in an angry scribble and followed Kirk to the lift.

The rooms were charming in a chintzy sort of way which matched the house. Each contained a double bed with a quilt covered in the same material as the curtains.

'You only get single beds in twin-bedded rooms these days,' Kirk said. 'These rooms can be let to couples who want to sleep together in the fullest sense, or to singles.' He paused and then added nonchalantly, 'Like us.'

Candy went to the window and stared towards the trees crowding to look over the end wall of the long garden. Although she had left the ship feeling tired, a sudden urge to explore came over her.

'Do let's go for a long walk in the forest!' she suggested eagerly.

Kirk got up and came to join her. 'Is that what you'd really like to do? I would have thought a drive would be better after the strenuous time we had this morning. There are lots of interesting places around here.' He slipped his arm round her shoulders and turned her to face him.

Her heart was thudding but she managed to answer coolly. 'It's a perfect afternoon for walk-ing—not too hot—and to me it seems ages since I was on land. *Please*, Kirk!'

'OK, you win.' He gave her bottom a friendly pat and moved towards the door. 'I'll change my jacket for a thin sweater and we'll be off.'

Candy was already in cotton trousers and a polo shirt, and she had only to change her shoes. As she put on the trainers she had brought with walking in mind, she wondered whether she should have been so insistent. Maybe Kirk hated walking? She didn't know anything about his tastes.

Perhaps his leg was hurting. She should have thought of that.

She asked him as soon as he returned but he assured her it was not seriously troubling him, and they set out, going by way of the garden and through a gate into the forest.

The scene was so beautiful that Candy was soon in a state of rapture. The trees were all decked in fresh green growth and there were tendrils of young bracken uncurling along both sides of the path, which was just wide enough for them to walk abreast. . .provided that they kept very close together.

Here and there, where the trees drew back a little, there were wild flowers—pink and white campion, and still a few late bluebells. Squirrels peeped at them from behind tree-trunks, and rabbits raced away into the undergrowth. New Forest ponies, well-used to humans, were feeding in the clearings, and birds fluttered overhead, their beaks full of food for their young.

'This is great!' Candy drew a long breath of delight.

Just for a moment she wondered how much of her pleasure was due to her surroundings, and how much to the presence of Kirk. Thinking about it, she came to the conclusion that the question was better left unanswered. She was happy and that was all that mattered.

'You aren't a country girl, are you?' he asked.

'Not really, though I have grandparents who farm in Kent. I was born in Canterbury and that's where I've always lived. All my life I've loved the country, though, so I suppose it's in my blood. How about you?'

'I suppose you could say the same about me, but my ideal countryside is different from yours. I told you about those idyllic holidays I spent on a Swedish island when I was growing up, didn't I?'

Candy nodded. 'They sounded wonderful—so much more exciting than anything I've known.'

They walked for almost an hour, hand in hand and talking intermittently, or sharing a silence which never became uncomfortable. Suddenly Kirk came to a halt.

'Don't you think we've come far enough?'

She hadn't even begun to think of turning back but she was willing to agree. 'I must admit that a cup of tea would be nice. Do you think they'll give us a proper old-fashioned afternoon tea with scones and cucumber sandwiches? It looks that kind of place.'

Kirk laughed and rumpled her hair. 'What a girl you are for food! I can't think how you keep that slender figure.'

'Hard work!' Candy said promptly, and they both laughed.

On the way back they had an animated conversation about some of their hospital experiences. Kirk had been a senior registrar in the neurology department of a famous London hospital before his skiing accident.

'Will you go back there?' Candy asked.

'I'll probably try to. I certainly want to return to the neurology field. How about you? You won't want to go on being a ship's nurse forever.'

'I've loved my first experience of a cruise, but I expect I'll begin to get tired of it after a while—probably because of all the other jobs I have to do. When that happens, I think I shall try for a job in London, preferably at the hospital where my friend works.'

Back at the hotel, they found it was too late for afternoon tea anyway.

'Think you can exist until dinnertime?' Kirk asked with a grin.

Candy laughed and assured him that she could. As they separated to shower and change for the evening, she told herself that it was a long, long time since she had felt so gloriously light-hearted. It had been a wonderfully happy afternoon and there seemed no reason why the rest of the short break shouldn't follow the same pattern.

Naked in front of the mirror, she surveyed herself critically. Kirk hadn't actually admired her slender figure but he had implied that he appreciated it, and just for a moment she wished she had brought the clinging green and white dress he had liked. It would have been far too dressy for this sort of hotel, though. The full-skirted floral patterned skirt and plain white silk blouse in her case were much more suitable.

Just as she was ready there was a tap on her door and she found Kirk outside.

'Shall we go down to the bar and have a drink?' He looked her up and down. 'Very nice, but not as sexy as the one you wore the other night—the dress you took off before you came to my cabin.'

'"Changed" would sound better,' Candy pointed out with a smile.

'So it would.' He put his arm round her shoulders and they descended the staircase side by side.

They sat for some time in the bar and then went into the dining-room. Compared with menus on the *Bergsen*, the food on offer was simple but it was also very good and both of them found it a pleasant change.

'You can soon get tired of those long, elaborate meals,' Kirk said, spooning up avocado mousse. 'Haven't you found that?'

'I'm just beginning to, but I expect our well-heeled passengers require them. I was talking the other day to a woman who spent her whole time wandering about the world and staying in famous hotels. Imagine it!'

'I prefer not to, thanks.'

They were silent for a moment. The mention of 'well-heeled' had reminded Candy of Sir George and Lady Wickham. The term certainly applied to them but there couldn't be much happiness in their lives at present or in the immediate future either. Although she certainly wasn't cold, an involuntary shiver passed over her, and Kirk looked at her enquiringly.

'Is something the matter?'

Hastily, she explained the direction which her thoughts had taken. 'She was such a courageous lady and I hate to think——'

Kirk stretched out his hand and put it over one of hers. 'Don't let yourself think about it. There's nothing either of us can do—or anyone else, for that matter—and you know as well as I do that the world is full of such cases. We'd never survive if we let ourselves dwell on them.'

'I know.' The feel of his warm hand was doing strange things to her and she had no difficulty in banishing the momentary sadness. Long before the end of the meal she had forgotten it.

They drank their coffee in the lounge, which was like a drawing-room with French windows opening on to the garden. From where she sat, Candy could see fairy-lights strung among the trees, and a half-moon shining brightly above. It was a night for love, for wandering along the shadowy paths with some beloved person and perhaps finding a remote summerhouse. . .

Candy's wayward mind took another leap. Supposing—just supposing—Barry could be her companion on such an occasion; would she enjoy strolling in the garden with him?

No! Definitely not. It might be only two or three months since the transfer of his affections to her mother had left her feeling hurt and humiliated, but there was no denying that her heart had healed with astonishing speed. It had never really been broken—she admitted that—but it had certainly been bruised.

The one thing she really wanted at that moment was to wander hand in hand with Kirk through the soft darkness of the June evening.

Abruptly, she put down her coffee-cup and went to stare out into the garden. The delicious and erotic scent of old-fashioned white pinks was wafted to her on a little breeze, and she could see their small, ghostly faces bordering the path. The beauty of it all was sending odd tremors down her spine. She shivered and clasped her hands tightly together to stop their trembling.

Suddenly she was aware of Kirk standing close behind her, his hands on her shoulders.

'It looks beautiful out there,' he said softly. 'Shall we take a stroll?'

Candy had no idea how she answered, but the next moment she found herself outside on the patio, Kirk's arm in hers. They went down some steps and began to follow the path which led towards the distant gate through which they had passed earlier. After the warmth of the house, the air was deliciously cool but after a few minutes Candy began to feel chilly in her thin silk blouse. She tried to hide it but he noticed almost at once.

'You're cold!' he exclaimed, putting his arm round her. 'Let's find a more sheltered spot.'

They left the path and went down a narrower one which led them eventually to a sort of arbour surrounded by climbing roses just coming into flower. There was a rustic seat apparently just waiting for them and they took possession of it by mutual unspoken assent.

Kirk's arm tightened round her. 'It really is a perfect night,' he murmured, his mouth close to her ear.

'It just needs a nightingale,' she pointed out, trying to speak lightly.

At that moment a wild, unearthly scream cut through the darkness from the direction of the forest. Candy jumped so violently that she nearly fell off the seat. 'What in the world was that?' she gasped.

'Only a shriek owl,' Kirk told her calmly. 'Haven't you ever heard one before?'

'I—I don't think so. I thought owls said tu-whit tu-whoo.'

'Not all of them.' He moved a little nearer and she felt the warmth of his breath on her cheek. 'You don't really want an ornithological lesson just now, do you?'

Candy was not at all clear what she wanted now that they were actually in the garden and alone. Her body was dictating one thing and her mind another. Emotionally confused, she could only decide to wait and see what happened.

For a while they sat quietly, very close together with his arm round her. Candy stopped wondering about what might be going to happen and allowed a strange dreaminess to take possession of her. When Kirk turned her head towards him and kissed her, she responded happily, her whole being stirred by his nearness and the feel of his lips.

They sat like that for some time, talking a little, kissing quite a lot, but with more sensual emotions held at bay.

Suddenly Kirk's grip tightened and she could feel the thudding of his heart mingling with the passionate beat of her own. He pulled her on to his lap and buried his face in the softness of her neck.

'You're very desirable, Candy, love,' he murmured seductively, 'and on such a night——'

On the verge of being carried away, Candy knew it was time for someone to regain control and she wanted it to be her. She began to struggle.

'I—I think we've been out here long enough, Kirk. Let me go, please.'

His arms relaxed their grip and she stood up. As he did not immediately move, she turned away and began walking briskly towards the house. She could see it in the distance, lights still streaming from the windows, but she couldn't remember the nearest way back. They had wandered considerably after they'd left the main path, and the one she was on now twisted and turned. It was dark, too, with the moon hidden behind a cloud and trees making a canopy overhead.

It was an extra-dark patch which was Candy's undoing.

She completely failed to notice a short flight of moss-covered steps, slipped on the top one and fell forward, to land painfully at the bottom on knees and elbows.

'Candy!' Kirk came down the steps in one bound and helped her carefully to her feet. 'Are you all right?' He steadied her by holding both her arms, peering anxiously into her face.

He'd said something funny, though quite without meaning to, and Candy felt she ought to laugh. Unfortunately she felt much more like crying. How could she possibly be all right after such a fall?

'I—I don't think I've broken anything.' She moved her limbs cautiously and they all seemed to work.

'Thank God for that!' He smoothed her hair

back with a gentle hand. 'If only you hadn't been in such a hurry to escape from me——'

It wasn't Kirk she had wanted to escape from—at least not exactly—but she let it pass.

'We'd better get back to the house and assess the damage in a good light,' Kirk resumed. 'Have you got any first-aid kit with you?'

'I don't normally take it on a one-night break!'

'No, of course not—silly question.' He took her arm firmly and they began to walk slowly towards the house. 'I've got some in the car, though, and as soon as I've seen you safely to your room I'll fetch it.'

It seemed a very long way to Candy. As soon as they started she was aware that her left ankle was hurting, and only Kirk's arm prevented her from limping. It was not long before he, too, became conscious of her difficulty.

'Do you think you've sprained your ankle?' he asked, looking down at it in concern.

Candy was already worrying over the possibility but she refused to admit it. 'I expect I twisted it a bit but it'll be OK tomorrow after a night's rest.'

He made no comment but she sensed that he was dubious. How absolutely awful it would be, she thought unhappily, if she returned to the ship with a bandaged ankle and covered in bruises! She'd never live it down.

Fortunately they reached the first floor without meeting anyone. It was fairly late and those guests who had not gone to bed were in the bar. Candy subsided thankfully into her armchair, and Kirk put on all the lights and came over to her.

'I can see that plenty of plaster is going to be

needed.' He picked up first one arm and then the other, and blood dripped down on to her skirt. 'I'll get the first-aid kit and in the meantime you're not to move from that chair.'

Candy promised meekly, torn between a desire to look at herself in the mirror and an even stronger longing just to do nothing. She was beginning to ache all over and her grazes throbbed and smarted horribly.

She was not alone for very long, and as soon as he returned Kirk pushed her chair close to the washbasin and started work. He put disinfectant in the water and washed her arms thoroughly, ignoring her occasional protests. When she was clean and plastered, he turned his attention to her legs.

'I'm afraid your tights have had it,' he observed. 'To put it frankly, they're a bloody mess. Can you manage to take them off yourself? If not, I'll willingly do it for you!'

Ignoring the offer, Candy stood up, dragged her skirt up as far as it would go, and pulled down the tights. They had already started to stick in places and she was obliged to compress her lips to avoid crying out. Gradually, grazed knees and shins came into view.

Kirk gave them the same thorough attention that her arms had received and then came at last to the swollen ankle. He examined it carefully, his fingers firm but gentle, and then gave his diagnosis.

'I don't think it's even a minor sprain. You appear to have given the inner ankle-bone a very severe knock, which is making it hurt like hell.

I'll put a cold compress on and we'll see how it is in the morning.'

Candy received the information with relief. With any luck she would have stopped limping by the time she was on board again. She looked down at Kirk's bent head as he struggled with the bandage, and smiled tenderly. Doctors were never very good at that sort of thing. She longed to touch the bright hair and feel its softness beneath her fingers, but restrained herself. What with one thing and another there had been enough emotion for one evening.

Kirk looked dubiously at his handiwork, gave it a final pat and stood up. Candy smiled up at him and thanked him politely.

'I don't know what I would have done if you hadn't been there.'

The idiocy of the comment struck her at once and she wasn't surprised when he laughed.

'If I hadn't been there, you wouldn't have fallen.' Their eyes met and he was suddenly serious. 'This is no time for post-mortems. Would you like a drink before I help you to bed?'

CHAPTER SEVEN

IT WAS a long time before Candy fell asleep. She had refused the drink and also Kirk's offer of assistance. The emotional state caused by the shock of the fall and his ministrations afterwards was already severe and she needed to be alone to recover.

Slowly the smarting and throbbing eased and her limbs began to relax. Not so her mind. Muddled thoughts, all in some way connected with herself and Kirk, bubbled to the surface and sank again before she could come to grips with them—only to be replaced by others equally disturbing. One moment she was sure she was falling in love with him, and then, remembering how wrong she had been about Barry, she was full of doubts.

As for Kirk's feelings towards herself, it was obvious that he was attracted in a physical sense but she didn't think it went any deeper than that.

Did she want it to? She couldn't be sure.

When weariness finally conquered her, she fell into such a deep sleep that a gentle knocking on her door failed at first to rouse her. Struggling halfway back to consciousness, she thought she was on the ship and a passenger was disturbing her in the night with some problem which might, or might not, be serious. With a groan, she rolled over and peered at her watch, vaguely aware that daylight was peeping round the curtains.

That couldn't happen on the *Bergsen*. Suddenly Candy knew where she was; her vision cleared and she saw that it was nine o'clock. At the same moment the knocking came again.

Her wounds now seemed fairly quiescent. Forgetting about her ankle, she slid out of bed and then winced as it took her weight. Not bothering to put on a robe, she limped to the door and unlocked it.

Kirk was standing there, dressed, shaved and with his shining hair neatly brushed. He smiled down at her but his eyes were anxious.

'How's my patient this morning?'

Candy returned the smile, trying to hide the fact that she was balancing on one leg. 'Fine!'

'Liar!' He looked her up and down, and she hoped her nightie wasn't as diaphanous as she feared it might be. 'I'm quite sure you must be stiff and sore, but that'll soon pass. I'm more concerned about your ankle.'

'It still hurts a bit but I'm hoping it'll be OK by the time we start work again.'

Kirk looked dubious but made no comment. 'I'm just going to ring for room service,' he announced instead. 'What do you fancy for breakfast?'

'Room service?' Candy looked wildly round at her clothes scattered over the floor. 'I'd really much rather go down to the restaurant.'

'Like that?' He gave her a wicked grin and stepped into the room, putting his hands on her shoulders and holding her prisoner.

The ribbon straps on her nightdress were no

protection from the warmth and intimacy of his touch, and Candy had to repress a tremor.

'It would take you ages to get ready,' Kirk went on, 'and I'm starving. I woke up early but didn't want to disturb you. I suggest you put on a robe—for the sake of the waiter—and come along to my room, which is reasonably tidy. OK?'

'All right.' She was breathless and struggling to conceal it. 'I'll be there in a few minutes.'

Kirk ran his finger down her cheek in a caressing gesture. 'Good girl! But you haven't said what you want to eat.'

'Anything you're having. I don't care.' She was backing away from him, willing herself not to limp.

What Kirk was having turned out to be grapefruit, orange juice, porridge with cream, bacon and sausages with waffles, mushrooms and tomato, followed by croissants, the whole accompanied by a large cafetière of coffee.

Candy had never eaten breakfast in a man's bedroom before, and at first felt uncomfortable because of the implications. But the waiter was cheerful and polite, and appeared to notice nothing unusual in the situation. Kirk, too, was completely at ease.

For him, no doubt, it wasn't the first time.

Thrusting aside thoughts of that nature, she settled down to enjoy the food and, though she couldn't keep up with Kirk, she felt greatly restored by the meal.

When they had finished, he consulted his watch.

'We've got roughly five hours before we're supposed to be back on board. I prescribe a leisurely drive through the New Forest, with a short stop at some pub for lunch. Agreed?'

'Lunch!' Candy groaned. 'Don't talk to me of food after the breakfast we've just eaten. I shan't want anything else until tonight's dinner.'

He raised his eyebrows disbelievingly but did not argue, and Candy went off to get ready. It seemed to take twice as long as usual but she had finished by the time he reappeared.

'I want to look at your grazes before we go downstairs,' he told her. 'They'll do much better if they can be left uncovered. Are you brave at taking plaster off?'

Candy made a face. 'No more than any-one else.'

'Better let me do it for you.'

He took her arm in a firm grip and, before she had time to brace herself, ripped off the covering on her elbow. Ignoring her gasp of pain, he frowned down at the sore red patch.

'This will soon heal if the air is allowed to get to it. Keep it like this for as long as possible. Have you got any uniform dresses with long sleeves which you can wear when you start work again? As you know, any wounds still oozing must be covered in the surgery.'

Touched by his thoughtfulness, Candy agreed meekly. She had brought a few rather old-fashioned dresses with her in case it was cold, and they would do very well.

It was past mid-morning by the time they left the hotel. As they drove through quiet, almost traffic-free roads, she found herself wishing the time had been longer. It was all so peaceful, with dappled sunshine and shade, and forest ponies feeding without fear at the roadside, that her happiness increased with every mile.

Not much had happened to cause such a state of euphoria—she had to admit it. In fact, a good deal had occurred to have the opposite effect. It had been a very nasty fall, and she still felt sore and bruised. There was the problem of her sprain, too. She just had to be mobile on board.

So why did she feel so happy?

Shying away from the answer to that, Candy abandoned self-analysis and concentrated on enjoyment.

On board the *Bergsen* it was still fairly quiet. Some passengers had arrived but the coaches bringing most of them were not yet due. Candy went straight to her cabin, using the lift instead of the stairs, and put on one of her long-sleeved dresses.

Surveying herself in the long mirror, she thought she looked dowdy and outdated. Her normal dresses were well-cut and emphasised her curves. These were button-through and appeared to have been made with no idea of fitting anybody in particular.

With a shrug of resignation, she turned away. It would only be for two or three days, and she needn't keep the dress on just now. Ripping it off, she substituted a pair of white cotton trousers and a long-sleeved polo shirt in pale blue silk jersey.

The ship did not remain quiet for long. From

three-thirty onwards coaches began spilling out
their passengers below on the dock—smart, well-
groomed women and men in expensive casual
wear. They all seemed to have mountains of
luggage, and crew-members were kept busy
transferring it all to the waiting staterooms or
well-appointed cabins prepared for their new temporary owners.

Candy hovered in the embarkation area, ready
in case she was needed but hoping very much that
she wouldn't have to exercise her ankle.

Among the passengers streaming past, she
noticed a pair who didn't seem to belong in this
cosmopolitan throng. One was an attractive girl
with pale blonde hair hanging nearly to her waist.
She was wearing jeans and carrying two lots of
hand luggage, and was followed by a woman who
looked about fifty and was very quietly dressed
in a brown linen suit. It hung loosely on her thin
frame, and Candy, noting this, was also aware of
the lines of pain etched on her face.

The two of them slipped to the back of her
mind as soon as they were out of sight, but later,
when the turmoil had subsided, Emma brought
them back to her attention.

'Guess who's on board?' Her brown eyes were
alight with amusement and something Candy
couldn't give a name to. 'Julie Markham!'

'Who's she?'

'Oh, sorry—I forgot you'd probably never
heard her name. She was your predecessor as
nurse, but she broke her contract so abruptly that
they had to get a temporary replacement to fill
in for a couple of weeks.'

Candy looked at her blankly. 'What on earth's she doing here now?'

'She's a passenger. I had a word with her and apparently she's looking after her aunt who's been very ill. They've got a stateroom—just imagine it! The aunt must be well off even if she doesn't look it.'

'I think I saw them,' Candy remembered. 'Is she a blonde—the girl, I mean?'

'Very much so.'

'It was only for a moment.' Candy paused and then added deliberately, 'Julie must be the one who left because she'd fallen for Kirk.'

Emma gave her a sharp look. 'Who told you that?'

'I believe *you* did.'

Emma's eyebrows shot up. 'Really? I ought to be ashamed for spreading rumours—not that there wasn't good foundation for what people were saying. Julie made no secret of her feelings for Kirk but she did have another reason for leaving. The poor girl wasn't a good sailor so she was a bit unreliable as a ship's nurse.'

With a wave of her hand she departed, leaving Candy feeling oddly disturbed. Nothing in Emma's flow of information had given her a clue as to Kirk's feelings towards his one-time nurse. Maybe Julie had had some encouragement to fall in love with him?

The flow of passengers had ceased and Candy decided to go to the purser's office and get some Spanish money. Trying hard not to limp, she set off. A little later, she was crossing the magnificent maroon carpet in the reception area when a small elderly lady with elaborately dressed grey-blonde hair came hurrying down the stairs and rushed up to her.

'Can you help me, please? I've lost my little grandson.' Her voice—definitely American—was rising in panic. 'His mother is expecting another child and she's been told to rest, so I offered to take Junior with me on my cruise. Oh, God—I'll never forgive myself——'

Candy interrupted as gently as she could. 'What's the little boy's name, how old is he, and what is he wearing?'

'He's called Earl after his daddy—Earl Hammerson—and he's four.' She wrinkled her finely plucked brows. 'He was wearing red jeans and a white short-sleeved top, and he's got fair hair and brown eyes. He's a real little bundle of mischief—one minute he was in the cabin with me and the next he'd vanished.'

'We'll broadcast a message on the Tannoy,' Candy said, 'and I'm sure he'll soon be found. Come with me, Mrs Hammerson, and I'll arrange it.'

They were busy at Reception but Candy soon attracted attention. A few minutes later a dis-embodied voice rang out in every corner of the ship, giving a description of the missing child and asking if anyone had seen him.

There was nothing to do now but wait.

Candy persuaded her charge to sit down on one of the comfortable settees, but Mrs Hammerson remained rigidly upright, her hands tightly clasped. Conversation was difficult but somehow Candy kept it flowing by concentrating on the family at home in the States.

Neither of them was looking towards the stairs, but something must have alerted Mrs Hammerson for she suddenly leapt to her feet with a squeal of excitement.

Kirk was descending the stairs carefully with a red and white bundle in his arms. For one dreadful moment Candy thought the child was unconscious, but a movement of the little fair head on Kirk's arm killed that fear. The little boy was sobbing quietly, though, and clutching his left elbow with his other hand.

Mrs Hammerson hurled herself towards the pair, questions pouring from her, and Kirk hurried to reassure her.

'He's bruised his elbow rather badly, poor little chap. Bumped his head too, but he'll soon be OK.' He looked over the top of her head towards Candy. 'Come down to the surgery and we'll assess the damage. I think a nice, interesting bandage might do a lot of good psychologically.'

'But where did you *find* him?' the distraught grandmother panted as Kirk strode towards the lift.

'In the most likely place.' He gave her one of his charming smiles. 'The lifeboats are an irresistible attraction to children, and when I heard the announcement I went there first. It didn't take me long to find one which had an occupant. It's not easy to get into them and Earl had fallen and hurt himself, making it impossible to get out without help.'

Candy went ahead and unlocked the hospital.

She steadied the little boy's arm while Kirk made a careful examination.

'There's no fracture,' he said, 'and, in any case, it would only have been a greenstick break, which is merely a partial fracture which is common with children and heals well. Nurse will immobilise the arm and I'm sure a clever little boy like this one will soon get used to being one-handed. In a few days we'll give him a sling instead.'

'Thank you, Doctor,' Mrs Hammerson said, 'but what about his head?'

'There's no real damage done but he'll have a mighty fine bruise. I'll give you a mild sedative for him so you both get a good night.'

They departed, the elderly American still gulping her thanks, and Kirk gave Candy a rueful grin.

'Last cruise we had Steve pouring with blood right at the start, and now this has begun with a lost child. Life's full of excitement!'

Candy smiled and agreed. The mention of Steve had reminded her of what she had been about to do when Mrs Hammerson had intervened, and she told Kirk. To her surprise, he frowned.

'It's a long way from here and you've done enough walking for the present. Much better to go to your cabin and rest that ankle.'

His concern for her produced a warm glow in the region of her heart, but she protested nevertheless. 'I thought I'd find out if they've got any news of Steve. He might have seen his doctor this morning.'

'Even if he did, he's unlikely to have found out anything,' Kirk pointed out with a slight show of impatience. 'We all know he'll have to have a number of tests.'

'Yes, of course. I just wondered, that's all. I was very sorry not to have said goodbye to him yesterday and wished him luck, but the Harris baby made that impossible.'

'Your concern does you credit,' Kirk said lightly.

Was he being sarcastic? Candy wasn't sure, and made no reply. Almost immediately he returned to his former manner and continued speaking.

'I'll go to the purser's office and change your money for you, and I'll even ask about Steve, though I'm sure it's pointless.' He put his finger under her chin and tilted her head. 'So be a good girl and do what the doctor ordered. I'll be back before long.'

She felt a butterfly kiss on her mouth and he was gone.

Locking up with fingers that trembled a little, she wondered whether he knew about Julie and, if so, what his reaction had been. He hadn't appeared to have anything on his mind, but perhaps he would have regarded her reappearance as a matter of no importance and not worth mentioning. After all, although apparently everybody knew his nurse had been in love with him, no one had hinted that he had reciprocated.

Even so, in spite of so much logical thinking, Candy felt uneasy.

When Kirk returned, she was sitting upright on her bed with one pillow behind her and her foot resting on another, and he gave her a nod of approval.

'Here you are.' He put a pile of coins and some dingy notes on the dressing-table. 'They've got a nice chap named Alan Bainton in Steve's place. He's older and going grey a bit, but he looks quite healthy.' He paused and then added casually, 'Steve hadn't phoned, so there won't be any news now until we're back at Southampton.'

Candy thanked him for the money and made no comment on the information. Kirk was now sitting on the edge of her bed and looking at her critically, and his nearness was arousing emotions which she felt unequal to coping with at the moment.

'That fall shook you up pretty badly, didn't it?' he said thoughtfully. 'You must try and rest as much as possible today and tomorrow. No dancing this evening.'

'I couldn't anyway,' she pointed out, 'because of my ankle. I asked if I could have a sedentary job and was told to help Dawn at the roulette table. I don't know anything about it, of course, but——'

'I'm sure she'll do her best to put you in the picture.' Kirk got up again and moved towards the door. 'By the way, I'll hang around for a short while when the surgery is open, just in case you run into anything you can't handle easily. Not that I expect any patients, but you never know.'

He closed the door before Candy could find the words to thank him, and she sat for a moment staring resentfully at the dowdy long-sleeved dress hanging on her cupboard door. How many days would she have to wear it? Two? Three?

All too soon it was time to put on the horrible

garment and go next door to the hospital. Kirk had not yet arrived and, to her surprise, she had a visitor almost at once—not a patient but a passenger who had lost his supply of insulin. He was a nice man and very distressed.

'I can't think how it happened, Nurse. I had it in my pocket, just as I always do when on a journey, and it must have slipped out somehow.'

'Do you think you lost it on the ship?' Candy asked.

'I must have because I used it soon after I came aboard. I'm all right at present, of course, but you don't need me to tell you that a diabetic can't be without it for long.'

'No, of course not——' Candy broke off as Kirk entered, and she quickly explained the situation.

'What you have to do,' he told the anxious-looking man, 'is to go to Reception and ask for their help. They'll broadcast a message on the Tannoy. Someone is almost sure to have spotted your insulin container lying around, and you may even find that they have it waiting for you.' He smiled. 'Don't worry; we'll soon get it sorted.'

But when they were alone, Kirk gave vent to his real feelings. 'It's amazing how bloody careless people can be! That man's life depends on his insulin. You'd think he would look after it better.'

'We've got some here,' Candy reminded him.

'Yes, but I don't want to start using it when we've only just sailed.' He opened a copy of the *Lancet* and began to turn the pages. Candy had brought a guide to Santiago with her, and for a while there was silence in the surgery.

Suddenly a sound from the corridor caught Kirk's attention.

'I think we may be going to have another visitor,' he said, abandoning his magazine.

Candy put down her book. They were both facing the door when it was pushed wide open and Julie Markham appeared.

She stood poised on the threshold, her long pale hair gleaming like wintry sunshine and her lips curved in a radiant smile. For a split-second no one said anything but there was time for Candy to glance at Kirk. It was as though a screen had come down over his face and hidden all trace of feeling. Except for a tautness round the mouth, he was utterly without expression.

'Hi, Kirk!' Ignoring Candy after one swift glance, Julie advanced into the room. 'Aren't I a lovely surprise?'

His eyebrows twitched slightly. 'You're certainly a surprise.'

'Don't you want to know why I'm back on the *Bergsen*?'

'I've no doubt that you're about to tell me,' he observed drily.

She came nearer and perched on the desk, swinging one leg. 'I'm a customer this time. My aunt Stella—she's Dad's sister and she married a man with pots of money but she's a widow now—has been ill and she thought a cruise might do her good. She didn't care what ship she picked and, as I'd offered to go with her, I suggested the dear old *Bergsen*. We were lucky enough to get a stateroom cancellation.'

'A stateroom indeed! Rather different from

your previous accommodation next door to where we are now.'

'You can say that again,' Julie agreed happily.

Candy was beginning to get tired of being ignored, but at that moment Kirk turned to her.

'You two girls might as well get to know each other. Julie, this is Candy. She's just starting her second cruise.'

The two nurses said 'Hello' with a marked lack of enthusiasm, and Candy was conscious of being very thoroughly scrutinised. If only she had been wearing her normal outfit she wouldn't have cared, but she was unhappily aware that she was looking absolutely nothing like a nurse on a luxurious cruise ship.

Julie hesitated in an affected sort of way, and then said with apparent diffidence, 'I don't want to interfere or anything, Candy, but I do think you're going to find that uniform awfully hot when the ship reaches the Mediterranean. Personally, I always wore short sleeves even in the Baltic, and much thinner material. You can always add a cardigan if it's chilly.'

Candy drew a deep breath and smiled sweetly. 'It's very kind of you to worry about whether I'm too hot, but there's no need. This isn't my normal uniform. I have to keep my arms covered just now because I was idiot enough to slip on some steps and I've got some rather bad grazes.'

She saw Julie's gaze dart towards Kirk, but all she said was, 'That was bad luck,' in a doubtful sort of tone.

Candy agreed, and then forced herself into

making an attempt at friendliness. 'It must feel strange being an ordinary passenger with nothing to do except enjoy yourself.'

'It's going to be great!' Julie's large blue eyes opened wide. 'I'm really looking forward to it.'

Kirk had paid no attention to their brief exchanges. His face still wore that deadpan look. But now he glanced up and asked whether they were likely to meet the aunt professionally during the cruise.

Julie shrugged. 'She's brought her usual medication with her but I suppose something might crop up. She has gastric trouble and her doctor ordered rest and a light diet. She's a lot better than she was.' She hesitated and then added uncertainly, 'At least she says she is.'

'Hasn't she had any X-rays?'

'I honestly don't know. Though we live in the same town, I don't see much of her. I've been away recently on an agency job.'

Kirk stood up with an air of terminating the conversation. 'Nice to see you again,' he said lightly. 'I hope you and your aunt enjoy your cruise.'

Julie slid off the desk and thrust her arm through his, looking up into his face appealingly. 'You can't dismiss me just like that after— well, after we worked so closely together. The least you can do is to buy me a drink before dinner.'

It was now ten minutes past the surgery's closing time and Kirk had no reason to refuse, but Candy thought that he hesitated before leaving with his ex-nurse.

More perturbed than she would have cared to admit, she locked up and went to her cabin. Kirk had shown no sign of pleasure when Julie appeared, but that might mean he had himself well under control.

She surely wouldn't have fallen for him as badly as people seemed to think without *some* encouragement—like sessions on the observation deck, for instance.

Learning how to operate a roulette wheel was a new experience for Candy. She had not looked forward to working with Dawn, but to her surprise the dark-haired courier was friendlier than usual. At first she confined herself to giving instructions, but as they waited for people to drift into the Fiord bar after dinner she asked Candy an abrupt question.

'What's Julie Markham doing back on the ship? I heard she was escorting an invalid aunt but I don't believe that's her real reason.'

'It seems to be,' Candy said cautiously.

'Why do you say that?' Dawn leaned forward and fixed her eyes on Candy's face. 'Have you met her?'

'She came to the surgery to—to see Kirk, and then dragged him off to buy her a drink.'

Dawn muttered something Candy didn't catch and frowned down at the wheel with its numbers and brightly coloured sections of red and black. She seemed to be hesitating but eventually she asked an obviously reluctant question.

'How did he react to her reappearance? Surely he wasn't—pleased?'

Candy shook her head. 'I don't think so but it was hard to tell because he played it very cool indeed.'

The sound of voices and laughter heralded a surge of smartly dressed men and women into the bar. After ordering drinks, they gathered round the table. As Candy tried to fix her concentration on what was happening, she was conscious that at the back of her mind, visible only to her inward eye, there was a picture of Kirk and Julie in the main lounge at that very moment, dancing in each other's arms.

Was Dawn's imagination following the same path? She was laughing and flirting with the men, so it was hard to believe. But then Candy herself was doing the same thing—it was part of the job—but underneath it all she was far from happy.

It was impossible to believe that the return of Julie wouldn't have *some* effect on the developing relationship between herself and Kirk.

She was tired when the evening ended at last, and her ankle ached, so she went straight to her cabin. Morning brought a lifting of her spirits, though nothing happened to cause it except that she was too busy to think about anything except work. During the surgery hour they were never without a patient, and after that she was on duty in the library.

They were now well into the Bay of Biscay and the sea was noticeably rougher. Just to be on the safe side, she took two of the pills Kirk had mentioned when she'd come on board, and was relieved to find that she still felt perfectly well.

A proportion of the passengers had disappeared into their cabins but no one asked for medical assistance. Not at first, anyway. . .

CHAPTER EIGHT

AT TWELVE-thirty, Candy was locking up the library when a middle-aged woman approached her and she recognised Julie's aunt Stella. Seen close to, she looked even thinner and paler than she had done yesterday, but her manner was calm and composed. She wore beautifully cut fawn trousers and a cashmere sweater to match, but her grey hair was cut short and looked as though she washed it herself.

'Excuse me—someone told me you were the nurse. . .'

'That's right.' Candy smiled and indicated her name-tag. 'Can I help you?'

'It's not me. I'm a good sailor, I'm glad to say, but my niece is feeling dreadfully ill, poor girl. She wanted me to fetch the doctor but I don't know how to contact him, and, in any case, one hardly likes to bother him over a simple case of seasickness.'

'I don't expect he would have minded,' Candy assured her, wondering if it was true. 'Has your niece taken any medication of her own?'

'I don't think so, but she started feeling a bit queasy in the night so I couldn't be certain. Is it important?'

'It could be.' Candy came to a decision. The staterooms were on the same deck as the library so it wouldn't take long to check. 'I'll come with

134

you and ask her, and then find the doctor. He would need to authorise any issue of drugs.'

Julie was in no state to revel in luxury today. She lay on her bed, ashen-faced and motionless, her eyes closed.

'I'm sorry you're feeling so poorly,' Candy said, meaning it and thankful that she wasn't in the same state. 'Have you taken anything?'

Julie made a moaning sound which sounded like, 'No,' and then roused herself slightly. 'It wasn't too bad at first and I thought that if I stayed in bed maybe I'd be all right.' She opened her eyes and peered at Candy. 'Why didn't Kirk come?'

'I just wanted to assess the situation, and now I'm going to find him.'

'Thank you, Nurse.' The aunt led the way to the door and opened it for her.

'Please call me Candy, Mrs—er——'

'I'm Stella Kennedy,' she said with a wan smile.

In the big lounge people were sitting around with pre-lunch drinks, and Candy found Kirk with a glass in his hand chatting to Marie, the dancer who had a grumbling appendix. She sat down next to him and plunged straight into an account of Julie's suffering.

'I can't say I'm surprised,' he commented when she had finished. 'What really puzzles me is why she came back. She knew she'd got to cross the Bay of Biscay.' Glancing across at Marie, he apologised for talking shop. 'We were discussing your appendix before Candy joined us. Are you really expecting me to believe you haven't had even the smallest twinge of pain since you recovered from that bad bout?'

'I'm really expecting you to believe it,' Marie said solemnly, her dark eyes smiling.

'There's no harm in expecting!'

They both laughed and Kirk stood up, putting his glass down on a small table. 'I'd better go to the surgery and get that poor girl some pills.'

Candy debated whether to offer to go instead. It was the obvious thing for a nurse to do but she hesitated. Kirk might be intending to spare her ankle the long walk back to the veranda deck. Or, on the other hand, he might actually *want* to visit Julie to reassure himself about her condition.

'I'll go if you like,' she said uncertainly, looking up at him.

He waved a nonchalant hand. 'It's OK—I don't mind a little exercise—and it wouldn't be the first time I've had to take Julie some pills! By the way, if you see that youngster who caused such a fuss yesterday, you might check that his bandage is secure.'

Candy promised to do so and looked after Kirk thoughtfully. Other people—mostly women— were doing the same as the tall doctor with his Viking good looks made his way through the crowded lounge. Some of them, no doubt, would lose their hearts to him in a mild sort of way before the end of the cruise. It wasn't surprising that those who worked with him—his nurses— seemed to fall like ninepins.

Horrified at the path her thoughts had taken, Candy tried to snatch them back. Julie had been a victim, if everyone was to be believed, but there was no need for her successor to become one too. She might be in danger—even teetering on the brink—but she hadn't yet fallen.

Or had she?

'You've got a very peculiar expression on your face,' Marie said curiously. 'You're not feeling seasick, are you?'

'Goodness—no!' Candy broke into an awkward laugh. 'I was just wondering whether to go in search of a little boy called Earl Hammerson.'

'Why bother? He'll turn up at lunchtime, won't he?'

'Sure to, I should think.' Candy stood up. 'Let's go and have ours.'

During the night, the ship docked at Vigo, on the north-west coast of Spain. The passengers were to go on various tours, and Candy was booked to escort the all-day one to Santiago de Compostela. On the way to the embarkation area she met Julie going in the opposite direction. She had obviously quite recovered.

'Those pills Kirk brought me did a lot of good,' she said in answer to Candy's polite enquiry. 'I shall have a lazy day, though, after what I went through yesterday, but Aunt Stella's going on the Santiago trip.' She frowned slightly, looking prettily worried. 'I hope it won't be too much for her.'

Candy promised to keep an eye on Mrs Kennedy, and they set off punctually at half-past nine. It was a long drive to Santiago, where they were to visit a famous cathedral, and she had plenty of time for thinking. A guidebook lay on her lap and sometimes she turned the pages, but mostly she thought about Kirk.

She had been attracted to him right from the beginning of the first cruise, and the fact that they were both escaping from unhappiness had seemed to draw them together. Gradually ordinary liking had developed into something deeper. . .

Reaching the point where she always brought herself up with a jerk, Candy looked at her watch and discovered it to be coffee-time. At first it had taken her ages to serve drinks on a coach, but now she could accomplish it with speed and no spillages, and she was glad to have something to occupy her mind.

Soon after that they reached the outskirts of Santiago.

Stella Kennedy gazed at the ancient cathedral in awe. 'It's so famous,' she murmured, 'and pilgrims have been coming here for centuries, but though I'm quite an experienced traveller I've never been here before. I'm very grateful to my niece for suggesting this cruise.'

So it had been Julie's idea all along. Interesting.

The cathedral was huge, dark and crowded with tourists of all nationalities. The Spanish guide gave them strict instructions to keep together and they began their tour, moving in a tight group from one spot to another.

As they stood staring at a giant censer, a woman who had been with Stella on the coach came up to Candy.

'I'm sorry to bother you but I can't see Mrs Kennedy anywhere. We've been keeping together, both being singles, but she seems to have disappeared.'

Candy felt as though a cold hand had clutched her heart and was slowly squeezing it. The thing she most dreaded had happened.

She moved swiftly towards the guide. 'Please don't move on for a moment. I'm told someone is missing.'

'Missing? Never have I had this happen!' The guide glared at Candy, her black eyes full of reproach. 'Please to find her at once.'

Candy sped off. It was easy to travel quickly alone and she began a methodical search. Fortunately, she remembered, Stella was wearing a white cardigan, which would make it easier.

Quite suddenly, in the region of the high altar, she came face to face with her.

'Mrs Kennedy!' Candy seized her by the arm. 'I'm so thankful to have found you! However did you get separated?'

Stella clung to her and looked as though she might faint. 'Oh, God—I was so frightened—I couldn't think what to do——' She took a deep breath and tried to steady herself. 'It was when we came in single file through that narrow passage to the high altar. If you remember, it took a long time for us all to emerge, and I was so tired I just had to sit down. It—it seemed to ease the pain, too.'

'Pain?' Candy asked sharply.

'Not really pain—just a little discomfort. Anyway, there was a group of Germans near and I started to listen to the commentary. I know

German fairly well and got quite absorbed. When I looked round, you'd all vanished.'

She was so penitent that Candy could only feel sorry for her. Making no comment, she hurried her captive back to rejoin the party.

For the rest of the day she kept a careful eye on Stella and was concerned to note her increasing weariness. As soon as they got back to the ship, she showered and went along to the surgery. There might be time to discuss what had happened at Santiago with Kirk before passengers with medical problems began to arrive.

Kirk, immaculate in his white jacket, was sitting at the desk and she noticed, with an oddly sinking heart, that his face wore one of his inscrutable expressions.

He said abruptly, 'Julie cornered me when I was on my way down here. She wanted to make a serious accusation about you.'

'What?' Candy stared at him in dismay. Her conscience was clear. 'I don't understand.'

He frowned down at his hands which lay idly on the desk-top. 'She claims that you were careless and managed to lose one of the passengers in your care—namely, her aunt.' Glancing up suddenly, he fixed his eyes on Candy's face. 'I had to promise to look into it.'

Of course—she ought to have guessed. Candy felt her cheeks flooding with angry colour, but her voice was well under control.

'I suppose you're willing to listen to my version?'

For a moment the blank look vanished and she saw some sort of emotion in his eyes.

'That's what I'm waiting to hear,' he assured her.

She drew a long breath and prepared to defend herself, explaining how she had watched the passengers going one by one—including Mrs Kennedy—into the narrow passage, and then followed after them. 'She admits it was her own fault that she got separated from the party at the other end.' Defiantly, she tilted her chin and held his gaze. 'I wouldn't mind betting she told Julie so.'

Kirk got up and crossed to the door, which was standing wide open. He pushed it almost shut and then came back and put his hands on Candy's shoulders. The deadpan expression had gone, and now his face was full of warmth and tenderness.

'I'm very much afraid you may be right about Julie, but I had to go through the motions. She doesn't seem to like you very much. I can't imagine why.'

Candy could have told him but she had no intention of doing so. Instead, she said, 'It doesn't matter—just so long as *you* don't think I was to blame.'

His reply was eminently satisfactory.

'Of course I don't, love, and I shall tell her she's got it all wrong at the first opportunity.' He kissed the top of her head. 'Did you get the impression that Mrs Kennedy was feeling ill as well as tired?'

Candy nodded. 'She let slip that she'd had a bit of pain.'

'We know she's got gastric trouble,' Kirk said thoughtfully, 'but according to Julie she's supposed to be on the mend. There's nothing we can do about it. If she wants to keep her internal problems private, that's her privilege.'

'But she might have an ulcer, or gallstones, or—or cancer.'

'True, but I don't think Julie would fail to let us know if her condition worsened.'

A gentle knock at the door caused them to spring hastily apart. The patient was an elderly man who had managed to get a splinter down inside his thumb-nail. Candy steadied the trembling hand while Kirk gently drew out the sliver of wood.

Their heads were very close together and her fingers accidentally touched his. Involuntarily, she raised her lashes and found herself studying the tiny laughter-lines at the corners of his eyes.

No doubt he had laughed a lot when he was with Nicola. Candy had definitely got the impression that they had been friends as well as lovers. Suddenly, an upsurge of emotion caught her by the throat. There was no reason for it, except that it had been a long, worrying and tiring day, and Julie's accusation had been the last straw.

'I don't think that will give you any more trouble, Mr Forman,' Kirk was saying pleasantly, 'but please come and see us at once if it does.'

They were alone after that and he took the opportunity to ask Candy how her wounds were progressing.

'My ankle's almost back to normal.' She stretched out her leg and twisted the foot round. 'And I don't think I need cover myself up as though I had leprosy any longer. With your permission I'm going back to my proper uniform tomorrow.'

'Let's have a look at those grazes.' Kirk stood up and waited while she rolled up her sleeves.

'They've healed very well.' He ran his fingers up and down her arm, and she had to bite her lip to restrain a shiver. 'I won't ask you to pull down your tights and show me your legs.' His eyes twinkled. 'It wouldn't look good if we had a late customer.'

'They're OK,' she said quickly, without meeting his eyes. 'So it's all right if I revert to my normal gear in future?'

'I shall look forward to it,' Kirk said solemnly, and glanced at his watch. 'You can go off if you like and get ready for the captain's cocktail party. You've remembered that it's tonight?'

She hadn't, actually, but now that she could wear what she liked she felt more interested. Thanking him for locking up, she hurried to her cabin and hesitated over the contents of her wardrobe. Eventually she chose a long dress of filmy white voile with ruffles at the hem and a very low neckline.

Everyone had dressed up for the occasion. Julie looked wonderful in sapphire-blue, and as she stood talking to Kirk, their two blonde heads very close, they made a spectacular pair. Averting her eyes hastily, Candy found a fortyish, rather overweight man named Ivor Hodgson at her side. He had a red face and an obvious hairpiece, and monopolised her until the party ended.

'I'll look out for you when the dancing starts.' He squeezed her hand.

Candy forced a smile and reminded herself that it was part of the job.

The entertainer was good, with a repertoire of conjuring tricks and impersonations, and for a while Candy forgot all about Ivor Hodgson. When the dancing began she managed to avoid him for a while by vigorously carrying out her social duties as far from him as possible.

It was not until people began to drift off to bed that he managed to corner her.

'You've been very much in demand,' he grumbled, drawing her into a clutch so tight that she could feel him breathing.

'It's what we're supposed to do—dance with as many people as possible, I mean.'

'Well, now you've done your duty—and done it nobly, if I may say so—we can enjoy ourselves.' His fingers moved on her back and began a slow, would-be erotic massage.

Candy endured it for a moment and then made a small sound of protest. 'I wish you wouldn't do that.'

'You don't like it?' He stared at her in genuine surprise. 'I've always been told my technique is rather good.'

'It's your dancing technique you should be thinking about just now.' Candy winced as he stumbled over her foot.

'I'm a bit rusty at doing this old-fashioned stuff. Disco-dancing is more my line.'

Candy longed to say, Aren't you a bit old for that? but restrained herself. She was gritting her teeth and steeling herself to endure his unwanted attentions when he suddenly bent his head and pressed his sweaty cheek against hers.

It was too much. She jerked her head away violently and as Ivor spluttered, 'What the hell's the matter with you?' she heard a quiet voice behind her.

'My turn, I think.'

Kirk stood there, magnificent in the dark blue uniform with epaulettes on the shoulders which he had donned especially for the cocktail party. His golden hair gleamed in the spotlight and he looked more than ever like a Viking. Calmly, without another word, he held out his arms and Candy, finding herself abruptly released, slipped into them.

Ivor seemed stunned by the other man's laid-back attitude, but he did manage to mutter, 'Maybe you'll have better luck than I did, mate,' before disappearing among the other dancers.

'An unpleasant type,' Kirk remarked conversationally.

'I suppose we're bound to get one now and then, but most of the passengers seem very nice, as they were on the Baltic cruise.'

Candy had spoken in as tolerant a tone as she could manage, but something in her face caused Kirk to look at her searchingly.

'That guy didn't really upset you, surely?'

'Oh, no, of course not—it's only. . . .' She allowed her voice to die away, fearing that it might suddenly display a shame-making quiver.

'There *is* something the matter,' he persisted. 'You've been in an odd mood ever since you came back from Santiago.'

She hadn't felt right since Julie Markham joined the cruise, but she wasn't about to tell him that. Instead she said defensively, 'I was very worried about Mrs Kennedy's disappearance.'

'But you seem to have found her without much trouble, and now it's over and done with.' He was still looking into her face with a puzzled expression on his own.

Candy made no reply, and after a moment Kirk steered her off the dance-floor and towards the nearest exit.

'I prescribe a breath of fresh air,' he said softly.

It was beautiful out on the promenade deck. The lights of Vigo still blazed and there was a faint sound of music. Above their heads the fairy-lights strung high up on the ship displayed their varying colours, and down below the dark water twinkled with diamonds.

At first they merely wandered along the deserted deck hand in hand. It was so lovely and so romantic that Candy felt more churned up inside than ever. She tried to take deep breaths to slow down her racing pulses, and all the time she could feel her emotions getting rapidly out of control. To her horror, she was suddenly on the verge of tears.

Still struggling for calm, she drew an extra-long breath but it ended in a sort of gasp that was half a sob and only too audible.

Kirk stopped abruptly and swung her round to face him. He cupped her face in his hands. 'Candy, love, you're crying! There *must* be something the matter.'

'There's nothing special—honestly there isn't.

I expect I'm a bit depressed. Everybody feels like that at times.'

He murmured something that sounded like, 'You poor darling,' but she couldn't be sure and, anyway, she was now beyond control. As he put his arms round her and drew her close, she pressed her face against his chest and let her tears flow freely.

After a moment, Kirk said wryly, 'I'd just as soon you didn't soak the front of my best jacket.'

'I'm s-sorry——' Candy raised her head and was promptly kissed.

He moved one of his arms but continued to hold her with the other. Groping in his pocket, he produced a large white handkerchief and mopped her face.

'Better now?'

'Yes, th-thank you.'

'You've made my face nearly as wet as yours.' He rubbed it vigorously.

The storm of tears had eased her tension but left Candy feeling very vulnerable. She needed more than the kind and gentle comforting she had received—something bigger and stronger which would absorb her body and soul, something which in her secret heart she called love.

Kirk had been standing silent, still holding her tightly but apparently deep in thought.

Suddenly he said quietly, 'I know a very good cure for depression.'

Her heart missed a beat. 'Do you?'

'You know what I'm talking about, don't you?' His voice was only a murmur but so seductive that Candy thrilled to the sound of it. 'Making love—that's what I mean.' He looked searchingly into her face.

Excitement caught her by the throat, just as tears had done a moment ago. Her body was urging her to agree to what he asked. And yet she hadn't changed her mind about sexual pleasure being something special, the natural result of love as well as physical desire.

If only Kirk had said, I love you. But he'd been honest and made no attempt to pretend.

Candy's troubled thoughts stopped with a jerk. She had a strange feeling of being on the verge of a great discovery, but just then Kirk bent his head and captured her lips. Passion leapt between them and evidently he sensed her arousal and took it for granted that she was willing to continue.

'Oh, my darling——' He hugged her to him and, taking her hand, drew her towards the companionway. Candy's head was spinning and she almost lost her balance. She wondered if she had, in fact, lost her emotional balance. As they climbed up to the boat deck, she struggled to regain it, to reach out for that little bit of extra strength which would enable her to make the right decision.

'Here we are.' Kirk unlocked the door to his cabin and switched on the light.

Candy took a deep breath of the cool night air and went in. And, as she saw that the cabin was in its usual state of disarray, the burning passion which had held her in its grip was replaced by a great wave of tenderness. Macho he undoubtedly was, but he was also dear and sweet and very, very human.

Apologising, Kirk collected the scattered clothes and stowed them away in various places, and Candy even managed to make a gently teasing comment.

'It can't be your Swedish blood that makes you so untidy. Stockholm was a beautifully kept city.'

'I expect it's the wild, romantic Celt in me. Did I tell you my mother's a real mongrel—a mixture of Scottish and English, with a bit of Welsh thrown in?' He banged the cupboard door shut. 'Would you like a drink? I've got a bottle of Chianti somewhere and I always keep two glasses in the toilet annexe.'

He must be in the habit of entertaining people in his cabin. Another officer perhaps? Candy would have liked to believe that that was the answer, but she was painfully aware that it could have been Julie who had used the second glass. Maybe even Dawn.

This was downright stupid, she scolded herself. She had enough on her mind without bothering with useless conjecture.

And suddenly—with absolute certainty—all Candy's doubts were dissolved and she knew that she was *not* going to make love with Kirk. Physically she still wanted to—oh, God, how badly she wanted it!—but with mind and heart now united against it there was no way that she was going to give in.

He might be angry and might even accuse her of misleading him, but she hadn't really. He had simply assumed her agreement, which wasn't surprising considering how close she had been to it.

One thing was for sure—he would demand her

reason for taking such a stand, and she still hadn't worked out what she was to tell him. It couldn't possibly be the truth—that, for her, lovemaking was impossible when one person was seriously in love and the other merely enjoying light-hearted dalliance.

Seriously in love. Candy repeated the words in her mind and marvelled at them. They were wonderful and frightening both at the same time, and at that moment she could see no further ahead than the next few minutes.

'Cheers!' Kirk clinked his glass against hers and sat down beside her on the bed.

Their shoulders were touching but nothing more. It could have been just an ordinary visit, except that, if it had been, they would have been more talkative. And there wouldn't have been this terrific tension which Candy could feel building up between them.

She drank her wine slowly but the glass was empty at last. In silence she gave it to Kirk, and he put it, and his, on the dressing-table. Sitting down again, he took her hands in his and looked deep into her eyes. Hastily she lowered her lashes in case he should read her secret written there, and summoned all her courage. If only she could be sure of finding the right words!

The telephone started to ring.

CHAPTER NINE

'HELL!' Kirk buried his face in the softness of Candy's neck. 'What a moment to choose! I feel very tempted to let it ring.'

'You're a doctor. You know you can't do that.' Candy said quietly.

'Of course not.' He heaved himself on to his feet and snatched at the phone. 'Dr Nielsen.'

An agitated female voice burst into speech, and though Candy couldn't make out what she said she managed to catch the name Marie.

'Did you get any of that?' He replaced the handset. 'It's Marie—she's got a recurrence of the pain.'

'Oh, dear, that doesn't sound at all good.' Candy slid off the bed and smoothed down her dress. 'Shall I come with you to see her?'

'Please.' He slipped his arms into his jacket. 'We'd better stop off at the hospital on the way and collect a few items.'

'That will give me a chance to change.'

They set off together, not speaking until they stepped out of the lift and began to walk down the long corridor.

'Marie seemed OK during the performance this evening,' Candy said over her shoulder. 'As far as I could judge, anyway.'

'An inflamed appendix makes its own rules. She's had two bouts of severe pain—one on the

151

ship and one before she came—which ought to be warning enough for anybody. I wish now that I'd insisted on her seeing her own doctor during the break between cruises, but she probably wouldn't have obeyed me——'

'So it wouldn't have made any difference if you had.'

They had reached the hospital and Candy went into her cabin to change into jeans and a polo shirt. They emerged at the same moment, Kirk carrying a miniature doctor's bag, and went down the nearby stairs, down into the depths of the ship.

Kirk's tap on the door of the cabin shared by Marie and her friend Annette brought the blonde dancer instantly to let them in. She was looking pale and worried, and greeted them with relief. Marie, wearing a négligé, was curled up on her bed.

As they entered, she opened her eyes and murmured faintly, 'I'm so sorry, Doctor. . .'

I'm sorry you've got this pain again.' Kirk sat down on the edge of the bed and looked down at her thoughtfully. 'I'll have to examine you, Marie, so can you uncurl a bit?'

He went on talking as Candy helped the girl to turn on to her back. 'When did you first notice the pain? Tonight, I mean.'

Marie had her lips pressed together and it was Annette who answered. 'She didn't seem very well when we were dressing for our first number, but she said she was OK. After that, I forgot about it until, when we came down here to go to bed, she suddenly groaned and collapsed into a heap, like she was when you came in.'

'Thank you,' Kirk said politely, 'but I would like Marie to tell me herself when the pain came on.'

The dancer winced as his hands explored her abdomen, but she answered coherently enough. 'I felt a twinge almost as soon as we started dancing. By the end of the programme I was really beginning to feel ill, but I got through somehow and came down here as soon as I could. I didn't want Annette to call you but she insisted.' She looked into his face with imploring dark eyes. 'Oh, Doctor, you must give me something to stop it so I can carry on—please! I can't be ill—I just can't.'

He gave her a sympathetic smile. 'I understand how you feel, and certainly no decisions can be made tonight. We'll see how you are in the morning. In the meantime I'll give you an injection which will help you to sleep.'

While he was preparing it, Candy took the patient's temperature. She had noticed the heat of Marie's skin and wasn't surprised to find it alarmingly high. Carefully schooling her expression, she shook the mercury down and replaced the thermometer in Kirk's bag.

'There's just one other thing, Marie.' He stood with his hands on his hips, looking at her thoughtfully. 'You're an awfully long way from medical help down here. I hope the injection I've given you will see you through the night, but I'd be easier in my mind about you if we moved you to the hospital. Candy's cabin is next door and you could summon her in a moment if the pain got worse. You wouldn't mind?'

A rebellious expression flashed across the dancer's face and then was gone. Candy guessed that she just hadn't the strength to protest, and she hurried off to fetch the wheelchair. When she got back, Annette was putting a few toilet articles into a polythene bag, and Marie lay limply on the bed, her eyes closed.

Somehow they got her into the chair and transferred her to the hospital. Candy kept a bed always ready for occupation, and as soon as she was curled up on it Marie fell fast asleep.

'I was surprised you gave her a pain-killer.' Candy said as they withdrew. 'You refused last time.'

'That was because I didn't want to do anything which might confuse the situation. The pain went away and she carried on as normal. I don't think that's going to happen on this occasion.' Kirk paused, waiting at the door as Candy switched off the main lights. 'This time I'm almost certain I shall have to operate, but it would have been cruel to tell her that tonight. What was her temperature, by the way?'

'Thirty-nine degrees.'

'Not too good, but it's only to be expected.'

Candy halted outside her own door. 'Poor Marie—she's in for a terrible shock in the morning—if not before! And even if she feels better tomorrow, she won't be able to dance again this cruise. I suppose Rose will have to take her place.'

'Temporarily, but I expect the company will fly a dancer out to join the ship at some convenient port. Anyway, none of that is our problem.' Kirk came nearer and put his hands on her shoulders, looking down into her eyes. 'I'm very sorry it ended like this, love. May I hope for better luck next time?'

But Candy had regained her sanity, and she wasn't sure whether there would ever be a next time.

'I—I don't know. I—I'm so tired I can't think.' She drew a deep breath and managed to steady her voice. 'If I get a summons from Marie, do you want me to call you?'

'Yes, please, but I don't think you'll be disturbed.'

He bent his head and kissed her on the lips. The feel of his mouth, firm and warm, almost set Candy on fire in spite of her weariness, but with a murmured, 'Goodnight,' she slipped away from him and disappeared into her cabin.

She slept fitfully that night, very conscious of the patient next door. Once she got up and went quietly to make sure that there was no change in Marie's condition, but she found her asleep, though rather restless.

At six o'clock she was so wide awake that it was impossible to stay in bed any longer. A hot shower removed the last of the tiredness from her limbs, and she dressed quickly in her uniform and paid another visit to the hospital. This time she found Marie half awake, and a light touch on her forehead—still very hot—woke her up completely.

'How do you feel this morning?' Candy produced a thermometer and shook it down.

'I—don't quite know.'

'Think about it while I take your temperature.'
She popped the thermometer into Marie's
mouth—noting dry, cracked lips—and put her
fingers on the slender wrist.

It was like working in a big hospital except that
there was no chart to fill in, a little matter which
hadn't occurred to her during last night's drama.
In fact, she didn't think the company had supplied
any charts. People weren't supposed to remain in
hospital on a cruise-ship long enough to need a
proper record of their condition.

Marie's temperature hadn't altered much—not
a good sign as it would normally be lower in
the morning. But at least it hadn't gone any
higher—or dropped a lot, which would have been
even more ominous.

'I've still got that horrid pain,' Marie said in a
small voice. 'I do wish the doctor would give me
some medicine to take it right away.'

'You'll have to talk to him about that when he
comes to see you. I expect he'll be here soon.'

'I'm thirsty. Can I have some water, please?'

This was a hurdle which Candy knew she had
to surmount. If Marie was to be operated on that
morning she mustn't have even a sip.

'I don't think I ought to give you any until the
doctor's seen you,' she said firmly. Going into the
annexe, she got a large bath-towel out of one of
the cupboards. 'I'm going to give you a good wash
now and you'll feel much fresher.'

'I'd much rather be left alone.'

Candy smiled and continued her preparations.
When the patient and her bed were both clean and
tidy, she turned her attention to other important

matters. Experienced as she was in theatre work, it was impossible not to be a little nervous on this occasion, with only two pairs of hands to do everything.

She located the drugs required for pre-med and put them handy, and then went into the little theatre to check the anaesthetic equipment. It was while she was busy with this that Kirk came quietly in and asked the inevitable question.

'She's much the same as she was last night,' Candy told him. 'Temp, pulse, respirations—the lot.'

'You haven't said anything about the possibility of an operation?'

'Oh, no!' She was shocked at the suggestion. 'But I did refuse her a drink. She didn't make the connection, of course.' She looked up into his serious face. 'Are you definitely operating or will you wait a little longer?'

'I'll make my mind up when I've seen her, but I really can't see the point of waiting.' He thrust both hands into his pockets, frowning down at his feet. 'She's obviously got an extremely inflamed appendix and if we delay we expose her to the risk of peritonitis. On the other hand, it cleared up last time and could do so again.'

'She's worse than she was then,' Candy pointed out.

They had been talking quietly in the surgery, and she remained there briefly while Kirk went off to visit his patient. She could hear a low murmur of voices, and then a high-pitched exclamation from Marie. Judging this to be her cue, she went swiftly to join them.

Kirk was sitting on the edge of the bed. Marie, her dark eyes wide with horror, turned to Candy and burst into agitated speech.

'He says he wants to take my appendix out! I didn't think you could have operations on a cruise-ship. Why can't I wait until I get home? It might get better before then and I wouldn't have to be operated on at all.'

'Listen, Marie.' Kirk captured one of her waving hands and held it firmly. 'You have an abscess on your appendix, a very small bit of you which is completely useless. If it's removed, you will never again have that awful pain. On the other hand, if it's ignored, the abscess will probably burst and then you'd be in real trouble.'

'You'd still have to have the operation,' Candy put in, 'and it would take much longer to get over it. Your career would be seriously interrupted. This way, you'll be back at work in quite a short time.'

Tears rolled down Marie's flushed face and she gave a huge sniff. Feeling very sorry for her— she might be missing her mother—Candy handed her a tissue, and they waited until she had regained control.

'OK—I give in.' Pathetically, she added, 'I'll try not to make any more fuss.'

'Good girl.' Kirk patted her hand and released it. 'Candy will give you something to make you sleepy, and in another hour or so we'll do the operation. It won't take long.'

'Why can't you get on with it now?' Marie demanded with a show of spirit.

Candy knew that they would be busy getting the theatre ready, but she was not surprised when Kirk ignored the question.

'You won't notice the time—you'll be too dopey. Just lie still and let your pre-med do its work, and it'll be all over almost before you realise it.'

Marie swallowed the tablets and obediently closed her eyes, and Candy could see that she was relaxing already. There was no reason why she shouldn't be left on her own for a short time. She had a telephone in the unlikely case of need.

'Breakfast first,' Kirk said as they walked along the corridor. 'I don't like operating on an empty stomach.'

Candy smiled but disagreed. 'My priority is to take a look at the outside world, just to make sure it's still there.'

She had given so little attention to their where-abouts during the last few hours that she was momentarily surprised to find the ship in the River Tagus, and about to dock at Lisbon. The Portuguese capital lay before her eyes, white and green and sparkling in the early morning sunshine.

She was supposed to be escorting a half-day tour of the city, she remembered suddenly, ashamed of her forgetfulness. She would have to find the staff captain at once and apologise for giving him so little notice.

To her relief, the blonde giant of a man— Swedish, like most of the officers—was already aware of the situation, and had altered his arrangements accordingly.

'Dr Nielsen has told me,' he said calmly. 'There

is no need for you to worry. Please give my good wishes to the dancer.'

There was just time to snatch some breakfast and then she must get busy.

Candy had turned the air-conditioning up as high as possible but it was still hot and claustrophobic in the miniature theatre. Clad from head to foot in green, except for the white masks they wore, she and Kirk seemed to have lost all individuality. They were like people in a play, acting their roles.

Actually, she was the only one playing an unfamiliar role. Theoretically, she knew something about anaesthetics. But she had never been an anaesthetist before. Fortunately she could concentrate on it entirely, since Kirk had declared that he didn't need an assistant for such a routine operation as an appendicectomy. He was quite capable of picking up his own instruments.

It all seemed to be happening very quickly. Kirk had made the incision with supreme confidence, and the retractors were in place, holding it open, almost before Candy, anxiously watching her gauges, had realised he had begun. In no time at all the appendix—looking just as unhealthy as they had expected—was lying in a kidney dish.

'The operation was definitely necessary,' Kirk murmured. Above the mask his eyes, blue and smiling, met Candy's. 'Patient OK?'

'Fine! When shall I stop the anaesthetic?'

'As soon as I've done the suturing.' He was already preparing the needle. 'In view of her profession, I shall have to do my very best embroidery.'

'I expect she'll be upset about the scar—it's only natural.'

'It's not on a part of the anatomy which is normally displayed by a dancer—or not on a cruise-ship, anyway. Besides, it will soon fade.'

In a very short time Marie was transferred to her bed, still deeply asleep.

'We shan't be able to leave her alone until she comes round,' Kirk said. 'Would you like to go and get some lunch while I keep watch?'

'You go first,' she suggested. 'I'll keep an eye on Marie while I'm tidying up, instead of just sitting beside her reading—reading a guidebook to Lisbon.'

Kirk touched her lightly on the cheek, his fingers gently caressing. 'It's a shame you had to miss your tour.'

'It doesn't matter. I shall have other opportunities.'

He nodded and went away. Alone, Candy stood still and took a long, hard look at herself. Inside her head, so clear, she almost feared she might have said it aloud, there was another sentence. Unless I have to leave the ship because I've been such a fool as to fall in love with the doctor.

The words had come out of the blue, completely unexpected, and they hit her with the force of a severe blow. She had known she was in danger, but not that she had reached the point of no return.

It was ironic, to say the least, that she had run away from one distressing experience only to land herself in another.

*   *   *

When Candy returned to the hospital after lunch, she found Annette there, talking to Kirk.

'We've had an offer of assistance,' he said, getting up.

'Not until Marie comes round,' the dancer put in quickly, 'but as soon as she's properly awake I'd be quite willing to sit with her for an hour or so. I know you have other things to do as well as nursing.'

'Nursing comes first, but that doesn't mean I'm not grateful. Could you come back at, say, three o'clock?'

'Nice girl,' Kirk commented when Annette had gone. 'It was a shock to her when I broke the news about Marie's operation earlier today, but she seems to have rallied.' He put his fingers on Marie's wrist, checking the pulse, and then moved towards the door. 'She's showing signs of coming round so you ought to be able to leave her safely by the time her friend comes back.'

Almost as soon as he had gone, the patient opened her eyes and Candy propped her up with pillows, talking to her as she did so. Eventually she got a coherent reply, and she was delighted when Marie made no mention of either headache or nausea. She must be a better anaesthetist than she had feared!

When Annette appeared, Marie—though still dopey—was delighted to see her, and Candy left them with a free conscience.

On the promenade deck she found Stella Kennedy stretched out comfortably with an unopened book on her lap. She looked very pale, with dark shadows beneath her eyes, but she greeted her visitor with a smile.

'I hope you're none the worse for your adventure at Santiago.' Candy sat down beside her.

Stella shrugged and ignored the question. 'I've been very good today and not attempted an excursion. It's a nuisance, though, because I'd hoped to do some shopping in Lisbon. I have a number of nephews and nieces, much younger than Julie, and I would like to take them presents.'

Candy glanced across at the customs building, only a hundred yards away. She had noticed that morning that part of it housed a number of souvenir shops which looked quite attractive. After hesitating a moment, she pointed them out to Stella.

'They may not be quite the sort of shops you had in mind, but if you'd like to go and have a look I'd be happy to come with you. I haven't been ashore myself yet.'

'That's very kind of you.' The thin, wan face brightened at once.

Candy felt pleased that she had made the suggestion but Stella immediately thought of a difficulty.

'Oh dear, I haven't any Portuguese money. Will they take English?'

'The big shops in the city might have done, but I don't think they would here. But not to worry. If you give me some notes, or a traveller's cheque, I'll go to the purser's office and get some escudos for you.'

Candy found Alan Bainton, Steve's temporary replacement, very willing to oblige.

'I'm enjoying this cruise,' he confided, counting

automatically. 'I wish poor old Steve all the best, of course, but I wouldn't mind working on the *Bergsen* a bit longer.'

Candy almost said, Perhaps you'll get your wish, and then decided against it. Instead, she gave him a friendly smile, thanked him, and departed.

Walking very slowly, she and Stella set off. Strangely, the expedition turned out to be as tiring for the escort as for the shopper. To stroll along so extremely slowly made Candy feel extraordinarily weary, but once they began shopping she managed to buy a few presents herself, which helped to pass the time.

At the end of an hour, Stella announced that she had had enough. She had certainly spent a great deal of money and bought some very pretty things.

'Thank you for being so kind to me,' she said as they toiled back across the dock. 'I'd like you to accept this as a small memento.' Opening one of her numerous paper bags, she produced a beautiful hand-painted fan.

Candy was delighted and a little embarrassed. She knew the fan had cost a lot of money, but there was no possibility of refusing it, even if she had wanted to. Murmuring fervent thanks, she opened it out and admired the delicate decoration.

It was as they were climbing slowly up the gangway that she noticed Julie watching them from the top.

'Where on earth have you been?' Julie demanded angrily as they reached her level.

Candy took it upon herself to answer. 'Just a little shopping expedition,' she said airily.

'But my aunt's not up to it. She was supposed to rest today. You had no right to take her off on your own like that.'

Before Candy could think of a reply which wouldn't disclose that she was about to lose her temper, Stella interposed.

'I'm a grown woman, Julie, and I make my own decisions, but I must admit that I'm tired now. I intend to go to the cabin and lie down.'

'Would you like a cup of tea?' Candy asked.

'No, thank you, dear. Tea always gives me indigestion.'

As soon as she was out of earshot, Julie burst out again. 'Did she give you that fan?'

Candy raised her eyebrows. 'As a matter of fact, she did. Any objection?' Once more in control of herself, she looked challengingly at the other nurse.

Julie was clearly bursting with objections, but before she could think of the best one to be put into words Candy changed the subject.

'I don't want to pry into family matters, but it would help if we knew a little more about Mrs Kennedy's illness. Has she had any X-rays?'

After a moment's hesitation, Julie made an effort and replied without too much animosity, though grudgingly. 'I told you I'd been away on an agency job and I don't know if she's had X-rays or not. She said she'd got gastric trouble and it seemed a good idea to take her away on a sea voyage.'

To Candy it seemed a crazy idea, and she

couldn't help wondering whether Julie had really thought it would benefit her or whether she was making use of her aunt for some purpose of her own.

She said casually, not really wanting to appear inquisitive about Julie's private life but strangely uneasy, 'Whatever made you pick on the *Bergsen* after leaving the ship so abruptly?'

The other girl started, and said defensively, 'I thought it might be fun to see Kirk again.'

'I see.'

'No, you don't. You don't see anything at all.' Julie came to a sudden halt. Judging from her expression, she seemed to be involved in an internal conflict. She hesitated, started to speak and then broke off again.

Eventually she tossed back her long hair and tilted her head defiantly. 'I didn't mean to tell anybody, but, the way things seem to be turning out, I think you ought to know.'

'Know what?' Candy was utterly lost.

Julie's eyes met hers for a moment and then were veiled. She was twisting her hands together nervously but she had obviously made up her mind.

'Everybody was puzzled when I broke my contract but I'd got a good reason. It was because I thought I was pregnant and I needed to do something about it quickly. Actually, it turned out to be a false alarm and I wished I hadn't been in such a hurry.'

Candy stared at her, utterly appalled. Julie couldn't possibly have been disappointed with the effect of her bombshell, and it was clear from her expression that she was aware of it.

There was triumph in her face, and in her voice too, as she delivered the final blow.

'I've no intention of telling you who the father would have been, but I expect you can guess, can't you?'

For the rest of that day Candy was simply going through the motions. She smiled, talked and did what was required of her with speed and efficiency, and all the time—behind the façade—her mind plodded round a treadmill of unhappy thoughts.

She did not for a moment doubt that Julie's oblique reference had referred to Kirk. His virility must have led him into one or two sexual incidents since Nicola died. It would be absurdly starry-eyed to imagine anything different.

But one thing was for sure: she—Candy—had no wish to be another. She was now more than ever relieved that their lovemaking had been interrupted by the summons to visit Marie. In future she would avoid with all her skill situations which could lead to a similar temptation.

She saw little of Kirk that evening. Prior to opening the surgery she was busy with her patient—washing her, remaking the bed, and persuading a steward—whose English was minimal—to bring her a milky drink. The shipping company had provided everything possible for a little hospital—except a miniature kitchen.

Kirk had started surgery before she was free to join him, and they were so busy with trifling ailments that there was no opportunity for conversation, which was just the way Candy wanted it.

'Time to shut up shop,' Kirk said at last.

She was in the act of closing the door when Stella Kennedy appeared.

'Oh, dear, am I too late?' she asked in dismay.

'No, of course not. Come in.' Candy stood back to let her pass.

Kirk was politely on his feet and waving her to a chair, and she sat down with a sigh of relief.

'I've never been so far below on a ship before and it seems very strange without any windows. I don't think I would care for being a patient in your hospital—if you'll forgive my saying so.'

'I hope you won't be,' he said with a smile.

'Well, no, I hope so too.' Stella paused to recover her breath. 'I expect you're wondering why I'm here. I've got gastric trouble, you know, and the white medicine my own doctor gave me doesn't seem to be doing any good. I wondered if you have something—er—stronger?'

There was a pause and Candy glanced at Kirk. His expression told her nothing but she could guess at his thoughts. Eventually he leaned forward with his arms on the desk.

'I'll be honest with you, Mrs Kennedy. The stomach medicine we have here is likely to be much the same as your own, and I would hesitate to give you anything else without more know-ledge. Have you seen a specialist?'

She started and a faint colour appeared in her pale cheeks. 'I'm afraid not. My doctor wanted me to—he thinks I may have an ulcer—but I'm

such a coward. I have this stupid dread of operations, and so when my niece suggested this cruise
I—er—escaped and came away instead.'

'I don't think,' Kirk said carefully, 'that you're
enoying it very much, are you?'

'N-no, not at all. I hate this invalidish sort of
life, and being unable to do any proper sightseeing. I wish we hadn't come.'

'I take it that you didn't tell your doctor about
your fear of being operated on?' She shook her
head, and Kirk smiled and continued quietly,
'That's a pity, Mrs Kennedy, because then you
would have learnt that ulcers can nearly always
be cured medically these days. They are only very
rarely removed surgically. All the same, it
wouldn't be wise to neglect the matter any longer.
I recommend that you see a specialist at the
earliest opportunity.' He stood up and came
round the desk. 'Think it over and then phone
your doctor from Gibraltar, asking him to make
an appointment for you.'

Stella rose shakily to her feet, looking dazed.
'You really mean that? I've been worrying myself
unnecessarily?'

'It's very probable.'

She drew a long, quivering breath but her voice
rang out with unexpected strength.

'I won't only ring my doctor from Gibraltar,
I'll leave the ship and fly home. My niece won't
be pleased but that can't be helped.' She held out
her hand. 'I can't tell you how grateful I am, Dr
Nielsen.' Her gaze took in Candy. 'And you too,
Nurse. You've been very kind to me.'

When she had gone, they looked at each other,

and Kirk said ruefully, 'I wonder what it feels like to have all that money?'

But underneath her pleasure because Stella's health problems were probably going to be solved, Candy was thinking about Julie. It was wonderful news that she was going away again, but how much better it would have been if she had taken her secret with her.

Or would it? Perhaps it was just as well that she had let it out.

CHAPTER TEN

ANOTHER beautiful morning. Candy stood at the rail and gazed entranced at the wonderful, breath-taking sight of the famous Rock of Gibraltar outlined against a vivid blue sky. It was so exactly like the pictures she had seen of it that it scarcely seemed real.

She had already visited Marie and found her in good shape after her operation and anxious to get up.

'I suppose you'd like to go and practise some dancing,' Candy had teased.

'I'm not that daft! When I went to the toilet my legs felt as if they were made of cotton wool, and my tummy's pretty sore too.'

'It's bound to be for a few days, but your legs will quickly get stronger.' Candy had helped her patient out of bed and steered her towards a chair she had placed at the washbasin. 'I expect the doctor will want you to make the hospital your base until the end of the cruise. Your own cabin is so very out of the way.'

'I don't mind. It's much more comfort-able here.'

Reviewing the conversation while, at the same time, admiring the view, Candy found she had been joined at the rail by Kirk, and she relayed it to him.

He grinned at the contrast between Stella's

opinion of the hospital and the dancer's. 'I'm glad someone appreciates what we have to offer. I suppose it all depends on what you're used to.'

'I wonder how Mrs Kennedy will get on with her telephoning?'

'I expect one of the couriers will fix up her flight for her, but she'll have to ring her doctor herself.'

'Have you seen Julie since her aunt decided to abandon the cruise?' Candy asked diffidently.

Kirk shook his head. 'It's a bit rough on the poor girl to have her holiday snatched away from her at the halfway stage. I feel sorry for her.'

The words dropped like lead into the pool of awkwardness which had suddenly developed between them. She had asked for it, Candy thought unhappily, by asking that stupid question. She muttered something about it being breakfast-time, and slipped away.

When Kirk came into the dining-room she was deep in conversation with Emma, and he took an empty seat next to Dawn. She was suddenly reminded of her first meal on board the *Bergsen*.

What a lot had happened since then! The two cruises, which she had feared might be rather bor-ing at times, had proved amazingly eventful medically speaking, but the biggest surprise had been the change in herself. She had arrived feeling bruised and unhappy, but her heart had healed so rapidly that she had been obliged to admit that it hadn't been very severely damaged after all.

Unfortunately she was still very far from happy.

Shrugging away such unprofitable thoughts, Candy finished her breakfast and went to open the surgery. They were busy right up to closing time with a succession of minor ailments, but the last patient departed promptly. Candy was about to close the door when she heard someone approaching.

Julie came storming in like a tornado.

'I suppose *you* put Stella up to this ridiculous idea!' She tossed back her long, straight hair and glared at Candy. 'Who gave you the right to mess up other people's arrangements?' Her face was scarlet with rage.

'Of course I didn't put her up to it! I wouldn't dream of such a thing,' Candy said indignantly. 'I was as surprised as you must have been when she told us what she intended doing.'

'You would say that, of course,' Julie sneered. 'I'm afraid I don't believe you.'

'I don't care whether you believe me or not!' Candy clung desperately to her rising temper. 'It happens to be the truth.'

Kirk had been looking from one to the other in blank astonishment, but now he intervened. 'For God's sake, Julie, stop behaving like a maniac. We were both present when Mrs Kennedy made up her mind to leave. It was a very sudden decision, I admit, but that doesn't mean either of us tried to influence her. It was entirely her own idea.'

Julie's anger dropped from her like a discarded garment. She stood drooping before them, biting her lip. 'I suppose I'll have to believe *you*,' she muttered.

He came round the desk and stood looking down at her. 'Cheer up, Julie—it's not the end of the world. You'll be spared the Bay of Biscay on the homeward run, anyway.' He took her by the arm and propelled her gently towards the door. 'I reckon your aunt'll be needing your help with the packing, so off you go and don't let us hear any more of this nonsense.'

He had spoken to Julie as though she had been a schoolgirl, Candy thought, and suddenly felt sorry for her. Her own temper had died just as quickly and she felt glad that the unpleasant scene was over.

Suddenly she felt Kirk's hands on her shoulders and he turned her to face him.

'I was quite surprised to see you on the verge of losing your cool,' he said thoughtfully. 'These last few days you seem to have been a bit lacking in your usual spirit.'

'Oh—er—have I? I expect it's because I've been so busy. Life has been a bit hectic, you must admit.' She tried to escape his grasp and felt his hands tighten.

'Are you sure that's all it was—just that you were busy and preoccupied?' Kirk persisted.

'I don't know! If I'd realised I was going to be questioned like this, I'd have got my answers ready.' Candy managed to wriggle free. 'I've got to escort a tour round the Rock soon, and there's Marie to see to and——'

'OK, I get the message, and I agree this is neither the time nor the place for a conversation of this sort.' He gave her a long, hard stare. 'But I'm sure there's something wrong, Candy, love, and I mean to find out what it is.'

She looked up at him, her heart pounding,

but could think of nothing to say.

'Tomorrow,' Kirk went on, 'the ship will be at Málaga and will spend twenty-four hours there, so that passengers can dine ashore if they wish. There are plenty of attractive eating places within a short taxi ride of the dock. Provided the office knows where we are, there's no reason why I shouldn't invite you to have a meal with me. Do you like seafood?'

'Oh, yes—I—I love it.' She bent her head to hide the radiance in her eyes which had nothing whatsoever to do with the prospect of eating seafood. 'I was supposed to go on the long trip to Granada but I altered it—because of Marie—and now I only have to do the morning tour. So there's no reason why I shouldn't dine with you, and thank you very much.'

Her prim politeness sounded absurd to her own ears, but Kirk only said, 'Good,' and gave her one of his special smiles.

Later on, they met briefly as she was hurrying to the embarkation area to join her passengers on the coach.

'I forgot to tell you I'm going ashore this evening to dine with an old colleague of mine who's now at the Naval Hospital. I've cleared it with the staff captain but it's no problem really. I can be reached by phone within seconds.'

'Have a good time,' Candy said lightly, 'and don't forget we sail at midnight for Málaga.'

They were standing behind one of the huge screens covered with photographs, momentarily unobserved. Kirk moved nearer and gently touched her cheek; slowly and sensually his fingers stroked her skin, causing tremors of delight.

'I'm hoping to have an even better time tomorrow evening,' he said softly.

Candy flushed and hurried towards the gangway. He didn't mean it, of course. It was just one of those things men said to girls when they had invited them out.

She did not see him again until they met at morning surgery, when she asked him if he had enjoyed the dinner with his friend.

'Very much—we had a lot to talk about, and he showed me round the hospital, which was very interesting.' His tone was abstracted, as though his thoughts were following a different line from his spoken words.

Their first patient was Earl Hammerson, the small boy who had fallen into a lifeboat. This time he had managed to push a foreign body into his ear but Kirk was able to extract it without difficulty. It turned out to be a bead from a necklace belonging to his grandmother which he had broken.

They were busy after that and then it was time for Candy to set off with a coach party along the coast. The scenery was typically Mediterranean, but the area was all built-up and she did not enjoy it as much as her other tours.

The evening came at last and she put on the green and white silk dress which Kirk had once admired. He was looking very smart himself in pale fawn trousers and a cream summer jacket, and when they reached the bottom of the gangway he slipped his arm through hers as they strolled through the crowds.

It was a cosmopolitan scene, with snatches of conversation in all languages assailing them from every side. The mild evening air was laden with the mingled odours of cooking and women's perfume, fishing nets and the scent of unknown flowers. Candy had no wish to talk; it was sufficient just to be there, enjoying the foreignness of everything—and enjoying it with Kirk.

Before long he stopped outside a small restaurant from which issued a stream of flamenco music. Three young men in vaguely Spanish costume were playing guitars and singing something with a strong beat, but the place was not crowded because it was, for Spain, still early. Their table was in an alcove, from which they could see most of what went on and yet retain an illusion of privacy.

'This is nice,' Candy said happily.

'I hoped you'd like it.'

Kirk picked up the menu and they gave their attention to choosing food and wine. That done, an odd little silence descended on them, and he broke it by suddenly introducing the subject of his visit to the Naval Hospital at Gibraltar.

'I told you it was interesting but I didn't go into details.' He broke off as the wine-waiter appeared with a bottle of red wine and poured a little into Kirk's glass. Tasting it, he nodded approval and returned his attention to Candy.

'Ken—that's my doctor friend—had just returned from a short visit to London, and he'd visited our old hospital, where I used to be a

registrar on the neurology team and he was an
orthopaedist. While he was there he heard on the
grapevine that my job will soon become vacant.'

Candy's blue-grey eyes widened as she gazed
at him across the table. She said hesitantly, 'Does
that mean you intend to try and get it back? Oh,
Kirk, do you think you're fit enough?'

'I reckon I am. I was a wreck when I came on
board but that was two months ago.'

'Would you be able to break your contract?'

'I'd like to see anyone stop me!' He laughed but
was quickly serious again. 'Actually, I probably
wouldn't need to. I've only got another month
to run.'

Candy's had another two months. She tried to
imagine the ship without Kirk and her heart sank.
'So what do you intend to do?' she asked.

'Drive up to London as soon as the *Bergsen*
gets Customs clearance at Southampton, and visit
my hospital.' He paused, holding her gaze with
blue intentness. 'What about you? I had
hoped——'

'I think I should visit my mother. After all,
I've completely stopped being hurt and upset
about—about what happened.' The fact that she
had replaced her distress with a different kind of
pain had nothing to do with it.

Laden plates had appeared in front of them,
almost without their noticing. The three young
men came and serenaded them, and Kirk bought
one of their tapes. They began to eat and Candy
wondered what had happened to her appetite.

Kirk said suddenly, 'Do you really want to go
all the way to Canterbury? Wouldn't a letter do

instead, or maybe a phone call?' Giving her no time to reply, he went rushing on. 'I was hoping we could spend the short break together, only without you falling down steps like last time, but this job situation which has cropped up really is important.'

'Of course it is,' she said warmly. 'It must definitely be your first priority.'

Kirk put down his knife and fork. 'You didn't comment on my suggestion about contacting your mother.' He waited but Candy kept her eyes on her plate. 'If you'd agree to do that instead of going to see her, we could spend the night in London instead of in the New Forest. What do you think?'

Her heart was thudding so violently that she could hardly speak. As she struggled to find the right words with which to put the question which she had to ask, Kirk leaned forward and answered it.

'As far as I'm concerned, it wouldn't matter much where we were—provided we were together in the fullest sense. You know what I mean, don't you?'

She knew very well and the knowledge intoxicated her. For a moment she was assailed by a temptation so strong that she wilted under its power. Why shouldn't she accept the invitation and enjoy what was being offered? Why did she want so much more?

Cautiously she raised her lashes and stole a glance at his face. He was beginning to look concerned at the long silence, but she couldn't convince herself that it was due to anything more than the possibility of disappointment.

He said quietly, 'What's the matter, Candy?'

Abruptly, without the slightest warning, she lost her temper.

'Matter? I'm being stupid and outdated, that's what's the matter! And I don't care. I suppose you make a habit of asking your nurses to spend the night with you—perhaps Dawn, as well. There was Julie—and probably the girl who came in between us. I don't care for being part of that sort of relationship. To me, lovemaking is more important than that.' She sprang to her feet. 'I've finished my dinner and I'm going back to the ship!'

Kirk stood up too. He started to say, 'You were willing enough a little while ago——' but it was too late.

No one took any notice of Candy's whirlwind departure. Her temper lent speed to her feet and she soon reached the dock. But as she climbed the gangway and felt the cool sea-breeze blowing on her hot cheeks, her fury began to subside.

How *could* she have let fly like that? It was unforgivable! If only she hadn't loved Kirk so much it wouldn't have happened, but she couldn't bear to think that she was no more to him than just a girl—one of several—whom he found attractive.

There was dance music coming from the main lounge, but on the whole the ship was unusually quiet. Candy climbed rapidly up the companionways until she reached the observation deck, and then made her way to the far side, away from the town.

It was there that Kirk found her. He came straight to where she stood, leaning on the rail with bowed head, and put his arms round her. With a sob, she turned and leaned against him, her face hidden.

'My darling——' His voice was deep with concern. 'What did I say to upset you like this?'

'I'm sorry,' Candy wept. 'I should never have behaved so badly—it was dreadful of me.'

'Never mind that.' He kissed the top of her head. 'Why did you do it?'

'I—I didn't want to be another Julie.'

'Another Julie? What on earth are you on about? Julie's nothing to me. I would have thought that was pretty obvious.'

Candy raised her head and looked up into his face. Her eyes were wet but the tears had ceased to flow. 'I'm talking about when she was working as your nurse—it was different then. Everybody seems to think so.'

'Everybody be damned! I wish people would mind their own business!' Kirk exclaimed furiously.

'But there must have been *some* foundation for a rumour like that,' she persisted.

He hesitated, and then said reluctantly, 'Since this seems to be the moment of truth, I must tell you that I came near to sleeping with her once. It was some time ago and I was still deeply depressed, both because of my injuries and the loss of Nicola. Luckily I came to my senses in time, and I very much regretted letting myself get even that far.'

Candy made no comment but her mind was

busy. She accepted Kirk's assurance absolutely and experienced a flash of anger because Julie had deliberately misled her. Her suspected pregnancy remained something of a mystery. Presumably she had had a one-night stand with somebody—a passenger, perhaps—caused by her frustration over Kirk.

Above their heads, the fairy-lights danced in a pattern of rainbow colours, and although the shore was brilliantly lit the view from their side of the ship showed only dark water and a star-sprinkled sky. It was so beautiful and so romantic, and Candy knew that she had come near to spoiling it all.

'Oh, Kirk,' she said sadly, 'can you ever forgive me for standing you up like that?'

'It's already forgotten. We've got far more important things than that to talk about.' His voice shook with emotion. 'Oh, Candy, darling, I love you so much! I was going to tell you at the end of the cruise but I can't go on any longer without knowing how you feel about me—not after what we've been saying to each other tonight.'

'You—love me?' she repeated in a wondering tone. 'I'm not quite sure I know what that means.'

'It means a lot of things, not merely that I want to go to bed with you, though certainly that's high on the list right now.' His arms tightened convulsively. 'It means that I think you have a beautiful body, and I like your company and your independence, and I even love you when you lose your temper. In other words, I love *all* of you and I want to marry you when we can both find the time.'

'Oh, Kirk——' Candy reached up and put her arms round his neck. Her heart was thudding and she could feel his beating in time with it. 'I love you too, so very much. I've never, ever felt like this before, so I know it's for real, even if we haven't known each other very long——'

'What has time got to do with it?' he broke in passionately. 'I'd known Nicola nearly all my life but it wasn't the same as the feeling I have for you——'

'But you were going to marry her.'

'And we would probably have had a good marriage on the surface because we knew each other so well. She was, quite literally, the girl next door, but we both knew that the vital spark which means that a couple are romantically *in* love as well as loving each other was missing. Can you understand?'

'I think so,' Candy said thoughtfully, 'and thank you for telling me.'

'There's something you haven't told *me*,' he pointed out gently. 'I still don't know whether you've accepted my proposal of marriage.'

Candy laughed joyously. 'I just hadn't got around to it, that's all. I accept with all my heart, Kirk, darling. Does that satisfy you?

'If you'll come down to my cabin,' he murmured, 'I'll show you how I feel about it. . .'

The last three days of the cruise seemed like a dream to Candy, though she appeared to be functioning normally as a nurse-courier. The ship

visited Tangier and then set sail for home. On
the morning of their arrival, she went to the office
to collect her passport and heard someone calling
her name. It was Alan Bainton.

'I've got news for you!' He waved a piece of
paper. 'I wrote it all down so I that wouldn't
forget anything.' Seeing her look of astonishment,
he added hurriedly, 'There was a phone call
from Steve.'

'Steve?' She was immediately interested.
'How is he?'

Alan studied the paper. 'He has a rare form of
glandular fever. He'll need treatment but will be
fit again eventually, and I was to be sure to thank
you and the doctor for organising his tests.'

'It was his own doctor who did that. We merely
set the ball rolling.' Candy beamed at him.
'Thanks a lot, Alan.'

He looked at her curiously. 'You're positively
radiating cheerfulness. Got something nice to look
forward to?'

'You could say that!' She laughed and went on
her way.

An hour later she was *en route* to London in
Kirk's white BMW.

The M3 was busy and they did not talk much.
In London the traffic was horrendous but Kirk
found his way to a small hotel where he had
booked a room for the night. A double room.

To Candy the thought was intoxicating, but she
understood when Kirk seemed abstracted while
they were eating a light lunch. He was to visit his
old hospital that afternoon and so much
depended on it.

'Good luck, my dearest love,' she said as he prepared to set off. She hugged him and then stood back to admire his smart appearance in a well-cut grey suit and his hospital tie.

'Don't expect too much,' he warned her. 'They can't offer me the job right now, you know. It'll have to be advertised.'

'I understand that, but I still think you'll have a good chance of getting in by the back door.'

He was gone for hours. Candy had a long conversation with her mother over the phone and another, even longer, with her nursing friend. To neither of them did she give any details of her present situation. Time enough for that when she'd got used to it herself!

In her mother's case it was easy to dodge personal questions because she was eager to talk about her own wedding plans. Her friend was more difficult, inclined to ask a lot of questions, but Candy steered the conversation in a different direction, giving a vivid description of life on board ship, and somehow managing to convey the impression that she was phoning from Southampton.

That done, she was at a loose end and it seemed an age before she heard Kirk's tap at the door. One look at his face told her that he had good news.

'Everything's OK!' He seized her and whirled her round, holding her high in the air.

'Put me down!' she commanded, and he lowered her gently and kissed the top of her head. 'Now, tell me all about it. Is it really all settled,

Kirk? I can hardly dare to believe it.'

He sat down in one of the two comfortable armchairs and drew her on to his lap. 'The chap who was appointed to my job has been offered a consultant's post, and will be off very soon. It all happened very suddenly, but the situation was confused by my having gone off to work as a ship's doctor. Now that I've appeared and assured them that I'm fit again, just in the nick of time, they're going to fix it so that I can take over.' He was suddenly very serious. 'Oh, Candy, love, I— I can't tell you what it will mean to me to get back to my own field again.'

'I think I can guess.' Her voice shook with emotion. 'It's marvellous news—I'm so thrilled for you.'

They talked for a long time, making plans, altering them, and then Kirk looked at his watch and asked her what she would like to do that evening.

'See a show? Dine at the Savoy? It's your choice.'

'Would we get tickets as late as this?'

'Maybe not, so that leaves dining out— unless——' He broke off, hesitating.

'Unless what?'

His arm round her tightened. 'I was just thinking it would be quite a good idea to stay here and have room service—with a bottle of champagne, of course. We've got a lot to celebrate.' Kirk's eyes twinkled. 'This room is very pleasant and we've got the TV if we're—er—bored.'

Candy twinkled back at him. 'Do you think we're likely to be?'

It wasn't a question that needed answering and he kissed her instead. It was hard for them to come down to earth and choose from the menu which was brought them, but somehow they managed it. They dined early, finishing the champagne, and by mutual consent went early to bed.

Tomorrow they would be back on the *Bergsen*, ready to start a new cruise with new passengers, but tonight was theirs—to love each other and be happy.

Barbara

DELINSKY

A COLLECTION

New York Times bestselling author Barbara Delinsky has created three wonderful love stories featuring the charming and irrepressible matchmaker, Victoria Lesser. Worldwide are proud to bring back these delightful romances – together for the first time, they are published in one beautiful volume this September.

THE REAL THING
TWELVE ACROSS
A SINGLE ROSE

Available from September   **Priced £4.99**

W⊕RLDWIDE

Available from WH Smith, John Menzies, Volume One, Forbuoys, Martins, Woolworths, Tesco, Asda, Safeway and other paperback stockists.

MILLS & BOON

LOVE ON CALL

The books for enjoyment this month are:

STILL WATERS Kathleen Farrell
HEARTS AT SEA Clare Lavenham
WHISPER IN THE HEART Meredith Webber
DELUGE Stella Whitelaw

♥   ♥   ♥   ♥   ♥

Treats in store!

Watch next month for the following absorbing stories:

NOTHING LEFT TO GIVE Caroline Anderson
HIS SHELTERING ARMS Judith Ansell
CALMER WATERS Abigail Gordon
STRICTLY PROFESSIONAL Laura MacDonald

Zoë Barnes was born
legend has it her skirt o
of 'Dido and Aeneas'. According to her mum, sh
making an exhibition of herself ever since.

Her varied career has included stints as a hearing-aid technician,
switchboard operator, shorthand teacher, French translator, and
the worst accounts clerk in the entire world. When not writing
her own novels, she translates other people's and also works as a
semi-professional singer.

Although not in the least bit posh, Zoë now lives in Cheltenham
where most of her novels are set. Fatally bitten by the love bug,
Zoë now shares a home with her husband Simon, and would
rather like to be a writer when she grows up.

Zoë Barnes is the author of six bestselling novels including
BUMPS and HITCHED. The others are HOT PROPERTY,
BOUNCING BACK, EX-APPEAL and LOVE BUG also
published by Piatkus. Zoë loves to hear from her readers. Write
to her c/o Piatkus Books, 5 Windmill Street, London W1T 2JA
or via email at zoebarnes@bookfactory.fsnet.co.uk

Also by Zoë Barnes

Bumps
Hitched
Hot Property
Bouncing Back
Ex-Appeal
Love Bug

Just Married

Zoë Barnes

PIATKUS

Copyright © Zoë Barnes 2003

First published in Great Britain in 2003 by
Judy Piatkus (Publishers) Ltd of
5 Windmill Street, London W1T 2JA
email: info@piatkus.co.uk

This edition published 2003

The moral right of the author has been asserted

*A catalogue record for this book is available
from the British Library*

ISBN 0 7499 3384 4

Set in Times by Phoenix Photosetting, Chatham, Kent

Printed and bound in Great Britain by
Mackays of Chatham Ltd, Chatham, Kent

For anyone who's ever embraced marriage, contemplated it from a distance, or punched it on the nose and run away.

Prologue: The bridal suite, Brockbourne Hall, Christmas Eve

'Twas the night before Christmas . . .

But no ordinary night. My wedding night, thought Mrs Emma Sheridan, who only a few hours earlier had been plain Miss Emma Cox. And now she was lying in a four-poster bed in the poshest of posh hotels, while her new husband slumbered peacefully beside her, still endearingly pink and wrinkly from falling asleep in the Jacuzzi.

Small wonder he was exhausted; it had been a long, long day. After going out for the best part of seven years, Emma and Joe had finally tied the knot on Joe's birthday. In comparison to all the build-up, the actual event had passed like lightning. She could almost have believed it hadn't happened at all if the evidence wasn't all around her. An ivory-coloured basque lay where it had been flung, her raw silk dress formed a rumpled heap on the armchair, and one lace-topped stocking snaked across the carpet like an escaping python.

She felt for the plain gold band on her finger. So it really had happened! She was married at last, to the gorgeous bloke she'd adored ever since he was the school hunk and she was a scabby-kneed new girl, longing for him to notice her existence. In the moonlight filtering between the brocade curtains, she saw her faint reflection in the dressing table mirror, little more than a monochrome shadow. Do I look different now I'm Joe's wife? she wondered. I don't *feel* very different.

vii

'Joe,' she whispered, 'are you awake?'

He murmured sleepily as she kissed him on the cheek, but didn't stir; and she hadn't the heart to wake him just to tell him that she couldn't sleep. So she slipped out of bed, put on her new silk robe and slid her feet into her slippers.

With a backward glance and a smile, she stepped out into the corridor and closed the door softly behind her.

Hiring an entire wing of Brockbourne Hall for two whole days at Christmas was ridiculously extravagant but, as Joe pointed out, with him doing so well now they could afford it, and it was the best time of year for getting all the family together. Besides, after such a long wait it would have seemed bizarre to whisk the whole thing through in a ten-minute register office ceremony. It had to be special; more than special.

And yet ...

She pushed open the door of the Hatherley Suite and stepped into a silent world which, only hours earlier, had been full of relatives and friends dancing and getting pleasantly drunk. Now it was a *Marie Celeste* of abandoned party nibbles, half-drunk glasses of wine, crumpled napkins.

Over there was the precise spot where she and Joe had kissed, to the accompaniment of ribald cheers, as they stepped out together for the first dance. Funny, it had been a wonderful day, yet it still felt like it had happened to somebody else.

Pink and silver balloons still floated above the remains of the wedding cake, beside the place card that read: Mr and Mrs Joe Sheridan. Mrs Joe: what a silly idea, as if a husband could still own his wife, the way they'd done in the old days. Why, she wondered, hadn't Joe become Mr Emma Cox?

An opened bottle of champagne still sat in an ice bucket. She picked it up; it was half-full. Here's to us, she declared as she drank a silent toast. At last I'm what I want to be. So why do I still feel like ordinary old me?

She laughed and took another swig of flat champagne. Like everybody, she'd expected far too much. Life would go on, pretty much the way it always had. After all, all she and Joe had really done was say a few words and sign a bit of paper.

Such a little thing couldn't really change your whole world. Could it?

1

On a chill, damp evening in late February, Emma Sheridan screwed up her face in concentration and forced a last rebellious strand of hair into the big butterfly clip. There was rather a lot of hair to tame: thick, honey-blonde layers that framed her heart-shaped face and fell in soft waves onto her shoulders. One of these days, she really would have to get it cut; being a nurse it was only sensible. After all, she'd lost count of the number of times it had escaped from captivity and got spattered with sick, blood or something worse, not to mention the days when she'd worn it longer and a drunk had tried to strangle her with it. Ah, the romance of the A&E department – just like on the telly, but a lot smellier.

Just as she was doing up the last button on her uniform tunic, she heard the sound of Joe's key in the front door and skipped out of the bathroom to greet him. Maybe in twenty years' time she might be more blasé about his coming home at night, but at the moment it was lovely being loved up, revelling in the novelty of being Mrs Emma Sheridan instead of plain old Miss Cox, spinster of some other parish.

Funny how she'd imagined married life would be just like the single version, only with a bigger grocery bill: here they were only two months in, and already it seemed to have changed everything.

'Joe!' She sprang into his arms, and he spun round laughing, making her legs fly out like ribbons on a maypole. She was a normal-sized five foot five, curvy in the right places and pretty strong from her job, but in her husband's embrace she felt like a seed off a dandelion clock, a tiny little puff of nothing. At six two with shoulders you could hang an elephant on, Joe spent most of his life looking down at the top of her head, while she had a crick in her neck from gazing up at him adoringly.

But there was so much to adore in that face: the soulful, golden-brown eyes; the dimpled chin; the close-cut, tawny hair; the Sheridan family nose that had kinked ever so slightly to the left since he fell off his bicycle, aged fourteen. A face that was handsome, yet not afraid to be lived in. The face she loved.

'Hiya, Squeaky.' She reddened with embarrassed pleasure at his pet name for her. She'd once tried to think up one for him, but none of her ideas had stuck; whereas she'd been landed with 'Squeaky' the first time Joe had heard her breathless, high-pitched squeak of a laugh. She'd hated it at first, but now embraced it as though it were a caress: something special, that only Joe ever gave her. He gave the tip of her nose a lick and set her down. 'How's my gorgeous darling wife?'

'All the better for seeing her gorgeous darling husband.' She noticed how tired he looked. 'Busy day at work?'

'Mental. Tim Rawlings ballsed up the automated ordering system, and we ended up with only three cabbages between here and Wolverhampton.'

She smoothed a gentle hand down the side of his face, slightly stubbly after a long day's area sales-managing for Unico, Britain's fourth largest supermarket chain. 'But you sorted it all out, right?'

Joe preened modestly. 'Just doing my job.'

'Well I bet you did it better than anybody else would've done.'

'You'd say that even if I didn't.'

'Of course I would, you're my big hunky hero.' She rubbed herself up against him like an overexcited eel. 'My lovely gorgeous irresistibly sexy hero.'

'Does that mean I can look forward to an evening of unbridled lust with my adoring wife?' he asked hopefully.

Emma smiled. 'I wish.' Detaching herself, she reached for her coat. 'I'm on duty tonight, remember?'

'Not necessarily.' Joe slid a coaxing hand underneath her tunic, and gave her bum a squeeze. 'You could call in sick.'

She giggled. It was so, so tempting. She'd only been in her current job since just before the wedding, and already she'd had two weeks off for the honeymoon – still, what difference would one more night make? But she knew what would happen if she started off down that route. One night would turn into three, and before she knew it they'd have chucked her out of the nursing bank for being unreliable.

And just because she'd given up a good job in a London teaching hospital to come back to Cheltenham and marry Joe, that didn't mean she'd stopped caring about her career – even if she did have to keep reminding herself of that occasionally.

'You know I can't.'

'Why not? Everybody else does it.' She knew he wasn't playing a game; he really meant it. 'And it's not as if we're desperate for the money.'

That was true enough, thought Emma. And even if they had been, her pitiful salary wouldn't make much of a dent in Joe's pizza bill, let alone the mortgage on this snazzy apartment.

'I'll see you in the morning,' she promised, jumping up and dotting a goodnight kiss on his forehead.

There was just a hint of a pout in Joe's response. 'I might have gone to work by then.'

'In which case I'll see you in the evening, won't I?'

'Yeah, for about ten minutes.'

She sighed. 'You don't make this easy, do you? Hey remember, only three more nights and then I'm off for five.' She headed off down the passage to the front door, past a row of Chagall prints and a life-size Spiderman cut-out, and Joe followed, pulling off his tie and flinging it over Spiderman's shoulder.

'Yes, well, just don't expect to be getting any sleep, OK?'

'Promises, promises.' She turned and blew him a kiss. 'There's a lasagne in the fridge, I made it this afternoon; and a bag of ready-made salad. And why don't you put your cardboard friend in the spare room, along with your Baywatch posters? I'm sure he'd be much happier.'

'But I like having Spidey here.' Joe flicked the end of the tie. 'And he's useful too, see?'

'You want a hatstand for the hall? So let's go out and buy one. One we both like.'

'But I—'

She wagged a teasing finger under his nose. 'Yes, well *I* live here now too, Mr Sheridan, and it's bad enough having to share the bathroom with the Starship Enterprise. So how about it? Hmm?' She fluttered her eyelashes prettily.

'Well . . . maybe. We'll see.'

3

'You bet we will. Right, gotta go now, see you in the morning.'

Joe's face fell. 'Oh. OK, 'bye darling. Be good.'

And then she was gone, leaving Joe looking as if the wheels had just fallen off his skateboard.

It was a quiet night in the A&E department at Cotswold General. So quiet, the receptionist had even switched off the electronic display that usually read: CURRENT WAITING TIME FOUR HOURS.

Emma's mouth opened in an enormous yawn, and somebody pushed a Quality Street into it.

'What's this for?' she mumbled through a mouthful of choc-olate toffee.

'To keep you awake.' Eileen, the nursing assistant who'd been at Cotswold General since King Arthur had his tonsils done, nodded towards a massive tin on the reception desk. 'Courtesy of a satisfied customer, apparently.'

'I didn't think we had any of those. Just dead ones and ones who make complaints.'

Eileen laughed. 'Who's had too many late nights recently?' She gave Emma a suggestive nudge in the ribs. 'Go on, girl, don't keep it to yourself. I'm dying of suspense.'

'Eh?'

'Married life! You know, rumpy-pumpy. Must be good, you obviously aren't getting any sleep.'

Emma tried – and failed – to suppress a blush that started at her chest and ran right to the tips of her ears. 'Eileen!'

'I know, I know, mind my own business.' She heaved a sigh of grey-haired nostalgia. 'Takes me back to my own ...'

'Your own what?' enquired Lawrence the charge nurse as he passed through on his way to return the ECG machine to its bay. 'Teeth? That must've been a while back.'

Eileen swatted him with a disposable glove. 'I was talking about when I was first married! Emma was about to tell me all the juicy bits about her sex life, weren't you, Em?'

'Nice try,' laughed Emma. 'Dream on.'

She had a sneaking suspicion it was either Eileen or Ray the night porter who'd tied an inflatable stork and baby bootees to her peg in the staff changing room, the day she came back off honey-moon, but she knew she'd have to put up with that kind of thing at least until the novelty wore off and somebody else got hitched.

4

When people spent their working lives among blood, guts and tragedy, they had to get their laughs somehow.

As she checked over the resuscitation trolley for the nth time, just for something to do, Emma couldn't stop her mind sneaking back to the lovely cosy apartment where Joe would be dolefully eating his lasagne and watching reruns of *Robot Wars*, before climbing into the king-size bed. All on his own.

He's right, she thought. I could've rung in sick tonight – they'd never have missed me. God knows, they'd probably have been grateful. Even allowing for the differences between London and Cheltenham, and the fact that it was a dull, damp Wednesday in February, this was a quiet night. Normally, anyone with minor injuries was in for a long wait on a wobbly plastic chair, with nothing but anti-drugs posters to stare at. Tonight, the minute a minicab driver came in with a cut finger, three nurses and a junior house officer had all pounced on him at once.

Just as she was wondering if she could fake a migraine and get sent home, the phone rang and all hell broke loose.

The charge nurse slammed down the receiver, all trace of merriment gone from his face. 'Major traffic accident on the motorway,' he announced. Everybody sprang instantly to attention.

'How many injured?' asked one of the junior doctors.

'Sixteen, four serious, coming our way in around,' Lawrence glanced at the clock, 'five minutes. So if anybody wants a pee, go and do it now. Looks like it's going to be a long night.'

'Emma?' A voice called through the open door and down the passageway. 'Emma dear, this door knocker could do with a bit of Brasso. Emma, are you there?' The voice paused but no reply came. 'Joe?'

Joe had just put Emma's rather fine home-made lasagne into the microwave (he couldn't be arsed using the real oven, it took far too long), and was singing along to J-Lo on the radio when his mother put her head round the kitchen door.

'Joe, darling. I let myself in with that spare key you gave me, you don't mind?'

Joe opened his mouth to remind her that she was supposed to have given them the key back when they returned from honeymoon, but what the heck. After all she was his mum, not a cat burglar. 'Hello there.' He gave her a peck on the cheek. 'How's Dad?'

'Fine since he started on the new tablets, and don't let him tell you he isn't.' Minette Sheridan glanced around as though there might be somebody lurking in one of the kitchen cupboards. 'Where's Emma?'

'She's on nights again, Mum, didn't she tell you?'

Minette's diminutive body stiffened, matching the ruthless symmetry of her chin-length ash-blonde bob. 'On nights? Again?' The ping of the microwave oven punctuated the outraged silence. 'And she's left you to make do with some horrible TV dinner? Oh Joe, that's just not right.'

Joe protested, albeit weakly. 'It's a lasagne, Mum, Emma made it h—'

But it was pointless; Minette had already made up her mind. Seizing the plate from Joe's hand, she slid the contents straight into the kitchen bin. 'Right! You're coming home with me for a decent meal.'

'But Mum ...'

'I've made a steak and kidney pie. And apple crumble to follow.'

That swung it for Joe. He'd always been a sucker for his mum's home cooking, perfectly respectable though Emma's might be. And besides, his dinner was in the bin now and he had to eat something, didn't he?

'I'll just get my coat, then.' He was drooling already.

Emma peeled off her disposable latex gloves and dropped them wearily into the bin.

'You OK?' asked Lawrence, laying a hand on her shoulder.

She nodded. 'Fine. Just a bit bushed, that's all.' It was more than that though, she reflected; a mixture of acute physical exhaustion and an adrenalin high that wouldn't let her come down for hours. She was glad she had Lawrence to talk to; he was the kind of bloke you'd trust with your life. Emma's boss or not, in the couple of months she'd been at the General, they'd become really good mates. And mates were in pretty short supply since she'd left all of her old ones back in London.

He stepped away and leaned his back against the door frame. 'It's been quite a night,' he observed.

'Do you reckon the kid'll make it?' she asked, thinking of the fourteen-year-old with the ghostly white face and the twisted legs, who'd thought it would be such a great idea to take his brother's car for a drive.

The charge nurse shrugged. 'Hard to say, isn't it. But we did our best, like we always do. And if it wasn't for you being so quick off the mark, that old lady with the aneurism would probably be dead.'

She looked up. 'You reckon so?'

'I know so. You're good at this job, Emma.' He lowered his voice. 'To be honest we're lucky to have you, but I didn't say that, OK?'

She smiled. 'Say what?'

'Now for God's sake get yourself washed and changed, woman. From what I hear there's a sexy young man waiting for you at home, and he doesn't want you turning up smelling of puke.'

2

'That you, Rozzer? Hang on a minute.' Joe held the mobile to his ear as he squeezed through the Unico warehouse, taking care not to get economy ketchup on his new Armani. Like his ex-army dad, who still ironed creases in his jeans, Joe liked to look smart. And anyway, it was part of the job to look good – especially when you were on the management fast track with no intention of stopping till you hit Success Central.

Hand muffling the receiver, he gestured to the store man in the brown coat. 'Those fifty pallets to Abingdon by four, or I'll want to know the reason why.' His voice returned to normal volume. 'You still there?'

Rozzer Wilkinson – christened Roswell by his UFO-mad parents – replied through what sounded like a mouthful of crisps. 'Yeah. Just having a bevvy in the Two Foxes before the afternoon rush. What's up?'

'You and Toby fancy coming round on Friday night? There's a big match on satellite. Gary's coming,' he added, by way of an additional incentive.

'You sure it'll be all right?' asked Rozzer doubtfully.

Joe scratched his nose. 'How d'you mean, all right?'

'With Emma. You know, the new lady of the house? I mean, you've only just got back off honeymoon, you might want to ... do something else.'

Joe chuckled. 'Of course it's all right with Em, she'll be cool about it. Hey, we're not at it like rabbits every minute of the day you know.'

'More fool you,' quipped Rozzer.

'So – you coming round then?'

'OK, half-eight all right? Only I've got to close up the shop and then it's football practice.'

'Fine. See you then – oh, and don't forget the beer!'

Joe rang off and clipped the phone back onto his belt. He felt a little thrill of domesticated excitement as he thought of Emma. His lovely new wife. Of Emma, and of the nice warm bed they'd be sharing again after she'd finished this run of nights.

Hmm. Joe smiled to himself. Emma, a soft bed, a bottle of champagne . . . Rozzer definitely had something there.

Emma finished suturing the two-inch gash in the little girl's forehead, and sat back to examine her handiwork.

'There,' she smiled. 'That didn't hurt, did it?'

The corners of the little mouth quivered, but the child shook her head.

'And you were ever so brave!' Emma turned to the harassed-looking mother, still dressed in her pyjamas and blood-spattered dressing gown. 'Wasn't Sara-Jane a brave girl, Mum?' Mum smiled weakly, no doubt still recovering from the shock of having a brick thrown through her bedroom window in the middle of the night. 'I think that deserves one of our special certificates.'

She fetched one from the drawer in reception and filled in the girl's name in red felt pen. It read: This certificate is presented to Sara-Jane for being very brave in hospital. 'There we are.' She handed it over. 'Well done.'

'Say thank you to the nice lady, Sara-Jane.'

'Fank oo.'

'You're very welcome. Now, I'll just fetch a leaflet for your mummy, so she knows what to do if you feel poorly later on.' She looked the mother up and down. She wasn't saying much, and she was white as a sheet. 'Are you OK? Would you like the doctor to have a look at you too?'

'No, I'm fine. Really. It's just the shock.' She swallowed. 'I've just been thinking. About talking to the police . . .'

'That's OK, I can call them as soon as you're ready.'

'Actually.' The woman laid a protective hand on her daughter's shoulder. 'I've changed my mind. What I mean is, well, I don't want to make a fuss. In fact I don't think I'm going to bother reporting this at all, thanks.'

9

Emma cocked her head questioningly. 'But someone tried to hurt you. And your little girl. What if—'

'Never mind what if.' The woman's dark eyes met hers, and the look was suddenly diamond-hard. 'Look love, I live on the Meadows Estate,' she said. 'There's things you do and there's things you don't. It's talking to the police that got me in this mess in the first place. Now, if you've done with Sara-Jane, we're going home.'

'Hey, c'mon.' Joe refilled Emma's wine glass and set it back down on the edge of the bath, where it nestled among the overflowing bubbles. 'You're supposed to be in the grip of unbearable sensual ecstasy. Or am I doing this all wrong?'

'What? Oh, I'm sorry darling.' She sat up in the bath and gave him a foamy kiss. 'You're not doing anything wrong, I was just thinking.'

'Well, don't!' Joe pulled off his socks and sat down on the edge of the bath. Candles flickered around them in the half-light, casting romantic shadows. This was Emma's first night off, and he was determined it was going to be one to remember. 'You've got to stop imagining you can sort everybody else's lives out for them.'

'I know, and I don't, but I—'

'Yes you do! You've got a heart as big as a house and people take advantage of that.' He stroked her honey-blonde hair back from her face. 'Look, sweetheart, you had a word with the charge nurse, let him deal with it. If he thinks he ought to talk to Social Services or whatever, he will. It's not your responsibility, OK?'

'I—' He threw her a warning look. 'OK, ancient history.'

Emma flopped back into the foam and he started nibbling her toes, making her giggle. He was right of course, and she knew it. If there was one thing nursing had taught her, it was not to get personally involved. You'd go mad if you thought too hard about the person behind every bruise or dislocated toe. Professional detachment, that was what you had to aim for; even a first-year student nurse knew that.

To be honest, she'd thought she had the balance just about right; but that was before she'd moved back here from London and her whole life had turned inside out, leaving her feeling curiously vulnerable and adrift. She was so lucky she had Joe, her paradise

10

island in an ocean of uncertainty, even if Joe was the cause of the upheaval – in the nicest possible way.

'This is so strange,' she heard herself murmur.

Joe looked up from her pampered toes, crestfallen. 'I thought you liked it.'

'I do!' she replied, smiling at his expression. 'I didn't mean what you're doing, I mean life.'

'Oh God,' Joe sighed dramatically. 'Now she's a philosopher.'

She splashed him playfully. 'I'm serious! It's such a strange time in our lives, don't you think? Everything's different, so . . . new.'

'Of course it is.' He ran a finger lightly up her leg, teasing her beneath the waterline. 'But it's wonderful, not strange.'

'Both.' Detaching herself, she rolled over onto her belly and dotted kisses on Joe's bare thigh. He really is beautiful, she thought as she tasted the hint of salt on the smooth, toned flesh. He could have any woman he wants. How did I ever get so lucky? 'All those years we went out together, and we never really started to know each other till now. I never even knew you were allergic to celery!'

'So what? Hey, the getting to know each other bit is half the fun. Squeaky, love – what's brought this on?'

'Oh, nothing. Take no notice.'

'You are happy, aren't you?'

'Yes!'

She looked up into his eyes and felt the thrill of knowing that he was hers, really hers at last, and she was his. Everything else – the newness, the strangeness, the not quite fitting in – would sort itself out, because what really mattered was that they were together.

'Darling,' she whispered, drawing his face down to hers.

'Hmm?'

'Do you remember that big sunken bath we had that time in Tunisia? The one with room for two?'

Joe's smile broadened. 'Do I ever.'

'And do you remember what we got up to in it?'

'Of course I do. What about it?'

She kissed him. 'I'm not sure I can recall all the details. Maybe you'd better climb in here and remind me.'

Emma was still towelling herself dry when the phone rang.

'I'll get it,' said Joe, flicking back his still-damp hair. A moment

11

later he reappeared in the doorway of the bathroom, portable phone in hand. 'It's for you – the hospital I think.' He mouthed, 'Tell them to bugger off,' but Emma just stuck out her tongue at him.

'Hello? Emma Co—' she halted herself just in time, 'Sheridan speaking.

'Hi, this is Jennie from the Nursing Bank. Just thought I'd let you know where we're assigning you next week.'

'Oh,' said Emma, slightly taken aback. 'I thought I was staying on A and E.'

'Well, as you know Sister Murphy's coming back off sick leave and we'll be fully staffed for nights, so we're transferring you to days on ...'

Emma brightened considerably. Days on A&E, that was even better. And if she could stay on days until a permanent job came up ...

'... Milbrook Ward.'

For a moment, it didn't quite register. Then an alarm bell went off inside Emma's head. 'Milbrook? Isn't that a geriatric ward?'

'Female medical, strictly speaking, though a lot of the patients are long-stay elderly. A few of them have psychiatric issues as well.'

'Oh.'

'Is that a problem?'

'Er ... no,' lied Emma. Not that she had anything against elderly patients; it was just that she'd slogged her guts out to pass those courses in A&E and Intensive Care. That was what she loved. That was what she was *good* at, what she'd always wanted to do. And that was what she'd given up to come here.

'What's up?' mouthed Joe.

'Could you hold on a moment?' She cupped her hand over the receiver. 'They're transferring me to days next week.'

'Great!'

'On geriatrics.'

Joe shrugged, uncomprehending. 'Does that matter? Hey, we'll actually get to spend some time together!'

Emma turned back to the phone and took a deep breath. 'No problem at all, Jennie. When do you want me to start?'

The following day, the last of Emma's adrenalin ran out and the accumulated tiredness of eight consecutive nights hit her like a brick wall. She spent most of the day slopping around the flat in her Miffy pyjamas while Joe raced off to Evesham to find out why cheese sales had slumped by twelve per cent.

Yet again she had to admit that Joe had a point. Milbrook might not have been her choice, but it would be nice to do days again, not to mention sleeping in the same bed as Joe – at the same time.

As she lounged on Joe's huge white leather sofa, eating some salami she'd found at the back of the fridge, the phone trilled into life.

'Hello?'

'Hello, love, it's Mum. How's my number-one daughter enjoying married life?'

Emma had to laugh. Her mum always called her that, despite the fact that Emma was an only child. Mr Cox's early death had put paid to plans for brothers and sisters, and Karen Cox had never remarried. She always said she was quite happy as she was, and now the guest house kept her too busy to think about men.

'It's great, Mum, but you might have warned me about the underpants!'

'The what?'

'One minute they're wooing you with their skintight Calvin Kleins, the next they've got the ring on your finger and the Scooby-Doo boxers come out of the closet! It wouldn't be so bad, but he sleeps in them.'

'Never mind, love,' laughed Karen. 'Just rip a few holes in them next time you do the washing, and blame it on the machine. That's what I used to do with your dad's long johns. How is Joe, anyway?'

'Working too hard, as usual. I'm on my days off now, so I thought I'd get a nice romantic video out, do some pizzas, and then we can have a cosy Friday night in, all snuggled up on the sofa.'

'Sounds lovely.'

'What about you, Mum?' asked Emma. 'I hope you've been having a rest.'

Her mother laughed. 'A rest! What about all my guests?'

'In January?'

'You'd be surprised, Blackpool's busy all year round these days, what with the new casino and the boom in the gay trade. Did I tell you I got taken to a transvestite show-bar last weekend?'

13

'Mum!'

'It was fascinating. One of them gave me the most brilliant tip for getting nail varnish on without it smudging.'

'Mum,' said Emma sternly, 'you really do have to rest. Go away for a nice winter sun break or something. You looked absolutely exhausted at the wedding.'

'Sweetheart, I'd just organised a reception for two hundred and fifty! I was hardly going to be swinging from the chandeliers. But I'm perfectly OK now.' Emma's mother paused. 'Anyway, enough about me – how are you?'

That caught Emma on the hop. 'Me? Fine.'

Karen must have heard something in her daughter's voice, because she followed that up with '*Really* fine?'

'Yes, really fine,' insisted Emma. 'Well, OK, I guess things are still all a bit *different*. And I feel kind of isolated sometimes. But that's hardly surprising. After all it's eight years since I lived in Cheltenham, I could hardly expect all my old school friends to be hanging around just waiting for me to turn up. Do you remember Jessica?'

'The girl with the curly hair and the pony? She wanted to join the police, didn't she?'

'I ran into her in the supermarket. Three kids by two different dads, dropped out of college, and I heard on the grapevine she's just been had up for passing dud cheques.'

'Good grief.'

'And you know Christine Freeman? The one who failed all her GCSEs and was going to be a model? Guess what – last I heard, she was doing a Masters in economics! Nothing stays the same, does it, Mum?'

'Of course it doesn't. Change is what makes life interesting.' Karen paused. 'It's just that sometimes things change a bit fast, or all at once, and then it's hard to keep up.'

'I guess it was right, what you told me at the wedding. Some things do take time.'

'Even wonderful things can take some getting used to, love. And you must be missing Mickey – have you heard from her since the wedding?'

As usual, Mum had gone straight to the heart of the matter. Michaela was Emma's best friend, had been ever since the day they made up their first hospital bed together. For the last six years they'd shared a ramshackle rented house in Hackney with two other nurses, Ellie and Sam, and latterly with Phoebe, an air stewardess; all the time knowing this period of their lives was bound to come to an end and all the time half believing it never would.

Leaving Mickey behind had been harder than all the other changes put together. Like amputating a small but precious part of her own life.

'Yes, she's rung me a couple of times. Mind you she's been a bit preoccupied lately with that new bloke of hers.'

'Rod?'

'Good grief no, Rod was ages ago. I'm not sure what this one's called, I've lost track.'

'But everything's OK down there?'

'Seems to be. They've got a new girl in my room now, can't remember what she's called, Lisa-Anne or Lisette or something. And Sam's been talking about moving out. Anyhow, Joe and I are going to go down and stay sometime, so I guess we'll get all the gossip then.'

She hadn't realised how morose she sounded until her mum said, 'Chin up, you and Mickey will always be friends, anybody can see that. Besides, think of all the new ones you're going to make with Joe.'

'Yeah,' she retorted. 'All the sales reps and rugby players I could ever hope to meet. Oh no, now I'm starting to sound like Eeyore!'

'No, love.' Emma could hear the smile in her mother's voice. 'You sound just like me, three weeks after I married your father.'

'Really?'

'Really. I mean, I know I only gave up the bacon counter at the Co-op, but it still felt like the end of the world at the time.'

'I am happy, Mum,' said Emma quietly. 'I mean, really happy. I love him ever so much, it's just that sometimes—'

'It's OK, you don't need to explain. Just remember this: if you love each other as much as I know you do, everything's going to be just fine.'

When Joe got home that evening, just before eight, the smell of home-baked pizza filled the apartment, and a bottle of crisp dry white was chilling in an ice bucket on the glass and chrome coffee table.

He looked around. 'Em?' Then took two steps towards the kitchen – only to be pounced on by a scantily clad figure emerging from the bathroom.

'Welcome home, darling.' Emma moulded herself enticingly to the front of his business suit and pressed her lips against his. She'd been practising this all afternoon and knackered though she was it was going to be bloody good.

'Hey, wow!' He came up for air and found his arms full of black satin negligée. 'You look fantastic.'

'I know,' she replied modestly. 'The thing is, seeing as you've been such a good boy I thought you deserved a present.'

He grinned broadly. 'Do I get to unwrap it?'

'Maybe ... later.' She licked her lips seductively. 'There's no hurry though, is there? We've got all night. I thought we could start off with—What's the matter?'

Joe's grin had frozen to his face. 'Ah,' he said.

'Ah? What do you mean, ah?'

'Ah, I think I might have forgotten to tell you something.'

Emma's eyes narrowed. 'Such as?'

'Such as, the lads are supposed to be coming round tonight.'

'What! When?'

'About half-eight. There's this big American football game on Sky. You don't mind, do you?' From the expression on Emma's face, Joe could hazard a pretty good guess. 'Only the lads always come round on a Friday night.'

'Joe!'

'Or at least, they ...er ... used to.' He smiled sheepishly. 'I should've asked you first, shouldn't I?'

Emma glared as she picked up the bowl of runny chocolate mousse and tilted it above his head.

'If I phone them and tell them not to come, will you forgive me?'

He never found out whether she would or not; because at that point, the doorbell rang.

16

3

The cursor sped across the computer screen, spelling out the next message from Mickey. *So what did you do then?*

Sulked, Emma typed back, grinning at the memory of Friday night's little confrontation. She was sure Rozzer had expected her to slice him into quarters with the pizza cutter, sprinkle him with Parmesan and have him for supper.

As her fingers rattled the keys, she wondered how she and Mickey could possibly have managed without this personal Internet chat room. Especially on nights like this, when Emma's body clock still thought it was lunchtime, while Joe was sprawled diagonally across the bed like a snoring octopus. Mickey, bless her, never went to bed before two am. Yes, this was the next best thing to sitting in the front room together, sharing a bottle of Bailey's.

Stomped off to bed and tried to sleep, she went on, *but the lads made such a racket trying to be quiet that I got up and joined in. It was quite fun in the end.*

Joined in what?!!! demanded Mickey.

Watching the American football, what do you think!

Suppose Joe's a world expert on that as well, is he?

What do you mean?

Come on Em, your Joe's an expert on everything. He's even worse than Sam for showing off. Just watch out he doesn't take up nursing.

The very thought of that made Emma laugh out loud, and she had to stuff the sleeve of her dressing gown in her mouth. *YOU ARE KIDDING! Remember that time in Southend? When that wasp got into his trunks and he got stung on the bum?*

Oh yeah, he fainted. What a wuss.

Watch it, that's my beloved husband you're dissing! The cursor flashed lazily for a moment, then she added, *So what about YOUR latest bloke then? Is it love?*

Hardly. Mental midget. Think I might dump him soon.

Not still saving yourself for Jude Law are you? quipped Emma.

Nah, anybody with cheekbones and a brain. When you coming down to see us?

Soon.

Better be. Going to bed now, say hello to Joe for me.

OK.

And tell him I'll bake him another chocolate cheesecake if he fixes the gears on my bike. Night-night, be good.

I'll try. 'Night.

And with a yawn and a stretch Emma switched off the computer and went to gently roll Joe off her side of the bed.

To her relief, Milbrook Ward turned out to be a lot better than Emma had expected. True, it was old-fashioned, and most of the patients were elderly, but there were some real characters among them. Like Kitty the eighty-five year-old streetwalker, who couldn't be trusted within five yards of a good-looking doctor. And then there was Miss Crawford, who had taught at the Ladies' College just after the war and regarded the nurses as errant fourth-formers with bad deportment.

All in all, Emma wasn't too unhappy to be there for a week or two – as long as that was all it was. And it was nice to have patients who were well enough to hold a conversation.

It was a darkening winter afternoon, and snow was lashing against the windows. Inside, everything was running smoothly. An assortment of visitors were chatting to patients, the occasional loud laugh cut short by the realisation of where they were. A toddler was sitting on the end of its grandma's bed, covering the bedspread with chewed-up digestive biscuit. And Miss Crawford was telling the young girl in the bed next to her how the demise of the liberty bodice had contributed to the permissive society.

Emma had just finished attending to a seriously ill patient in one of the side rooms, and was about to go back into the ward office, when the sound of raised voices stopped her in her tracks.

At first, she thought one of the visitors was getting out of hand, but they had all stopped chatting or pinching grapes, and were unanimously gazing at the curtains drawn round a bed in the middle bay.

'Mrs Daley,' came the irritable voice from behind the curtains. 'No, no, I won't let you . . .'

'For pity's sake you old . . . Look, this is for your own good—'

'No, don't hurt me, no, Nurse! Nurse!'

Flinging a quick smile at the visitors, Emma reached the curtains in two long strides. 'Excuse me?' She eased the curtain aside a little way and stuck her head in. A young female doctor was bending over the patient in the bed, a tiny, shrunken figure whose face wore an expression of abject terror. 'Is there something wrong, only I heard—'

The words all collided in her brain as the doctor swished her dark ponytail, stood up and looked straight at her. No! No, it couldn't be, not *Zara*. Don't hyperventilate you silly girl, Emma scolded herself. It couldn't be Zara, not here; it must just be somebody who looked incredibly like her.

She might even have made herself believe that if it hadn't been for the look on Zara's face. A look of startled – and not exactly pleased – recognition.

'She's trying to hurt me, Nurse.' Mrs Daley twisted her arm free from the doctor's grasp, and Emma saw how tightly the doctor's fingers had pressed into the old lady's flesh, leaving reddening marks.

'Don't be ridiculous,' sighed Zara. Emma saw the badge on her white coat; it read DR ZARA JEFFRIES, SENIOR HOUSE OFFICER. 'I told you, Mrs Daley. You're very dehydrated. I'm just trying to put up a drip, for goodness sake!'

Emma stepped inside and drew back the curtain behind her. 'Everything's all right Mrs D, nobody's going to hurt you.' She took the elderly lady's hand and gave it a reassuring squeeze. It was cold and trembling. 'The doctor just wants to help.' She looked across at the doctor, who was exuding irritation. 'Could I just have a quick word outside, Doctor?' Zara didn't move, so she added, 'Now?'

'If you'd read Mrs Daley's notes,' said Emma with slow deliberation, 'you'd have—'

'If I'd *had* Mrs Daley's notes, maybe I'd have been able to read them!'

They were squaring up by the desk in the ward office, across half a doughnut and a cold cup of coffee, each of them avoiding mentioning that they had recognised the other, neither wanting to be the one to crack open the thin veneer of professional courtesy.

'There are only three of us on the ward this afternoon,' Emma went on, 'and my two nursing assistants had just gone on their break. In any case, Mrs Daley's notes are right here on the desk.' She pointed them out, in plain sight beside the telephone.

'Exactly! Instead of in the trolley where they belong.'

'With respect, you'd have seen them if you'd come in here first instead of barging straight in with your hypodermic.'

A white label, stuck to the front of the buff cardboard folder, read: PHOBIA: NEEDLES.

Dr Zara's exceedingly pretty mouth tensed. The expression said: I do not like being told what to do by anybody, and especially not by some know-it-all staff nurse whose husband I used to go out with.

'It must be nice to know everything,' she commented acidly.

'I wouldn't know,' replied Emma. 'But when I don't know something, I ask. Now, would you like me to stay with Mrs Daley while you put up her drip?'

'I think I can just about manage on my own, thanks.' Zara whisked the patient's notes out of Emma's hand. 'Haven't you got bedpans to polish or something?'

'Good day?' enquired Joe, emerging from the kitchen with his pinny on. The flat was filled with the comforting smells of fresh coffee and something tasty cooking slowly on the stove.

Emma kicked off her shoes, threw off her sodden coat and stomped across the room, shaking like a wet terrier. 'What does it look like?'

'Aw, never mind, come here and let me cuddle it better.'

She squelched gratefully into his arms and luxuriated in a huge hug that felt like being cuddled by a warm polar bear. 'You know,' she sighed, 'this is the nicest thing that's happened to me all day. Not that it's got much competition.'

Joe stroked her hair. 'Somebody been nasty to you? I'll beat him up for you.'

'I wouldn't if I were you. Besides, he's a she. Snotty cow, losing her temper with the patient and then trying to blame me.'

She tilted back her head and gazed up the nine inches that separated her from the top of Joe's head. 'Bet you can't guess who, either.'

'One of the patients?'

'Nope.'

'That nursing officer that used to be a prison sister? The one with the enormous hands and the hairy chin?'

'Wrong again. Think doctor. Think Miss World contestant. Think somebody you used to know very, very well.'

She never thought he'd guess, so when he replied, 'What – you mean Zara Jeffries?' she almost fell over backwards.

'You knew!' she exclaimed. 'You knew she was working there all the time, and you never let on!'

Joe looked puzzled. 'Should I have?'

Emma wondered if the man she had married could really be that emotionally dim. 'Joe, this is Zara we're talking about! The girl you were practically joined to at the hip for five years.'

'Four and a half,' he corrected her. 'And we didn't really start going out properly till she was fifteen.'

'Four and a half, five, what difference does it make? You were like the Posh and Becks of Lansdown Comprehensive. Every boy wanted to be you, every girl wanted to be her.'

Joe smiled. 'Except you.'

'Yeah, except me,' agreed Emma, making her way into the kitchen and lifting the lid of a saucepan. 'I just wanted to kill her. What's this?'

'Lamb and apricot casserole. I finished early today, so I thought I'd cook my lovely new wife a nice dinner.' He slipped his arms round her waist and nibbled her neck. 'You see, I do have my uses.'

'Well all right,' conceded Emma, 'I'll let you off. But I still think you could have warned me. I mean, I haven't seen the woman for years; I thought she was still up north somewhere.'

'She was,' said Joe, stirring the casserole and licking the spoon. 'Then this job came up at the General and she decided to come back.'

Emma frowned. 'How come you know so much about all this?'

Joe looked up. 'Hmm? Oh – we keep in touch off and on. Exchange the odd e-mail, that kind of thing.'

'That's the first I've heard of it! Are you sure that's all you've been exchanging?' she added, only half jokingly.

He looked at her and his brown eyes twinkled. 'You're not still jealous of Zara? You *are*, you're jealous!'

'No I'm not!' she protested, giggling as he tickled her into breathless submission.

But as they kissed and the stew bubbled over the edge of the pan, a part of Emma's brain was still wondering how many other things Joe hadn't bothered telling her about.

4

Joe whistled to himself as he drove to the next store through the pelting rain, thinking fondly of central heating, big mugs of hot chocolate and his nice warm wife.

Ah, married life. There was nothing like it. Success was important, of course it was; but it was ten times better if you had somebody to share it with. And he loved sharing it with Emma, loved looking after her and being her protector against all the nasty things in the Big Bad World. He was sure his mum was right; there was nothing a girl liked more than feeling safe and secure.

Tonight, he thought to himself, he might just slope off early from that boring meeting in Gloucester and pick up Emma from her shift at the hospital. Perhaps they'd go to the pictures and have a bite to eat at the French bistro on the way home. It was so nice having her around all the time; not having to cram everything into weekends or holidays or the odd day off.

As he turned off into the private slip road that led to the back of the Newent store, his mobile phone rang; quickly he parked and answered it.

'Joe Sheridan.'

He didn't recognise the man's voice on the other end of the line. 'Damian Lee here, Fiona Tiverton's PA.'

The group personnel director! He could count on the fingers of ... well, actually on one finger, the number of times he'd had any contact with her – and it had never been a cause for rejoicing. He wondered what he'd done wrong now. 'Er ... hi.'

'Ms Tiverton wants to see you in her office at four thirty today.'

'Today? But I've got a meeting in Ba—'

'Today, Mr Sheridan.'

Joe didn't scare easily, but he was starting to feel distinctly rattled. 'Can I ask what this is about?'

'Four thirty,' repeated the voice. 'And don't be late, Ms Tiverton has a very tight schedule.'

Despite the clattering of enormous pans and the ever-present reek of chip fat, the staff canteen at the Cotswold General was an oasis of tranquillity for anyone who'd had just a bit too much of being nice to the general public.

Or their colleagues, mused Emma, grateful to get her evening break after missing out on lunch. It was just after seven, all the patients had been fed and the drug round done, and nobody looked in danger of dying before her shift ended at half past eight. She ought to have been relaxing with her cup of stewed tea and looking forward to going home, but the truth was she felt like climbing up on the roof and having a good scream.

For one thing, there was Joe's mum. Now, Emma was quite willing to accept that Minette wasn't the worst mother-in-law in the world, and on occasion they'd even enjoyed the odd ten minutes of each other's company. But promise or no promise, Emma was not in the mood for 'popping in' to the Sheridan residence on her way home, delivering their copy of the wedding video and submitting to a half-hour explanation of why Joe had to have his sprouts cut up for him.

But all of this was as nothing compared to Zara.

'She's got it in for me, I really think she has,' lamented Emma.

Lawrence, who regularly ate in the canteen when he was on nights, made dubious noises through a mouthful of spaghetti carbonara.

'No, really!' she assured him. 'If you'd seen the look on her face ... I'm telling you, everywhere I go, she's there. And I wouldn't care, but she's on the surgical team, she shouldn't be working on medical at all!'

'Maybe that's the problem,' suggested Lawrence. 'Maybe she's pissed off because she's having to do Dr Das Gupta's job while he's in America.'

'Then why take it out on me? Just 'cause he got to go on some crappy exchange and she didn't?'

'She probably isn't. From what I hear, she's like that with everybody.' He leaned over and added confidentially, ' The porters on A and E call her Miss PMT.' He swallowed a mouthful of Pepsi and stifled a burp. 'Chin up, kid, I'm sure it's nothing personal.'

'So why is it that every time I make a mistake, I turn round and she's smirking at me? And of course, *she* never does anything wrong, does she?'

Lawrence sighed. 'Look, love, I'm no expert, but don't you think you might be overreacting a bit because of, you know, what went on in the past? You did say she and Joe went out together for a long time, and nobody could blame you for being, well, jealous.'

Emma couldn't really deny that Lawrence had a valid point. 'I suppose. But that's the point, don't you see? She's probably never forgiven *me* for going out with Joe, and now he's actually *married* me ...'

'Gawd help us.' Lawrence shook his elaborately highlighted head. 'And I thought I agonised about *my* love life. Take my advice, darling, put the silly tart out of your mind and just enjoy the fact that you've got a big strong sexy man who thinks the world of you.'

He sounded so wistful that Emma realised how self-centred she was being. 'Sorry, take no notice of me; got to pay a duty visit to the in-laws tonight.' She took a sip of tea. 'So – how's life with you?'

'Oh, fabulous.' He looked at her over the rim of his cardboard cup. 'My sister's left her boyfriend again and moved into my place with the kids, and now Duncan says he thinks he might be straight. Ah well, some day my prince will come.'

'You've made me feel all guilty now,' said Emma reprovingly.

'Good! A bit of angst's good for the soul. Now, are you going to perk up or what?'

'Oh all right then, seeing as it's you.' What would I do without you, Lawrence? wondered Emma, feeling better already. It was impossible to stay depressed around him for long. Stupid people might avoid him because he was camp as a row of tents, but to Emma he was a revelation: the big brother she'd never had.

He got up, flicking breadcrumbs off his white uniform tunic. 'Listen, the word is, Janice Clark's up the duff and we're going to need someone permanent on A and E soon. Plus, there's another reorganisation in the offing and I might just be moving to permanent days. So be good, Cinders, and Uncle Lawrence might just be able to whisk you away from Milbrook after all.'

There was a limit to the amount of time you could put things off, and Emma had decided that she might as well get the whole thing over and done with. Consequently, by half-past eight she was standing in the drizzle outside the door of Number 43, Orchard Way, framed on one side by a conifer in a square planter and on the other by a sign that read: BEWARE OF THE POODLE.

If she'd turned and looked across the road, she'd have seen the house where Mr and Mrs Jeffries had lived with their daughter Zara, a decade or so ago. But Emma was in no hurry to relive her spotty, buck-toothed schooldays, when she'd felt like some kind of mutant compared to the girl from Number 40.

She rang the bell, and after a few seconds she heard a voice call down from upstairs, 'Door, Alan. I'm just vacuuming the dog.'

The door duly opened and a tall, straight-backed, middle-aged version of Joe appeared, carrying a copy of *What Investment*. 'Come in love,' he boomed affably. 'Minette'll be down in a minute. Minette, it's Emma, shall I use the best cups?'

'Don't be silly, Alan, she's family now. Don't do anything, I'm coming down.'

Minette's imminent arrival was heralded by an apricot-coloured, yelping fuzzball which shot down the stairs, into the kitchen and vanished into the garden at the speed of sound.

'There he goes,' mused Alan as the dog flap banged shut. 'He hates it you know, sometimes I wonder why we don't just get him a flea collar.'

'Hello, Emma darling.' Minette came down the stairs and gave her new daughter-in-law a peck on the cheek. Standing back a couple of feet, she looked her up and down. 'You're still looking very peaky, you know – Alan, isn't she looking peaky?'

'I ... er, well ...'

'Yes, very peaky. That's what comes of working all those night shifts. Still, now you're working more civilised hours you can build up your strength.' She smiled. 'And you'll need all your strength to deal with our Joe, he can be quite a handful with all those socks he gets through. Have you got a proper mushroom, by the way?'

Emma looked at her blankly. 'A what?'

26

'A mushroom, dear. A wooden one for darning. You *must* have one, otherwise how are you going to do his mending?'

Mending? thought Emma, not daring to admit that the moment Joe's big toe poked through his sock he chucked it in the bin, then went out and bought another ten identical pairs.

'Um, well—'

'Never mind, dear, I expect I've got a spare one in my sewing room somewhere. Remind me later.'

'I can't stay long,' Emma said hastily. 'I just popped in to let you have this.' She handed over their copy of the wedding video.

'I hope they've edited out the bit where the organist lost his place,' commented Minette. 'It was so amateurish, and everybody started sniggering when his music fell off the stand.' She turned to Emma. 'Now dear, Earl Grey or Lapsang?'

Emma smiled despairingly. 'I don't suppose you've got any PG Tips?'

She only stayed half an hour, but as half-hours went it was one of the longer ones.

For a start-off there was the inevitable gentle probing about grandchildren: when, where, how many, and how come you're not pregnant already since our Joe is undoubtedly the most fertile man in the Western hemisphere? Then there was the home-baked apple pie and the bottle of vitamins Minette pressed into her hands as she was leaving, because 'he always seems so hungry and with you both working I do wonder if he's eating properly.'

But undoubtedly the worst feature of her visit – worse even than Minette's CD of tone-deaf Amazonian pygmies – was Minette's delight at discovering that Zara Jeffries was back in town.

'Emma darling, you can't imagine how surprised I was when Joe told me!' she enthused.

'Not half as bloody surprised as I was,' muttered Emma.

Minette's eyebrows lifted quizzically. 'Pardon?'

'Sorry, I was just saying ... yes, it was quite a surprise, wasn't it?'

Minette sat back in her seat, teacup elegantly poised, reminiscing about her favourite daughter-in-law who never quite was. 'Ah yes, such a lovely child. Always beautifully dressed you know, never a hair out of place. A wonderful actress and singer too. And such a sweet nature.'

27

Emma nearly choked on her macaroon. 'You think so?'

'Oh, *definitely*. You probably don't recall, but Alan and I remember that really cold winter when she and Joe organised food parcels for all the elderly people in Leckhampton. Not to mention the crèche she ran for working mums in the summer holidays.'

Move over Mother Teresa, thought Emma.

'I rather hoped she'd settle down and have babies. She'll make a wonderful mother one day – fabulous with children you know.'

Of course she bloody is. Emma smiled through clenched teeth, feeling positively mutinous.

'In fact at one point I even,' she giggled and nudged her husband, 'thought that she and our Joe might...' Her smile receded. 'But that was before he started going out with you, of course.'

'Never mind,' said Emma with forced gaiety, 'she seems to be doing very well for herself.'

'Well of course she is, dear. She always was a cut above.' Minette sighed nostalgically. 'You know what I regret most, dear?'

'What?' enquired Emma.

'If only I'd known before that she was back in Cheltenham, we could have invited her to your wedding! Wouldn't that have been just perfect?'

The funny thing about Minette was that, even when she was at her most preposterous, her words sometimes contained a grain of truth. And in truth, Emma mused, it was nice being back on days, even if she did miss the cut and thrust of A&E like crazy. It was nice just to be able to spend some quality time with Joe.

As she padded up the hall and pushed open the kitchen door, the only thing she could say was, 'Wow!' All the lights were off, and the whole of the dining area seemed to be filled with the soft, flickering light from dozens of candles, stuck in everything from wine bottles to eggcups.

'Welcome home, darling.' Joe enfolded her in his big warm bear-hug, lifting her off the ground so suddenly that she let out a trademark squeak of pleased surprise. 'Good day?'

'OK, I guess.' She blinked, her eyes still accustoming themselves to the smoky light. Joe smelt of aftershave and shower gel, which wasn't at all like Joe after a long day spent haranguing staff all over Gloucestershire. Something was definitely afoot, and judging from the amount of trouble he'd gone to it must be something really bad. 'Something's happened, hasn't it? Something awful?'

Joe laughed. 'Don't be silly! I can pamper my lovely wife if I want, can't I?' He whisked a bottle of champagne out of the cooler he'd improvised from the bathroom bin, and indicated two plates of salmon mousse. 'Hope you like it, it's only M and S I'm afraid, didn't have time to do anything else.'

Emma sat down slowly, never taking her eyes off Joe's face. 'What's going on?' She put her hand over the top of her wine glass, forcing him to pause in his mad flurry of activity. 'Joe, I want to know!'

'All right, but let me pour you a drink first.'

Reluctantly she conceded. 'Now tell me.'

Sitting down opposite her, Joe took both her hands in his and kissed them. 'You're right, darling,' he said. 'Something has happened.'

She caught her breath.

'But it's not something bad, it's something brilliant. I got called to head office today to see Fiona Tiverton, and you'll never guess what – I'm being promoted.'

'Promoted!'

'Yes – to regional sales manager!'

Emma was just plain stunned. Seizing her glass of wine, she downed half of it in one gulp. 'Joe! I can't believe it!'

'Neither could I – apparently I'm the youngest regional manager Unico has ever had. You are pleased, aren't you?' he asked anxiously.

The thought that she could possibly not be pleased made Emma laugh so hard that she almost choked. 'Pleased? Joe, it's wonderful!' Springing to her feet, she ran round behind his chair and threw her arms round his neck. 'Want to know something? You're the cleverest, most talented, gorgeousest husband in the whole world, that's what you are.'

She felt his body relax in her arms. So he really had been worried that she might not greet the news with enthusiasm. She wondered why.

'There'll be a new company car of course,' he went on, 'and the extra money will come in useful, though obviously I'll have to work extra-hard for it. But you know how I love a challenge.'

Emma felt the pause in his voice rather than heard it. 'But?' she prompted.

'Not but, not exactly.' Joe reached for her hand and brushed his lips against it. 'The thing is, with this being a more senior job, with responsibility for a bigger geographical area ... well, there'll be quite a lot of travelling.'

'You travel a lot already,' Emma pointed out.

'Yes, but I'm always back the same day, aren't I? With this new job, I'll have to travel down to London a lot and maybe further afield for sales conferences and things, and I'm bound to be away overnight quite often. Sometimes I might be away for several days at a time.'

'Oh,' said Emma, her arms slackening about Joe's shoulders.

He half turned to look at her. 'I know it's a bummer, what with us being just married and all that,' he said, his eyes asking for her approval, 'but it won't be so bad really.'

'No,' said Emma faintly. 'I suppose not.'

Maybe he didn't catch the disappointment in her voice, or he chose not to hear it. Either way, when Joe spoke again he was full of boyish enthusiasm. 'This'll be really good for both of us, I know it will. And just think how much more we'll appreciate being together when I *am* home.'

'You're right, Joe, it's great news,' she said, pulling herself together.

'Really?'

'Really.'

And she sat down and toyed with her salmon mousse, although strangely she didn't seem to have much of an appetite any more.

5

Minette couldn't wait to tell the world about her brilliant son's latest news. In fact, she spent so much of Saturday on her mobile that by the time she'd finished it was red-hot and Alan told her she'd probably just irradiated the entire left side of her brain.

But Minette didn't give a damn about that. She'd happily have died for Joe, if dying would have got him any further up the corporate ladder. Having three other sons who'd made passable careers for themselves carried little weight compared to the dazzling successes of her darling youngest. Joe had always been the special one, not that she'd ever have admitted it openly: mothers weren't supposed to have favourites, after all.

In her eyes, go-getter Joe had always been 'the brainy one', the only one of her four children to have passed his A levels (albeit only just) and gone on to higher education, where he'd taken a business and management course whose title alone was so incomprehensible that you couldn't help but feel proud.

Minette always reckoned he'd got all that natural authority from his father; after all, Alan had spent nigh on twenty years in the Royal Engineers, admittedly only as a corporal, but you didn't even make it past private unless you had a bit of something about you, did you? And of course, since he'd left the army, Alan had built up a natty little business of his own selling reconditioned laptops – with a little help from Minette.

Helping was something Minette excelled at; in fact she saw it as the prime duty of a mother and a wife. How could a man fulfil his potential without constant subtle shoves in the right direction? And who better to administer those shoves than the woman who cooked his dinner and chose his ties?

31

And now that she'd, as it were, delegated that task to Emma, Minette felt bound to make sure that Joe's new wife realised her duties too.

Giving the two-foot-high porcelain tiger a final polish, she put down her duster, took off her Marigolds and dialled up the flat. After three or four rings a voice answered.

'Hello?'

'Emma, oh good, I caught you in! You work such bizarre hours I thought you might not be there.'

There was an audible yawn from the other end of the line. Clearly Emma was devoting far too many hours to that thankless job of hers; small wonder there was never any fresh pot-pourri in the en-suite loo. 'No, I'm off today and on a late tomorrow. Was there something, only I—'

'Actually yes, dear. I just wondered if you might like to come shopping with me tomorrow morning.'

There was a long and rather stunned silence, filled with unspoken question marks.

'Shopping?' said Emma at length.

'Yes, dear. Joe's little niece is being christened next month, and I really could do with someone to help me choose the right outfit. Afterwards, why don't we treat ourselves to lunch at that lovely tearoom I told you about?'

'Er, well ... tomorrow morning ...'

'You did say you were off until late tomorrow,' Minette swiftly reminded her. 'Shall we say half past nine outside Seuss and Goldman?'

Shopping with Minette: the best you could say was that it was an experience. Up till now Emma had always been careful to avoid it, but this time she'd walked right into the trap and there was no escape.

As she trailed around hat shop after hat shop, Emma mused that it wasn't so much the shopping she dreaded, as the unlimited potential for putting her foot in it.

'What do you think of this one?' demanded Minette, adorning her head with something between a large blue plant pot and an overstuffed waste paper basket.

Emma had to think fast. Tell the truth and risk offending her new mother-in-law, or lie and let her be a laughing-stock?

'It's ... er ...' She crossed all her fingers and toes. 'Pretty ghastly actually.'

'Yes, it's vile, isn't it,' agreed Minette, and Emma nearly died of relief. 'I don't know how they've got the nerve to charge five hundred for it. See,' she smiled, giving Emma's arm a chummy squeeze, 'I knew you and I would see things the same way.'

All the way round the chi-chi shops of Montpellier, Emma had the distinct impression that there was some hidden agenda behind all this girly togetherness. It was something to do with the throw-away comments Minette kept making about 'being part of the family now', and how important it was to 'keep up standards' – or maybe she was just being oversensitive. Most probably all new wives felt like this: as though marriage was some kind of bizarre recruitment process, in which you got the job first and then had to suffer the interviews for months afterwards.

Around half past twelve, when Emma's head was starting to spin and Minette had finally decided on a grey thing swamped in feathers, they headed for the Elgar Tea Rooms, a cod-Edwardian place of pilgrimage for the terminally genteel that nestled in the shadow of the Ladies' College.

Emma felt suddenly underdressed as they were ushered to a window table by a girl in a floor-length floral dress and a white mob cap. This was undoubtedly the sort of place where you ought to wear white gloves and sit with your knees together, and Emma's best black jeans blended in like pole dancers in a nunnery. Minette, of course, was greeted by the owner like a long-lost relative.

'Mrs Sheridan, how lovely to see you again! Will it be your usual?'

'Not today thank you, Maureen,' replied Minette, handing Emma the handwritten menu. 'We're treating ourselves. This is my son's new wife, by the way: I'm sure I mentioned her to you?'

I do have a name you know, thought Emma, and chipped in with 'Hi, I'm Emma.'

'Oh yes, the big wedding you were telling me about – how super for you, dear.' The middle-aged proprietor adjusted her pinny. 'Well I'll leave you to choose what you'd like to eat; can I get you any drinks in the meantime?'

Before Emma could open her mouth to say, 'Yes please, I'll have a hot chocolate with cream and extra marshmallows,'

Minette got in first with, 'A pot of camomile tea for two please – that'll be lovely and soothing after a hard morning's shopping, won't it, Emma?'

Ugh, was Emma's immediate reaction, but she smiled and echoed, 'Lovely,' making a mental note to be quicker off the mark when it came to the food order.

As they sipped their tea and Emma made an effort not to grimace, Minette rattled on about the christening, and her new hat, and the matching gloves and shoes she'd have to buy. This was easy stuff; all Emma had to do was smile and nod, and make the occasional appropriate noises.

'Another grandchild already!' Minette's eyes brimmed with sentimental pride. 'A whole new generation ... family's so important, don't you agree? Well, of course you do, otherwise you wouldn't have got married, would you?'

'Right,' said Emma, wondering where this might be leading.

'I really do think it's so sad, the way marriage has declined in the days since Alan and I tied the knot. So many couples living together, splitting up, women behaving like men and neglecting their children, and some not even wanting children at all!'

'Well, not everybody—' began Emma, but she might as well not have bothered, since the only thing Minette was listening to was her own voice.

'It's just not natural.' Minette shook her head with a kind of sorrowful conviction. 'Still, that's never been a problem with my family and I'm sure it never will be in the future, will it dear?'

Emma was starting to feel distinctly uncomfortable. 'Sorry? I'm not quite sure what you're getting at.'

'Marriage, dear, marriage and family life. It's obvious you care about it just as much as I do. And that you know how terribly important it is to be there for Joe, to support him and—'

'To support each other,' cut in Emma.

'Yes, of course.' Minette smiled, just a hint of tension appearing at the corners of her mouth. 'But in different ways. Man hunts and gathers, woman nurtures and nest-builds, and makes a happy home. It's the natural way of things – just look at ...' Minette waved a hand vaguely, 'penguins!'

'Male penguins incubate the eggs on their feet while the female ones go off hunting for food,' pointed out Emma, who had seen a programme on the Discovery Channel on that very subject. She was not at all sure that she liked the direction of this conversation. 'They stand in the snow for months on end, freezing their feathers off.' Minette looked flustered.

'Yes, well all right, perhaps penguins aren't the best example. Cats and kittens, then.'

Emma thought it wise not to point out that a tom cat's sole involvement in feline family life was at the moment of conception, after which he buggered off and left Ms Pussycat to get on with being a single mother. 'Yes, but people are a bit different from animals,' she ventured.

'Not *that* different,' Minette assured her. 'Nature is nature, you can try changing it but it always asserts itself in the end. Like grass growing through concrete.' She patted Emma's hand. 'Don't worry my dear, I know you'll make Joe a wonderful wife. And you know you can always count on me for help and advice, don't you?'

'Thank you,' said Emma. It seemed the safest thing to say.

'I expect you'll need all the advice you can get,' mused Minette, 'now that Joe's got this promotion. After all, if he's going on to great things he's going to need a strong wife behind him – and one who can be a first-rate hostess and housekeeper. It wouldn't do for a future chairman of Unico to turn up for work without a properly ironed shirt!'

Emma wished she could have replied, 'Actually Joe does all the ironing,' but unfortunately that would have been a complete lie. Joe's attitude towards ironing had always been to buy things that didn't need it.

'Of course I'll support Joe,' said Emma, as sweetly as she could manage through a mouthful of vile herbal tea. 'And he'll support me too; he knows how important my career is to me.'

'Of course he does, dear.' Minette beamed indulgently. 'And it'll be such a useful thing for you to go back to once the children are at school. Oh look, here's Maureen – are you ready to order?'

Ready to order maybe, replied Emma in the silence of her thoughts. But I'm sure as hell not ready to lie down and be a domesticated doormat – whatever you may think.

Minette's 'advice' notwithstanding, things soon started to look up for Emma at the hospital.

As Lawrence had predicted, Janice announced that she was

pregnant just as A&E was being reorganised, and once Lawrence had moved over to the day shift, he found himself short of staff. Consequently, within a few weeks Emma was back doing the work she liked best, courtesy of his quiet word with the Nursing Bank. And best of all, if Janice decided not to return after maternity leave, as she was threatening to do, that might well lead to a permanent vacancy.

On the surface at least, things were going great. Joe was the man of the moment at Unico, the young go-getter with all the new ideas, and Emma was back in the job she was born to do. There was just one fly in the ointment: the newly-weds weren't exactly spending much time together.

At least one night a week, Joe made a special effort to get home before eight, and they usually went out for a meal and maybe took in the late-night film at the multiplex. Barring disasters, he'd be home all weekend. The only problem was, Emma wouldn't. She might be on days now, but that didn't mean her hours were much less unsocial.

Joe nibbled reflectively on his prawn toast. 'You know, Emma, I've been thinking.'

'Ooh, you want to be careful doing that,' quipped Emma.

'No, seriously. I've been thinking. About us – well, about you mostly.'

Emma spooned more egg fried rice onto her plate. 'I jolly well hope you have. We've only been married three months!'

'Listen, please,' he implored, kissing one of Emma's fingertips and using it to mime a zipper running from one corner of her mouth to the other.

Emma listened, though she really didn't like it very much when Joe came over all serious. He wasn't a naturally serious person, though she supposed he must have to pretend he was when he was at work. She'd always been the fretter, the worrier, the one with the overactive imagination, who pondered over whether falling trees in deserted forests made a noise or not. Joe was the one who said 'no problem' and meant it. That was why he made her feel so safe.

'I've been thinking,' he repeated. 'About these hours you're working.'

Emma groaned inwardly. Not that old chestnut. She really thought he'd have got used to her being a nurse by now. 'They come with the job, Joe.'

He washed down the last of the prawn toast with a swig of beer, and a waitress in an embroidered silk dress whisked his plate away. 'Not necessarily.'

'Meaning what exactly?' She caught the look in his eyes and pounced before he had a chance to reply. 'Because if you're suggesting I should give up my job...'

'No, of course I'm not.' He took her hand and gently stroked the finger with the bright, shiny wedding band. 'But maybe there are other nursing jobs you'd enjoy just as much.'

She was really on the defensive now. 'Such as?' she bristled.

Joe sighed. 'Look love, I'm only suggesting it because—'

'—your mum suggested it.'

'No! Well, not exactly. She just pointed out that with you working part of most weekends and me away most of the time during the week, we're hardly getting to see each other. And she's right, Em. She really is. We're married, we ought to be together.'

'I know.' The crestfallen look on Joe's face tugged at her heart strings. 'But you know how much my nursing means to me.'

'Exactly. Which is why I've brought,' Joe fumbled around in the pocket of his crumpled suit jacket, 'this.'

He took out a folded square of newsprint, unfolded it to reveal the Sits Vac page from the local paper, and spread it out on the table. One of the advertisements was circled in red biro, but he pointed to it anyway.

She read what it said. *The Regency Clinic, Cheltenham's new state-of-the art private hospital, seeks experienced nursing staff for a variety of posts. Flexible hours to suit. Excellent pay and working conditions.*

Joe waited anxiously. 'So – what do you think?'

'I like the job I'm doing!' she protested, more than a little suspicious about the origins of the advert. It had Minette's fingerprints all over it.

'But you like being with me too, don't you?'

That was a direct hit below the belt. 'Of course I do! But working in the private sector, oh Joe, you know what I've always said about that.'

He squeezed her hand so tightly that she gasped. 'Just think about it, Emma. What harm is there in applying?'

She didn't supply an answer, because she couldn't think of one.

'Go on, Squeaky,' he urged. 'You know it makes sense.'

6

Mickey was most insistent. 'So you're definitely coming down this weekend. You are, aren't you?'

'We'll try,' promised Emma. 'I mean, I've managed to swap my shifts to get the weekend off.'

'Great!' The phone line crackled with enthusiasm. 'And so have I, so that's settled. It'll be just like old times.'

Emma hated to dampen her enthusiasm. 'But Joe keeps saying we get so few weekends off together, it ought to be just the two of us – you know, go off somewhere quiet and romantic. You can see his point.'

'But you promised, Em.' Mickey's voice suddenly sounded very small, childlike and distant.

Emma frowned. 'Is something wrong?'

'Yeah, my so-called best mate doesn't want to come and spend the weekend with me 'cause now she's an old married lady she can't think of anything but ... cushion covers!'

'Don't talk daft!' giggled Emma. 'I haven't had a brain transplant you know. And of course I want to come – I just have to persuade Joe that he does too.'

'Leave him at home and come on your own!'

Emma sighed. 'Then he'd moan all week about us not spending any time together. Don't worry, I'll persuade him.'

'Well, mind you do,' warned Mickey. 'Or me and the girls'll be buying you a subscription to *My Weekly*.'

All the way down to London in the car, Joe pouted like a Gressingham duck with an overbite.

'We could have been in the Lake District by now,' he sulked as they sped down the motorway into the gathering dusk.

'But it's only March and it's freezing! No thanks.'

'All right, Paris then. Or somewhere warmer – you can get great weekend breaks to Madeira, Portugal, anywhere you like. But oh no, we're going to the Château Fleapit to spend the weekend with a bunch of chain-smoking hyenas.'

That was just a bit too much even for Emma's heroic patience. 'Hey, those "hyenas" happen to be my mates!' she protested. 'And I know they smoke too much, but a lot of nurses do. It's the stress of the job.'

She knew she'd played right into his hands the moment the words left her mouth and a glint of triumph appeared in Joe's eye.

'All the more reason for you to get a job that's less stressful.'

'Perhaps,' she hedged, peering out of the window at a coach-load of singing pensioners in party hats, no doubt on their way to somewhere more exotic than Hackney.

'Not perhaps, definitely.'

'Don't try and bully me.'

'Who's bullying?'

'You know what I get like when you bully me. I dig my heels in.'

They drove along in silence for a while after that, the plastic wedding horseshoe still tied to the rear-view mirror dangling mournfully on the end of its tangled white ribbon. It was all very well saying get a less stressful job, thought Emma, but it wasn't going to be less stressful if she didn't like it, was it?

On the other hand, Joe was right. Up to a point anyway. Working at the Regency Clinic would pay well, she bet all the equipment actually worked, none of the patients reeked of meths, and she'd be able to see as much of Joe as she wanted. Maybe it really was time to listen to reason instead of adrenalin. Trouble was, she didn't want to.

After a while, Joe said, 'I'm sorry.'

She shrugged. 'It's OK.'

'I only want the best for you. For both of us.'

'I know.' She turned and smiled at him. 'Don't worry, it'll all work out.'

He signalled to leave the motorway at the next junction.

'You're really looking forward to seeing Mickey again, aren't you?'

A huge grin split Emma's face from ear to ear. 'What do you think?'

'I think you've got three months of accumulated gossip to get rid of, and that's not going to happen until you're half-pissed on cheap plonk and Mickey's shown you her latest tattoo.'

She settled more comfortably in her seat. 'Ah, you know me so well.'

'Better believe it, kid.'

'But you forgot the bit where Ellie burns the pasta and we have to ring up for a takeaway, and Sam gets the Twister board out at three in the morning, only we're all too wrecked to work out which arms and legs are which.'

'No darling, I was just *trying* to forget that bit.' He shook his head like a very wise old grandfather. 'And you actually *miss* living like that?'

'No, of course I don't!' And it was true, well, ninety per cent true. She leaned over and kissed him on the cheek. 'But I do miss Mickey.' She squeezed his arm. 'Thanks for coming with me.'

'' S OK. What's a weekend in Paris when you can eat burned pasta?'

Ah, Hackney *mon amour*. A huge wave of nostalgia washed over Emma as they drove past the skateboard park and the disused gasometers, and turned into Magenta Street.

As the car bumped over a pothole, and Joe winced in sympathy with his beloved suspension, Emma bounced up and down and waved like a mad thing. 'Mickey! Yoo-hoo! Look, Joe, she looks exactly the same!'

'Emma love,' he reasoned, 'it's been three months, not three years!'

'Yeah, I know,' admitted Emma, 'but she might have had a haircut or something.'

'What, Mickey – have a haircut? Get real, Em, that girl doesn't cut her hair, she has it culled.'

Magenta Street (which intersected with Azure Road and Heliotrope Terrace) was a lot less colourful than its name suggested. It consisted of a double row of typical Victorian terraces, some smart as a TV makeover programme, others still resolutely run-down, with peeling front doors and sash windows whose frames were as full of holes as an Aero bar. Number 44 came very definitely into the second category.

As Joe slowed down to park, a small, busty, crazy-haired figure with a cute bum and boots like tractor tyres leapt across the pavement to whisk away a clutch of traffic cones reserving the parking space. There was nobody quite like Michaela Jones, thought Emma fondly. With the big chest and the seventies' prog-rock hair, the overall effect was an oddly successful hybrid of Barbara Windsor and Harpo Marx.

Flinging open the passenger door, Emma hurled herself out and the two girls pogoed around the pavement, hugging each other and squealing. Joe sort of hung around on the sidelines, jangling the car keys and making little ahem-ing noises in the back of his throat.

'It's you!' exclaimed Emma.

'Yes, it's me – and you!'

'I can't believe it.'

'Me neither. Isn't it fantastic?'

'Brilliant!'

Lordy, thought Joe. Goodness only knows what they'd be like if they hadn't seen each other for a year.

'Hi Joe.' A voice was hailing him from somewhere above and he swivelled round and looked up to see a gamine, cocoa-brown face framed by short, jet-black hair. Ellie was leaning out of her bedroom window, waving a tea bag. 'Fancy one?'

'Too right I do, you're a life-saver.' He made a bee-line for the front door. At least somebody round here had their priorities right. Hurrah for Ellie and her magic teapot.

Ellie jumped down the last three stairs and met him, breathless, in the hallway. ''Fraid next-door's cat got the last of the milk,' she said. 'Do you want to go to the shop? It's only about ten minutes' walk.'

Sod that, he thought. If this had been his world, next-door's cat would just have got a swift kick up the backside, but it all too obviously wasn't. So he supposed he'd better make the best of things. 'It's OK, I'll have it black with sugar instead.'

'Actually, I think we're out of sugar, will golden syrup do?'

Inwardly despairing already, he followed her into the kitchen, where a thin girl in a pink bra and Snoopy knickers was bending over the sink, plastering her hair with something that looked like boiled spinach pureé. 'Don't mind me,' Sam said cheerily, her voice echoing around the metal sink, 'I'm just doing my henna, only it stains the bowl if I do it upstairs.'

'Sa-am,' hailed a voice from upstairs. 'Have you had my new jacket?'

'No,' came the reply, in a tone that sounded more like 'I may have done but I'm not admitting it.'

'Well it's not where I left it….'

'Ask Feebs,' replied Sam, sticking a disposable shower-cap over her spinach-laden head and disappearing in the direction of the downstairs loo. 'Or Lisette.'

'Lisette?' enquired Emma, coming into the kitchen with Mickey.

'New girl,' explained Mickey. 'Trainee physio. She's nice, you'll like her.'

No I won't, thought Emma with a sudden surge of childish jealousy. She's in my old room, in my old bed, and I'm not going to like her one bit. 'Yes, I expect I will,' she replied with a forced smile. 'By the way, where are we sleeping tonight? In the garden shed?'

'My room,' replied Mickey, popping a chocolate-chip cookie into her mouth. 'I'm taking the sofa, it's not really big enough for two. And before you thank me with tears in your eyes,' she added, 'it's OK. I'm expecting you to take me out on the town and lavish vast sums of money on me.'

A horrified squeal came from upstairs. 'My jacket!'

Sam stuck her head out of the loo, green streaks running down her face. 'Found it have you? '

'Don't play the innocent with me! It was hanging in your wardrobe! How did it get there – fly?'

'Search me,' replied Sam cheerily, disappearing back into the toilet as a cushion whizzed past her head.

Everybody laughed – except Joe. Mad, he thought gloomily. They're all mad. Not to mention hopelessly immature. It's a good job Emma's not living here any more. He tried not to notice the mooning garden gnome on the shelf next to the biscuit tin, but he was sure it was dropping its trousers just for him.

Emma was positively radiating girlish excitement. She looked, thought Joe, about fourteen. 'Isn't this great, Joe? Isn't it?'

'Great,' he agreed. 'Any chance of that cup of tea?'

'Tea?' snorted Mickey. 'You don't want tea! This is supposed to be a celebration. Ellie, whatever happened to that bottle of Bolivian champagne?'

'We drank it – about five minutes after Feebs brought it home.'

'Ah well, never mind. Looks like another trip to the offie. Hands in your pockets girls.'

Emma intervened. 'Put your money away, this is on us. Isn't it Joe?'

And she nudged him, and he smiled for all he was worth.

That night in bed, Emma snuggled up close to Joe and wrapped her arms around him. Not that she had much choice in the matter: Mickey's bed wasn't exactly the biggest in the world, and the big dip in the mattress had the effect of rolling everything into the middle.

'Isn't this romantic?' she murmured.

Joe fidgeted uncomfortably, manoeuvring his bottom around a protruding spring. 'My arm's going numb,' he complained.

'Oh Joe, don't grumble,' Emma chided him. 'It's really kind of Mickey to give up her bed for us. I mean, it can't be much fun bedding down on that crappy old sofa.'

'We could've stayed in a hotel,' he countered. 'I did say before, didn't I? Didn't I say it'd be like this?'

'No we couldn't, it wouldn't have been the same at all. You know that.' She nuzzled into the crook of his shoulder and let her fingers slide lazily down his warm, firm body. 'Besides, this is exciting and you know you like me best when I'm *excited*, don't you?'

Instead of rolling her onto her back and flattening her to the bed in a surge of conjugal passion, Joe shifted position and swore under his breath.

Emma propped herself up on her elbows. 'What's the matter now?'

'I think I've pulled something, sitting on that stupid beanbag all evening. Why can't they get chairs like everybody else?'

'Same reason they don't go on Caribbean cruises or buy their clothes at D and G. Dosh, love. Moolah. Money.'

'God knows why anybody'd want to work for the NHS,' Joe sighed. 'Have you thought any more about that job?'

43

She put a finger on his lips. 'No pestering me about it; you promised. Now, big boy, am I going to get up and play Ludo all night with Mickey, or are you going to find some other way of entertaining me?'

It was awfully early for a Sunday morning. Even health freaks Lisette and Feebs hadn't surfaced yet. But already Joe was sitting fully dressed in the living room, having an animated conversation about gherkins on his mobile.

Yawning with the effort of putting one foot in front of the other, Emma slopped down the stairs in her old slippers and the top half of Joe's pyjamas. There didn't seem much point in trying to get back to sleep. Once Joe was awake he never came back to bed, and besides, he was right: it was definitely a contender for Lumpy Mattress of the Year.

As she was rifling through kitchen cupboards full of Ryvitas and Mars Bars for the coffee jar, she heard the downstairs loo flush, and a moment later Mickey appeared in the kitchen, looking tousled and pale.

'You're not usually up this early,' commented Emma. 'You look awful.'

'Good,' said Mickey, flopping onto the nearest chair. 'I'd hate to think I looked great, feeling like this.'

Finding the coffee, Emma took another mug off the hooks on the wall. 'You look like you could use one too.'

But Mickey grimaced. 'Coffee? God no, just the thought of it makes me feel queasy.'

This was big news to Emma. Out of all the housemates, Mickey had always been the caffeine freak, the one whose breakfast was likeliest to consist of three double espressos and a cigarette.

'You really are ill, aren't you?' Emma flicked on the kettle and sat down at the table, next to her friend. Close up, she looked even worse – white skin and pink-rimmed eyes with dark circles underneath. Emma kicked herself mentally for not noticing before.

Mickey shook her head and smiled ruefully. 'Not ill, just bigtime nauseous. Have been every morning for the past two weeks. Work it out, love, you're a nurse.'

When the penny dropped, it didn't so much fall as base-jump. 'You're not ... no, you couldn't be.'

'Oh yes I am.' Mickey patted her stomach, positively concave

44

under her Real Madrid nightshirt. 'About two months' gone, as far as I can work out.' She paused for a moment, then a huge, artless grin illuminated her face. 'Great, isn't it?'

Emma's brain reeled. She was glad she was sitting down, because if she hadn't been she'd almost certainly have fallen over. In the background the kettle came to the boil and switched itself off, unheeded. 'Let me get this straight – you're *pregnant*?'

'Yep. And before you ask, yes it was a mistake and yes, I really am thrilled. Never been so excited in all my life.'

The next question leapt automatically into Emma's head. 'And what does what's-his-name think about it?'

The ensuing silence virtually answered the question for her.

Eventually, Mickey said, 'Gavin? He doesn't know. I dumped him a couple of weeks ago, just after I told you I was going to.'

Emma's jaw dropped. 'Oh Mickey! You mean you dumped him before you knew about the baby?'

'Oh no, I already knew, I did a home test. Matter of fact that was more or less why I called time on the thing with Gavin. It was never more than a fling, Em, I told you that. One of those things you have between proper relationships 'cause there's nothing better on offer. The last thing I wanted was him going all serious and trying to make an honest woman of me or something!'

It took a while to digest all this. 'But you're going to tell him. Aren't you?'

'Well … yes, I suppose so,' conceded Mickey. 'Eventually. Not that I think he'll be much of a problem, I don't think he even likes kids.'

Emma was seeing Mickey in an entirely new light, and it took some getting used to. 'You – a mum?'

'Yes, yes, I know. How can somebody who bites her own toenails off and has an overdraft the size of Madonna's album sales make a decent mother? Well, looks like I'm just going to have to show you!'

'I didn't mean … Mickey, I think you'll make a great mum,' said Emma, with perfect honesty. 'I just never thought you felt the time was right.'

Mickey shrugged. 'I didn't. But you don't choose things like that, do you? They choose you, at least that's how I see it.' She looked at Emma. 'So now you can see why I was so keen for you to come down this weekend. I couldn't just tell you on the phone. Matter of fact you're the only person I've told so far.'

Emma put an arm round her best friend's shoulders, feeling for the first time in a long while the streak of vulnerability that ran not so far beneath that carefree, confident surface. 'Have you thought what you'll do for money or how you'll cope with your job and everything?'

'Things'll work out. I'll make them!'

'You know you can call on me though, don't you? Whenever, whatever?'

This provoked a smile. 'Of course I do, Em. In fact I'm bloody counting on it!'

7

Mickey's startling news wasn't easy for Emma to get her head round. It wasn't just that Mickey had seemed the least likely of her close friends to go in for kids; it was the weird fact that people her age had already started investing in new lives when, strictly speaking, they'd hardly begun to explore their own.

Emma wanted children though, most definitely she did. And she and Joe had always said they were going to have them while they were still young enough to enjoy it. But somehow the reality of Mickey's impending motherhood made the whole thing feel disturbingly close to home, in a way it had never done before.

Not that there was much time to ponder the whys and wherefores of early parenthood. On her first day back at work after a well-oiled weekend, just when she was kind of hoping for an easy ride, A&E managed to lay on an outbreak of food poisoning, a severed finger and half a dozen cases of smoke inhalation. There was, as Dr Jeffries snidely remarked on her way into Resuscitation, 'no rest for the wicked'. Needless to say she was looking in Emma's direction when she said it.

There were no breaks that day, unless two gulps of coffee behind the door of the plaster room counted as a break. It wasn't until the end of her shift, at a quarter to five, that she had a chance to get her breath back. As she pushed open the door of the staff changing-room, she caught the middle of a conversation.

'How about the White Hart for a few jars and then on to the Casbah?' It was Terri the nursing assistant's voice, coming from behind an open locker door.

'Cool,' replied third-year student Diane, who at forty-four was five years older than Lawrence and was often mistaken by patients for the sister in charge. She freed her plum-coloured hair from its elastic band and shook it out. 'But there'd better be some decent talent this time. I'm not being landed with some spotty nerd again!'

Emma slipped off her navy-blue uniform trousers and grabbed her jeans from the locker. 'What's this – celebrating somebody's birthday?'

Terri closed her locker door, buttoning a white nylon blouse over her truly gargantuan breasts. 'No, just one of our regular wild nights out. Everybody on A and E's going – Dan, Ivan, Satja, even Janice.'

'Everyone except Lawrence,' pointed out Diane. 'All those lovely straight boys aren't really his scene.'

They giggled.

'Oh,' said Emma. 'So everybody else is going then?'

There must have been a note of utter pathos in her voice, because Terri and Diane exchanged guilty looks.

'Ah,' said Terri. 'You mean you wanted to come too?'

'We didn't think you'd be interested,' Diane cut in. 'Not seeing as you're ... you know.'

'Seeing as I'm what? Terminally unhip?'

'No! Just, you know, married.' She enunciated the word as though it were a cross between religious orders and a communicable disease. 'I mean, hey, we're going to get totally rat-arsed and do embarrassing things with total strangers,' she added. 'People don't really go in for that kind of stuff once they're married, do they?'

Emma did up her jeans, flung aside her stained white uniform tunic and stuck her head through the neck of her favourite blue jumper. 'It doesn't matter,' she shrugged, though it patently did.

'You're very welcome to come,' said Terri.

'Yeah, go on, come,' urged Diane.

Emma swung her locker door shut, turned the key and dropped it into her pocket. 'No, you're right,' she sighed. 'It probably isn't my scene.'

But as she put on her coat and made for the car park, a little part of her still wished that it was.

It was already dark outside, and the air was as cold as frozen vodka. Emma halted in the open doorway for a moment, reluctant to part company with the last of the hospital warmth, then took a step outside and let the doors swing shut behind her.

'My God, look at that face,' said a voice just behind her in the shadows. 'If that's what married bliss does for you, I'm glad I'm gay.'

She swivelled round, and saw Lawrence leaning up against the wall in the corner, arms folded, cigarette defiantly drooping from his bottom lip. The rule was, strictly no smoking anywhere on hospital premises; but then again, nurses weren't supposed to run in the corridors, or wear orange socks on duty, and Lawrence didn't take any notice of those rules either. As far as he was concerned, anything that didn't harm anybody but himself was nobody's business but his own.

'What's up?' he asked.

'Nothing's up,' she replied, joining him in his corner.

'Don't give me that, if you sag any more your knuckles'll be scraping the ground.'

She let out a rather pathetic sigh. 'Have you ever felt suddenly very, very old?'

Lawrence let out a short, almost triumphant laugh. 'Sweetheart, I *am* very, very old.'

'No, seriously. You know what I mean. When was the first time somebody said something, or did something, and you thought, "Shit, I'm not the carefree young kid I thought I was?"'

'Ah,' said Lawrence. 'That'd be the time I went into Top Man for some trousers, and the assistant asked me if I was buying them for my son. Duncan thought it was hilarious.' He peeled the cigarette from his lip. 'So who's rattled your cage then?'

'Oh, nobody; take no notice. I just didn't get invited to the staff piss-up, that's all. Everybody seems to think being married turns people into sad gits.'

Lawrence put an avuncular arm round her shoulders. 'Listen, prune-face. The only reason that lot are running around all night like Club 18-30 reps is 'cause they haven't got anybody to go home to. And the only reason I'm not running around with them,' he added, 'is that I've more chance of meeting my ideal man at a WI sewing circle than on Ladies' Nite at the Casbah.

'So believe me, Em, if anybody round here's a sad git, it sure as hell ain't you.'

*

49

''Bye darling.' Emma stood on tiptoe for her goodbye kiss, and Joe gathered her up in his big strong arms.

''Bye sweetheart. Be good, see you tonight.'

'Don't be too late, I'm going to have a go at that recipe for creamy Italian chicken.'

'Yum yum, can't wait.' That much was obvious – Joe was already halfway to the top of the stairs that led down to the underground car park. 'Got to rush, kiss kiss, 'bye.'

And with the clattering of feet on uncarpeted stairs, he was gone.

Joe's presence was so powerful, so apt to fill an entire building let alone a single room, that the sudden disappearance of it seemed to leave a peculiar void behind. Somehow silence seemed more silent, spaces bigger and emptier than they had only moments before.

Emma collected the post and the milk from downstairs, and slopped back into the flat in her dressing gown and slippers. It was nice to have a day off, a day to lounge around and indulge in blissful idleness, but it would have been nicer if Joe could have had one too. There was no avoiding the truth: she was missing him already, and he'd only been gone two minutes. She could still smell his aftershave in the bathroom, and his coffee cup was still standing warm on the draining board, alongside his empty cereal bowl.

Lawrence was right though, she decided. It was the others who were the sad gits, not her. After all, she had what everyone wanted: a nice home and somebody she loved to go to bed with every night.

She hummed happily as she showered, dressed and thought domestic thoughts. Much as she deplored unnecessary exercise, she probably ought to do something housewifely. Change the bedlinen, that's what she'd do this morning; make everything smell lovely and fresh.

As she opened the antique linen-chest Joe had bought on a business trip up north, her hand reached automatically for the duvet set with the blue and gold floral design. She knew what Joe would say. He'd groan, roll his eyes and complain, 'Not that thing! What's wrong with all the other duvet covers?', but she didn't care. This was her favourite, and he'd just have to live with it – again.

It wasn't until she was stripping off the old pillowcases that it dawned on Emma just why she was so attached to what was, essentially, a four-metre length of rather ugly poly-cotton. This duvet set was one of the few things in the flat that had actually belonged to her.

She straightened up and looked around her, taking stock. Alarm clock: Joe's. Chrome and glass bedside tables: bought with Joe's money after a recommendation from one of Joe's colleagues. Futuristic bed: OK, they'd chosen that together, but it had been Joe's money that paid for it. As for the carpet, that had come with Joe's brand-new luxury apartment, along with the entire contents of the kitchen – right down to the matching bread bin and kitchen-roll holder.

I'm living inside somebody else's life, she thought suddenly. Joe's endowed me with all his worldly goods, and I haven't got any to endow him back. And she sat down on the end of the bed, instinctively surrounding herself with her shabby old duvet cover, feeling like a foreigner.

No, that was silly; this living together permanently, this being married thing, was brand new for both of them, not just her. Like her mum had said, it was bound to feel a bit strange at first. And if Joe earned a lot more than she did, it was only natural that he'd have done more of the advance nest-building. Wasn't it? Well yes, Emma conceded; but at least Joe hadn't had to change homes, towns, jobs ... Good grief, even most of their friends in Cheltenham were really Joe's.

But Emma wasn't one to mope, and things would soon change once she'd been here a while, settled in. Besides, it was only when couples didn't understand each other properly that things went wrong; and after all these years Emma felt sure that Joe understood her almost better than she understood herself.

It was after ten when Joe got home that night, and the creamy Italian chicken had long since turned drier than a cowpat in Arizona.

'Oh Em, I'm so sorry.' Joe flung his briefcase into a corner, tore off his tie and undid the top button of his shirt. 'Like I said on the phone, the meeting dragged on and then I had to rush off to Nottingham because some old dear had slipped on a grape and was threatening to sue.'

51

'It's not your fault,' sighed Emma, because after all it wasn't. 'Is she OK?'

'Hmm?'

'The old lady, is she all right?'

'Oh, I don't know, I think so. I got halfway there and the store called to tell me she'd gone off happy with a bunch of flowers and an apology.' He yawned so wide his jaw almost cracked. 'Is dinner ruined?'

'Completely. I'll stick a pizza in the microwave, shall I?'

'You're a star.' He watched her walk off into the kitchen and smiled. 'And devastatingly sexy with it. By the way ...' He snuck up behind her as she bent to reach into the freezer, and slid his arms round her. 'I've got something for you.'

Despite her earlier annoyance, Emma giggled. 'I thought you were hungry!'

He laughed. 'I am! I didn't mean that. I meant, I wanted to make it up to you for tonight, so on the way home I bought you a little surprise.'

Intrigued, she stood up and turned round. 'A present?'

'Uh-huh. Bet you can't guess what it is.'

'Give me a clue.'

'All right. It's something you've been hankering after for ages.'

Emma's heart skipped a beat. Oh bless him, she thought, loving him even more than ever; he knows how much I've been wanting one, and now he's gone out and bought it for me. 'A camera!' she squeaked. 'You've bought me that fab digital camera!'

Joe's face fell momentarily. 'What camera?'

'The silver one in Dixons' window! The one I always go on about whenever we walk past.' Emma clocked Joe's expression and felt like a big-mouthed idiot.

'Do you? Oh no, not that – this is something much better! Something we can enjoy together. Do you want to see?'

He was holding something behind his back. 'Show me.'

'Might do. If you're nice to me.'

She made a grab for it. 'I'm always nice to you! Give it here!'

Joe whisked it above his head, out of reach. It was a big silver envelope. 'Sure you've been good enough?'

Emma was helpless with laughter. 'Joe, if you don't give it to me I'll ... I'll ...'

'You'll what?'

He kissed her, and she dissolved. 'Probably love you forever anyway,' she admitted.

'Oh go on then,' he relented, presenting the envelope to her with a big smile. 'I got you the platinum one,' he added eagerly as she ripped it open. 'It was more expensive but you get a lot more personal attention.'

She found herself staring at a glossy card, bearing a picture of two muscular Hitler Youth-alikes dressed in matching red exercise gear. The legend proclaimed: *Welcome to a Great New You!* 'What is it?'

'It's an annual membership to my gym!' Joe replied excitedly. 'I don't like us being apart any more than you do, and now we can exercise together.' He grabbed her hands and swung her round. 'Won't that be great?'

'At least he cares,' pointed out Diane the next morning, as Emma supervised her dressing a scalded hand. 'My Adrian bought me an iron last Christmas.'

'An iron? Ordinary or cordless?'

'I'm serious. Twenty-three years we've been together, and boy, does it show. Just you wait till the gilt's rubbed off *your* gingerbread.'

Emma grunted. 'At least an iron is useful – what am *I* going to do with a platinum gym membership?'

'Women!' snorted the plumber whose hand was being treated. 'You sound just like my missus. She drones on and on for months about what a fat bum she's got, and then when I buy her a nice exercise bike for a surprise, she bursts into tears and says I don't fancy her any more!'

'No, it's not that he doesn't fancy her, Mr Grimley,' explained Diane, encasing the injured hand in a sterile plastic bag. 'It's the fact that he hadn't got a clue what she really wanted. That's it, isn't it, Emma?'

'Frankly,' replied Emma, 'I'm not sure I want my emotional life analysed, thanks very much! I wish I'd never mentioned it now. And watch what you're doing with that strapping, you'll cut off his circulation.'

'Yes, watch it,' agreed Mr Grimley, following Diane's less than elegant efforts. 'That's a craftsman's hand you've got there. Been round more U-bends than you've had hot dinners.'

This delightful image was still fresh in Emma's mind when she heard a shout through the cubicle curtains. 'Where is she? I know she's here.'

Then Tully the porter's voice, calm and steady: 'You can't go in there, Mrs Wilson, why don't you come with me and – ow! Somebody page Security.'

Emma scarcely had time to match up the voice with the name when the cubicle curtain was wrenched back.

'You bitch,' spat Sara-Jane Wilson's mother, her eyes mad, dark circles of rage in a dead-white face. 'You lying bitch. It was you, wasn't it?'

Emma's mind reeled back to the little girl with the gash on her head, and the frightened woman from the Meadows Estate who had so not wanted to talk to the police. 'What's wrong?' she began, but the woman wasn't listening.

'Just couldn't keep your mouth shut, could you? And now they'll think it was me that went to the police and Sara-Jane and me'll be in more trouble. I'm going to fucking kill you.'

As the fist aimed for her face Emma managed to parry the worst of the blow, and a second later Tully and a burly security man had dragged the woman away.

'Oh my God,' gasped Diane. 'Are you OK?'

'I'm fine,' Emma snapped, though she could taste blood on her lip.

Mr Grimley jumped up off the examination couch. 'Here love, have a lie-down. Looks like you need it more than I do.'

It wasn't much of an injury, not compared to the broken noses and heads A&E saw on an average Saturday night. But try as she might, Emma couldn't cover up the three parallel gouges on her left cheek; and at the end of her shift, when she tried to do up the buttons on her coat, she found that her fingers were still trembling.

'I'll drive you home,' offered Diane, but Emma shook her head.

'Thanks, but I'll be fine. See you tomorrow.'

All the way back to the flat, Emma rehearsed what she was going to say to Joe when he got home that night. 'Hello darling, I've just been attacked by another patient.' Whichever way she put it, he wasn't going to be pleased. Still, he wouldn't be in till late; she had time to have a nice relaxing bath and curl up on the sofa with a soothing CD.

At least, that was the plan. But when she got to the front door, she found it standing ajar, and when she caught a whiff of Minette's Chanel No 19, she very nearly turned tail and fled.

But at that very moment the door opened wide and Minette stepped out, talking over her shoulder to somebody in the flat. 'Tell Emma to put it on Regulo four, and don't forget to get her started on those folic acid capsules. Oh, and—' Minette walked slap-bang into her daughter-in-law. 'Emma! What on earth have you done to yourself?'

Emma groaned. 'Nothing, honestly.'

'That you, Emma?' Joe appeared in the doorway behind his mother. 'I got the afternoon off. Jesus, Em, what's happened?'

Wearily, Emma padded into the apartment, Joe supporting her like an invalid granny and Minette trailing her like a bloodhound with a fresh scent. As the front door closed, she knew she was well and truly scuppered.

'Look, before you say anything, it's only a couple of scratches and she didn't really mean it.'

'She?' Minette's ears pricked up.

Emma sat down. 'A patient. She thought I'd told the police about what had happened to her and her daughter. The poor woman was beside herself.'

'Poor woman!' Joe could hardly believe what he was hearing. 'Some lunatic attacks you, and all you can say is "poor woman"?'

'You're pressing charges, of course?' Minette cut in swiftly.

Emma avoided Joe's gaze; but her silence spoke volumes.

'Em, listen to me,' he ordered her. 'You *are* pressing charges.'

'It's not her fault,' Emma protested. 'There's a hate campaign on her estate because she spoke to the police in the past – and now this. She was in tears when she left, I can't drag her through the courts as well.'

'Oh for Christ's sake!' exclaimed Joe.

'Be sensible, Emma,' urged his mother. 'You can't just let people get away with this sort of thing. I'm sure the police want you to have her charged.'

This was, indeed, true; and part of Emma knew she ought to be standing up for hard-pressed A&E workers everywhere. But the look in that poor mother's eyes wouldn't leave her. 'Maybe so,' she said quietly. 'But what about what *I* want?'

Taking off her coat, she draped it over the back of the white leather sofa. 'Now if you don't mind, I'm feeling really tired. I think I'll go and have a sleep.'

Later, when Minette had left in a flurry of solicitous whispering, Joe slipped quietly into the bedroom.

Emma was lying under the covers, fully clothed, staring up at the ceiling. 'I've not changed my mind.'

'I didn't think you had.' He wriggled under the covers beside her and took her hand in his, and they lay there side by side. 'Hey, I know you, remember?'

'You sure about that?'

'OK smarty-pants, I thought I did. Did you really want a digital camera?'

'It doesn't matter.'

'Yes it does, I should have realised. I'll get you one next time I want to give you a surprise, huh?'

'Then it won't be a surprise,' she pointed out.

'It will be if I tell you I'm buying you a ... a pink hippopotamus.'

'Can you get them in yellow? I think I'd prefer yellow.'

They lay there in companionable silence for a little while. The tremor had gone from Emma's hands, but they felt cold and stiff.

'It's no good, you know,' said Joe quietly. 'How many times is it that some loony's taken a swing at you? I can't cope with it, it makes me so angry.' Emma knew what was coming next, even before he had a chance to say it.

'OK, OK,' capitulated Emma. 'I'll apply for that job at the Regency Clinic. But no promises, agreed?'

She felt his entire body relax. 'Agreed. Oh Squeaky, it'll be so great if you—'

'There's something else we haven't talked about for a while,' Emma interrupted him.

'Oh? What?'

'Well, we've always said that once we were married we'd buy a place together, haven't we? A little house, with a bit of garden; you know, the full suburban bit.'

There was a pause. 'Yes,' agreed Joe.

'But?'

'But there's no tearing hurry, is there? I mean, this apartment –

it's in such a brilliant location. And the longer we hang on to it, the more it's going to appreciate in value.'

'And ... you can't bear to leave it? Is that what you're saying?'

'No, of course not! I just can't see any point right now, that's all. You like it here too, don't you?'

Emma thought carefully before she answered. 'It's a lovely flat,' she said, 'but it's *your* flat. Don't you think it's time we had something that was ours, something we've chosen together?'

'Of course I do,' replied Joe, rolling onto his side and wrapping his arm around Emma. 'And we will – just as soon as the time is right.'

Since Joe's promotion, he had less time (and energy) for wild nights out with the lads, but Friday at the Two Stags had become not so much a night out as a sacred monthly ritual.

'Here's to Joe's old ball and chain eh?' quipped Gary, raising his Peroni in an ironic toast. 'Letting him out for good behaviour.'

Taking a long, satisfying swig of Guinness, Joe burped contentedly and slid just a little further under the table. 'She's not a ball and chain, she's a gem among women,' he said, wagging a reproving finger.

'Yeah, all right, she's a bit of a babe is your missus.' Toby tossed up a pickled egg, caught it in his teeth and downed it in a series of gulps like a snake swallowing a frog. 'Gawd knows though she's put ten years on you already – look at those love handles!'

Joe submitted to prodding good-naturedly. 'Get out of it – what love handles?'

'And is that a bald patch he's getting round the back?' ventured Gary with a malicious twinkle in the grey eyes that had seduced a thousand barmaids – or so he claimed.

'Ah well, you know what they say about bald men,' philosophised Rozzer, draining his glass and giving his own thinning scalp an affectionate pat.

'Yeah, and you're the exception that proves the rule,' replied Gary, causing general mirth.

'I dunno Joe,' mused Toby, spinning coins on the sticky table top. 'What are you – twenty-eight? And married! I mean, she's a great girl and all that, but what d'you want to go doing that for?'

'Cheaper than paying for it!' winked Gary salaciously.

'And you'd know,' retorted Joe.

'You won't catch me getting myself tied down before I'm forty,' declared Toby. 'And even then she'll have to be a super-model.'

'A blind supermodel,' commented Joe.

Rozzer laughed along with the others. But as they took the piss out of Joe's newly-married state, anyone who'd cared to observe more closely might have wondered why Rozzer looked ever so slightly sad.

8

The following Tuesday, Emma stood despairingly in the middle of the living room, hands on hips. 'Joe.'

His head popped round the bedroom door. 'Is it important? Only I'm working on that report for the meeting tomorrow, haven't a clue how I'm going to get it finished in time.'

'Shouldn't you have thought about that *before* you invited the three horsemen of the apocalypse round for the evening?'

He snorted. 'They're not that bad.'

'No?' Emma held up half a rasher of greasy bacon. 'Well I just found this down the back of the sofa. Honestly, they're the biggest bunch of slobs I've ever met.'

'Oh come on,' protested Joe, 'what about the Hackney House of Horrors? It's totally gross down there.'

'That's the landlord's fault!'

'Sweetheart, I don't think you can blame the landlord for the state of their fridge. There's that much mould in it you could lose David Attenborough in there.'

Emma went on wearily dabbing at the grease stains on the white leather. 'This isn't going to come out, you know,' she warned.

'What isn't?' Faintly alarmed, Joe came out to inspect the damage. 'Oh that's nothing,' he concluded in relief, 'just a couple of grease spots, you won't even see them once the cushions are back on.' He rubbed his eyes, reddened from Gary's chain-smoking and far too much TV. If a candle could have had more than two ends, Joe would have burned all of them simultaneously. 'I can hardly keep my eyes open – is there any of that Java coffee left?'

'Are you sure that's a good idea?' Emma picked up a discarded pizza box and stuffed it into a bin liner along with a host of empty beer cans and the cigarette ends somebody had stubbed out in her orchids. 'You'll be up all night.'

'The way this report's going, I will be anyway.' Joe stretched, and Emma noticed just how worn out he was looking.

'You do realise you're doing too much?' She followed him back into the bedroom, where he flopped wearily back down in front of the computer. 'If you carry on like this you'll make yourself ill.'

'Like, I have a choice?'

'Actually yes.' Standing behind his chair, she put her arms loosely round his shoulders. 'For a start-off, you could cut down on the late-night sessions with the lads.'

'But they're my mates – and everybody needs a bit of relaxation. Besides,' he added, inputting a string of numbers to a spreadsheet, 'I didn't actually invite them tonight, they just called round on the off-chance.'

'Exactly!' Emma stooped to rest her chin on her husband's shoulder. 'They seem to think they can turn up without warning any day, any time, swan in here like it's their place, stick their feet up on the coffee table, and demand an endless supply of crisps.'

Joe stopped keying in figures. 'I thought you liked my mates. They like you,' he added rather accusingly, as though there ought to be some kind of automatic reciprocity at work. 'Toby says you're a babe.'

Toby, reflected Emma, had the brain of a peanut and the sexual mores of a degenerate chimpanzee; still, she supposed it was nice to be appreciated, even by a lower primate. 'They're OK in their own way,' she hedged, 'it's just that they act like they own the place. Can't you ask them to phone before they turn up? Or agree on certain days for them to come round?'

Joe looked deeply disappointed, like a small boy who'd just been told he couldn't have the wheels off his granny's wheelchair for his go-kart. 'It's not very spontaneous,' he commented. 'What if they're out sometime and they just fancy dropping by?'

'What if *I* just fancy an early night?' Emma countered. She was starting to find all of this a bit irritating. After all, she was the one who had to clean up after Joe's mates, and Joe wasn't the only one forced to endure Rozzer's tuneless renditions of 'You'll Never Walk Alone'.

Joe turned his head to look at her. 'Oh, I get it. This isn't about me, it's about you!'

'Joe love, it's about both of us. We've both got jobs to do where we have to be wide awake and not make mistakes. I'm not saying don't have your mates round, I'm just suggesting maybe we don't want them barging in whenever they feel like it.' She half-laughed. 'The way things are going, you'll be giving them their own front-door keys next.'

Joe had never been any good at dissembling. The look on his face said it all. 'Oh Joe, you haven't!'

'Only Rozzer,' he said defensively. 'Just in case I get locked out or something.'

Emma despaired. 'Your mum and dad have got a spare key, the man next door's got one, you've got one hidden in the car – why don't you just take the locks off the door and tell everyone in Cheltenham to help themselves?'

'Now you're just being silly,' chided Joe.

'Not half as silly as you.'

He scratched the top of his head with a pencil. 'I don't get it: this is my home, why can't I have my mates round when I want?'

'*Our* home, Joe,' Emma corrected him; but on reflection she was half-inclined to believe he'd got it right the first time.

As Joe and Emma drove across Cheltenham a couple of evenings later, Emma found herself mentally dividing her husband's friends up into two categories. On the one hand there was the ever-present bunch of feckless lads, and on the other … there was Will.

If someone had tried to design an exact opposite of a Gary or a Toby, they would have come up with someone like Will Morgan. While Gary's *Who's Who* entry might list his favourite pastimes as paintball, cheap booze and expensive women, Will's was more likely to include nappy changing, burping and making one modest civil service wage stretch to feed three mouths.

'Remind me – how old is it now?' asked Emma as they neared the house. She realised with slight embarrassment that she couldn't even remember if the sprog in question was a boy or a girl.

'Six months. And she's a baby, not an it!'

'Ah, so it's female then?'

Joe directed a playful swipe at her head. 'You know damn well she is! Liddy – Lydia, after her grandma. Don't tell me you can't remember.'

Emma didn't. But she couldn't. 'Oh yes, that's right.' She dimly recalled the blurry picture Joe had e-mailed her of a red blob in a knitted hat. Whether the blob was male, female or indeed human had been difficult to tell.

'Real bobby-dazzler by all accounts. Smiles all the time.' He caught the look of incredulity in Emma's eye. 'Yes, yes, all right, I know it's wind really but if you were her mum you'd want to give her a good press, wouldn't you? Besides, Will says she's gorgeous.'

'Of course he does, he's her dad!'

'Don't come the cynic with me, Em, you know as well as I do you'll go all gooey the minute you set eyes on her.'

Will and Kathy lived in a two-up two-down terraced house just off the wrong end of the High Street – the bit the council had recently rechristened the 'West End' in a wave of municipal optimism. It might not be the ultimate des res, but after all the work they'd put in, it shone like a beacon of cosiness among all those identical, faceless houses.

As Emma got out of the car and Joe locked it, she looked up at the front of the house, rendered now in a cheery shade of ice-cream pink, and at the cute window-boxes that would be bursting with sweet peas and pansies come spring. It was the very image of blissful domesticity. Even the white cat on the doorstep had spotless paws.

She felt just the tiniest pang of envy. Ah well, in a few months' time she and Joe would probably have their own house too – though Emma was willing to bet that Joe would angle for something glamorous with lots of bedrooms, overlooking the racecourse. Either that or a minimalist loft development in Gloucester Docks, with one entire wall dedicated to an enormous flat-screen plasma TV. Sometimes, perversely, she found herself wishing he'd not got that promotion, just so he'd be forced to lower his sights. But that was just plain silly. Who in their right mind would say no to more money?

They rang the bell and waited. From somewhere inside the house came a noise like the whistle on a steam engine, and Joe and Emma looked at each other.

'Good lungs for a little 'un,' remarked Joe.

'Watch out for exploding wine glasses if she keeps that up.'

But silence returned as suddenly as it had been shattered. Then the door opened, and Will ushered them inside with much grinning and hugs. Blond and floppy in a vaguely Hugh Grant way, he managed to combine immense eagerness with the drained look of a man who had not slept since Christmas. 'Guys! Great you could come. How's married life?'

'Fantastic,' replied Joe, saving Emma the trouble of answering. 'Should've done it ages ago, like you and Kathy.' He dipped into his pocket and pulled out a cuddly duckling. 'So where's my darling little princess?'

'I'm in here,' replied a disembodied voice.

They all laughed at the old joke, and Will led the way into the combined kitchen and dining area, where a jolly-looking redhead with pink cheeks was installed in a comfortable armchair, a bundle clasped to her robust chest.

'Hi you two,' said Kathy. 'Sorry I didn't come to the door, only Liddy said it was time for her din-dins.'

'And when Liddy says she wants something there's no saying no, is there, sweetie-pops?' Will chucked the infant lovingly under the chin. 'Rules our lives twenty-four hours a day, don't you Liddy? Who's a cute little tyrant? Yes you are!'

'Hi Kathy,' smiled Emma, bending to kiss her on the cheek. 'You're looking really…well.'

'Fat,' Kathy corrected her serenely. 'I'm looking fat. But Will says the earth-mother look suits me so who cares?'

Will nodded with enthusiasm. 'You know, I hadn't realised it before, but a big, womanly belly is so incredibly *sexual*.'

He's flipped, thought Emma. Must be sleep deprivation.

Joe looked up from waggling the toy duckling in front of Liddy's nose. 'Anyhow,' he announced authoritatively, 'a woman can't lactate properly without a bit of body-fat, can she?'

Emma laughed, more embarrassed than amused. 'Joe!'

'What?'

'Since when were you an expert on lactation?'

He shrugged modestly. 'Oh you know, just been reading the odd article on breastfeeding in our in-store magazine. Never can tell when you'll need to know that stuff, can you eh?'

It struck Emma that Joe wasn't very likely to need to know it *ever*, at least not unless he had some kind of pioneering sex-

63

change operation. And there was something very weird about seeing Joe's eyes light up at the mention of cracked nipples and cradle cap. She wasn't entirely sure she liked it.

Emma decided to change the subject. 'Anything I can do to help in the kitchen?'

Will looked apologetic. 'Actually, we thought we'd just phone for a take-away if that's OK with you.'

'I thought a nice simple pizza?' suggested Kathy. 'Anything with onions gets into my milk and then the poor darling's crotchety all night. And as for alcohol . . .'

'Oh. Yes, of course.' Emma shifted an economy pack of disposable nappies and made room for herself on the sofa. 'The two of you must be really knackered, what with all those sleepless nights and nappy changes.'

Will rested a hand on Kathy's shoulder, and they gazed into each other's eyes with mutual adoration. 'Oh, we don't mind any of that,' said Kathy. 'After all, it's not everyone who's blessed with a precious little angel sent straight down from heaven.'

Emma was about to burst out laughing when she realised – with a nauseous churn of the stomach – that Kathy was perfectly serious. 'Well . . . no,' she agreed, with a nervous smile. Let me out of here, she screamed silently. She cast an 'oh my God' look at Joe, expecting him to pull a face, but he wasn't even looking in her direction; he was gazing at the baby. Worse, the vacant grin on his face said: my brain has just been stolen and replaced with a pink fluffy rabbit.

'Can I hold her?' he asked eagerly.

'Of course you can,' beamed the proud mother, uninhibitedly detaching a sleepy, wet mouth from her right nipple. 'That's it, Liddykins, you go to Uncle Joe for a lovely big cuddle.' She sniffed her hand. 'Oh dear, better hand her back to Mum, I think we've just filled our nappy.'

Emma was stunned to hear Joe reply, 'No worries, leave it to us. We'll soon have her all lovely and clean, won't we, Em?'

Her jaw dropped. 'Sorry?'

'Come on, Squeaky, you're the expert. Grab the Pampers and show me what to do.' He gave her a jocular nudge and a wink. 'Hey, it'll be great practice for us, won't it darling?'

Kathy looked from one to the other, put two and two together

64

and clapped her hands delightedly. 'Oh Em! You're not? Already!'

'No,' replied Emma hastily. 'I'm not. *Definitely* not.'

Kathy reached out and squeezed her hand compassionately. 'Ah well, never mind, it's still early days. I'm sure you two will have your own little baby really, really soon.'

Emma had meant to tackle Joe about the baby thing as soon as they got home, but they were both tired and had to get up early the next morning, so she let it lie. Over the next couple of days they never seemed to be in the same place for long enough to have a proper conversation, and before she knew it, it was Friday night again and the lads were due round. Besides, Joe hadn't so much as mentioned babies since that night at Will and Kathy's; and Emma was inclined to put the whole Liddy thing down to the full moon or too many episodes of *Children's Hospital*.

All the same, the thought continued to niggle at her as she drove home from her late shift. Beyond vague references to having kids 'when the time seemed right', and enjoying taking his elder brother's kids for the odd kick-about in the park, Joe had never been one for baby-talk. He'd even moaned about the noise they made in restaurants. Surely he wasn't suddenly turning all broody on her?

Maybe she ought to talk to him about it after all.

As she unlocked the front door and trudged wearily into the flat, a cheer went up from the assembled bodies on the sofa.

'Yeeeeaah!' roared Toby, waving a Budweiser bottle. 'Go on my son!'

'Smash his bleeding head in, go on!' seconded Gary. 'Hit him where it hurts.'

And he did. In fact Emma came into the living room just as boxing glove made contact with nose, and blood spattered all over the ring. She winced at the televisual banquet that was two large, sweaty men in shorts, beating the crap out of each other.

'Oh God, not boxing,' she groaned, thinking of the poor A&E team who'd have to sweep up all the bits and sew them back together.

'Not just any old boxing,' Joe corrected her. 'The middleweight championship of the world. Live from the NEC.'

'Pay-per-view,' added Rozzer, who was clearly impressed by that kind of thing.

'That's nice,' yawned Emma, dead beat after a long evening of drunk teenagers and smelly tramps. 'I suppose that means they get a better class of brain damage.'

'They know what they're doing,' protested Gary. 'Besides, they're getting paid a packet. I wouldn't mind having my brain bounced around a bit for a couple of million quid.'

What brain? thought Emma, but managed to swallow down the words before they escaped from her lips. She headed for the kitchen, to deposit her coat and eat the contents of the fridge, but as she passed behind the sofa Joe caught her hand and pressed it extravagantly to his lips. 'Ah, 'tis the fair hand of my lady Emma, fragrant with the perfume of a thousand damask roses.'

'Actually, I've just done an enema,' she replied wearily. 'Now, anybody else want a bacon sandwich?'

'I'll be back in half an hour; well an hour, max,' promised Joe as he followed his three mates out of the front door. 'Just long enough to pick up that video from Toby's and come straight back.'

'Okey-doke,' replied Emma, returning his ketchup-smeared kiss. She didn't bother asking why anyone desperately needed to pick up a motorcycling video at one o'clock in the morning. Blokes were just like that, there was no point in trying to understand why. 'Just don't expect me to be awake. I'm on early tomorrow, remember.'

Joe pulled a face. 'Can't you throw a sickie? Just for once?'

'Sorry.' She kissed the wrinkles from his nose. 'Wish I could. Go on love, they're waiting for you.'

She listened to the sound of the taxi pulling away down the main road, then dragged herself to the nearest armchair and flopped in it. Sleep. That's what she needed. Leave the tidying up till tomorrow; it could wait. But even as she ordered herself to bed she knew she couldn't face getting up in the morning to another display of beer cans and congealed sausage fat.

Just as she was making a start, the doorbell rang. That was quick, she thought; Joe must've forgotten his key or something. But when she opened up it wasn't Joe standing on the doorstep, it was Rozzer.

'Thought I'd better ring,' he said, shuffling his feet awkwardly like an embarrassed schoolboy. 'You know, rather than use the key Joe gave me.'

'Did you forget something?' Emma looked around the flat but nothing sprang out at her.

'No, that is, not exactly. I thought I ought to come back and help you tidy up. Can I come in?'

Emma could not have been more stunned if a grand piano had fallen on her head. The concept of any of Joe's friends reducing mess rather than making it was novel to the point of unheard-of. 'Are you sure you're feeling all right?' she demanded as Rozzer finished collecting up rubbish and got down on his hands and knees to sweep crushed crisps off the afghan rug.

He looked up at her. 'Fine. I just thought I ought to help,' he said. 'Seeing as nobody else ever does. It's not right, expecting you to do everything.'

Taken aback, Emma sat down heavily on the arm of the sofa. 'Oh,' she said. 'Well . . . thanks. It's nice of you.'

'Trouble is, people end up taking other people for granted,' Rozzer went on. 'If I hadn't done that to Maxine, maybe she wouldn't have . . .' He stopped in mid-sentence, red from bull neck to the roots of his Number One.

'Just don't you let him take you for granted, you hear?' Rozzer got to his feet and wiped his hands on his trousers, looking for all the world like the runt of a pit bull litter. 'Or you can tell him he'll have me to answer to.'

9

'Joe,' began Emma, as they lay snuggled up in bed together under a jumble of Sunday papers.

He wriggled round to face her, and nuzzled his stubbly chin into the crook of her neck. 'Mmm, you smell nice. All buttery.'

She licked the last of the croissant crumbs off her lips. 'Joe, listen.'

'I am listening.' His hand slid down her back and underneath the old T-shirt she'd thrown on while she got the breakfast. 'You're seriously overdressed, you know.'

Emma giggled. 'I was cold!'

He pressed his mouth close to her ear and whispered, 'We have ways of warming you up. Want to find out how?'

It wasn't that she didn't like the sound of it, but it was hard enough to pin Joe down at the best of times, and this was probably the only decent opportunity she'd have to talk to him before next weekend. 'I've been thinking,' she said. 'About us.'

Joe jerked his head back and looked at her quizzically. 'That sounds a bit ominous! Don't tell me, a handsome plastic surgeon seduced you over an eyebrow-lift, and you're going to run away to LA and make faces together.'

'Oh ha ha. Listen, I was just thinking about our future, that's all. After seeing Kathy and Will the other night. And, you know, talking about families and stuff.'

His ears pricked up. 'Oh yes?' An exploratory hand slid up and down her tummy. 'Hey, Kathy wasn't right was she?'

'No!' She grabbed his hand and clamped it forcibly onto her bare buttock. 'What is this sudden obsession with me being pregnant?' She didn't wait for Joe to answer. 'Look, it's just that I

68

couldn't help noticing how those two are struggling to manage on one wage, and it got me thinking, that's all.'

Joe frowned. 'Will's only a junior clerk in the DSS, love. I hardly think we'll ever be strapped for a tin of beans.'

'Maybe not, but it's the principle of the thing.' She drew herself up as much as was possible when you were lying down with your husband's hand up your T-shirt. 'I've made up my mind, Joe: I want to pay my way.' She caught the expression on his face. 'Don't look at me like that, I'm serious!'

'I know you are.' Joe planted a row of kisses along her collarbone. 'And I love you for it. But you *do* pay your way, silly.'

'Darling, I hardly think pitching in with the odd tankful of petrol or basket of shopping is paying my way. I mean I want to do it properly – you know, set up a standing order to pay a share of the mortgage, that kind of thing.'

Joe propped himself up on one elbow, as baffled as he was amused. 'What on earth's brought this on?'

'Nothing,' she replied defensively. 'I've been meaning to talk to you about it since before we got married. Look, we're a real couple now, aren't we? Living together all the time.'

'Of course we are, we're married.'

'So we should be sharing things – the bills included.' Emma played her trump card. 'If you really want me to feel this place is my home, I need to contribute to the cost of it, otherwise—'

Joe cut her off just as she was getting into her stride. 'Sweetheart, you're my wife, not a lodger! What's mine is yours. And besides, I earn three times what you do.'

Maybe that's the whole point, thought Emma in a rush of inner clarity. Maybe I need to pay my way to show that I exist, that I'm worth something, or else vanish beneath the weight of my husband's superior credit rating. But if she said that aloud she was afraid it would just sound childish or worse. 'I still want to contribute,' she insisted, but Joe just chuckled softly and stroked her cheek.

'Darling Em, I know you mean well, and I really appreciate the offer, but honestly there's no point.' He kissed her benignly on the forehead. 'I can take care of everything, you just concentrate on being my lovely darling wife.'

'No, I'm not getting any weird cravings or anything,' Mickey assured her. It was Monday morning and Emma was alone in the

69

flat, wandering around with the phone tucked under her chin as she got ready to go on duty at twelve. 'I'm still feeling too nauseous to crave anything. Well, anything but a bucket,' she added as a dark afterthought.

'That'll pass off soon, I'm sure it will,' soothed Emma. 'You're not supposed to throw up much after the first trimester.'

'Yes I know, I've read *Nursing Care of the Ante-Natal Patient* too,' retorted Mickey. 'But remember that poor woman we had that time in Cas? The one who was five months gone and couldn't keep anything down, not even a glass of water? We had to admit her and put her on IV fluids.'

'Trust you to anticipate the worst,' smiled Emma, screwing up her face to concentrate as she applied a lick of mascara. 'I don't know, every zit an abscess, every freckle a malignant melanoma. Look on the bright side, they say if you're chucking your guts up it means it's a really secure, healthy pregnancy.'

'Nice. Whoever "they" are, I bet they're all men. Speaking of which, how's lover boy?'

'Joe?' Emma almost said "baby mad", but that was perhaps not the most tactful thing to say. 'Oh, you know, gorgeous as ever.'

'Lucky bastard.'

'I know I am.'

'Not you, him. Well, send him down to Hackney if you get fed up with him, I'm sure we could find a few shelves for him to put up.'

You're a braver woman than I am, Mickey, thought Emma as she put down the phone. Being pregnant and sick and solo couldn't be much fun, no matter how pleased you told everyone you were. She wished Mickey lived a bit nearer; and not just for Mickey's sake.

Hardly had she started on making up the other eye when the phone rang again. 'Were you on Joe's computer?' asked her mother. 'I've been trying for ages to get through.'

'Hi Mum. No, I wasn't on line, it was Mickey. She wanted a nice long girlie chat. How's things in the frozen north?'

'Oh, a bit slow right now. There's a big gay festival on in Brighton and half my winter clientele's disappeared off down there, so I'm rattling around here all on my own at the moment.'

'Good,' declared Emma. 'You work far too hard, it'll do you good to have a nice break for a week or two.'

Karen laughed. 'It's obvious you've never been self-employed with bills to pay!'

Emma winced. 'Mum! Don't you start on about household finances too. Joe and I were arguing about all that yesterday.'

'Surely you've not got money problems?' asked Karen, clearly surprised.

'Not those kinds of problems, no. And no problems at all, according to Joe.'

'Something tells me you don't quite agree.'

'How can I? Joe thinks it's perfectly fine for him to flash his money around and pay for everything, like I'm some kind of ... of ... *dependant* or something.' She hadn't meant to bend her mother's ear about it, but having an attentive audience made the whole thing spill out. 'And while we're at it, why don't I just give up my silly little job and stay at home having babies? After all, it's not like I have a *proper* career like he does.'

'Oh Emma,' chided her mother. 'I'm sure Joe doesn't think that at all.' She paused. 'He didn't really say that, did he?'

'Well, not the bit about the babies, not in those *exact* words,' admitted Emma.

'Aha,' said Karen.

'But that's what he meant,' she insisted. 'And all the stuff about him paying for everything, that's exactly the way it is. He says seeing as he earns so much more than I do, it's pointless me contributing to the household bills. In fact we might as well just call my salary pocket money!'

'Well I suppose he does have a point ...'

'Mum!'

'Only about earning so much more than you. But I can see why you want to make a contribution. And I'm sure he does too, he just thinks you're already making it by cooking and cleaning and all the other stuff you do.'

'That's what I'm worried about. I'm sure he's got this crazy idea in his head about me playing the perfect housewife and mother while he zaps around in a sharp suit, pulling off deals.'

'And I take it that's not what you want?'

'Mum!' squeaked Emma. A dreadful image of herself in a dowdy smock paraded through her mind, followed by a whole regiment of miniature Joes and Emmas; she shuddered at the prospect. 'Do you even need to ask?'

71

'Just checking.' Emma heard her mother take a deep breath. 'Emma love, you know you can talk to me about anything, any time. But don't you think you ought to be talking to Joe about this?'

'I would,' replied Emma, 'if he was ever in a mood to listen. Either he's too tired to talk, or he pats me on the head and tells me not to worry.'

Karen sighed. 'Maybe he's right, love. Maybe you are worrying too much. I mean, it's early days, isn't it? You're still learning to live with each other. And I'm sure Joe does understand how important your job is to you. Deep down.'

Emma wished she shared her mother's confidence. 'Mum, he's known me since I was fifteen, and he still thinks I spend all day mopping brows and emptying bedpans.'

There was a slight pause before Karen replied. 'Well, if he does think that – and I'm only saying if – whose fault is it?'

That took the wind out of Emma's sails. 'You're not taking his side?'

'No, love, I'm not taking sides at all, and I don't think anybody else should either, you included. The minute people start talking about sides, the whole thing turns into a silly confrontation. What I'm saying is, if Joe doesn't understand what you do, and why it's important to you, maybe that's because you haven't explained it to him clearly enough. And maybe he's not trying hard enough to explain things to you, either.

'The fact is, Emma, you're not kids any more; you're two grown-up married people. You have to learn to live for each other, as well as for yourselves; and you're bound to make mistakes along the way. But nobody can do that learning for you.

'Now, why don't you tell me all the latest hospital gossip? It's so quiet up here, I could do with a bit of excitement.'

That night, the phone rang just as Emma and Joe were sitting down to dinner. With a muttered 'Not again,' Joe got up and stomped across the room to answer it.

'Hello, Mickey. Yes, of course I guessed it was you, it's always you. No, as a matter of fact it's not very convenient actually, her dinner's getting cold. Here.' He held out the receiver. 'It's you know who.'

Half an hour later, when Emma returned from the kitchen with her warmed-up pasta, Joe was still glowering at the phone, as if daring it to ring again.

'That wasn't very nice,' commented Emma, plonking herself down on the sofa next to him.

'Too right, she's never off that bloody phone.'

Emma threw him a reproving look. 'I didn't mean Mickey, I meant you! Did you have to be quite so rude to her?'

Joe reached for the TV remote. 'I wasn't rude.'

'Yes, you were! It's hardly fair, especially when I make such an effort to be nice to all your slobbish mates.'

He flopped back into the sofa's yielding embrace. 'Look, I'm just knackered, OK? I've driven all the way to York and back today, just for a ten-minute meeting, and all I ask is a nice quiet evening with my wife. Why does Mickey have to be on the phone to you every bloody night?'

Emma hesitated. 'Because ... she needs me.'

'What in God's name is that supposed to mean?'

'She's going through a difficult time.'

'Oh really,' sniffed Joe. 'Go on, what is it this time – another argument with the latest poor sap of a boyfriend? Run out of her favourite colour of nail varnish?'

'As a matter of fact,' Emma replied quietly, 'she's pregnant.'

It took a lot to knock Joe off balance, but that did the trick. He gaped back at her, slack-jawed with a half-chewed Murray Mint lodged in the corner of his mouth. 'She is?'

'Having a baby. Yes. So you see, that's why she needs a lot of support right now, especially since she split up from the father.'

'My God. *Mickey*?'

'I would've told you sooner,' Emma went on, 'only she wanted me to keep it under wraps until she's had her three-month scan and knows everything's going fine.'

'Well,' gasped Joe. 'I knew she was a bit stupid, but that really takes the biscuit. I mean, how irresponsible can you get?'

It was Emma's turn to be startled. 'What do you mean, irresponsible?'

'Come on, Em, she's got no bloke, no place of her own, she works all hours, and now she's bringing a child into the world. If that's not irresponsible, I don't know what is.'

Half an hour earlier, Emma might have agreed that Mickey's circumstances weren't exactly ideal; but something in Joe's attitude really rankled. It felt oddly personal, as if by attacking Mickey, her best friend, he was getting at her. 'If you think that's irresponsible, what about Will and Kathy?' she demanded.

'What are you on about? They're married and they're buying their own house!'

'Yeah, and it's just about crippling them financially. Kathy admitted as much. God knows how they're all going to manage on Will's salary once she spawns the football team they're planning. At least Mickey's only got herself and the baby to support, she's got qualifications behind her, and she brings in more than Will does anyway.'

'Maybe she does, but what kind of home life is that kid going to have? And what's the dad got to say about it?'

'Not a lot,' admitted Emma. 'He doesn't know.'

Joe snorted and rolled his eyes. 'I knew it.' Sliding an arm round Emma's waist he drew her close. 'Thank God you and I had the sense to do things properly and get hitched.' He kissed her on the cheek. 'Don't take this the wrong way Em...'

She heard the 'but' coming before he spoke it.

'But, well, it's not that I don't feel sorry for Mickey and all that, and I know how close the two of you have been in the past; only maybe it's not such a bad thing that you're not living down there any more.'

'No? Why's that then?'

'Well, Cheltenham's your home now, isn't it? *Our* home.' Emma noticed how he neatly avoided adding 'and it looks like I've snatched you away from Mickey's dodgy moral influence just in the nick of time.' 'Lots of new opportunities, lots of things for us to share.' He leaned his head against hers. 'Lots of new friends to make, too. Friends we can share as a couple.'

'Like Kathy and Will?'

Joe didn't notice the irony in her voice. 'Yes, like Kathy and Will. Face it, Em, Hackney's in the past now. And everybody has to move on.'

The implication wasn't lost on Emma. 'If you think that means I'm going to drop Mickey!'

'I never said that,' parried Joe.

74

Emma wasn't having any of that nonsense. 'She's my best mate, Joe!'

'I know, but—'

She silenced him with a glare. 'No buts. Mickey's my best mate and she's staying that way. Whether you like her or not.'

10

It was a normal day on A&E. Two thirds of the people sitting on the chairs in the waiting area looked like there was nothing wrong with them, while the rest quietly dripped blood onto the stain-resistant carpet, or hunched miserably with bags of frozen peas clamped to their swollen faces.

On this particular day Emma was on triage duty. All the staff nurses took turns at it, making preliminary decisions about whether a smashed nose ought to be seen more quickly than a dislocated elbow, or whether a slight stomach ache might suddenly turn out to be raging peritonitis. There was always the thought at the back of your mind that you might miss something vital, though most of the time the job consisted of explaining to a man with a six-inch nail through his foot why he had to wait longer than a kid with a pebble up its nose.

She went to the door and called out the next name. 'Mr Stephens?' A young man in bloodstained jeans limped over. 'That's right, over there, take a seat. Now, what's the trouble?'

'What's it look like? Fucking dog bit me on the ankle.'

'Any pain?'

'Aches a bit, that's all.'

'Up to date with your tetanus shots?'

'Yeah, I think so. Had one a couple of months back, when I caught my finger in the hay-baler.'

Emma looked at the wound briefly. The skin was a little swollen, but it had stopped bleeding, so she marked him down as non-urgent and moved on to the next patient.

Four hours later she'd pretty much forgotten about him, until Zara Jeffries came crashing into the triage office and slapped a set of notes down on the desk. 'Who put this one down as non-urgent? Was it you?'

Emma glanced at the name: Paul Stephens. 'Dog bite, wasn't it? Yes, that was me. Why?'

'It would have been nice if you'd bothered to tell me the man's a bloody diabetic! He'd been sat that long out there, without so much as a cup of tea, that he was starting to go hypo by the time I got to him. Why the hell didn't you fast-track him?'

'Because he didn't tell me he was diabetic,' replied Emma simply, mentally cursing. 'Anyway, it's his job to make sure he controls his blood sugar levels. And I'm not psychic.'

Dr Jeffries' shapely upper lip curled. 'Yes, well, maybe you should give clairvoyance a try, it's obvious thinking's not your strong point.'

'Excuse me!' gasped Emma.

'Or you'd have realised how dangerous leg and foot injuries can be in the diabetic patient, particularly when they're insulin-dependent like Mr Stephens. You'd better pray it doesn't turn gangrenous. So, Nurse Sheridan, have you got any more nice little surprises for me, or can I go and get on with my job now?'

Bloody Zara. Bloody triage. Bloody every bloody thing. Emma was not in the best of moods as she swung the car out of the hospital car park.

She loved her job and she was damn good at it, she knew she was. Or at least, she'd known she was until Dr Zara came glowering onto the scene. It wasn't that she couldn't take criticism – when it was fair. She'd been moaned at before by everybody from senior consultants down to junior porters, and she liked to think she was adult enough to take it on the chin. But bloody Zara only had to arch one finely-tweezed eyebrow to make Emma feel like a clumsy first-year student all over again.

Why? thought Emma. Why has she got this mission in life to put the boot in at every opportunity she gets? OK, maybe I should have asked him if he was a diabetic, but it's not one of the questions on the form. Maybe it should be. Maybe if she's so shit-hot she ought to design a new form herself, in all that lovely spare time she's got. From what I hear, it's not as if she has a life or anything.

Swearing colourfully all round the one-way system took some

of the edge off Emma's annoyance, but she was still in a less than sunny mood when she got home.

To her surprise, Joe's car was parked outside the apartment block; then she remembered him saying something about working at home one afternoon this week. Normally she'd have been thrilled, but today part of her wanted to stick her head under the duvet and eat biscuits.

'Where's that giant pack of Mini-Cheddars?' she demanded as she slammed the front door, threw her coat on the floor and headed straight for the kitchen. 'I need junk food now.'

'Hello darling.' Joe popped up from nowhere, PDA in hand. 'Bad day or shouldn't I ask?'

Emma rooted manically through kitchen cupboards, getting all the spice jars jumbled up and knocking over an open bag of rice. 'Just tank me up with biscuits and tell me Zara's emigrating.'

'Oh, not again.' Joe ditched the PDA and slid his arms round his wife's waist. 'Who started it this time?'

'Guess.'

He nuzzled the back of her neck. 'You don't think ... I mean, it's not possible ... you might be just a teensy bit oversensitive? With her being who she is?'

Emma wriggled free, turned round and threw him a furious glare. 'Gee, thanks! Take her side, why don't you?'

'I'm not! Look, I'm sorry OK? It was a stupid thing to say.' Gently he tipped up her stubborn little chin. 'Hey, I love you, Mrs Sheridan.'

She relented at the twinkle in those lovely eyes. 'I love you too. But I still want biscuits.'

'And a hug?'

'Most definitely a hug.'

Sitting side by side on the living-room rug, with a *Scooby-Doo* cartoon on the telly and a bucket of Mini-Cheddars between them, Emma and Joe put the world to rights, the way they'd always used to before they were old and responsible and married.

'I still say Velma's dead sexy,' insisted Joe. 'I kid you not, behind those bottle-end glasses lurks a heart of untamed passion. And just look at those lusty thighs.'

'You're weird, you know that?'

He popped a biscuit into her mouth. 'Takes one to know

one.' They munched in silence for a little while. 'Feeling a bit better?'

'Much.' She reached out and took his hand. 'I've missed this, you know.'

'Me too. But with the new job and all this extra responsibility ... I mean, really I should be working now.'

She put a finger to his lips. 'I know. Just don't remind me, not right now. I like pretending sometimes.'

'Pretending?'

'You know, that we're just two kids again. Like that summer when we both worked on the pick-your-own farm.'

Joe cuddled her close and laughed at the memory. 'That was a good summer. God but I ate a lot of strawberries.'

'It was the summer you first asked me out. Before then I was never sure you'd even noticed I was alive.'

'As I recall, it was the summer you grew breasts.'

'Ah.' Emma nodded. 'I knew there had to be a reason for it. That, and you splitting up with Zara.'

Joe wagged a reproving finger under her nose. 'Ah-hah, I thought we weren't mentioning her any more.'

'Do you ever regret ... you know, you and her?'

He looked at her in astonishment. 'No! Of course not.'

'I think she does.'

'Hmm,' said Joe. 'Well if she does – and I bet she doesn't – she's going to be one disappointed doctor. Oh, by the way.' He got up, went out to the hall table and returned clutching an envelope, 'This came for you.'

He handed it to her and she saw the franking mark: The Regency Clinic: Caring for You and Yours. For a brief moment a little spasm of panic gripped her. Applying for a job was one thing; actually getting a letter back about it made it uncomfortably real.

'Go on, open it,' urged Joe. And she did.

'It says I've got an interview,' she said, feeling oddly flat as she handed it to him.

'Fantastic!' Joe pulled her to her feet and dragged her round the room in an absurd little dance. 'See? I knew you could do it!'

Emma didn't bother pointing out that this wasn't exactly a huge surprise, seeing as it was the Regency Clinic, not Chicago Hope; but his enthusiasm was infectious and the mildly pleased feeling grew on her by degrees. 'I didn't say I'm taking it though,' she reminded him, 'and that's assuming they offer it to me.'

'Of course they'll offer it to you,' Joe scoffed. 'They'll take one look at you and fall in love with you, just like I did. Just think, Em, if you work there you'll be doing civilised hours, you won't have to do weekends, it'll be great!'

'Well, maybe,' she admitted cautiously.

'And you're forgetting the best thing of all,' Joe added.

'What's that?'

'If you're working at the Regency Clinic, Zara Jeffries'll be out of your hair for good.'

Minette couldn't have been more pleased if slovenliness had been made a capital offence.

'Alan!' she exclaimed, putting the phone down and rushing into the downstairs cloakroom, where her husband was gazing intently into the mirror as he trimmed his moustache, 'Joe says Emma's got an interview!'

'That's nice,' said Alan, eyes narrowing as he steadied his hand ready to attack a rogue nostril-hair. 'What interview's that then?'

'For a job. At that lovely new private clinic on the way to Gloucester.'

'Ah,' nodded Alan, his face relaxing into a smile as he outsmarted the hair and snipped it into oblivion. 'But I thought she already had a job.'

Minette sighed. 'Alan love, you know perfectly well where she works. It's like a butcher's shop in Casualty on a Saturday night. And the language! Then there are all those disgusting tramps and alcoholics, and Lord only knows what sorts of diseases the girl could be bringing home to our Joe.'

'I suppose,' reflected Alan, tilting his head slightly to one side to check that the results of his topiary were symmetrical. There were few things worse, in Alan Sheridan's world, than unpolished shoes and a tatty moustache. 'Lad seems healthy enough to me though.'

'At the moment, maybe! Anyway, she's got an interview and I'm sure they'll give her the job. Or at least, I hope they will.' Her elation dimmed just a little as she reflected on Emma's haphazard dress-sense. 'Well, we shall just have to keep our fingers crossed and hope she does her best. It'll be so much nicer for Joe, knowing she's working with people who *deserve* to be treated.'

Alan grunted, whether in agreement or not it was difficult to tell. In any case he had just spotted the wiry grey hair sprouting out of a mole on the side of his neck.

'As for Zara, that lovely girl... She really ought to move to the private sector too. It's horrible to think of her working in that sweatshop, but if she will be a doctor. Well, that's what ambition does to young women these days. All work and exams. No wonder the poor girl never has time for boyfriends.'

She smiled to herself while Alan wrenched out his prey in triumph. 'Of course,' she reflected, 'Zara never did quite get over our Joe...'

11

Best shoes, crisp white shirt, smart black trousers. That was
Emma's standard interview outfit. As she stood in front of the
mirror-fronted wardrobes in the master bedroom, she wondered if
she ought to have branched out a bit and bought something less
boring – a posh skirt suit even? Joe would happily have paid for
out for something designer and chic. Heck, if he could have bribed
the interview panel to give her the job, he'd have done that too.

But no, she always felt frivolous and girly in a skirt; and
besides, if these people were going to employ her, they might as
well see the real Emma Sheridan from the word go.

If.

She looked back at herself from three different directions as she
angled one of the mirrored doors to take a critical look at her backside. No, it didn't look too vast and there wasn't anything stuck to
the seat of her pants. Reaching out for her black jacket, she slipped
it on, felt for the silly lucky black cat badge she kept permanently
pinned to the lining, and was about to walk out of the door when
the phone rang.

She almost ignored it, but the answering machine kicked in and
she heard Joe's breathless voice: 'Em? Emma, are you still there?
Oh damn, I wanted to say good luck.'

Emma snatched up the phone. 'So say it!'

'Thank goodness, I thought you'd already left.'

'Another ten seconds and I would've done. You left it a bit late,
lover boy!' She pouted in mock indignation. 'I was beginning to
think you didn't care.'

'Of course I care! Sorry darling, there was a bit of a flap on at
head office, we've only just sorted it out. Forgive me?'

'Oh ... go on, then.'

'Love you, you know.'

'Love you too.'

'Go get 'em, girl. You're worth ten of all the rest of them put together.'

She took a last glance at herself in the mirror and smiled. 'I know I am. But hey, listen—'

'I know,' he said. 'You're not promising to accept the job, right?'

'Right.' She didn't tell Joe that the thought of working at the Regency had started to grow on her a bit, despite her natural instinct to reject anything that Minette thought was a great idea. Nice hours, nice surroundings, nice patients, decent money ... The prospect was enough to make any nurse's socialist principles waver.

'Promise you'll think about it carefully though?'

'I promise. Got to go now, or I'll be late.'

'Love you lots.'

'Me too. 'Bye.'

'And over there, that's our health spa and hydrotherapy pool.' Emma's guide pointed to a glazed door, through which she could make out sparkling turquoise water and the dazzling glint of white tiles. 'Naturally all our staff are welcome to use the facilities when they're not required by patients. Oh yes – and our salary packages for nursing and medical staff come with free medical insurance.'

'Naturally,' echoed Emma, doing her best not to gape like an overawed peasant.

It wasn't easy though. This was all a massive culture shock. For a start, she was being shown round the Regency Clinic not by some grey-suited NHS administrator, but by a real-life *matron*. The genuine article, from the absurdly intricate lace-trimmed cap right down to the black shoes and the navy-blue dress that hugged her substantial frame like well-cut upholstery. Not that Matron looked at all anachronistic, not among the smiling ranks of black-stockinged nurses with their crisp white aprons and fob watches.

My God, thought Emma; they've staffed this place with extras from *Carry on Nurse*. And she could just picture the smirk on Joe's face when she told him about the black stockings.

Mind you, the uniforms were the only retro aspect of the

Regency Clinic. Everything else about the place ached with newness, from the state-of-the-art bone scanner to the mono-grammed furniture in reception, and the faint scent of carpet ad-hesive hanging in the air. No black scuff marks on the skirting boards here, no ancient copies of *The People's Friend*, or mangled patients making the place look untidy.

'Of course, all our in-patients are accommodated in single rooms with en-suite facilities,' Matron went on, striding out along the softly carpeted corridor. Knocking at a door, she pushed it open to reveal a middle-aged man in a dressing gown sitting up in bed with a tray of poached salmon, watching satellite TV. 'Good afternoon, Mr Godwin. This is Nurse Sheridan, she's thinking of joining our team.'

He raised his wine glass in salute. 'Good for her.'

'Off home tomorrow, I hear?'

Mr Godwin nodded. 'Mind you, I'll be sorry to go home.' He took a sip of red wine. 'Like a five-star hotel it is here, Nurse.'

'I can see that,' agreed Emma. 'Nice meeting you'; and then she was forced to set off again in pursuit of Matron, who was already halfway down the corridor.

'I meant to ask at the interview,' she panted when she finally caught up. 'What are the clinic's main specialities?'

'Well, we have a first-rate reputation in liposuction and laser treatment for short sight,' Matron enthused. 'And we do a lot of hip replacements.'

'Oh,' said Emma, less than overwhelmed. 'But that's not all, is it ...?'

'Goodness me no! We deal with all manner of elective general surgery, and then there are our Well Woman and Men's Health clinics, and our minor surgery day unit. As you saw, we have superb theatre facilities, and it's important to our business to ensure that they're kept busy.'

'What about emergency surgery?'

'No,' Matron smiled. 'Wherever possible, we prefer to refer emergencies to the Cotswold General.'

Hmm, thought Emma. I bet you do. Good old NHS, every-body's dumping ground. 'So what if a patient suffers compli-cations after an operation here?'

This clearly struck Matron as not the sort of thing the Regency Clinic could possibly allow to happen on its premises. 'Well, in the *unlikely* event of serious complications, we would arrange transfer to an NHS hospital with the appropriate specialist facilities.'

'So you don't have an intensive care or high dependency unit?'

'Dear me no, that would be terribly costly. But you mustn't worry; there's always a consultant on call in case of emergencies. You'd never be left to cope on your own.'

Emma didn't have a chance to say that, actually, having too much responsibility wasn't what worried her, because they had come back to the end of the corridor, and the open doorway to Matron's office. 'Do take a seat, Mrs Sheridan. Can I offer you some more coffee?'

'Thank you.' You didn't say no to free Blue Mountain.

Matron rested her elbows on her desk and pressed the tips of her fingers together. 'Well, Mrs Sheridan, after speaking with you and examining your references, I'm happy to tell you that the board has decided to offer you a post here.'

A weird feeling rushed over Emma: a mixture of excitement and gathering doom. Somehow, although she'd known this was going to happen, she still hadn't managed to prepare for it. 'Oh,' she said. 'I'm ... very pleased.'

'Of course,' Matron smiled. 'And in fact, we were so impressed with your experience and personal qualities that we would like to offer you a post as a junior sister.'

This time, Emma was genuinely stunned. 'A ... *sister*? Gosh, I—' Her mind whirled. All this time she'd been struggling to get a permanent staff nurse's post at the General, and suddenly these people wanted to make her up to Sister! 'In which treatment area?' She ran through the possibilities in her mind. There were no emergency facilities here, so ... theatre? General surgery?

'Outpatients.'

'Pardon?' Tell me I'm not hearing this, thought Emma.

'Outpatients,' repeated Matron. 'It's a key post, organising paperwork, ensuring notes are available and making sure our patients and consultants are kept happy.'

'Oh,' said Emma.

'And of course this is a daytime post, working Monday to Friday.' Matron brandished Emma's application form like a prosecution counsel's brief. 'You do say here that you're looking for a job with more regular hours.'

*

Joe's face turned white. 'You turned it down! What do you mean, you turned it down?'

Emma placed the serving-dish of roasted vegetables in the middle of the table. 'I told you,' she said quietly, 'I just couldn't do it.'

'I don't believe this!' Joe ignored the lamb chop cooling on his plate. 'They offer you a sister's job, just what you've always wanted, and you say no!'

'A sister's job on Outpatients,' she reminded him.

'Exactly! A Sister's job with nine-to-five hours, Monday to Friday, zero stress—'

'Zero interest.'

'All the holidays you could want ...'

'And no proper nursing, let alone anything skilled. I'd be a dogsbody, Joe. A glorified form-filler. That's not what I spent years training for.' She laid a hand on his. 'Hey, eat up, it'll go cold.'

He shoved his plate away across the glass-topped table, and stood up. 'I'm not hungry.'

'You said you were ravenous when you came in.'

'That was before you dropped your little bombshell. Oh Emma, you promised you'd think about it!'

'I *did* think about it.'

'Yeah, for about three seconds.'

'For as long as it took,' she replied firmly. 'And it wasn't just the job, Joe, it was the place. I can't work there, it's ... it's ...'

He marched into the living room and practically threw himself on the sofa. 'What – civilised? Clean? Full of people who don't abuse you and beat you up?'

'Soulless. Not like a hospital at all. Half their patients only go there because they don't like the shape of their nose.' She sat down beside him. 'Oh Joe, after all this time I thought you understood me.'

Joe glared back at her. 'So did I.'

Angry tears welled up in her eyes. 'What's that supposed to mean?'

'It means we're married, Emma. We're supposed to share things with each other, talk them over, make decisions together. I can't believe you could be so ... so selfish.'

The word hit home with such calculated force that for a few

moments it left Emma completely breathless. Then: 'Selfish? Me?'

Joe glowered. 'You heard.'

'Bloody hell, Joe,' she exploded, 'that's a bit rich, coming from you!'

'What?'

'I don't recall you "talking things over" with me when the company offered you a promotion and you knew you were going to spend half your life away from home! Oh no, you just said "thanks very much" and muggins here had to put up with it.'

'That was completely different! My whole career was at stake. I couldn't very well say no, could I?'

'Oh really? Well, come to that I don't recall you asking me if I minded your mates using our home as a social club, either. And while we're on the subject of careers, who was it that uprooted her entire life, left all her friends, gave up a job where she was valued, and all for someone who's never even had the decency to say "thank you"? Oh goodness me, who'd have known it, it's me!' Tears of furious self-pity overflowed and began trickling silently down Emma's cheeks.

'You're just twisting the facts,' protested Joe, his face thunderous. 'Don't you want us to have a good life together?'

When Emma looked into his eyes she saw the glint of something steel-hard and stubbornly unyielding. She completely understood for the first time how a man like him could have got so far in his job in such a short time. He wouldn't give up, wouldn't let go; not for anything, not even for her. The realisation was so horrible, so painful, that she began to sob.

'Of course I do! But if you won't let me have a good life of my own—'

'Don't talk rubbish! As if I've ever stopped you—'

'Do you really think that's a recipe for happiness?'

'—doing anything! Not that you'd take any notice if I did.' Joe got up and stalked across the room. 'Why the hell are you crying, anyway? I mean, it's not like you haven't got your own way.'

'What?'

'Well, you never had the slightest intention of taking that job, did you? You just went through the motions.'

'That's not true!' sobbed Emma.

They glared at each other, the clock in the background measuring out their misery in slow, agonised clunks. It was as though time had ground almost to a halt, stretching out the anguish to its sado-masochistic max. The only other sound was the occasional sniff of Emma's tear-filled nose.

All at once something inside her turned cold and clear-headed, and she broke free of the torture. Snatching up her handbag, she pushed past Joe and headed for the front door.

'Where are you going?' he demanded, lunging into life just a little too late.

'Out,' she snapped. And one door-slamming moment later, she had.

By the time Emma had walked all the way to the all-night garage shop, she was freezing cold and cursing the fact that she'd left her coat behind. At least inside the store, she could lurk among the aisles and find excuses not to go back.

Paracetamol, she needed paracetamol; and there were none in her bag. Her head was throbbing from all the crying, and when she caught sight of her reflection in a display of cheap bathroom mirrors, all she could see were two red-rimmed circles.

It was not the best moment to turn walk slap-bang into your mother-in-law. Particularly when that mother-in-law happened to be Minette, weighed down with car shampoo and oven cleaner. But fate, it seemed, had it in for Emma tonight.

'Emma, darling! You look dreadful. Are you all right?' Minette grabbed hold of her, drew her to one side and clamped a hand to her frozen brow. 'You're *shivering*. Are you coming down with the 'flu?'

'It's just a headache,' insisted Emma. 'Stress, I expect. A couple of painkillers and I'll be fine.'

The mention of stress deepened the frown of concern on Minette's face. 'Oh no, it wasn't the interview, was it? Didn't it go the way you wanted?'

'Well, not exactly.' It wasn't entirely a lie, and all Emma wanted to do right now was run away and hide.

'Oh dear, I'm so sorry.' Minette shook her head sorrowfully. 'Never mind, be brave. And perhaps next time you'll let me give you a few tips on personal grooming? Now, must rush – Alan's in the garage fiddling with that dreadful old Jaguar of his, and I simply must get the oven cleaned while I have the chance. Goodbye dear, chin up, give my love to Joe.'

I'd like to give him something, thought Emma, but I'm not sure it's love. Oh, but who was she fooling? Now the edge of the anger had worn off, all she really felt was sad and lonely and cold.

She bought a packet of headache pills and a coffee from the vending machine, then went and huddled by the window, where there was just enough space to sit on the ledge if you didn't mind perching on one buttock. I ought to go home now, she thought; but if I do, I'll just look stupid. Mind you, that's only fair. I am stupid.

As she tipped back her head to swallow the pills, she saw a familiar figure standing at one of the petrol pumps. A squat, balding figure in an ill-fitting sweater, lovingly filling up a cavernous orange Volvo.

There couldn't be two cars like that in Cheltenham; or two owners. Oh bloody hell, was the entire town out on the prowl tonight?

Rozzer's square head loomed over the top of the computer magazines just as Emma was trying to take cover behind a stack of growbags. 'How do Emma, fancy meeting you here!' He dug in his pocket for a twenty-pound note and handed it to the cashier. 'Where's Joe?'

'We're not joined at the hip you know,' she replied bitterly.

'Oh. Sorry.' He touched her hand. 'Jesus, you're half frozen. Where's your coat?'

'Came out without it.'

'Bloody hell,' said Rozzer, pocketing his change and looking her up and down. 'Are you all right?'

'Why do people keep asking me if I'm all right?' she demanded, loudly enough to make both the other customers turn and look at her. 'Of course I'm bloody all right!'

And then she burst into tears again.

Sitting in the passenger seat of Rozzer's Volvo, Emma gazed up at the apartment block, locating the precise rectangle of light that was Joe's ... no, their flat.

'I can't,' she said in a small voice.

'Yes, you can.' Rozzer gave her shoulders a surprisingly gentle squeeze. 'That's the mistake I made, not going back.'

She looked at him sharply. 'When?'

'When Maxine and I broke up...' Rozzer sighed. 'We were only nineteen, should never have got married that young. But I did love her. Trouble was, I took her for granted and eventually she thought, Sod this.. We had a big row and I walked out. If I'd had any sense, I'd have walked right back the next day. Only I didn't, 'cause I was stupid, so I lost her.'

'I'm really sorry,' said Emma. 'I didn't know ... not the details, anyway.' She sniffed into another of Rozzer's tissues. 'But ... y-you think I'm taking Joe for granted? You think he's right and I'm being selfish?'

Rozzer laughed quietly. 'Not you, you cretin. The other way round. When it comes to selfishness Joe wrote the book. He doesn't mean it, but ...' He shrugged. 'Neither did I. Let's just face it, most men are emotional retards.'

It was Emma's turn to laugh. 'You're not that bad.' She blew her nose. 'You really think I should go and talk to him?'

'Definitely I do. But listen.' He laid his hand on top of hers. 'I've never stopped wishing I'd stayed on at school and got myself a decent job, like you have. Don't let Joe bully you into accepting something boring, just because it fits with what he wants.

'If it's not what you want, you've got the right to say no.'

'Em! Oh my God, Emma, I've been out of my mind worrying about you!'

All the way up the stairs to the flat, Emma had been worrying what on earth to say when she came face to face with Joe again, but she needn't have. The moment he saw her, he ran to her and swung her up into his arms.

'Oh Joe,' she sobbed, 'I'm so sorry.'

'No, I'm sorry, I behaved like a selfish bastard.'

'Maybe I should've thought the job over a bit more before I turned it down, or at least talked to you about it ...'

He set her down on her feet again, but kept tight hold of her as he stepped back to look at her, as though afraid that if he let go for one second she might vanish again. 'Maybe there's stuff we should both have done differently, but it doesn't matter now. All I care about is having you back.' She gazed up into his eyes and saw the wetness of unshed tears glinting in the lamplight. 'Oh Squeaky, I thought you'd left me.'

She smiled through a curtain of snot. 'As if.'

'I guess this being married thing isn't quite so easy as we thought it was,' ventured Joe.

'Well, it is a bit different from the odd two weeks in Majorca,' Emma conceded. 'I suppose it's all about us each getting used to the fact that the other one's not going to go away, ever again. Does that sound terrible?'

'No,' said Joe. 'Actually I'm really glad about it.'

And, to her surprise, so was Emma.

It was around half past six the next morning, as Joe and Emma lay entwined in each other's arms, that the phone started shrieking.

Accustomed from years of night shifts to answering telephones in her sleep, Emma leaned over Joe and grabbed the receiver. 'Mmm?'

'Emma? It's Minette. Is Joe there?'

She was half tempted to reply, 'No, he's in a brothel in downtown Algiers,' but it was too early. Instead she elbowed Joe in the ribs until he rolled over and groaned.

'It's your mum.'

She flopped back onto her pillows and was looking forward to another half-hour's sleep when Joe said, 'I'll be right there,' slammed down the phone and jumped out of bed.

Abruptly wide awake, Emma sat up. 'What's up?'

'It's Dad.'

Her heart skipped a beat at the memory of her own father, and the day he'd gone to work and never come home. 'He's not ill, is he?'

'Worse.' Joe shoved his feet into his slippers. 'Some arsehole got into the garage in the night and nicked his Jag.'

'Is that all.' Emma sagged with relief.

'All? He's spent thousands restoring that car.' Grabbing a jumper from a chair at the end of the bed, he thrust his head into it. 'And I'll tell you what. If he gets his hands on whoever did it, I wouldn't want to be the one picking up the bits.'

12

Lucky I didn't take that job at the Regency Clinic, mused Emma as she drove into work early one morning. I'd have had even more free time to get lonely and bored in. It was a sobering fact that she'd never spent so much time alone in her life. That was the unsatisfying thing about the situation as it stood; you got all the crap bits of being single and not enough of the benefits of being married. But Joe insisted he was happy in his job, and in the end that had to be the most important thing. Didn't it?

When Emma walked into A&E, normally the most peaceful place in Cheltenham at seven o'clock on a Tuesday morning, she found Lawrence in animated conversation with a couple of police officers, outside his office.

'I need to interview them the minute they get here,' insisted the woman constable.

'Well you can't,' replied Lawrence, who could be as stubborn as a Ribena-stain when it suited him. 'Not till we've finished with them.'

'They're my material witnesses! I need statements.'

'They're my patients, and I need time to get them treated. I'm sorry, you'll just have to wait. And from what the paramedic said over the radio, the motorcyclist's in no fit state to give a statement about anything.'

'What's happening?' asked Emma, pinning her name badge on to her white uniform tunic.

'Road traffic accident,' replied the young male constable, so pink and well-scrubbed that he could have been hatched that very morning.

'Oh? Where?'

'On that really isolated road near Ledbury, the one with all the Z-bends. Stolen S-type Jag in collision with a motorbike. Must've happened in the small hours; a local farmer was out early and came across a great big hole in his hedge.'

'Bad?'

Lawrence nodded. 'Looks like one dead, two injured, one critically. Not sure how bad the other one is. They're bringing the live ones here,' he added. The charge nurse glanced at the large digital clock above the Aids poster. 'ETA fifteen minutes, so tell Diane to get cubicle nine ready, and I want the last of those minor injuries cleared before then. Got that?'

'I'll get on to it now.' Emma turned aside to head for the waiting room, then the PC's words registered and she turned back. 'Did you say S-type Jag?'

'That's right, nineteen sixty-three S-Type, flame red with wire wheels. Oh, and one of those customised hood ornaments – military badge or something.' The younger police officer smiled sheepishly. 'Bit of a car bore, sorry.'

A 1963 red Jag – with a military badge on the bonnet! Emma's pulse quickened. What had only been a vague notion before hardened into virtual certainty. The certainty that Alan Sheridan was going to be far from happy when he found out what had happened to his precious car.

He's just a kid, thought Emma as the paramedics ushered the boy straight past the reception desk and into the treatment area. Yet another stupid kid who'd thought he'd have fun with somebody else's car and wound up killing someone instead. He looked barely tall enough to reach the pedals.

She didn't really know why it still had the power to shock her after all this time. After all, joyriding accidents happened practically every night of the week. Maybe it was just the thought of whose car it was, and the fact that she'd actually sat in the back of it, being driven home from the station. Or it might have been the way the boy crumpled like a paper bag in the rain when they told him his girlfriend was dead, killed instantly as she sat beside him in the front passenger seat.

There wasn't much to be done for the boy; not physically anyhow. All he had was a sprained wrist and a bump on the head.

Besides, moments later a wheeled stretcher crashed through the front doors, IV bag swinging wildly from a hook above the blood-stained plastic mattress.

'Thirty-seven-year-old male, leg and chest injuries, possible internal bleeding, possible head and neck trauma, GCS eleven,' rattled off the paramedic. 'Fire crew had to cut the remains of the bike off him before we could stabilise him.'

The A&E team started working on him straight away.

'Bleep the surgical reg.'

'Take some blood for cross-matching. Where's that oxygen?'

The boy with the sprained wrist stumbled out of his cubicle and ran down the corridor before Terri could stop him. He stopped in his tracks and stared, panic-stricken, at the man on the trolley and the doctors and nurses clustered round him. 'Is he...dead?'

Emma caught him by the shoulder to prevent him going any nearer. 'Best keep back.'

He was shaking violently. 'I didn't mean ... I didn't mean it.'

The woman police constable stepped forward, an opportunistic gleam in her eye. 'If you've done with him ...'

The boy's eyes pleaded for a reprieve but none came. 'We was only having a laugh.'

The house surgeon glanced up disdainfully, a smear of blood on his cheek. 'I don't care what you do with him, just keep him out of my way.'

Lawrence reappeared at the last minute. 'Sorry folks, he's not going anywhere just yet, he could have concussion. Terri, take him back to his cubicle and wait there.'

'What's your name?' asked Emma as she began cutting off the motorcyclist's blood soaked leathers.

The stranger on the stretcher groaned again, but didn't open his eyes. With his neck immobilised in a rigid collar, he could scarcely have moved even if he'd been fully conscious.

'Your name,' she repeated. 'Can you tell me?'

This time the eyelids dragged themselves open. Not very far, because the poor man's head had swollen to twice its normal size, reducing his eyes to narrow slits. But even so, they were the most startlingly blue eyes Emma had ever seen. An intense, almost electric blue, so vivid that for a moment she half wondered if he was wearing coloured contacts.

'Richard.' A harsh, painful breath. 'C-clay. Bourne.'

Somebody wrote the name on a treatment sheet. 'Where are those bloods?' demanded the house surgeon. 'And get me the surgical reg *now*.'

The lips moved again. He was trying to say something but it was barely audible, muffled by the oxygen mask.

'Sorry?' Emma bent to listen. 'Say it again.'

'Cam ... era. Where's ... my camera?' His chest fluttered with the effort of getting the words out.

Emma glanced around her. There was no sign of anything that looked like a camera. Most likely it had been left at the scene of the accident – either that or somebody had half-inched it. 'Don't you worry,' she said rashly, attaching sticky electrodes to his chest. 'It's quite safe.' It was probably a lie, but it hardly seemed the right time to break bad news to the poor guy.

His heart was leaping and struggling in his chest like a trapped bird. And a couple of seconds later, as Emma was taking his blood pressure, every monitor started shrieking at the top of its voice.

'Shit, he's going off—'

'BP's falling—'

'He's arrested. Don't you bloody die on me, you bastard.'

You're not going to die, thought Emma as she rushed the trolley into Resuscitation. I won't let you.

But she had absolutely no idea how she was going to manage it.

'Call for you,' said Satja as Emma passed the reception desk, on her way back from Theatre. Richard Claybourne had arrested twice more on the way there, but had held on long enough to go under the anaesthetic. Now it was all down to the surgeons. Anyhow, he wasn't Emma's problem any more.

'Oh? Who?'

Satja put a hand over the receiver. 'I think it's your mother-in-law.'

Great timing, cursed Emma. Just as I was finally about to get a cup of coffee. 'Hi Minette, it's Emma.'

'I've told you before, dear, call me Mum.'

'Er ... yes,' said Emma reluctantly. 'Look, I can't really talk at the moment, I'm on the receptionist's phone.'

'I just heard, dear. About Alan's car. The police say it's a write-off!'

'I wouldn't know,' replied Emma. 'But it was a serious accident.'

'He wants to know if those young hooligans are there at the hospital. He wants to come down and give them a piece of his mind.'

Oh God, thought Emma. Corporal Sheridan on the warpath, that's the last thing we need. Alan threatening them with National Service, while Minette egged him on with cries of 'You tell them, Alan.' Well, Emma would've liked to tell Minette that the thirteen year-old girl was so terminally mangled they were still looking for some of the bits, and her boyfriend was so pathetically scared he'd wet his pants in the Relatives' Room. Unfortunately she couldn't.

'You know I can't discuss individual patients,' she chided Minette. 'It's not ethical.'

'But I don't want to know anything confidential!' she protested. Just—'

'And besides, the police have left now. You could always phone them down at the station. And I'm sure they'll be in touch soon anyway.'

'They'd better be,' sniffed Minette. 'It is Alan's precious car we're talking about, you know! He's invested a lot of time and money in that Jaguar.'

Emma grimaced as she handed the receiver back to the receptionist. She felt unaccountably tired all of a sudden. Working a fourteen-hour shift with no breaks was no problem compared to a two-minute phone conversation with Minette.

'Staff,' called a voice from the front door as Emma headed in the direction of the staff dining room.

Oh hell, she thought as she turned and walked back. 'What?'

One of the paramedics held up a black bag with a shoulder strap. 'I think this may belong to that motorcyclist we brought in. It's full of photographic equipment, looks quite expensive. Shall I hand it in?'

Before she'd really thought about it, Emma found herself reaching out to take the bag, and heard herself say, 'No, it's OK, I'll make sure he gets it.'

Well, well, Mr Claybourne, she said to herself, remembering those absurdly blue eyes. Maybe you are still my problem after all.

If you pull through.

13

Joe woke up with a start, convinced he was going to be late for the office. Then he opened his eyes, found himself nose-down on his computer keyboard and remembered he was already there.

Sitting up, he rubbed his eyes and tried hard to focus on the screen in front of him. All this getting up in the dark and driving to Birmingham every day got to you a bit after a while, no matter how young and fit and keen you might be. Not to mention all the meetings that kept springing up at opposite ends of the country. Joe sometimes wondered if there was a competition on at head office to see how far apart they could schedule two meetings on the same day. The current record was Plymouth and York, but he was pretty sure they could improve on that.

Stifling a yawn, he rummaged in his desk drawer for a chocolate guarana bar. A shot of instant energy, that was what he needed, then he'd be fine.

As he slumped in his chair and munched, glad that his secretary couldn't see through from her side of the door, he gazed around at the trappings of youthful success. Having his own office was the biggest status symbol of all – no poxy open-plan for the Regional Sales Manager, oh no. No 'hit your monthly target and we might give you a third wall for your cubicle'. OK so it wasn't a *big* office, but it had its own water cooler – and proper carpet too, not just ancient carpet tiles that curled up at the edges and tripped you up.

All in all it was very nice, but just occasionally even Joe had to admit it could feel a bit like a cell. Sometimes, when he was sitting there resisting the urge to play computer solitaire, a small, shameful part of him hankered nostalgically after the days of pies and pints with the lads at lunchtime. In those days it'd been 'us' and 'them' and it still was; the only difference was that now he was very definitely one of 'them'.

Still, it was no good whingeing. If you wanted to get on you had to stop wanting people to like you all the time. And that included the area rep he'd just had to sack for failing to get Unico products into motorway service stations.

He crumpled up the chocolate wrapper and aimed it at the bin. It hit the rim just as the intercom buzzed.

'I said hold my calls,' he complained.

'I know,' replied Shirley, his secretary, 'but I've got Sir Stanley on the line.'

'Sir Stanley!' All kinds of lurid imaginings filled Joe's mind. The distinguished chairman of Unico was not exactly renowned for his friendly little personal phone calls. 'Don't keep him waiting then, put him through.'

Instinctively he fiddled with his hair and sucked the bits of nut out of his teeth. A man like Sir Stanley could tell if you were wearing a tie just from the sound of your voice.

'That you, Sheridan?'

'Sir Stanley!' If Joe had grinned any harder his face would have split. 'What a . . . a nice surprise.'

The chairman chuckled gruffly. It sounded like an earth tremor with a Yorkshire accent. 'I doubt it.'

Joe swallowed hard. 'Is there something . . .?'

'If there wasn't something I wouldn't have rung up, would I?' The chairman left a sadistically long pause, then added, 'Relax, I'm ringing to say "well done", not "collect your P45".'

A warm glow of relief spread over Joe. 'Oh,' he said. Well that *was* a nice surprise.

'Don't sound so surprised. You're not daft, you know you deserve it. People think I spend all my time playing golf, but believe it or not I do notice things. Like the twenty per cent increase in wine sales since you took over the Midland region.'

'Well, I don't suppose it's all down to me,' Joe babbled modestly. 'I mean you have to take into account—'

'I don't care how you're doing it Sheridan, just keep it up. And while you're at it, see if you can get 'em to shift more luxury ready meals instead of all those economy baked beans.'

'I'll get right on to it,' promised Joe, who was already mentally working out how he was going to wean his customers off Unico's biggest-selling line.

'Good.' Sir Stanley paused. 'Mind you, there is one thing I've been meaning to have out with you.'

Joe's heart, which had been dancing in the sunshine like a pink helium balloon, promptly went pop and fell over. 'There is?'

'There is. And that thing is ... socialising.'

'Sorry?'

'Mingling, man; showing your face. God help us, Sheridan, you're not a bloody troglodyte, get out more. I know Unico's come a long way since my father set up in business, but I still like to see us as a family firm. And when families get together they like everybody who matters to be there. So the next time the company throws a staff party or a charity dance or whatever ...'

Joe was not slow to take the hint. 'I'll be there, Sir Stanley.'

'Glad to hear it. After all, I'm sure you want to be one of the ones who matter.'

Too right he did. 'Of course. I mean, anything I can do—'

'Right. Oh, and Sheridan.'

'Yes, Sir Stanley?'

'Don't forget to bring that lovely new wife of yours. I'm sure my Margaret's got lots of good advice to give her.'

After Sir Stanley had rung off, Joe relaxed back in his executive leather chair and swivelled smugly. Tick, gold star, teacher's pet. The only thing that took the edge off it was not having anybody to rush straight off and tell. Shirley had been PA to the last three regional sales managers; nothing short of ritual suicide impressed her. And it was no use ringing Emma: she was on yet another late shift, so that meant coming home to a cold flat and another microwaved dinner. Mum then? No, Wednesday was her afternoon for the charity shop. He could have called Dad, or even one of the lads, but they'd probably take the mick. Besides, Dad was still breathing fire over his beloved Jag – or what was left of it, which wasn't much.

No, if he rang anybody it'd have to be someone who'd listen, and smile, and tell him what he needed to hear: that he was good.

He'd almost given up on the idea when a thought ker-chinged into his brain. He did know someone like that; someone who – if his memory served him right – generally had a day off on a Wednesday.

Joe hesitated only momentarily as he picked up the phone. What could be more natural than dialling up an old mate? Besides, he hadn't spoken to Zara in ages, and they'd promised each other they'd keep in touch.

'I'm telling you, it's a jar of Bovril!' insisted Diane.

'You're making it up!' protested Terri, helpless with laughter.

'No I'm not! Cross my heart and hope to die.'

Behind the door of the sluice, many a patient's dark secret had been sniggered over through the years. But not many were weirder than the case of the elderly archdeacon's foreign body.

'Well?' demanded Terri as Emma arrived with something nasty in a bedpan. 'Is Diane telling porkies or what?'

''Fraid not,' she replied. 'His muscles have gone into spasm and it won't budge, so they're taking him up to theatre this evening.'

'Told you.' Diane licked her fingertip and scored an imaginary point in the air.

'Oh my God,' said Terri. 'Why would *anybody* ...?'

Emma shook her head, half in amusement, half in compassion. She'd seen it all: light bulbs, vacuum cleaners, fruit and vegetables, even a ball of string. 'Poor old sod,' she said, washing her hands. 'Can you imagine what kind of time he'll have up on the ward?'

Lawrence put his head round the door. 'Excuse me, ladies, but can we postpone the knitting circle till later? I need somebody to talk to the archdeacon's wife.' Everybody took a step back. 'Diane, you'll do.'

'Aw, why me?'

'Go on, hop it, you need the practice. And mind you keep it tactful.' Diane stuck out her tongue by means of a parting shot. 'Ah Terri, nice bit of projectile vomiting for you in cubicle six.' Terri's mouth opened. 'And don't complain, or you'll be helping Eileen delouse that vagrant.'

Terri went, leaving Emma looking expectant. But once the two of them were alone, Lawrence just deflated against the wall, as if someone had stuck a pin in him. 'God, I'm dreading the end of this shift.'

'Are you OK?' asked Emma.

'Nope.'

'Ill?'

He grunted.

She could see he was waiting for her to ask. 'So what's wrong?'

'One word,' replied Lawrence. 'Starts with D and ends with arsehole.'

'Duncan?'

'You guessed.' Lawrence slouched against the wall, elbow on the door handle.

'I thought you'd split up.'

'No darling, that was *last* week. Last week Duncan was exploring his sexuality, aka shagging everything with a pulse. *This* week he's definitely gay, and apparently we're back together and everything's hearts and flowers.'

'That's ... good,' commented Emma, wondering if it was.

Lawrence threw her a pitying look. 'Oh yes, terrific,' he snorted. 'Especially the bit when he turned round and asked me to marry him, the little shit.'

Emma blinked. 'Marry him? Wow, he must really care about you then.'

'Hah!' exploded Lawrence. 'He's only done it to fuck my brain up even more than he already has.'

'You really think so? So you turned him down then?' Lawrence didn't answer. He looked downright mournful, thought Emma, hardly like the blushing bridegroom-to-be. 'So why don't you tell him to move out? Tell him it's over?'

He looked at her as though she'd just said the dumbest thing in the world. 'Emma love, that's a great idea – only you've forgotten something. I'm head over heels in love with the manipulative bastard.'

Grabbing a disposable apron, he pulled it grimly over his head.

'You just don't know how lucky you are, kid, having a man you know you can trust.'

At the end of her shift, Emma was so tired that she didn't bother changing; just slipped her coat on over her uniform tunic and trousers.

Every instinct in her body told her to walk out through the double doors, get into her car and drive straight home to Joe. Or to the absence of Joe, if he hadn't made it home tonight. But as she picked up her handbag, she remembered Richard Claybourne's camera bag, still locked in the departmental safe. She'd promised to take it up the previous day, but things had intervened and she just hadn't got round to it.

You'll have to do it now you've remembered, she remonstrated with herself. Go on, take it up to the ward and let's be rid of it before it gets nicked or something.

Hauling the bag onto her shoulder, she plodded to the lift and waited a couple of centuries for it to arrive, dozing against the wall until the sudden 'ping' almost made her fall over.

'Claybourne?' said the Sister on ICU. 'Oh yes, Richard Claybourne. We transferred him downstairs to Marston Ward this morning. Sorry.'

As she plodded all the way back down the stairs, Emma mused that at least that meant the patient must be making some progress. Either that or they didn't expect him to survive so they weren't going to waste an ICU bed on him.

Marston Ward's vague odour of embrocation and jockstraps announced itself the moment you stepped through the swing doors. This was Male Orthopaedics and Trauma, in other words a ward full of young men who'd found imaginative ways to break bits of themselves. The concentration of testosterone in the air was so high that two breaths and you could feel the hair growing on your chest.

Almost colliding with a tall, blonde woman on her way out of the ward, Emma smiled a brief apology and headed for the nurses' station. 'I'm looking for Richard Claybourne,' Emma announced to the ward clerk. She nodded to the camera bag. 'Patient property.'

The clerk scanned the whiteboard list on the wall. 'He's in side room B, but there's not much point going in, I think he's unconscious. Shall I sign for that and put it in our safe?'

'Oh. OK then.' Emma signed and was just about to go when a staff nurse she vaguely knew popped out of the sister's office.

'Hi there – you're from A and E, aren't you?'

'That's right, Emma Sheridan. Just brought up some of Mr Claybourne's property. How is he?'

'Stable. Doing well. All we need now is for him to wake up, trouble is finding people to spend time with him.'

'Doesn't he get many visitors?'

'Just the one so far – tall blonde girl, his sister I think. She's only just left actually. I don't think he has any other family locally. He's new to the area, that's the problem.'

'Oh well,' said Emma, turning away.

'I don't suppose ...' A gleam appeared in the nurse's eye. 'I mean, you're not in a hurry to get off, are you?'

'Well, actually ...'

'Only we're so busy on here tonight, and if you could maybe just spend ten minutes in there, talk to him a bit?'

'But I don't know him!'

'That doesn't really matter. And he does need as much stimulation as possible. We've all been taking turns, but it's busy on the ward and the moment, and ...' She caught the look on Emma's face. 'No, you're right, it's a stupid idea. You get off home, you look knackered.'

That's because I am, thought Emma. But then again, what am I hurrying home to? An empty flat and a takeaway?

And what difference are ten minutes going to make to my life anyway?

Joe was glad to get home. More than that, he was ecstatic. Thanks to a bit of diary-juggling and calculated lying, he'd got away from the office in double-quick time. For once, he'd decided, a 0.1 per cent dip in customer satisfaction in Stourbridge could take second billing to a nice intimate dinner with his wife.

Bunch of flowers in hand, he scaled the stairs two at a time and bounded up to the door of the apartment. By his calculations, Emma would have been home for about half an hour; just long enough to have a soak in the bath and wind down. She'd be thrilled when he told her he'd booked that cosy corner table at Rico's for half-past nine, followed by the late-night comedy cabaret at the Pillar Room.

Pushing open the door with a flourish, he made his grand entrance. 'Da-daaa! Guess who?'

The flat echoed embarrassingly to the sound of his voice. That was odd; he'd expected a CD playing and the sound of contented splashing from the bathroom. Perhaps she'd fallen asleep in the bath and hadn't heard him.

But the bathroom was empty. In fact so was the rest of the flat.

Freesias wilting in his hand, Joe sat down on the end of the bed and kicked off his shoes. It wasn't supposed to be like this. Right now, Emma was supposed to be covering him in soapsuds and grateful kisses. He felt curiously bereft.

How could she not be home?

Emma glanced at her watch again and then down again at the figure in the bed. She wondered how much longer she ought to stay.

'I don't know what else to tell you,' she said aloud. It felt really weird, talking about everything and nothing to someone who was not only a stranger but an unconscious one to boot. 'Gosh, I hope this is doing you some good,' she added, ''cause you can't imagine how silly it makes me feel!'

Richard Claybourne lay motionless under the covers, blue eyes closed, mouth slightly open. He might have been quite good-looking before the accident, but he wasn't a pretty sight now: his entire head seemed to have swollen to twice its normal size and his eyelids looked like two Victoria plums, all bulbous and raw. What with the matted blood in his hair and the line of stitches running across the bridge of his nose, he wouldn't be winning any beauty contests any time soon. All the same, something about him compelled the eye.

'So you're a photographer then?' said Emma, swinging one foot gently against the other. 'At least I guess you are, from the size of that camera bag. Or a really good amateur anyway. I sort of wanted to be a photographer once, did I tell you that? Used to take a lot of snaps when I was at school, and we used to mess about in the darkroom a bit, but well, these adolescent things never come to anything do they? Only I suppose they must do for some people,' she mused. 'Still, I'm a good nurse, or at least Lawrence says I am. Did I—'

Whether she did or not was never established, because the figure in the bed suddenly moved and let out a kind of mumbled groan. Emma leant forward, listening for anything that might make sense, finger ready to press the bell for the nurse. 'Mr Claybourne? Richard?'

The sore, heavy eyelids fluttered, revealing a brief flash of sapphire blue. The cracked lips moved.

'Don't. Go.'

And then he was gone again.

*

104

Two beers later, Joe sat huddled on the white sofa with a big bag of crisps, staring despondently at the TV screen.

It wasn't fair. You made a really big effort to come home, and then when you got there, you rang round and eventually found out from one of your wife's colleagues that she was doing some kind of unpaid overtime on somebody else's ward! She hadn't even bothered to call him herself to let him know.

If he'd been thinking straight, it might have occurred to him that he should probably have phoned Emma to let her know he was coming home early. After all, she was probably bored stupid with sitting in the flat on her own, waiting for him to drag himself through the door at midnight. But he wasn't thinking straight, and he didn't feel reasonable. Not even a little bit.

So he picked up his mobile and was about to phone the lads when it rang.

'Hi, Joe here.'

'Joe it's me, Zara. How're you doing?'

'Well . . . I've been better.'

'Really? But you sounded so happy when we talked earlier. What's happened?'

'Oh, nothing much. Ups and downs of married life, you know.'

'Oh dear. Well, I only rang to see if you fancied coming out for a drink sometime. Of course, if you'd rather not . . .'

'No,' he cut in hastily, 'I'd love to. As a matter of fact I'm free tonight if you are. How do you fancy the late-night comedy cabaret at the Pillar Room? Just so happens I've got a spare ticket.'

14

'I did say I was sorry,' Emma called back from the kitchen, as she slapped butter haphazardly onto a slice of toast. 'I didn't think you'd be back for ages, otherwise I'd have phoned to let you know I'd be late.'

'Oh well.' Joe didn't look up from the Sunday paper, not that he was reading it. 'Whatever.'

'Still, you did say one of your mates took the tickets?'

'What? Oh, yeah. In the end.'

She smiled to herself as she cut the toast and piled it on a plate. 'I can't imagine Rozzer at an alternative comedy night. He has enough trouble understanding knock-knock jokes.'

With hindsight, Joe was glad Zara hadn't been free and he'd ended up giving the tickets to Rozzer. He wasn't sure his conscience could have dealt with taking Zara to the comedy night; and he certainly wasn't going to own up to Emma that he very nearly had, purely out of juvenile spite. He didn't like feeling juvenile – or guilty. And sometimes, without even trying, Emma could make him feel both at once.

'Toast,' she beamed, bouncing into bed beside him with bright eyes and buttery fingers.

'Hey, watch out,' he protested, 'you're getting butter all over my—'

'I know,' she purred. 'And l might just have to lick it off.'

Joe's eyebrows shot up to his hairline. 'Hey, what's got into you – spring fever?'

'Are you complaining?'

'Not bloody likely.' Joe seized the plate of toast, put it firmly on the floor and threw back the covers. 'Go on then, I'm all yours.'

'Not so fast, tiger, you'll have to ask me nicely.'

'You little tease!'

Giggling, Emma rolled over, taking the duvet with her, and they play-fought over it like amorous ferrets in a trouser leg.

'It is sooo nice having a proper Sunday morning lie-in with my gorgeous irresistible wife,' Joe whispered in her ear. 'I could really get used to this.'

'Mmm,' she sighed luxuriously. 'Me too.'

'Nothing to do, nowhere to go ...'

'Except the christening,' Emma reminded him lazily.

Joe groaned. 'Did you have to remind me? Anyway, that's not till this afternoon, it doesn't count.'

'Don't tell your mum that, she's been planning it ever since the poor mite was conceived.'

'Well we're not going to think about it right now, OK? We're just going to lie here and do exactly what we want. No work, no distractions.'

At which point, naturally, the phone rang.

They looked at each other, each willing the other to ignore it. It was Emma whose nerve broke first, conditioned as she was to all those emergency calls she had to take at work. Trying to ignore the look of betrayal on Joe's face, she reluctantly grabbed the receiver from the bedside table and yawned into it. 'Uh?'

There was an unimpressed silence at the other end of the line, then: 'I beg your pardon?'

The voice was unmistakable. 'Oh, hi.'

'Is that you, Emma?'

''Fraid so, do you want Joe?' She didn't wait for an answer. 'Hang on a minute. It's your mother,' grimaced Emma, throwing the phone at Joe and burying her head under the pillow.

'You can hardly blame her for phoning,' pointed out Joe as he struggled into his suit.

I can if I want, thought Emma, sticking the last bit of Sellotape on the christening present. 'I'm not blaming her, I just wish she wouldn't always call when we're ... in the middle of something. You know, your mother could market herself as a contraceptive.'

'Don't be daft, she just wants to make sure everybody's there and looking their best. Remember, this isn't just any baby we're launching, it's a Sheridan.'

107

Emma laughed. 'Oh, and that makes it something special, does it?'

'Too right it does!' An entertaining thought entered his head. 'Hey, just think, the next one could be ours!'

'Er . . . mm,' replied Emma, rather glad that her mouth was busy holding strands of metallic pink ribbon.

Joe swore, and let out an agonised breath that sent his zipper shooting back down to ground zero. 'You've been boil-washing these trousers, haven't you?'

'What! I took them to the dry-cleaner's round the corner, Gold Service just like you always have.'

'But they're . . . tiny! Look at them and tell me they haven't shrunk.'

She looked. It wasn't a pretty sight. 'Oh dear. Looks more like a case of who ate all the pies.' She deftly ducked a flying cushion.

'Hell, I'll have to wear my work suit instead, and it's so *boring*.'

'They do say it's a sign of contentment, you know,' she called after him as he went off in search of bigger pants.

'What is?'

'Putting on weight after you get married.' She glanced at her own slender figure in the mirror over the mantelpiece. If anything, she'd got thinner. 'Then again, it might just be a sign of too many takeaways.'

His head reappeared round the door. 'And whose fault is that?'

'It's nobody's fault! Besides, I can't help it if you keep sloping off to your mother's for roast dinners and big sponge puddings.'

'At least she's there to slope off to. Not like some people.'

'Hark who's talking!'

They both shut up abruptly, realising that their banter was on the verge of turning into something less playful.

'You look really nice in that suit,' commented Emma after a short silence.

'You reckon? You don't think it makes me look like an accountant?'

She slipped her arms around him and felt the warmth of his reciprocal embrace. This was much better. This was what being married was all about. 'Not unless they're making accountants tall, handsome and masterful these days.'

'Masterful? Does that mean I get to order you about and have you satisfy my every whim?'

'Don't push it, big boy.'

They kissed. 'S'pose we ought to finish getting ready and go.'

'Mm.'

'We don't want to be late.'

'Perish the thought.'

'It's an important family event.'

'Oh, absolutely.'

Neither of them moved.

Emma walked her fingers playfully up her husband's arm. 'I suppose there might just be time ... but then again ...'

'Darling,' he enfolded her in his strong arms and eased her determinedly towards the bed. 'Believe me, there's always time. And if there isn't, we'll make some.'

OK, so maybe Crystal Minette Mary Charisma Sheridan wasn't the most beautiful baby in the world, but she was definitely a contender for the most good-natured. Either that, or Minette had slipped her some of the dog's Prozac. At any rate, all she did was beam and gurgle, even when the vicar's arthritic hands slipped and he dunked the top of her head in the ice-cold font. Which was more than you could say for Will and Kathy's baby, who wailed, hiccupped and then filled the church with a foul stench and had to be taken out for a nappy change.

'How much longer?' hissed Joe, shuffling his feet during yet another hymn. 'There's live football on at three.'

Emma nodded towards Minette, tastefully resplendent in dove-grey Jaeger and ostrich plumes. 'Don't let your mum hear you say that, she's having the time of her life.'

Small wonder Minette looked on top of the world. She'd succeeded in getting the entire Sheridan family out on parade, well scrubbed and ironed; there was a mountain of home-baked scones waiting in the church hall; and they'd even managed to squeeze the oversized infant into the family christening robe, though admittedly it didn't quite meet at the back.

After the service, everybody milled about in St Ermin's church-yard while somebody's step-uncle fiddled with a digital camera and the doting parents posed with the latest addition to the Sheridan clan.

'Now the grandparents,' instructed the uncle, waving them over like a conductor bringing in the wind section.

Emma felt curiously out on a limb; not exactly an outsider, yet not quite family either – not so much a participant as an observer. Still, she supposed that feeling would gradually wear off as time went on. Calves aching from her three-inch heels, she surreptitiously grabbed a moment's relief by perching her bottom on the corner of a mausoleum.

A voice from nowhere made her jump. 'I bet you're ever so proud.'

She swivelled round. Colleen, the wife of Joe's eldest brother Stephen, was teetering towards her across the muddy grass, pencil skirt hitched up around her thighs.

'Sorry?'

'Proud, you must be really proud. You know, now you're married to Joe.'

'Proud?' For a minute she thought it was some kind of joke, but it was obvious from Colleen's expression that she was serious. 'How do you mean?'

This produced a look of surprise. 'Well, you know, with him doing so well for himself and everything.' She found herself a perch next to Emma and lowered her bottom onto it. 'And he's such a lovely bloke.' She gazed almost worshipfully at her brother-in-law, who was posing for the camera with his new niece in his arms. A soppy smile spread over her face. 'Aw, just look at him with her, he's a natural.'

'Yes.' Emma had to admit that Joe did look cute with a baby in his arms, even if the baby in question was the size and shape of a Ford Cortina. He'd even mastered the goo-goo-gooing and face-pulling, which she'd never really got the hang of. She supposed that came from having family to practise on. 'So, how are your two?'

'Oh, same as usual. Wayne's got nits again, Geena won't eat anything but sprouts and gravy.'

'What?'

'Yeah, I know, weird. And the other day I caught them trying to set fire to the tortoise.'

'Oh my God!'

'Still, you wouldn't be without them, would you?' beamed Colleen. 'I mean, family – it's what marriage is all about, isn't it?'

The village hall was so packed that Emma had to breathe in to squeeze her way through all the portly cousins and plates of

110

sausage rolls. Somebody pinched her bottom by the mushroom vol-au-vents, but by the time she'd managed to turn and glare, the mystery perpetrator had made good his escape.

She found Joe squashed into a corner by the stage, underneath a poster advertising stretch-and-tone sessions for the over-fifties; a plate in one hand and his mobile in the other. Two of his three 'big' brothers, new dad Matt and old-hand dad Simon, had him well and truly captive. She couldn't help smiling: standing together, the three of them looked like a set of Russian dolls, near-perfect replicas of each other in slightly different sizes, from hulking, rugby-playing Simon down to almost bijou Matt.

New baby or not, there could only be one topic when Joe was on hand to have his brains picked.

'So you reckon I ought to go for it then?' asked Matt eagerly.

'Hang on a minute,' parried Joe, 'I didn't actually say that.'

'Only if *you* think it's a good idea to buy it, I'll—'

'I didn't say that,' repeated Joe. 'I just said if you've got the spare money and you really think it'll generate more business ...'

'Which it will,' Simon cut in enthusiastically.

'Well, maybe. But listen, this isn't my field, I'm a salesman, not a financial adviser.'

'A salesman!' snorted Matt. The two brothers exchanged amused looks. 'Listen to him.'

'Makes you sound like you sell double glazing or something,' said Simon.

'That's my little bruv.' Matt clapped Joe on the back. 'Hiding his light under a bushel. So, how much do you reckon I should put into this new equipment then?'

'I don't,' protested Joe. 'What I'm saying is, I think you ought to go and see someone who knows what he's talking about. I mean, what do I know about landscape gardening?'

'It's all business, isn't it? And there's not much you don't know about that.' Matt caught sight of Emma. 'Well, if it isn't my new little sis! I think you'd better tell this husband of yours to stop running himself down, Em, he's too bloody modest for his own good. As usual.'

'Hey, careful – too much of that and he'll be unbearable. We've already had to have the door widened to get his head through!' She wriggled her way through to Joe and pinched a crisp off his plate. 'What's this, a seminar?'

'Matt's thinking of expanding the gardening business.'

'Got to think big, wife and new kid to support,' explained Matt.

'And he wanted some advice. Not that I'm the right person to give it to him ...'

'There you go again,' sighed Matt.

'I'm not! If you were going to buy a car you'd get a car mechanic to look over it, not a ... a ...' He turned to Emma.

'Greengrocer?' she ventured.

'Exactly.' His expression pleaded 'rescue me'.

Out of the corner of her eye, Emma saw Alan, mooching around disconsolately with a pint in his hand while Minette relentlessly chatted up the vicar. 'Talking of cars, your dad's still looking pretty down in the mouth.'

'It's the Jag, he's started saying he's not going to replace it,' said Simon.

'You're kidding!'

'Well, the insurance won't cover it and you know how Mum hated the thing anyway.'

'Bloody joyriders,' grunted Matt. 'And I bet the little sods get off with a pat on the head and a caution.'

Joe was stunned. 'Dad's not replacing the Jag? But he loved that car! He'd have slept with it if the bed was big enough.'

Simon shrugged. 'I know, but what can you do?'

'Yeah,' sighed Matt.

'I'll tell you what we can do,' replied Joe, with the rare mad glint in his eye that told Emma he was about to do something impulsive. 'We can buy him a new one!'

'Who can?'

'Us! Us three.'

'Hey, hang on,' Matt laughed nervously, 'nice idea but some of us have got kids and businesses to think about!'

'All right then – *I'll* buy him a new one.' Joe drained his glass. 'But it'll be from all of us. Agreed?'

The other two looked doubtful. 'I dunno. I like to pay my way,' said Simon.

'God knows what your mum'll have to say about this,' remarked Emma. 'Are you sure it's such a great idea?'

'Oh, she'll come round,' replied Joe, chewing animatedly on a cocktail sausage. 'She's had her posh christening with a cast of thousands, the least she can do is let Dad have his car.'

Like a genie summoned from a bottle, Minette suddenly appeared from nowhere, sheaf of baby photos in hand. 'Now now, boys,' she wagged a finger, 'are you talking about football again? Shame on you Matt, you're supposed to be over there with Lucy, showing off your lovely baby!'

'Sorry, Mum. Catch you later about you-know-what, Joe.' Reluctantly he drank up and headed off into the mob.

'You-know-what?' Minette looked expectantly from Joe to Simon and back again. 'That all sounds very mysterious.'

Joe waved the thought aside. 'Oh, he just asked me for some advice about his business.'

Minette smiled indulgently. 'Well of course he did, darling.' She tucked an arm through his. 'Isn't it wonderful having a genius in the family?'

Simon agreed that it was. Emma felt slightly nauseous on Joe's behalf, and slightly more resentful on her own. She was starting to feel a bit like a speck of dust, clinging to the hem of Joe's glittering robe.

His mobile phone rang. 'Joe Sheridan? Oh, hi. What? No, it's OK, if the traffic's not too heavy I'll be over there in ...' He consulted his watch. 'About an hour. Sorry folks.' He switched off his phone. 'Got to love you and leave you, bit of a crisis at the Abingdon store.'

Minette looked crushed. 'On a Sunday, darling? Can't they manage without you? I wanted to show you all these lovely photos Uncle Trevor's just run off on his printer.'

'Sorry, Mum.' Ducking below the ostrich plumes, he planted a kiss on her cheek. 'Why don't you show them to Emma? I bet she can't wait to see them.'

'Oh.' Minette looked a tiny fraction mollified. 'Oh, yes, I suppose I could. Actually ...' Grabbing Emma's arm, Minette towed her towards the mini-crèche of infants and small children that had developed in one corner of the hall. 'Kathy was saying that Chloë's got a bit of diarrhoea, and I said that seeing as you're a nurse you'd take a look at it. You don't mind, do you?'

Emma looked back over her shoulder and stuck out her tongue. Nice restful Sunday? Ha! I'll get you for this, Joe Sheridan, she vowed. Just you see if I don't!

Emma wasn't normally one for going in to work early, and frankly she'd never been a fan of wet Monday mornings, but for some

113

reason she found herself driving into the hospital car park with half an hour to spare.

Whatever was she going to do with those thirty precious minutes? Lounge around drinking coffee? Clock on early and give Lawrence a heart attack? Or go up to the ward and find out how Richard Claybourne was getting on ...?

Perhaps that had been at the back of her mind all along; at any rate, all that talk of Alan's Jag had certainly brought him back into her thoughts. Had he ever been completely out of them? Silly question, of course he had. All the same, she had promised him she'd visit again and it didn't do to break your promises.

She checked the list of patients on the whiteboard at the end of the ward. Well, he was still here. Tracking down one of the outgoing night staff with the drugs trolley, she nodded towards the side room. 'I know it's a bit early, but could I pop in and see Mr Claybourne for a few minutes? I promised him I would.'

'Yeah sure, go ahead.' The nurse turned back to the trolley, then remembered something. 'Hey, you didn't come yesterday did you?'

'No, why?'

'Oh, nothing really. Someone visited him and left a pair of gloves behind. Thought it might have been you.'

Emma knocked on the door and opened it gently. The figure in the bed was lying perfectly still, facing the window, and she was about to go off and leave him to sleep in peace when he spoke.

'Emma?'

She nearly fell over with astonishment. 'Yes. Emma Sheridan. How did you ...?'

Richard Claybourne rolled over, very slowly and painfully, until he lay on his back, panting from the effort. 'It's OK, I'm not psychic. I saw your reflection in the TV set.' Clearly exhausted, he lay there looking up at her, taking in every detail of her face so intently that she felt the colour rising to her cheeks. 'You came.'

'I said I would.'

'People often say things they mean at the time, but then after-wards they change their minds. There's a chair over there.' He raised a bandaged arm.

'I can't stay long, I'm on duty in twenty minutes.' All the same,

114

she dragged the chair over and sat down. 'I just wanted to see how you were.'

'So what do you reckon?' he asked her. 'You're the expert.'

'You look a lot better,' she replied.

That was something of an understatement. A lot of the swelling had subsided, and those remarkable eyes were no longer just slits of blue in a mass of bruised flesh. Someone had washed his hair, too, and it spread out on the pillow, all glossy and black and bohemian. Even the gash across the bridge of his nose looked less Frankenstein, more romantic duelling scar. Sometime in the not-too-distant future, this was going to be a good-looking man again.

'That's good, because I feel like someone threw me through the air and then ran over me a couple of times.' He smiled, a little painfully thought Emma. 'Oh yes, somebody did. How are they doing?' he asked. 'The kids who flattened my bike?'

'One's been discharged, one's still serious.' She thought it best not to dwell on the one who hadn't made it to the hospital at all.

'And the car?'

'Completely trashed. As a matter of fact, it belonged to my father-in-law.'

'Oh my God. How's he taking it?'

'He's gutted.'

'I know how he feels. From what they tell me, you could put what's left of my bike into a couple of carrier bags. Thanks, kids, you did a cracking job there.'

She shrugged sympathetically. 'Still, at least you're OK. Or you will be.'

'I wonder if they'll go straight out and steal another car,' pondered Richard.

'Surely not!'

'I wouldn't be so sure, you never can tell with kids.' He reached for a beaker of ice-water on the locker and Emma handed it to him. 'At their age, I probably would. I was a right little tearaway. How about you?'

'Oh, you know. Boringly normal.' It was the first time Emma had almost wished for a criminal record. 'The worst thing I ever did was get caught without a ticket on the Underground – and that was only because I lost it!'

'Not the type to take risks then?'

'Not really.'

'Oh, I bet you are. Deep down.' His eyes met hers. 'We all are.'

She gave a nervous laugh. 'Not me.'

'What about all that stuff you were saying about taking up photography? If you really want to do it well you'll have to put your soul into it for everybody to see, and I can't think of anything more risky than that.'

She blinked at him in surprise. 'You remember me telling you that? I thought you were unconscious!'

'Some of the time I was. You've got a lovely voice, by the way.'

'Thanks.'

'I'm not embarrassing you, am I?'

'No,' she lied, 'of course not.'

'That's good. I have this habit of saying the first thing that comes into my mind. I know it's bad, but I have this rule: never let yourself be tied down by other people's standards. Or their inhibitions.'

'It sounds a very ... bohemian way of life,' she commented.

He laughed, the sound cut off as he winced at the pain of his numerous cracked ribs. 'If bohemian means living from hand to mouth and never staying anywhere long enough to get on the electoral register, then yeah, I guess I am.'

Emma thought of the visitor he'd had the previous day, and her mouth slipped the question in before her brain had time to censor it. 'So what does your ... partner think of it all?'

'Partner?'

'You know, your wife, girlfriend?'

She thought she caught a glimmer of amusement in his eyes. 'Do you really think any sensible woman would stick with a penniless photographer who turns down lucrative wedding jobs so he can go off and spend three days photographing a wet rock?'

Emma smiled. 'Well, it takes all sorts.'

'And what sort are you?'

'Pardon?'

'What stuff do you like? Whose pictures? Which photographer would you be if you could be anyone you wanted?'

To her surprise, Emma found that it was easy to talk to Richard; far too easy. Before she'd got halfway through telling him about the exhibition of contemporary Danish photography she'd seen at the South Bank (the one Joe had snuck out of to go to the pub), she caught sight of the time and leapt to her feet.

'Oh hell ... look, I'm really sorry, but I've got thirty seconds before I'm late for work.'

Even as she grabbed her bag and sprang for the door, Richard's calm voice held her back. 'Will you come again? Please? I've really enjoyed talking with you.'

'I'll ... see what I can do.'

Closing the door behind her, she sprinted for the stairs and hoped no one would notice that she was blushing to the roots of her hair.

There was no escaping Minette when her mind was made up, and her mind was very definitely made up that *everyone*, however uninterested, was going to endure the Ordeal of the Christening Photos.

Secretly, Joe was quite pleased to have an excuse for going round to the old family home; to unlock the door and step into the familiar smells of shoe-polish, stewed rhubarb and pot-pourri that soothed his frazzled nerves with their own homespun brand of aromatherapy.

The job was great; of course it was. But it was also harder than he'd anticipated (and he'd anticipated that it would be hard), and he'd not bargained on Sir Stanley deciding he could handle regional marketing as well as sales, or the woman he'd been promoted over being quite so wilfully obstructive. This was stuff he couldn't really talk about to anyone: not Em, not his brothers, not his mates, and definitely not his mum and dad. He felt the burden of their expectations, and for the first time in his life he was actually starting to feel that it *was* a burden.

But at least here, in the house he still instinctively called home, he could crawl back into the womb of his childhood for a little while, devour his mum's steak and kidney pie and pretend that his biggest worry was getting his homework in on time.

His mother called up the stairs to him. 'Cup of tea, Joe. Shall I bring it up?'

'No thanks, Mum, I'll be down in a minute.'

He sat cross-legged on the floor of his old bedroom, sorting through the contents of the built-in cupboard. Ostensibly he was looking for his old marketing textbooks from college, but he kept getting sidetracked by the Aladdin's cave of artefacts that chronicled his life from zero to the day he left home.

School photos. Snaps of him with Zara – arm in arm, laughing, dressed in their costumes from *Oklahoma*. His old football shirt. A tattered copy of *Lord of the Rings* – ah, how many times he'd tried to read that book, and how many times he'd failed. A tiny, striped sock with an embroidered name-tape. He rooted through it all until he came to the stack of books he was looking for, pushed right to the back of the shelf.

And then his hand touched fragile, wooden struts and painted silk. His kite! His beloved dragon kite! It had lain in the cupboard ever since the day it had got snagged in a tree and lost half its tail. It had never been quite the same after that.

He closed his eyes and saw the red and gold silk fluttering high over Cleeve Hill, riding the wind; carefree, unfettered, thinking about nothing save the moment. Just the way he'd been, in those days.

Not like now.

But he was just a child back then. Now he had power, success, possessions, a wife, a whole glittering future in his grasp. Everybody told him so.

His fingers stroked the tattered silk and suddenly he felt inexplicably sad; as though he had just realised how much he longed for something that had gone, and could never again return.

15

Time passed, and spring popped its cautious head over the windowsill, thought better of it and went back to sleep. Fluffy lambs gambolled tentatively in muddy fields. Crocuses emerged and were promptly blown flat. Bikinis appeared in shop windows for people to laugh at. And Joe's mum went out and bought him a vest.

Despite Minette's frequent visits, being married was getting easier, thought Emma. No more silly arguments, no more childish tears; all was peace and domestic harmony. Mind you, they were cheating a bit. Joe's job seemed to take him away from home more and more often, and when he did manage to stagger home and spend a night in his own bed, he was so knackered he probably didn't have the energy to argue even if he'd wanted to.

Sometimes, Emma thought it must bear some resemblance to one of those terribly civilised Continental marriages, where the wife swapped coq-au-vin recipes with her husband's mistress, and they all went on holiday together. Only Joe's mistress wasn't some suspender-clad babe; it was his job. Just as well she had something to keep her occupied too. Or should that be someone?

'This is good,' said Richard, handing back the photograph. Emma saw how carefully he handled it, supporting it on his palm as though it were something valuable and not just a snap she'd taken of three cows on a Welsh hillside. He must have realised what was going through her mind, because he interrupted her question with, 'No, I'm not just saying it to be polite. I told you, I don't do polite.'

'Well ... thanks,' was all that Emma could say. Despite their regular talks over the last couple of weeks, she still hadn't quite

119

learned to relax with him, even though she found him fascinating company. There was always the faint apprehension that he was about to do something dangerous. Perhaps that was part of his appeal. That, and the fact that he reminded her of all the bizarre, unconventional people who used to wander in and out of the house in Hackney. Cheltenham seemed a bit short on free spirits.

He eased himself into a more comfortable position in his high-backed hospital chair. The orthopaedic team had worked wonders in sticking him back together, but it wasn't easy getting comfy when you had sutures all over, plus a plaster cast and a sling.

'The sea's not straight on that one of the Isle of Man, though,' he remarked. 'Makes it look like the fishing boat's going to slide off the edge of the photo.'

Her face fell. 'Not straight?' She inspected it more closely. 'Oh no, you're right!'

'You need to watch things like that,' he said firmly. 'Pay attention to detail. That kind of slip marks you out as an amateur.'

'That's OK,' she retorted. 'I am an amateur!'

'That's not the attitude I want to hear.' Richard wagged a finger under her nose. He might be only thirty-eight, but right now he sounded like her old headmaster. 'You told me you wanted to be a proper photographer, young lady!'

She squirmed, like the time one of her tutors had caught her drawing a smiley face in iodine on an obnoxious patient's bottom. 'I wish I'd never told you now! It was just one of those adolescent things ... I wasn't really being serious.'

'Well, you ought to be. Everybody should always be serious about everything.' He winked. 'Except being serious.'

Emma pulled a face. 'What's that supposed to mean?'

Richard shrugged. 'Search me.'

'You're weird!'

'Ah, but admit it; that's why you like me.'

Hmm, thought Emma. He's probably right. My life's certainly a bit short on weird at the moment. They sat in silence for a few moments, while the big clock on the wall thunked round towards half-past and the man in the next bed lectured his wife about not overfeeding the koi carp. Richard had been moved into one of the bays on the main ward as soon as he was on the mend, and now an empty suitcase was lying on the counterpane, waiting to be packed with his scant array of possessions.

'So they're discharging you today then?'

He nodded. 'Looks that way. I just have to see the doctor and get my outpatients' appointment, and then I'm a free man.'

'Is someone coming to pick you up?'

'Yeah, Lydia. She's the editor I told you about who's been giving me the odd bit of freelance work on *The Courant*. I don't know how I'd have managed in here if she hadn't brought me clean clothes and stuff; I hardly know a soul in Cheltenham.'

'Oh, right.' I bet she's the woman who left the gloves behind, Emma thought.

'That's the trouble with being new to the area.' He leaned forward. 'You've no idea how embarrassing it is, having to ask a virtual stranger to go out and fetch your underpants.'

'I think I have.' She smiled. 'When I was in hospital having my tonsils out, Joe had to go and buy me a big box of Tampax, and the way he went on about it, you'd think I'd asked him to have a sex-change. And we were engaged!'

'Ah, so this husband of yours is the macho sort then?'

'No, of course not!' She hadn't ever thought of Joe as macho, and the notion seemed a bit silly, but perhaps there was an element of emphatic masculinity in there somewhere. Though at the moment it was coming out more like emphatic grumpiness.

She didn't mention it to Richard, of course, but she really couldn't figure out what was ailing Joe lately. He swore he wasn't ill; everyone thought the sun shone out of his bottom; and it couldn't be jealousy about her little chats with Richard, he wasn't that immature. Anyway, she'd been careful not to dwell on them, just in case.

'Are you sure he isn't?'

'Well, all men are a bit like that about women's things, aren't they?'

'No,' Richard replied simply. 'Some of us are adults.' Before she had a chance to protest that that wasn't very fair, he added, 'I've been meaning to tell you – I really appreciate it, you know. What you've done for me.'

'I haven't done anything!'

'Of course you have. You've wasted hours talking to me when you could've been doing something interesting.'

She coloured slightly. 'Rubbish!' she retorted. 'I've just been picking your brains, so I can steal all your best ideas and become a famous photographer.'

'That's what I like to hear. Just make sure you learn to get your sea straight first.'

A well-thumbed copy of the previous day's evening paper lay on the bed, next to the suitcase and half a bowl of wizened fruit. Emma flicked through the pictures with a newly critical eye: they were the usual mix of giant vegetables, Rotary dinners, weddings and people looking angry about something the council had done to the drains.

A headline drew her attention: MOTHER DEFIES COURTS. Underneath was a photo of a young woman and a child, standing in front of a block of flats. Swiftly she scanned the story.

'Someone you know?' enquired Richard.

'Not really. Just someone we treated in the department. Poor woman – first she gets intimidated for talking to the police about the local drug-dealers… And now she's too scared to testify, so the *Courant's* putting the boot in. What a lovely world we live in.'

'Sounds like she's had a rough deal,' sympathised Richard. 'Good picture though – see the composition? The focus of the picture is exactly where the eye wants it to be, on the little girl's face.'

Emma tutted. 'Don't you ever think about anything except getting a good picture?'

Their eyes met briefly. 'I try not to.'

'Why?'

He shrugged his broad shoulders. 'Because I made a promise to myself – no more complications in my life. Nowadays I go where I want, I do what inspires me, I try not to get too … involved … with what's going on around me.'

'Does that include people?'

'Oh, especially people.'

'I guess that's why you move around so much then?'

'Yeah – that and my restless feet. I get bored if I stay in one place for too long, plus I don't want to start feeling … well, tied.'

Emma put her head on one side. 'You know, Richard, I can't decide if that's really liberating or really sad.'

He folded his arms. 'Do I look sad?'

'Well … no,' she admitted. 'Bit battered though. I don't think you'll be riding any motorbikes any time soon.'

'Ha! You try and stop me.' He slapped his plaster cast. 'The

122

minute this comes off, I'll be down the bike shop for something big and noisy.'

'Maniac.'

'You only live once. Might as well do it properly.'

The big hand on the clock clunked triumphantly onto the twelve. Now it really was time to go. She pushed back her chair and stood up. 'Sorry to rush off, but I daren't be late again.'

They could have shaken hands, but that would have been too formal. And a hug or a kiss on the cheek somehow felt too intimate. So they just looked at each other.

'Right,' he said. 'OK then.'

'Fine.'

'It's been fun.'

'Yes.'

'I'll see you around.'

'You bet.'

She walked away swiftly, knowing that of course she would never see him again. This happened every time you built up a friendship with a patient; no matter how promising it might seem at the time, the minute it escaped from the protective hospital cocoon it inevitably withered and died.

But maybe that was for the best. After all, it wasn't as if Richard Claybourne was natural friend material. And she was a married woman . . .

The brand-new hypermarket was a great place to shop: a glittering white palace, stacked to the marble ceilings with imaginative ways to throw away your money. And Joe just loved his retail therapy.

Which was why Emma was so baffled. This evening, all he seemed to want to do was trudge round the store with the trolley, head down, hardly even glancing at the tempting displays.

She pointed out all the lovely gadgets: the PDAs and portable DVD players, and the giant electric train set that, normally, she would have had to drag him away from. But she might as well have offered him a choice of knitting patterns for all the interest he showed.

'What about these leather cushions?' she suggested in desperation. 'They'd go really well with the sofa.'

'What?' He raised his head briefly, shook it and went back to contemplating his toecaps. 'Nah.'

They moved on, through Ready-Made Curtains, Electrical Goods and Kitchenware, and finally hit the Food Hall. Ah, the curry section, thought Emma with relief: Joe's spiritual home. Surely he'd come alive at the prospect of unlimited lamb rogan josh.

'Wow, look,' she enthused, 'they've even got ras malai. And crispy dhosas with coconut chutney! Shall I get some?'

Joe sighed. 'Whatever you want. Let's just grab what we need and head home, shall we?'

Emma put the food in the trolley, but all the time she was looking at Joe, trying to work him out. 'Are you going to tell me, or do I have to guess?' she asked finally.

'Tell you what?'

'What's wrong with you.'

'There's nothing wrong with me!' He affected surprise, but Emma wasn't convinced. 'Well all right, maybe I'm a bit tired.' He yawned. 'You'd be tired if you had to drive all the miles I do.'

'Yes, maybe I would,' she conceded. 'But I've seen you tired before, and this is more than tired. Something's really got to you, hasn't it?'

'I don't know what you're talking about.'

'Of course you do. You've been really peculiar lately.'

'Peculiar!' At the sound of the word, several shoppers turned round in interest, and Joe dropped his voice to an annoyed stage whisper. 'What do you mean, peculiar?'

'Exactly what I said ... peculiar. All tense and distant. You don't want to talk about things any more, and when I snuggled up to you last night you rolled over and turned your back on me.'

He turned his back on her again. 'Don't talk rubbish. You're seeing things that aren't there.'

'Oh come on, Joe, give me some credit. Has somebody upset you at work? Please tell me.'

He laughed but there wasn't much humour in it. 'Upset me? I'm not five years old, Emma, thank you very much. I'm perfectly capable of fighting my own battles – not that there are any to fight!'

'I'm only asking because I care!'

'Because you're a nurse, more like.' He practically hurled a kilo of basmati rice into the trolley. 'There always has to be something wrong, doesn't there? If you're not kissing it better you're just not happy.'

That stung. 'That's bullshit and you know it!'

'Do I?' He started off down the aisle with the trolley and she pursued him with an armful of ready meals.

'It *is* work, isn't it?'

The trolley came to a halt, and Joe turned round to face her. 'Emma,' he said, quite coldly and deliberately, 'for the last time, there is nothing wrong at work, there is nothing wrong anywhere else, in short, there is nothing bloody wrong. Have you got that?'

'Yes, thank you.'

'Now, have you got any more stupid questions, or can we get to the checkout and go home?'

Much later that evening, Emma decided it was safe to pop her head round the door of the living room. Joe was lying sprawled across the sofa, watching *Groundhog Day* with the lights off.

Creeping in in her pyjamas, she perched on the arm of the sofa. 'Is this a private viewing, or can anybody join in?'

He looked up and smiled. 'No, they can't; but you can.' He swung his legs to the floor and patted the seat beside him. 'Hey, is that Monster Munch?'

She hid the bag behind her back. 'Might be. Want some?'

'Might do.'

'Then tell me what's wrong.'

His smile clouded. 'I told you, I'm just tired!'

'Really?'

'Really.' He slid his arm round her and snuggled her head against his shoulder. 'Hey, even you get tired and grumpy sometimes. Remember that time you'd done ten nights on the trot and that builder was rude to you? I thought we were going to have to call the fire brigade to get his head out of the bucket.'

She giggled at the memory. 'Well, maybe. So work's really OK then?'

'Work's great. They're really pleased with what I'm doing.' This time, he sounded as though he really meant it. 'Hey, and don't forget, there's a free luxury weekend in a country house to look forward to, courtesy of Sir Stanley. Four-poster beds, Jacuzzis ...'

'What's the catch?'

'There isn't one – not for you. All you have to do is lounge around while I'm being nice to boring people. Think you can handle that, Mrs Sheridan?'

'I'll give it my best shot.'

It was so comfy there on the sofa that they fell asleep halfway through the movie. By the time Emma woke up the DVD player had put itself on standby, and the room was almost completely dark, save for an occasional swish of light from the windows as a late-night car rolled past.

She looked at Joe, so peaceful there with his mouth hanging open and crumbs of Monster Munch down the front of his sweatshirt. He looked about fourteen, all tousled and carefree and dumb and completely lovable.

Maybe what he'd said was true, and there really wasn't anything wrong at work. If so, she ought to have been pleased. But deep down she felt sure he was keeping something from her. There *was* something bothering him, she was sure of it.

And if it's not work, she thought with a dull ache, there's only one other thing it could be.

It must be me.

And that, of course, was an utterly ludicrous thought. So why did it bother her so much?

'Mickey,' declared Emma, 'you make me sick!' Flopping belly-down on the bed, she kicked off her work shoes and made herself comfortable. Joe might be away at some meeting yet again, but at least she could enjoy a long girly chat.

'That's charming!' Mickey spluttered down the line from Hackney. 'Did you hear that, girls, Emma says I make her sick!'

A faint voice somewhere in the background replied, 'You do the same to us, love, but she doesn't have to eat your cooking.'

'Oh shaddup.' The sound of something being lobbed across the kitchen was followed by a squeal and then peals of laughter.

'Well, you do!' protested Emma. 'Just listen to you – up the duff, no bloke, living in a madhouse on a crappy NHS wage, and you sound like you've just won the Lottery. I bet you haven't even got morning sickness any more!'

Mickey guffawed. 'You bet wrong. I'm chucking up for Britain, as a matter of fact.'

Somebody grabbed the phone and shouted down it. 'You should hear her – it's like the soundtrack from *The Exorcist*.'

Emma grimaced. 'Thanks a lot, Sam, too much information.' She heard Mickey wrestle the receiver back amid much laughter. 'You still there?'

'Just about. I dunno, the youth of today . . .'

'So despite all this puking and constipation and varicose veins, you're still *smiling*?'

'Of course I am,' replied Mickey blithely.

'That's disgusting! What's wrong with you, you crazy woman?'

'I'm having a baby!' laughed Mickey, as though Emma had just asked the stupidest question in the world.

'You're asking me to believe it's really that great being pregnant?' marvelled Emma.

'It's definitely the best thing that's ever happened to me. Hey, did I tell you I'm having a scan next week – I can't wait to show you the pictures!'

'My God, you've changed your tune! Who was it said Hell was a ward full of screaming babies?'

'I know, don't remind me! I think I've been hormonally brainwashed, Em. I can't stop looking in babywear shops and buying little woolly bootees. To be honest, I've not stopped feeling excited since I found out I was pregnant.'

'Hmm,' said Emma, 'lucky you.'

'What's that? A note of jealousy?'

'Hardly. Disbelief, more like. If I was single and pregnant I'd be terrified. I mean, have you thought it all through? Where are you going to live? How are you going to support yourself? Who's going to look after the baby while you're out at work?'

Mickey came back with a smile in her voice. 'Stop worrying! Everything's going to be fine, Em, I know it is. OK, I didn't plan for this, but now it's happened I've just got this really good feeling that everything will work out for the best. Wait till it happens to you, you'll feel just the same way.'

'H'mm, well, I'm in no hurry to go forth and multiply, thanks, even if Joe is.' Emma twirled the phone cord round her finger. 'But I wouldn't mind feeling excited once in a while.'

'Em,' exclaimed Mickey, 'you've just got married to your dream man, you're living in a swanky apartment on the obscenely rich side of town . . . How can you *not* feel excited!'

'Let's just say it'd be a lot easier if Joe wasn't away all the time and I had some kind of social life.'

'But you've got a social life, haven't you?'

'Not any more. Unless you count Minette inviting me round for cosy evenings watching gardening videos. And as for friends . . .'

'Oh God, hark at you,' said Mickey. 'Little Emma No-Mates. What am I, bonehead, if I'm not a friend? Second thoughts, don't answer that.'

Emma reached out to the tin of toffees on the bedside table and popped one in her mouth. 'What you are is bloody miles away. And everybody in Cheltenham's either out clubbing every night, married with hordes of kids, or half-dead.'

'It can't be that bad, surely!'

'No? You try making friends when you're half of a couple but the other half's never there! All the married women think you're after their husbands, and all the single ones think you're boring because you're married.'

'What about the half-dead ones then?'

'I'm not quite ready for the Conservative Club yet, thanks very much.'

'Hmm,' mused Mickey. 'Sounds like what you *are* ready for is a nice decadent weekend in Hackney.'

'Wish I could,' sighed Emma, 'but one of the staff nurses is off sick at the moment, and it's practically impossible to get two days off in a row.' She didn't add that in any case Joe sulked if she wasn't in when he got home, because Mickey would simply have told her to let him sulk. Or that on one or two occasions she'd actually volunteered for extra hours, just for something to fill her time.

'All right then,' declared Mickey, 'if you're going to be *difficult* about it the mountain will just have to come to Mohammed.'

'What mountain?'

'Get your spare duvet out, kiddo, Fatwoman's coming to stay.'

The next time the lads came round, they had to send out for pizza.

'She does a cracking plate of chips, your Emma,' commented Rozzer wistfully. 'Nice and golden brown and crispy, and all fluffy in the middle. Where did you say she was?'

'On another late,' replied Joe, turning on the sports channel.

'I thought she was supposed to be working more civilised hours now,' said Gary.

'So did I,' replied Joe darkly. 'But the Blessed St Lawrence has only got to say he's short-staffed, and the next thing you know he's got her doing double shifts.'

'Bloody queers,' grunted Toby. 'Wouldn't let him lay a finger on me, I'm telling you.' Rozzer looked at him sharply. Joe looked embarrassed. Gary just went on catching peanuts in his teeth.

'Don't reckon he'd touch you with a bargepole, Tobe,' declared Joe. 'The man's got better taste.'

Gary sniggered.

'Oh ha ha, very droll,' said Toby. 'You know, I reckon you ought to be laying down a few ground rules. Face it, she's married now, she can't just bugger off doing whatever she wants whenever she wants.'

Joe looked doubtful. 'Well ... it's not as if I'm exactly home much myself at the moment,' he pointed out.

'All the same.'

'Don't you think you're being a bit unreasonable?' ventured Rozzer. 'I mean, she's entitled to her own life and all that, isn't she.'

Gary munched and swallowed. 'Oh my God, Rozzer's turning into a feminist. He'll be wearing a bra next.'

Everybody laughed except Rozzer.

'Ah well, I expect she'll be back by half-ten,' said Joe. 'Besides, she hates American football. We might as well make the most of it while we can, her friend's coming to stay next weekend.'

Gary's ears pricked up. 'Which friend? Hey, not the air hostess with the lovely bum?'

'No. Mickey.'

He pulled a face. 'The short, hairy one with the big mouth?'

'Oh yes. And guess what: she's pregnant as well.'

'Oh terrific,' grunted Toby. 'Why didn't you tell her she can't come?'

'This is Emma's home too,' Joe reminded him, at the same time reminding himself. 'Besides, she's not that bad and it's only for a couple of days. Now budge up Tobe, and stop hogging the margherita, you fat bastard.'

At half-time, when Toby and Rozzer were arguing the toss about line-outs, Joe went into the kitchen to fetch some more cans of beer from the fridge. As he turned round, he all but collided with Gary. 'Blimey mate, you made me jump.'

'I'm not surprised,' said Gary. 'It's because you're way too uptight. If you ask me, you need to chill out a bit more.'

Joe cracked open a can of lager. 'No, actually it's because I'm knackered,' he replied. 'It's called doing an eighty-hour week, because you're worried if you don't you'll lose a grip on your job.'

'Ah,' nodded Gary, 'I used to be like that, knackered all the time and barely coping. Now I can work eighteen hours straight and it doesn't bother me. So I might just be able to help you there.'

'How? I mean, short of a spare brain and two extra pairs of hands.'

Gary reached into his pocket and took out a small plastic bag. 'There you go mate. Enjoy.'

Joe glanced down at the round, white tablets. 'What are these?'

'Just something to pep you up, sharpen your wits.' He winked. 'And I bet Emma'll notice the difference too.'

Joe's mouth dropped open. 'I can't take these!'

Gary curled Joe's fingers over the packet. 'Don't be an idiot, mate, it's a rat race out there. Everybody else is doing it. Why should they have all the advantages?'

Emma walked up the steps of the public library, a new resolution in her step. Mickey was right: if she didn't have a social life she damned well ought to. So she'd made up her mind to acquire one before Mickey came to stay the following week.

It just so happened that all the local colleges and adult education centres had put up displays in the foyer, advertising their courses for the summer term. It wasn't hard for Emma to find what she was looking for: she'd read about it in *The Courant*. Nevertheless, she hesitated before she took a deep breath and walked across to the Hambrook Centre stand.

'Can I help you?' asked the lady on the stand, putting down a book on origami. She had long, grey hair almost to her waist and the biggest Navajo earrings Emma had ever seen.

'I'm ... er ... interested in the creative photography course. It is for complete beginners, isn't it? Only I don't know all that much and it's a long time since I had a decent camera.'

'I'm sure you'll have no problems at all. It's one of our most popular courses, you know – and last year we enrolled an old gentleman of ninety-seven who'd never taken a photo in his life.'

'Gosh,' said Emma, duly impressed. 'How did he get on?'

'Well, actually he turned out to be allergic to developer and we had to give him a refund, but nevertheless I'm sure he'd have done really well. And so will you.' The lady pushed up the sleeve of her enormous cable-knit sweater and stuck out a hand. 'Melanie Greenwood, I'm the course tutor.'

'Pleased to meet you.'

Ms Greenwood whisked an enrolment form out from under a stack of prospectuses. 'Now, would you like to enrol today?'

'Well ...' She thought about how difficult it would be to get the same two nights off every week, and how Joe would moan if she wasn't there to snuggle up to when he got home. And the humiliation when she turned out to be utterly crap at photography.

'There are only two places left. A couple of days more and they'll be taken.'

Emma slipped a hand into her jacket pocket and fingered the snapshot that Richard Claybourne had said was good. Had he really meant it? Had he – despite his protestations – just been polite? Oh sod it; what was the point of agonising?

'OK,' she said. 'How much is it, and where do I sign?'

Joe stood in the bathroom and looked at the little plastic packet in his hand. Four round white pills with smiley faces looked back at him, innocuous as happy aspirin. Gary's right, you're completely washed out, he reasoned: It's good of him to try and help. No it isn't! he reminded himself. Gary's an irresponsible idiot, and the sooner you flush these damn things away, the better.

One, two, three ... He watched them drop silently into the antiseptic blue waters of the toilet bowl. Just one more to go and he could forget about them.

You never know, he thought; if things get worse at work, if Sir Stanley keeps piling the pressure on and you really can't cope ... But no, he'd never actually *take* this crap, not in a million years.

All the same. Maybe as a kind of talisman, a just-in-case ...?

Flushing away the other three pills, he went back into the kitchen and dropped the last one into an old egg-cup at the very back of one of the cupboards. It was surprising how much better he felt.

16

Emma wriggled her arms into her denim jacket, peered out at the leaden sky and grabbed an umbrella. 'Are you sure you don't mind me going?'

Joe kissed her on the cheek, through a mouthful of sticky jam doughnut. 'Of course I don't.'

'Only I know you hate rattling around the flat on your own.' Go on Joe, she willed him. Beg me to stay home with you, then I won't have to go to the photography class and make an idiot of myself.

'No, you're right.' Joe wiped the jam off her cheek, reminding himself of the talking-to Rozzer had given him and the new leaf he'd resolved to turn over. 'I can't expect you to sit around waiting every night,' he said with a slightly forced smile, 'just on the off-chance I might get home before you're in bed. You go and enjoy yourself.'

'Well, if you're sure ...'

'Hey, you're not getting cold feet about this course, are you?'

'As if!'

'All right then, off you go.' He patted her lightly on the bum, nudging her towards the front door. 'And remember, I'm expecting you to have your own exhibition by next week.'

Emma saw him waving from the balcony as she got into her car and headed out of the centre of Cheltenham, still dogged by the heart-in-mouth feeling that she might be making a really stupid mistake. After all, you could hardly claim major artistic talent on the grounds that one person had vaguely liked one of your photos. And from what she'd seen of tutor Melanie Greenwood's work, there wasn't a wonky horizon in sight.

132

The Hambrook Centre stood on the south-eastern outskirts of the town, just where the suburbs petered out and became countryside. A large, redbrick building with a half-timbered upper storey, bits of the centre had originally formed part of a medieval banqueting hall – though its last incarnation had been as a second-hand furniture warehouse. One major restoration programme later, it now hosted everything from lacemaking classes to Tantric yoga, and the sign outside proclaimed: PROMOTING PERSONAL AND SPIRITUAL GROWTH THROUGH CREATIVITY, underneath a picture of a happy-looking yogi.

Two women in expensive exercise gear walked past as she was locking the car, engaged in animated conversation.

'Narinder says if I want to attain the highest levels of consciousness, I have to stop suppressing my hostility. But you can't just go round hitting people, can you?'

'Have you thought about the yogic flying workshop? Janice says it's done wonders for her hot flushes.'

'Really? Actually, I was thinking about kick boxing ...'

Hmm, thought Emma. I'm not sure about this; all I want to do is learn how to take a better photo. Still, you've paid your money, kid, so you'd better get in there and face the music.

To her relief, the bright, modern foyer was devoid of incense and people in saffron robes. Instead, a balding man in a woolly sweater and shapeless green cords was directing students like a traffic cop on point duty. 'Cooking for One? Upstairs, turn right, straight ahead. Sculpture? Through the double doors, ground floor of the annexe round the back. I'm sorry madam, I know we promote free expression, but you can't smoke that in here ...'

'The Creative Camera?' enquired Emma.

'Second floor, third door on the right past the toilets,' replied the man without pausing for breath. He turned aside. 'No sir, I'm afraid you've got the wrong night. Better Time Management is on Tuesdays ...'

Rather than cram into the tiny, crowded lift, Emma decided to take the stairs. At least running about at work kept her relatively fit. She was so intrigued by the snake mural that spiralled all the way up the stairwell that she stepped onto the second-floor landing without looking where she was going, and collided with a woman in a frumpy brown coat.

'Oh, sorry!' exclaimed Emma, deftly catching the woman's camera before it hit the ground and returning it to her.

'No, no, *I'm* sorry,' she insisted. 'My husband, Gerald, always says I'm in the wrong place at the wrong time.'

'I'm sure you're not.' Emma eyed up the camera: a fearsome, industrial-looking old thing festooned with spare lenses. It made her point-and-shoot APS look like a space-age toy. 'Beginners' photography?'

The woman nodded her mouse-coloured perm. 'You too? Oh, I am glad. I've been hanging around here for ages, wondering whether to go in or not. I mean, it'd be just like me to blunder into completely the wrong room ...'

'It does say "Creative Camera" on the door,' pointed out Emma. 'Come on, we can make fools of ourselves together.'

She pushed open the door and was confronted by a sudden, expectant hush as eight people stopped talking simultaneously and turned to stare at the newcomers.

'Nah, that's not her,' grunted a man in a Didcot Railway Museum sweatshirt, three sizes too small.

'Are you sure?' asked his neighbour, fiddling with the lens-cap on his Leica.

'Of course I'm sure, she signed my limited-edition print.'

'Where *is* she?' A woman strode up and down in front of the window, very dowager-duchess in her tweed skirt and twinset. 'It's nearly half past, and I was *assured* that Mrs Greenwood always starts on time. I have to get back and feed my dogs, you know!'

People shrugged and stared at their feet.

'Er, hello everyone,' said Emma, breaking the silence. 'I'm Emma Sheridan, and this is?'

'Treena Jones.' Her new companion smiled apologetically. 'It's short for Katrina, but my husband Gerald says that's too affected.'

'He says a lot of things, your Gerald,' observed Emma, who was already beginning to dislike him intensely.

'Oh yes,' beamed Treena. 'He's ever so clever. It was his idea for me to come on this course, you know. He says—'

Emma was about to learn another of the Thoughts of Chairman Gerald when the door opened and the bald man in the woolly jumper walked in.

The man in the overtight sweatshirt nudged Emma hard in the

ribs. 'That's Griff, the centre manager,' he informed her out of the corner of his mouth. 'I had him for Industrial Archaeology last year.'

With a clap of his hands, the man in the jumper summoned up attention. 'I'm afraid we had some bad news yesterday,' he announced. 'Mrs Greenwood won't be able to take this term's Creative Camera course after all.'

'What!' spluttered the woman by the window. 'But I've *paid*!'

'Yes, we realise that.' Griff nodded. 'But I'm afraid Melanie has been called over to America for a couple of months at short notice. *Force majeure*, as they say. A very prestigious residency.'

Everybody groaned. Aha, thought Emma: saved! I'm going to get out of here with a refund *and* my credibility intact.

'However,' he went on, 'I'm pleased to announce that we have managed to obtain the services of an excellent substitute.' Turning back to the door, he stepped out into the corridor. 'If you'd like to come in now, I'll introduce you to your students.'

A tall, spare, broad-shouldered shadow fell over the lecture room. The shadow of a man with a walking stick.

'Ladies and gentlemen,' the manager announced as he smiled for all he was worth, 'Naturally Mrs Greenwood is a great loss to the course, but it just so happens we've had a stroke of good fortune. An immensely talented and experienced photographer has just moved into the area, and as he's convalescing from a major accident, he's looking for a teaching post to tide him over until he's well enough to work in the field again.

'I do hope you'll join me in warmly welcoming Mr Richard Claybourne.'

'But you will still be leading the two-day weekend workshop on photographing wildflowers, won't you?' demanded Mrs Twinset and Tweeds.

'I think we might have to put that one on hold, Mrs Franks.' Richard lowered himself gingerly onto the edge of one of the desks, evidently still in some discomfort. 'Can you really see me crawling around the Cotswold uplands in this state?'

'But ... but we've *paid*!'

He shrugged his broad shoulders unconcernedly. 'I'm sure they'll give you a refund downstairs if you're not happy. 'Besides, wildflowers aren't really my speciality.'

'So what is then?' asked Lola, a husky-voiced blonde who could probably make a railway timetable sound suggestive.

Richard took in the semicircle of students with one sweep of his bright blue eyes. 'Cutting the crap,' he replied.

Several people giggled. Mrs Franks muttered, 'Well!' Emma couldn't take her eyes off Richard. 'What exactly do you mean by that?' she heard herself enquire. And for the first time since he had entered the room, they found themselves looking straight at each other. She half expected him to wink at her or make some witty comment, but he gave no sign of recognition.

He picked up the course programme and held it up for all to see. 'See this? "Self-actualisation through photo-montage"? Crap. "The photograph as mirror of the soul"? Crap. And what about this: "Painting with light"?'

'Crap?' ventured eager anorak Terrence, who was swiftly establishing himself as a would-be teacher's pet.

'You're catching on fast.' Richard put down the leaflet. 'Look, I'm not saying this whole course is no good, far from it. And from what I hear Mel Greenwood's a class act as a photographer. But you're rookies, not art-school students. What you need is *technique*. Right now, you couldn't self-actualise yourselves out of a paper bag.'

'But I've got a GCSE grade C!' protested a man in a suit.

'Congratulations.'

'So what are you saying?' asked Colin. 'You're going to give us a load of boring lectures about f-stops and focal length?'

'No, I'm going to give you a few *interesting* lectures, and then you're going to find out a load of stuff for yourselves; and by the end of this term's course you'll have a good enough grasp of the craft – because that's what it is – to go out and actually achieve some of the things you want to with it.'

'What sort of things?' asked Lola.

'Whatever inspires you. But until you know what you're doing, you'll just be messing about. Right, before we get down to finding out all about each other, I must give you your homework.'

Noses wrinkled. 'Homework? Already? We haven't even started!'

Richard hauled a large bag up off the floor and plonked it on the desk. Reaching in, he took something out and threw it at Colin.

'What's this?'

'Single-use, disposable camera. Thirty-six shots. Virtually idiot-proof. I want each of you to take one of these, go and point it at some things that sum up something about your life, and bring the prints in to Friday's session. Now, let's start with you, Emma.' You bastard! She thought. 'Why don't you tell us all what you're hoping to get out of this course?'

As Emma drove home, her head was whirling – and definitely not from the bottle of apple juice she'd had at the after-class drink.

As it turned out, she'd been quite glad of the camera class mob, and especially Treena, hanging on her arm like a nervous maiden aunt and monopolising all her attention. Otherwise she might have had to get into a conversation with Richard, and right now she felt dim-witted and far too tongue-tied to make sense. It had been bad enough in class, when he asked her why she liked photography, and she'd gone bright red and mumbled something pretentious about Ansel Adams, instead of admitting it was because she liked bringing out the shapes in things where nobody else could see them.

Mind you, she thought, at least I'm not Roger, only here because I can't get the nipples in focus on my 'glamour' shots, or – like poor Treena – because my husband won't let me anywhere near the family camera in case I break it.

'Poor Gerald,' Treena had lamented sadly.

'Why poor Gerald?' asked Emma. 'Why not poor you?'

'Because he has to put up with me ruining every photo I take! I'm all fingers and thumbs. Between you and me,' she confided over a small sweet sherry, 'I don't think he's quite forgiven me for cutting off the Bishop of Leicester's head.'

As she pulled into the car park at the apartment block, Emma glanced at the disposable camera sitting atop the dashboard. Stupid idea. Silly gimmick. Typical Richard. What was the point of it? And whatever would she take pictures of anyway?

Hey, probably she wouldn't even bother going back for the second session. But all the same, when she got out of the car she made sure to pocket the camera.

When she got back, Joe was draped across the bed and the whole flat smelt of cabbage.

'You're back!' enthused Joe, grabbing her by the hand and

137

pulling her down on top of him. 'I thought I was going to have to watch *When Fish Go Bad*. Did you learn loads?' he asked her through a big, hungry kiss.

'Only that some really strange people take photography classes. Oh, and the teacher's upped and left.'

'Already! You really must be a scary lot.'

'So they had to get a substitute.' She didn't mention who. 'I might not bother going back.'

'Coward!' Joe tickled her in the ribs and she dissolved into a giggling, squirming ball.

'Am not!'

'Are!'

She rolled out of his reach, gasping for breath. 'You only want me to go out so you can have the flat to yourself for your depraved orgies.'

'Damn, you guessed. So you'll go then?'

Emma whacked him with a cushion, and he retaliated with a copy of *TV Quick*. It was fun. They hadn't play-fought like this for ages; in fact she hadn't seen Joe so relaxed and happy since he started his new job.

She sniffed the air. 'What *have* you been eating? It smells like cabbage!'

Joe turned very slightly shifty. 'Er . . . yes.'

'But you hate cabbage!'

'Only sometimes,' he countered feebly.

'You mean, when *I* cook it?' The penny dropped. 'Oh, I get it – Minette's been round here again, hasn't she?'

'Actually, Mum did pop round with a bit of a snack. Liver and onions, three veg, and one of those big rice puddings she does. I was going to tell you . . .'

Emma scowled. 'So that's why you're in such a good mood! For God's sake Joe, when are you going to tell your mum she can't just "pop round" with food parcels whenever she likes?'

'Er . . .'

She took in his embarrassed expression. 'You told her, didn't you? You deliberately told her I was going to my class so she'd think, "Poor baby, he's going to starve to death." Well ta very much, I'm sure!'

'Aw, don't be annoyed,' wheedled Joe with a cabbage-scented burp. 'I saved you some rice pudding.'

Emma relented a little. It was, after all, very superior rice pudding. 'I should bloody well hope so!'

'And Mum brought something for you as well. It's in that box, over there.'

She followed his gaze to a large, round box by the wardrobe, resplendent in candy-pink stripes. 'It looks like a hatbox!'

'That's because there's a hat in it.'

A horrible thought entered Emma's head. 'Oh no, not ... not *the* hat. That awful grey one with the ostrich feathers?'

'Mum thought, seeing as we're going off on that posh country-house weekend, you'd want to look your best.'

Emma extracted the great, quivering mass of plumage from the box and plonked it on her head. 'Darling, if I wore this on a country estate, they'd think I was a pheasant and shoot me.'

'It's ... not that bad.'

They looked at each other and both burst out laughing. 'Oh yes it is!'

'Well all right, maybe it is, but it was a nice thought. Just tell her you wore it, she'll never know.'

Consigning the hat to its box, and the box to the top of the wardrobe, Emma kicked off her shoes and put on her comfy slippers. 'Did Mickey ring up to say what time she's arriving on Friday?'

'Oh, I don't know,' admitted Joe. 'Not that I noticed, but she might have called while I was on line. I haven't checked for messages.'

'God knows how you ever got to be a manager!' Emma went out to the phone in the hallway, dialled 1571 and, sure enough, there was a new message.

'Hi, it's me. Sorry but I can't come this weekend after all, something's come up. I'll be in touch. 'Bye.'

'Message from Mickey,' Emma called. 'She says she's not coming.'

Joe didn't actually grab his mum's hat and throw it into the air, but he might as well have done for the look of joy on his face. 'Not coming!' Joe swiftly covered for himself. 'Gosh, that's a pity.'

Emma stood in silence in the bedroom doorway. 'Something's wrong,' she said, shaking her head.

'Did she say so?'

'Not exactly. She just said "something's come up", and she'll be in touch.'

139

'There you are then.'

'What?'

'It'll be a new bloke, won't it? She's met some nutter who fancies short, hairy, pregnant women with attitude and she'd rather spend the weekend with him than with us. Which is just fine by me.'

Maybe he's right, pondered Emma. But as she replayed the message, she couldn't help noticing how flat Mickey's voice sounded; how different from the last time they spoke.

'I'd better just check she's OK.' Emma picked up the receiver and dialled Mickey's mobile.

'Well?' asked Joe.

'It's switched off, I got her voicemail.'

'For goodness sake stop fretting.' Joe patted the cushion next to him. 'Of course she's OK. She's probably looking forward to the same thing I am.'

'A weekend in bed with a good book?' enquired Emma with a smile.

'Not unless it's the *Kama Sutra*. He slid an exploratory hand underneath Emma's T-shirt. 'Darling, I don't suppose you can remember what we did with the rest of that chocolate body paint …?'

17

By the second session, the Creative Camera group had dwindled to eight; but Emma surprised herself by turning up dutifully on the dot of seven thirty, complete with her wallet of embarrassingly mundane photos.

'I know they're not very interesting, but I didn't know what else to take,' she explained as they were passed around the group.

'But you work in Casualty,' puzzled Roger.

'So?'

'So you've got it all there: blood, gore, human misery – God, I wish I had fantastic subject matter like that!' He made an imaginary frame with his fingers and thumbs and peered through it. 'I can picture it now: graphic scenes of birth, death, pain, degradation. You could make a whole exhibition out of that lot.'

'No thanks,' replied Emma firmly. 'I've no desire to be sued by my patients. Or lose my job.'

'You'll never be a success with that attitude,' sniffed Roger.

'I don't want to be a success, I just want to have fun and take a decent photo once in a while!'

'Quite right too.' Treena nodded approvingly. 'Everybody's so ruthless these days, they just don't care who they hurt, you know.'

Emma grabbed back the sheaf of prints, wiped off Roger's sticky fingermarks, and handed the photos to Richard. 'I suppose you'd better have these. Thirty-six pictures of our sofa.'

'Your sofa?' Richard raised an eyebrow. 'So that's what inspires you, is it?'

'Well ... not inspires, no. Obviously.'

'You said we can't take pictures of what inspires us until we know our arses from our elbows,' Lola reminded him sweetly.

141

'Oh, I think I could help you with that one, love,' leered Roger. 'The arse bit, anyway.' To his disappointment, Lola promptly got up and moved to another chair, putting Colin's wobbly bulk between them.

'Lola's right,' agreed Emma. 'You said just to take pictures of things that said something about our life, so that's what I did. And at the moment, my life revolves around that sofa.'

Kathleen Franks rolled her eyes. 'How can anybody's life revolve around a sofa?'

'Well, either my husband's flat out on it, fast asleep because he's just worked a fourteen-hour day, or it's empty and lonely-looking because he's in the *middle* of working a fourteen-hour day.' Emma folded her arms defensively. 'Anyhow, whatever. I did my best.'

'You did OK,' replied Richard. 'These are quite poignant really.'

'Poignant!' Suddenly Emma felt like the saddest of sad gits – which was ludicrous for a blissful newly-wed. 'They were supposed to be ... ironic. Or something.'

'Well at least they're all in focus, unlike ...' Richard held up a blurred picture of an Afghan hound. 'This.'

Mrs Franks tensed with righteous indignation. 'What was I supposed to do? Grand Champion Misty Rainmeadow III was wagging her tail in my face!'

'Which just goes to show that animal pictures are a bugger to get right. Best to start off with something that doesn't try to eat the camera, eh Colin?'

Colin's bullfrog torso swelled visibly at this hint of approbation. His pictures might not be imaginative, but the detail in them was so sharp it could have been excised with a scalpel. 'Ah well,' he sighed fondly, 'it's like I always say: you can't beat the sheer, architectural majesty of twin bogeys on a nineteen forties' steam locomotive.'

Roger sniggered something suggestive about twin bogeys, Lola told him to grow up, and Mrs Franks asked if somebody could please explain the joke.

'So, what do you think of my "Fat businessman on the toilet"?' asked Terrence eagerly.

'I think you're lucky you didn't get your face punched in,' replied Richard. 'And it's overexposed.'

142

'You can say that again!' guffawed Roger. 'Frozen assets or what?'

Terrence bristled. 'At least my photos weren't impounded by the chemist.'

Roger coloured. 'Only until the police have finished looking at them,' he protested. 'Just a formality, they said.'

Two hours later, Emma felt no nearer being a photographic genius, but at least she'd learned what single lens reflex meant. And that was a start.

'Are we all going down the pub then?' asked Terrence, scooping up the mysterious green shoebox that seemed to accompany him everywhere.

'Not tonight,' said Colin. 'Stuff to do.'

'Me too.' Roger rubbed his caterpillar-thin moustache. 'Ladies' night at the camera club tomorrow, got to clean my lenses.'

'Pubs really aren't my thing you know,' confided Mrs Franks. 'Besides, I have give Portia Tippytoes her bath, she's in the Two Years and Under Bitch class at Worcester on Sunday.'

Everybody else just sort of drifted away.

'Looks like just the three of us tonight then,' beamed Terrence, looking expectantly from Emma to Richard and back again. 'Nice and cosy. Where shall we go – the Black Boar?'

Emma was tempted to remember some pressing engagement, but abandoning Richard to Terrence would have been a pretty mean thing to do. So she let herself be crammed into a corner of the smelliest pub in town, slowly kippering in a haze of other people's cigarette smoke.

'It's great in here, isn't it?' enthused Terrence, clutching a half of shandy in one hand and his shoebox in the other. 'So much ... atmosphere.'

Emma and Richard exchanged looks, and she struggled to keep a straight face as his right eyebrow made a break for his hairline. 'Well there's certainly a lot of it,' she managed to say, coughing discreetly into her dry white wine.

'Well, well,' said Richard, eyes fixed on Emma. 'Fancy you being in my class.'

'Fancy you being my teacher.'

'Do you two know each other then?' asked Terrence.

'I didn't expect to see you again,' Richard went on, completely ignoring Terrence's interjection. 'At least, not so soon.'

143

She smiled. 'That was my line.'

'Really glad I have though.'

That pleased Emma more than perhaps it ought to have done. 'Funny,' she remarked, 'it was quite a shock seeing you somewhere other than in a hospital bed. It's like ... like people exist in one place and only in that place.'

'Yeah, we have a habit of pigeonholing people. So when you see them somewhere different it really throws you. Like they've broken the rules or something.'

'Mm.' she nodded eagerly. 'That's it, exactly.'

Richard ripped open a packet of peanuts and offered her one. 'Are you enjoying the course so far?'

'Oh yes, I'll say,' replied Terrence.

'Glad to hear it,' said Richard. 'But what about you, Emma?'

'Well ... I think so. Yes.'

'Only I noticed you were a bit quiet tonight, and I wondered—'

Terrence leaned forward, his head completely obstructing Richard's view of Emma. 'I bet you're wondering about *this* too, aren't you?'

Emma and Richard both stared at Terrence. 'What?'

'This. My box!' He laid it reverentially on the table top. 'Everybody does.'

'That's nice,' said Richard. 'So anyway, Emma, I was wondering if there was anything wrong.'

'You can ask me what's inside it if you like,' hinted Terrence.

'Oh. Right. I'll bear that in mind.'

'Of course, I won't tell you. Because it's a secret.'

Emma could see a fat vein beginning to pulse on Richard's normally smooth temple. 'Fine, then I won't bother asking.'

'But I suppose if you were to ask me very nicely ...'

Momentarily, Emma had the distinct impression that Richard – crocked body or not – was going to pick up Terrence, and his cardboard box, and drop-kick them straight out of the nearest window. But in the event he merely ran a finger around the inside of his shirt collar, as though it had suddenly grown too tight.

'Terrence, if you don't mind I'm a bit tired just now. And I was in the middle of asking Emma a question. So if you could just shut up for two seconds ...'

144

'Oh,' said Terrence, the wind temporarily taken out of his sails. 'Well, pardon me for breathing.'

'Nothing's wrong,' said Emma in the short silence that ensued. 'If that was what you were trying to ask me.'

'Are you sure? You look a bit drained, that's all. Like there's something on your mind.'

'No, not really. Well ... nothing much. It's just that a friend of mine was supposed to be coming to stay for the weekend, and she cried off suddenly without telling me the reason. And I'm not sure why, but I've got this really bad feeling about it.'

'Bad? What sort of bad?'

'I don't know.' She felt a bit silly now. 'I'm just sure there's something wrong.'

Joe arrived home about five minutes after Emma, and found her hanging on the telephone in the hall.

'Hi honey, I'm home!' He slung his briefcase into the corner and planted a huge smooch on her cheek.

She put a hand over the receiver. 'Good day?'

'Knackering. I need food, beer, and a cuddle, not necessarily in that order.'

'Be right with you, I just need to speak to Mickey and check she's OK.' A voice came on the other end of the line. 'Mickey? Mickey, is that you?'

'Mickey's in her room, Em.' It was Sam.

'Oh, OK, could you run up and get her for me?'

There was a short pause. 'Actually what I meant was, she's in her room with the door locked, and she won't come out.'

'What! Why?'

'Search me. She came home from work, didn't say a word to anyone, and just vanished upstairs. We've tried talking to her through the door, but she just tells us to go away.'

'So what are you going to do?'

'Do? What can we do? Wait till she comes out, I suppose.'

'Oh my God,' said Emma as she replaced the phone on its hook.

Joe emerged from the kitchen, a can of beer in his hand. 'Go on, what's she done now?'

'Locked herself in her room, and won't come out.'

'Good grief – how old is this woman? Twenty-six going on fourteen?'

'Don't, Joe, this is serious. I'm really worried about her.'

Joe sighed, slipped an arm through Emma's and led her gently but firmly towards the sofa. 'Sit.'

'But—'

'Sit. Take off shoes. Submit to foot massage. Doctor's orders.'

She flopped down into the squishy white leather. 'But you're not a doctor.'

'Yes I am, I'm a doctor of luurve-ology.' He set to massaging her feet. 'How's that? Is it de-stressing you yet?'

'It's lovely,' she admitted, 'but you're not going to stop me worrying about Mickey. There's something really wrong, I know there is.'

'No there isn't, she's just being ... hormonal. You're a nurse, you know how weird pregnant women can get. Remember that one you told me about who suddenly took up shoplifting?'

'That's hardly reassuring!' pointed out Emma. 'Besides, Mickey's not like that. She's never been the hormonal type. And she was so bubbly and happy last time I spoke to her – looking forward to her scan, and going off to look at a cot, and all that mumsy stuff.'

Joe worked assiduously on Emma's little toe. 'You do realise this is supposed to be your pleasure zone, don't you?'

'Hmm, so?'

'So start melting with ecstasy, you hard-hearted hussy! Look, I expect Mickey's just having an off-day – maybe she's feeling fat and frumpy, and having second thoughts about being a single mother. Perhaps she's actually wised up at last. It won't be easy being on her own, will it?'

'No, I suppose not,' conceded Emma. But in her heart of hearts, she knew that couldn't be the whole answer.

The conversation she'd had in the Black Boar lingered on in Emma's mind. After Terrence and his shoebox gave up and left, Richard had given her plenty of food for thought. Issued her with a challenge, even: 'If you're really that bothered about your friend, then prove it. Get off your backside and do something about it.'

It had seemed harsh at the time, rude even – after all, she hardly knew him, what business was it of his to tell her what to do? But the more Emma thought about it the more she started seeing sense in what he'd said. Claiming to be worried about someone was easy; it cost nothing and it salved your conscience. Proving it meant actually putting yourself out.

And when she rang the house and Pheebs told her that Mickey was still locked in her room, Emma knew the time had come to prove that she cared.

She phoned Joe at work, in the gap between a nosebleed and a sprained ankle.

'I've had a word with Lawrence,' she told Joe. 'And he's rearranged my off-duty so I can have the whole weekend off.'

'That's brilliant!' exclaimed Joe. 'Didn't I always say he was a top bloke really? How on earth did you get round him?'

'Oh, he was really good about it when I explained about Mickey.'

There was a short pause at Joe's end of the line. 'What's Mickey got to do with you having the weekend off? It's not as if she's coming to stay.'

Emma took a deep breath. 'No. I'm going down to Hackney.'

'What!'

'Just till Sunday night.'

'The hell you are!' He moderated his initial anger. 'Oh come on, Em, how often is it you get a whole weekend off? Don't you want to spend it with me?'

Oh Joe, please don't be like this, Emma pleaded silently. Don't you think I feel guilty enough already? 'I'm really sorry, Joe,' she said, 'but I have to. Mickey's my best mate.'

'And I'm your husband. Or doesn't that count for anything?' The hurt in his voice really stung, but she'd burned her bridges now and she'd just have to live with the consequences. Besides, they were both grown-ups, and there would be lots of other weekends; he'd soon get over it.

'Of course it does! And I'd much rather spend the time with you. But if I don't find out what's going on I'm just going to keep on worrying, and that'd spoil the weekend for us anyway.'

'So. You're going then.'

'Yes, straight after work. I'm just going to pop home for an overnight bag and then hit the road.'

'No matter what I say?'

'Please, Joe …'

'Fine. Guess I'll be seeing you, then.'

And with those parting words, he put the phone down on her.

18

It was late evening by the time Emma managed to battle her way through the London traffic and reach the house in Hackney. Ah well, at least she'd managed to contact Sam on the way down, so with a bit of luck there'd be a warm bed and a cup of tea waiting for her.

Magenta Street looked almost attractive in the dark. For one thing, you couldn't make out the graffiti, or the bullet-hole above the door of the offie, and the sulphur-yellow light from the street lamps cast a soft, romantic haze over the burned-out Astra by the halal fried-chicken shop.

A wave of nostalgia washed over Emma as she headed up the front path, reached for the key she'd still not got round to returning, and turned it in the lock.

'Hiya – anybody home?' She took a couple of steps into the hall and closed the front door behind her. 'Mickey?' She paused. 'Sam?'

Nobody answered. Everything seemed unnaturally quiet and still; but then it was Friday night. Only the very, very sad and the exceptionally married stayed at home on a Friday night. Which probably meant that all the girls – Mickey included – had piled off down to some pub or club, leaving her to twiddle her thumbs and reflect on a wasted journey.

The lights were on in the kitchen, so she gravitated towards the kettle and threw her coat and bag onto the table. Propped up against the Betty Boop cookie jar was the cardboard insert out of a pair of tights. On it was scrawled, in Sam's handwriting: *She's still in there, best of luck. Jammie Dodgers in jar, you're on the sofa tonight, Sam.*

Still in there? Emma found herself gazing up at the ceiling, as though she could see right through the plaster and joists and floor-boards, and into Mickey's thoughts. Time to find out exactly what was going on. She headed for the stairs, got halfway there and went back for the cookie jar. Mickey might not be hungry, but she sure as heck was.

'Just go away,' repeated the voice from the other side of the door. 'Please.'

It was the P-word that really put the wind up Emma. Mickey never said 'please' – 'sod off' was much more her style. And her disembodied voice sounded so flat and weedy, even allowing for an inch and a half of solid Victorian pine.

'I'm not going anywhere,' declared Emma, plonking herself down on the multicoloured landing carpet outside Mickey's room. 'Not until you open this door and let me in.'

'You'll have a long wait then.'

Emma eyed up her gargantuan supply of biscuits. 'Fine.'

'Whatever.'

Emma ate another biscuit, thinking what tack to take. 'Everybody's worried about you, you know.'

'I don't want people to be worried about me, I just want you all to leave me alone.'

'Sorry, no can do. Or at least, not unless you do a deal with me.'

There was a short silence, then: 'What deal?'

'Come out here and prove you're OK, and then I promise I'll go away. If you still want me to.'

This time, the silence lasted a lot longer. 'I just want to be alone, Em, *please*.'

That word again. Emma crawled closer to the door, pressing her cheek hard against the wood as if that would somehow force Mickey into connecting with her. 'Something's wrong, Mickey, I know it is. Don't try to push me away, we're supposed to be mates.'

'We *are* mates. And I'm not pushing you away, I just ... can't. OK?'

'Whatever it is it can't be that bad, surely,' coaxed Emma. 'Just tell me.'

When Mickey's reply came, it was in a tiny, faraway, half-choked voice. 'Emma, don't make me. Please don't make me.'

Knees drawn up, Emma hugged herself into a little ball of concern. 'Why, Mickey? Why?' Her throat tense, she uttered the words she'd been dreading saying. 'This is something to do with the baby, isn't it?'

A tiny, stifled sound that might have been a sob came from inside the room. 'Emma. Don't.'

The cold, dark waters that had been lapping at the distant edges of Emma's mind began to creep in closer, like a chill winter's tide. 'You can't stay in there forever. Sooner or later you're going to have to come out and tell someone about this.'

Silence ticked away, to the racing heartbeat of techno music coming through the wall from the house next door. Emma wondered what she was going to do next. Short of fetching an axe and chopping down the door, she was pretty short on options.

Then she heard the bolt on the inside of the door draw slowly back. And the door opened.

Mickey was in jeans and a crumpled T-shirt, her hair hanging in lank spirals on either side of her white face. Her eyes were red-rimmed and puffy, and she looked as if she hadn't slept for a week.

'Oh Mickey,' gasped Emma, 'you look terrible.'

A wan smile twitched the corners of Mickey's mouth. 'Thanks.'

Emma seized her by her cold, limp hands. 'Tell me what's going on,' she begged. 'Tell me what's wrong with the baby. Was there something wrong on the scan?'

A single, fat bead of moisture welled up and spilled from Mickey's eyelid, plummeting down her cheek. She raised her head and looked Emma straight in the eyes.

'There is no baby,' she whispered.

'What!'

'Well, there might as well not be.'

They sat side by side on Mickey's bed, arms round each other for comfort; Emma too shocked to cry.

'No,' she said, again and again, 'of course it's not your fault. Of course it's not. How can you think that?'

Mickey's face was glossy with silent tears. 'It must be,' she said. 'Who else's?'

Emma seized her by the shoulders. 'It's nobody's fault, Mickey. Stop blaming yourself, you're a nurse; you know these things happen. You've seen them happen dozens of times.'

'But not to me,' replied Mickey quietly. She sniffed and swallowed a throatful of salt water. 'Anencephaly. Makes it sound just like flu, or verrucas or something, doesn't it? But my baby doesn't have a brain, Em. She's just an empty shell inside me. And I want to know why, I *have to* know why ...'

Emma hugged her tightly and rocked her like a child. 'I know Mickey, I know. But sometimes there aren't any answers.'

'It feels like I'm being punished.'

'But you're not. You know that really, don't you?'

Mickey met her gaze, defied it for a long moment, then nodded. 'But a termination, Emma. I don't know how I'm going to get through it. I don't care if it's only an empty body, it's alive inside me and I'm letting them take it away.'

'You'll get through it because you're strong,' Emma assured her, gently stroking her cheek. 'The strongest person I know. And besides, you do realise I'm coming to the hospital with you on Monday?'

Mickey wiped the back of her hand across her eyes. 'You can't stay here with me, Em, you've got a job to go back to. And what about Joe?'

'Joe knows where the microwave is, and as for the job, Lawrence will understand. He'll have to. 'Cause if you think I'm letting you set foot in that hospital without me, you've got another think coming.'

Joe was not a happy bunny.

As if it wasn't bad enough being abandoned by your wife in favour of a wire-haired leprechaun, the DVD player had jammed and now refused to play anything but the same five seconds of *Terminator 2*, over and over again.

When the phone rang, he very nearly didn't bother answering it. Much as he loved his mother (and her roast dinners), he really wasn't in the mood for one of her 'nice cosy chats'. On the other hand, he didn't much fancy her turning up on the doorstep because he hadn't answered the phone and she was worried about him. So his nerve went after the first couple of rings.

'Hmm?'

'That you, Joe?' It was unmistakably Gary on the line, six-foot-one of spring-loaded testosterone. 'Hope you're ready big boy, 'cause we'll be round in ten minutes.'

Joe wrinkled his brow. 'Ready? Ready for what?'

'D'you hear that, lads? He says what for!' The sound of general hilarity came crackling down the line. 'To party, what else!'

'Oh,' said Joe, belatedly remembering something about Gary's cousin's best mate's stag do, and some rash comment he'd made weeks ago. 'Actually, I'm not really in the mood.'

'Then you *definitely* need to party, mate. Nothing like free beer and a couple of dog-rough strippers to get your pecker up, know what I mean?' He laughed dirtily. 'Hey, the little woman's not acting up is she? Trying to lay down the law? 'Cause if she is—'

'Emma? Don't be stupid, of course not.' There was a knot of something between dejection and anger stuck, like a discarded Polo mint, at the back of Joe's throat. 'Matter of fact she's not here. She's gone away for the weekend. But look, I don't really think I want to go out.'

Gary was not a man to let a little thing like total lack of interest stand in his way. 'So the cat's away? Wa-hey! Sorted. Right man, get your clubbing shirt on, it's about time we took you out on the town and reminded you what it's like to have a good time.'

Mickey lay on her back on the bedroom carpet, staring up at the glow-in-the-dark stars she'd stuck on the royal-blue ceiling. 'They're back,' she commented at the sound of a key turning in the lock on the front door.

'It's OK, I'll talk to them.' Emma reached out and squeezed her hand. She got to her feet. 'You're sure you want me to?'

Mickey nodded. 'Yes, I want them to know, but I ... I just don't think I could tell them myself. That's how I ended up in here in the first place, I just didn't know what to say. And the thought of the looks on their faces ...'

'I'll go and do it now,' promised Emma, reaching into her bag for her mobile. 'I'll just give Joe another try first.'

She dialled up the flat and waited. Waited. Waited some more. But there was no reply, just the annoying sound of own voice, telling her to 'leave a message and we'll get back to you'. So she rang off.

'He must be working late again,' she said, 'with me being away.' And for a split second she felt a pang of guilt, imagining him coming home to an empty flat and a TV dinner. Then she remembered how downright unreasonable he'd been, and it vanished as quickly as it had appeared.

She could have tried him on his mobile, but she didn't. If he wanted to sulk at work and imagine her living it up in the London fleshpots, then fine. Let him. Right now, there were more important things than Joe.

Left to his own devices, Joe wouldn't have had anything to do with Justin or Jason or whatever his name was's stag night, but even he had to concede that the lad knew how to party. Free beer, kebabs all round, even a WPC strippergram with an aerosol can of whipped cream.

By the time they reached the third or fourth pub (Joe had lost count after his fifth pint) Gary was wired and crazy, and Toby rattling off dirty jokes like they were going out of fashion. Even Rozzer was having fun in his own way, belly-dancing round the pub in an enormous bra and pink tutu. The only fly in the ointment was Joe.

'For God's sake cheer up,' urged Toby, tipping a double whisky into Joe's beer. 'Go on, drink it down, it'll put a bit of lead in your pencil.'

With a heavy heart, Joe glugged down a good half-pint. 'She just upped and went,' he said. 'She did, you know. Didn't matter what I said.'

Gary wagged a finger in Joe's face. 'You didn't ought to have let her. Should show her who's boss. They like a bit of discipline, you know.'

Joe took another gulp of whisky-flavoured beer, and contemplated the sticky marks on the bar counter as they moved queasily in and out of focus. '"I'm going," she says. Just that. "I'm going, deal with it." No "do you mind" or anything.'

'It's not right,' said Toby, burping into the sleeve of his purple satin shirt.

'No,' said Joe morosely. 'It's not right at all.' All at once he didn't feel angry any more, just immensely depressed. How long had they been married? A few scant months. And already Emma would rather spend time anywhere else but with him.

The young woman had been sitting alone at a corner table for well over an hour, sipping occasionally from a glass of red wine but mostly just drawing doodles on a beer mat.

She'd come to the Prince of Denmark for a bit of peace and anonymity; a refuge from work and life, and a place to sort out her thoughts. Normally it was a bit on the quiet side as pubs went, the kind of dive where old men congregated to talk about pigeons. But she hadn't reckoned with an invasion of stag-night revellers. Or the fact that one of those revellers was Joe Sheridan.

She was gladder than ever that she'd hidden herself away in the corner. Joe she might have coped with, but definitely not his boozed-up mates.

Looked like she'd just have to sit tight and wait for them to move on.

'Didn't I tell you?' said Gary. 'Never should've got married, my son. Biggest mistake of your life. Should've stayed fancy-free like me.'

Joe gazed into the depths of his pint glass and saw a dark, bottomless pit. Gary's words had taken root in his brain, and a terrible, twisted reasoning was at work in there. 'She doesn't love me any more,' he said bleakly.

Gary cupped a hand to his ear, straining to hear over the noise. 'What?'

Slowly and deliberately placing his glass on the counter, Joe rose unsteadily to his feet. 'Listen.' Nobody took any notice, so he thumped on the counter with his fist until they did. 'Got an announcement to make. GOT AN ANNOUNCEMENT TO MAKE.'

The ribald laughter subsided.

Joe swayed, steadied himself against the bar and assembled the jumbled words in his mind into some sort of order. 'My wife. You listening? She doesn't love me any more. Got that? SHE DOESN'T FUCKING LOVE ME.' From the looks on their blurred faces it was pretty clear that they had. 'Is that fucking sad or what?' Seizing his glass he raised it in an ironic toast. 'To the groom. See sense before it's too late, man.'

There was an uneasy silence. Then Gary laughed and swigged from his bottle of Red Square. 'I'll drink to that.'

Sitting in her corner, Zara just stared open-mouthed, and wondered if what Joe had just said might possibly be true.

19

Bright and early the next morning, spring sunshine hacked its way through the gap in the bedroom curtains, raced across the duvet and lasered its way through Joe's fragile eyelids.

'Oh God, no,' he moaned, as he rolled over and the nauseous throb of pain hit him with gleeful force. 'Squeaky … Squeaky, what the hell's wrong with me?'

Arm flailing, he patted the empty pillow beside him. And then he remembered. Or at least, half-remembered. And what he did recall made him wince even more than the thunderous pain in his head.

Exactly how much he'd had to drink the previous night, he couldn't say; but there'd definitely been an awful lot of it and it showed. He just about remembered the lads forcibly marching him down to the Bear & Billet, pouring a few jars down him at the Royal Oak and then the four of them moving on to some other pub … but the rest of the evening was little more than a hopelessly blurred home movie, punctuated with lurid Technicolor stills.

He sat up in bed, agonisingly slowly, one hand clamped to the side of his head in case it parted company with the rest of his skull and fell off. A horrible, uneasy feeling bubbled like molten lava in the pit of his stomach – and not just because he'd stripped off its lining with a mixture of cheap whisky and kebabs.

I'm sure I did something, he told himself, struggling – and failing – to dredge it up out of his memory. Something I really shouldn't have done. But what the hell was it?

Even after forcing down a bacon butty and promptly throwing it up, Joe felt little better. It didn't help that Emma wasn't there to tut at him and fill a tea towel with ice cubes for his head. He hadn't felt so alone since his first day at infants' school. He'd thrown up then, too.

He tried turning on the TV, but the Saturday-morning cartoons hurt his bloodshot eyes. Maybe he should ring Emma? But if he did that, she'd probably accuse him of checking up on her or something; besides, he had a nagging conviction that whatever he'd done the previous evening had had something to do with her.

In the end, he dragged his throbbing carcass to the phone and rang the only person he trusted to give him a straight answer.

'Rozzer?' The phone kept on ringing. 'Pick up the phone, Rozzer, I know you're there.'

Just as the answering machine message was coming to an end, Rozzer answered. 'Oh, it's you. So you're not dead then?'

'I wish I bloody was. How much did I drink last night?'

There was a short but discernible pause. 'Too much.'

'Thanks, I worked that one out for myself. Listen, you've got to tell me: was I really embarrassing?'

Rozzer cleared his throat nervously. 'Don't you remember?'

'Would I be asking you if I did? Rozzer, I want you to answer me a question – and be honest.'

'Oh,' said Rozzer unenthusiastically.

'Did I do something I might regret? Yes or no?'

This time the pause was so large you could have slotted an elephant into it. A fat elephant. 'That depends,' Rozzer said eventually.

'Depends? What the hell is "depends" supposed to mean!"
He groaned. 'It means I did, doesn't it?'

Rozzer was audibly getting more and more uncomfortable. 'Look mate, you were drunk, probably best to forget about it.'

'How can I forget about something I can't remember?' pointed out Joe, who was feeling increasingly edgy.

'You don't want to, mate, trust me.'

'Just tell me what the hell I did!' yelled Joe in frustration, and immediately wishing he hadn't. 'Or I'm coming right round and ripping your head off.'

'All right,' sighed Rozzer. 'You ... said some stuff. Loudly. In the middle of the Prince of Denmark.'

'Stuff? What kind of stuff? Stuff as in, "Let me buy you all a pint", or stuff as in "I'm a gay necrophiliac and I fancy your dad"?'

157

'Worse.'

'Shit. How much worse?'

Rozzer swallowed hard. 'Stuff . . . about Emma.'

The words fell on Joe like a concrete avalanche. His hand tightened around the telephone receiver. 'Go on,' he said, his head beginning to spin. 'Tell me the gory details.'

'Believe me, you don't—'

'Just tell me.'

And Rozzer did. When the grisly tale was done, Joe sat down in the middle of the hall floor and wondered how – even drunk – he could have turned into such a total tosser. Not to mention what was going to happen if one of his so-called mates ever told Emma what he'd said about her.

Rozzer put down the phone and went off to get ready for another tedious Saturday in the betting shop.

Not that it was work that was bothering him. The burden of friendship was getting increasingly heavy to bear, and – for all that he'd been Joe's faithful sidekick ever since they were in their prams – he was starting to see his best mate in ways he really didn't want to.

The worst bit was seeing himself mirrored in Joe. Not Rozzer as he was now, Rozzer as he'd been at nineteen: stupid and callous and taking everything for granted. Now, every time he saw Joe carping at Emma, it reminded him of the way he'd treated Maxine. And at least he'd had the feeble excuse of being just a stupid kid; what was Joe's excuse?

Joe, he said to himself as he donned his horrible polyester uniform blazer, you'd better wise up your act and make it snappy. Otherwise, you might just end up like me.

And I wouldn't wish that on anybody.

Joe fell asleep again, and didn't wake up till the middle of the afternoon, with a tongue like old carpet and breath fit to strip the paint off doors. Still, at least his head had stopped thumping; but that was a mixed blessing, since it enabled him to concentrate on his own idiotic behaviour.

Picking his robe up off the bedroom floor, he struggled into it and dragged his aching body to the bathroom. It was only on the way back that he noticed the light flashing on the answering machine.

158

'Joe? Joe are you there?' His heart beat faster; it was Emma. 'Oh. Well, I suppose you must be at work again. Look, I'm really sorry about Friday, but I was right ... it's terrible, Mickey's ... well let's just say she's lost the baby and she's really suffering. I can't go into details on the phone, but I'll tell you about it when I get back. I'm staying on an extra day. Back Monday night all being well, there are sausages in the freezer, 'bye.' There was a long gap, and then, 'Love you.'

Oh God, thought Joe. Poor Mickey. He picked up the phone and got halfway through dialling Emma's mobile, then chickened out. Just hearing her voice on the answering machine made him feel guilty. What was it going to be like when she fetched up on the doorstep?

Minette hummed to herself as she swabbed the dog's bottom with an antiseptic telephone wipe. He didn't like it much, in fact he'd probably go and hide under the sideboard for the rest of the day, but that was just too bad. In her daily war against microbes, Minette took no prisoners.

Once the offending sphincter was squeaky-clean, she released the yelping bundle, snapped off her disposable gloves and dropped them into the kitchen bin with a sigh of satisfaction. If the Angel of Death chose to take her right there and then, she mused, he wouldn't find any bits of fluff behind *her* cooker.

She was so engrossed in dusting the bottles in her store cupboard that she didn't hear the doorbell. In fact it wasn't until Alan came in through the back door, dishevelled and muddy from the garden, that she gave a thought to the outside world.

'Feet!' she squeaked, pointing at Alan's mud-caked wellies.

'But—'

She swiped the newspaper from his hand. 'For goodness' sake stand on the *Daily Telegraph*. I've only just washed those tiles you know!'

A second head appeared in the doorway. 'Hello, Mum.'

Minette's eyes widened. 'Joe! What on earth's happened?'

For a fleeting second she thought she caught a furtive expression sneaking across her favourite son's face; then it was gone and she told herself it was probably only wind from all that unhealthy food he ate.

159

'Nothing's happened! I just thought I'd pop round and see my favourite mum. Shall I go away again?'

'You most certainly will not!' replied Minette. 'Come in and sit down and I'll put the kettle on.'

'What about me?' enquired Alan.

'You can sit down when you've taken off those horrible trousers.'

'I can't take my trousers off in the doorway, woman, the neighbours'll see!'

'Then go and take them off in the garage, and come in through the side door. Oh – and don't forget to take your boots off first.'

'I guess I'd better take my shoes off too,' said Joe, bending to undo the laces. But Minette turned to her son with an indulgent smile.

'Don't you worry about those, darling, they're not that dirty and anyway, I can wipe the floor later. Now, come in and tell me all about everything. Where's Emma? Gone off to work and left you all on your own again?'

'Er, no. She's in London.'

'London!' The look on Minette's face made it amply clear that such behaviour could not be acceptable in a dutiful spouse. London was, after all, The Fount of All Vice. 'When she could be spending the time with you? Oh dear darling, you really will have to have a little chat with your wife.'

'Actually, I think there's a bit of a crisis down there,' Joe cut in. 'Her friend Mickey—'

'I don't care what goings-on there are,' replied Minette firmly. 'Family's family and once a girl's married she can't go on just doing what she pleases. Still,' she sighed, 'I expect she'll come round in the end, once the little ones come along.' She took Joe's hands and looked him up and down. 'You're looking peaky,' she observed.

I'm feeling peaky, thought Joe. Peakier than you can possibly guess. But he smiled, and protested: 'I'm fine.'

'Hmm, well, you don't look it. Here,' Minette rummaged in one of the kitchen drawers and took out a bottle of multivitamins, 'take two of these, I'm sure you've got a deficiency. Is she feeding you plenty of broccoli, like I told her to?'

'Loads,' Joe assured her. 'And cabbage.'

Minette shook her head. 'You always were a terrible liar.' She

160

smiled, pinching his cheek so hard it went pink. 'But that's my Joe all over. Such an honest little boy you were. Always standing up for what was right, and saying what you really thought. We were so proud of you.'

Joe returned her smile weakly, reflecting on the fact that standing up and saying what he thought had not stood him in very good stead the night before. Particularly since what he'd said was a load of old drink-sodden rubbish. And as for being proud of himself . . .

'Don't embarrass the boy,' grunted Alan, sidling into the kitchen in his underpants, muddy trousers neatly folded over his arm. 'Now, do I get a cup of tea or what?'

'Go and cover yourself up and I'll think about it,' replied Minette, reaching her caddy of Special Tea down from its cabinet. She rattled on as she spooned tea into the pot. 'Now Joe, dear, which would you rather have: scones or gingerbread? I made them fresh today. You look like you could do with feeding up. Have you been overworking again?'

'I'll only be a minute, Mum, just going to have a quick word with Dad.' Minette was so engrossed that she probably didn't even notice him slip out after his father and follow him upstairs into the spare bedroom. He found him rummaging through the contents of an overstuffed bin liner.

'Bloody women,' grumbled Alan. 'You put something down for five minutes and the next thing you know, they've put it out for the jumble.'

'Dad,' said Joe tentatively.

'I ask you – nice pair of cavalry twill slacks, smart, years of wear left in them.'

'Dad, can I ask you something?'

Alan found what he was looking for, and straightened up. 'You can ask, son, but don't expect me to know the answer. It's your mother who's the fount of all knowledge, you know.'

Joe shuffled from one foot to the other, hands thrust deep in his pockets. He hadn't felt this awkward since his father's agonised attempts at sex education. 'You know you and Mum?'

Alan raised a grizzled eyebrow. 'I ought to, we've been married long enough.'

'When you were just married, was it . . . easy?'

'Was what easy?'

Whatever else might be easy, thought Joe, this certainly wasn't. 'Did you ... you know ... did you ever have rows and stuff? Or say things you wished you hadn't?'

Light dawned on Alan's face. 'Oh, *that*. What've you done, accidentally let slip that her rice pudding's not a patch on your mum's?'

'Not ... exactly. We just had a bit of a disagreement, and I, well, let's just say I should've kept my big mouth shut.'

Thoughtfully, Alan slid a leg into his trousers. ''Course, your mother reckons we've never had an argument in thirty-five years of marriage.'

'No?'

'But that's 'cause she always gets her own way.' He chuckled. 'Or thinks she does. That's the way to handle women, you see – let them think they're in charge. Mind you,' He reflected, inserting the other leg. 'Most of the time they are. Except in the shed. No woman should ever defile the sanctity of a man's shed.'

Joe sat down on the edge of the bed. 'I think I've been a bit of a dickhead,' he confessed.

Alan ruffled his hair. 'Never mind, son, we're all dickheads. You just ask your mother.'

It was just about the longest long weekend of Joe's life. Oh, nothing else bad happened, just a sniggering phone call from Gary and that was it. Luckily he'd never been to the Prince of Denmark before in his life, and he wasn't planning to go there ever again, so with a bit of luck the whole thing would just lie down and die. And when Emma phoned him on Sunday night, she apologised again for leaving him on his own. But that just made him feel worse.

In the end he went in to work ridiculously early on Monday morning, and spent the whole day immersed in the most brain-crunchingly complex tasks he could set himself, just to take his mind off the amount of time that was left before Emma got home. It didn't work. His secretary kept coming in with cups of coffee and asking him if he was all right, but if she'd hoped he might confide his troubles to her motherly bosom, she was sorely disappointed.

On his way back home in the car, he rehearsed over and over again what he might say. 'I really missed you.' 'Emma, I'm a prat.' 'Would you like to hit me now?' All serviceable possibilities, but none of them quite conveyed how miserable and edgy he felt.

He called in at the best florist in Montpellier, squeezing in through the door just before they closed. 'I want a bunch of flowers.'

'What sort?' asked the girl.

'A big one.'

She looked at him in the same long-suffering way as the assistant in the lingerie shop, the night before Valentine's Day. 'No, not what sort of bouquet, what sort of flowers. Freesias, carnations, roses, gladioli, anemones ...?'

Joe suddenly realised that he was surrounded by an Eden of possibilities and couldn't even remember the name of Emma's favourite flowers. 'Er ... yellow ones. She likes yellow. Just give me everything you've got that's yellow.'

'*Everything?*'

'And put lots of ribbon round it.'

He could barely see through the back window as she drove the rest of the way home. As he parked, he saw that Emma's car was already outside. Damn, he'd been so sure she'd be back late, leaving him plenty of time to fluff the place up and stick Minette's casserole in the oven.

He climbed the stairs two at a time, leaving several mangled flower heads in his wake as the enormous bouquet swayed like a portable thicket.

'Emma?' His mouth dried as he unlocked the door and stepped inside. 'Are you there?'

'In here.' A small voice answered him from what seemed like miles away, but he found her sitting bolt upright on the edge of the sofa, a wet tissue twisted around fingers that were white with tension. And when she raised her head to look at him, he saw that her eyes were red and haunted.

'Oh, Em.' Seeing her like that, he felt utterly inappropriate standing there with his enormous bouquet. 'Em, I'm so sorry.'

'What about?'

'Everything. Every stupid thing in the whole damn world.'

She took a long sniff and wiped her tired face on the arm of her shirt. 'Me too.'

'God, I was an idiot, going off on one like that. Trying to lay the law down about London. I just didn't realise.' Joe dumped the flowers on the coffee table and sat down beside her.

163

'You weren't to know my instincts were right about Mickey,' she pointed out flatly.

'I should have known.' He put his arms round her shoulders and felt her flinch, then sag, as though the effort of holding herself upright had finally become too much to bear. 'You're always right.'

'Huh. It doesn't feel like it.' Was that a note of accusation in her voice? 'Sometimes it feels as if I can't do anything right.' All at once the flood-gates burst and she was sobbing on his shoulder. 'It was terrible, Joe, she wanted that baby so much and I had to leave her like that. All empty and lost. I said she could come back here with me, but she wouldn't, she just wouldn't . . .'

He gently stroked her hair. 'I know, I know. But you couldn't make her. You've done all you can for her.'

'I know,' she whispered, dripping tears down the back of his neck. 'But sometimes all you can do just isn't enough.'

The following afternoon, after work, Emma decided to walk home via the park. She didn't know quite why; maybe it was just because it was a nice sunny day. Or because she needed some space where other people's demands weren't pressing in on her. A neutral place, somewhere to think and just *be*.

She chose a bench beside the oblong lily pond and sat down to watch a mother duck marshalling a whole flotilla of fluffy brown ducklings. They all seemed to want to dash off in different directions, getting themselves stuck in bits of weed or lost behind lily pads, but everything seemed solvable with a maternal quack and a quick riffle of feathers.

Maybe motherhood really was that easy. Maybe like some people said, it was a basic instinct that you were born with. You might not think you were maternal, but the minute that miniature human popped out of you, you just knew straightaway what to do.

Or not.

What happened if you went into it thinking everything was going to be fine, and then you had the child and found you'd made a terrible mistake? What if you thought you were ready to start living your life for this miniature human being only to realise that you hadn't finished living it for yourself?

What if you left it too long and then you tried and nothing happened?

What if?

She slid back on the bench and swung her feet back and forth. After a morning spent racing round A&E yesterday seemed unreal, and yet she was still trembling from her share of Mickey's pain. And if that wasn't enough, when she'd finally managed to get to sleep Joe had woken her up at three am to tell her he'd been thinking.

'What about?'

'About how you don't know how desperately you want something until you see someone else lose it.'

Still sleepy, she rolled over to face him in the half-light. 'What?'

He took her hand and squeezed it really hard. 'I really think we should do it, Em. Have a baby. Now. It's the right time, I just know it is.'

And she'd been so taken aback she'd not said a word; just stared at the darkened ceiling while Joe went on about how wonderful it would be, until at last he wound down like a clock-work rabbit. And fell blissfully asleep.

'Penny for 'em,' offered a voice behind her.

She opened her eyes and blinked in the sunshine. 'Rozzer! Hi. What're you doing here?'

'I always bring my sarnies here. If I didn't get out of that madhouse for half an hour, I'd end up ramming a TV monitor over some punter's head. Mind if I join you?' He indicated the seat beside her.

'Be my guest.'

Rozzer peeled the lid off a plastic box. 'Cheese and Marmite?'

'No thanks.'

He took one bite, speed-chewed it and then slowed his jaws to a steady chomp. 'Are you OK? You look awful.'

'I had a bad weekend,' she confessed. 'A friend of mine has some problems. Big ones. I guess I'm still feeling a bit sad about it.'

'Oh.' He looked genuinely concerned. 'But you ... and Joe. You're OK?'

She shrugged. 'I guess.' Despite herself she laughed at Rozzer's furrowed brow. 'Yes, we're fine. He just gave me something to think about, that's all. A decision to make about us. And I really don't know what I'm going to say to him when he asks me about it again.'

Rozzer contemplated her for ages, while the ducklings peeped and bobbed about among the lily pads. 'It's none of my business,' he admitted, 'but can I say something?'

Puzzled, she threw him a sidelong look. 'Sure. What?'

'Whatever this decision thing is, Em, just be sure he's worth it.'

20

The staff dining room at Cotswold General was one of those places that never sleep. No matter what time of day or night it was, you would always find somebody there eating lukewarm lasagne and mainlining pints of black coffee. On this occasion it was only eleven o'clock in the morning, but Emma still thought she must be dreaming.

'Joe!' she exclaimed in astonishment as he walked up to her table. 'What on earth are you doing here?'

Joe wrinkled his nose in distaste as he sat down opposite her. 'I don't know how you can stand to work in this place. Even the food smells of disinfectant.' He reached into his pocket and produced a bunch of keys. 'I was on my way out and saw these on the hall table.'

'Oh no!' Emma realised now why she'd had that nagging feeling at the back of her mind all morning. Still shaken up over Mickey, she was having trouble focusing on anything at the moment and had very nearly catheterised the wrong patient. 'Thanks for bringing them over, I'd have looked a right prat having to climb in over the balcony.' She clocked the suit and the shiny shoes. 'I thought you were working from home today.'

'That's the other reason I came to see you – they've brought forward the York meeting to this afternoon, so don't wait up.'

Emma's morale dropped another notch. 'But I've already bought the tickets for tonight!'

Joe didn't seem exactly devastated. 'The play…I'd forgotten. Never mind – we can go another night.'

'It's only on till Thursday. And I've been looking forward to it for weeks. I thought you had, too.'

'All right, how about tomorrow?'

Does this man take notice of anything I say? wondered Emma. 'I told you, I've got to do another late tomorrow because of all the time I had off over the weekend.'

'Great, another night in on my own.' Joe rolled his eyes.

Emma's eyes flashed right back at him. 'Yeah, well maybe now you'll know what it feels like.'

'Hang on – you make it sound like I *want* to spend my life tearing up and down the bloody motorway.' Joe was starting to sound distinctly exasperated, but Emma wasn't in the mood to give him the satisfaction of an apology – even if heads were starting to turn in their direction.

'Well you do!' she snapped back. 'It makes you feel ... important.'

He snorted. 'Yeah, right – like emptying bedpans makes you feel important? Travelling about is part of the job and that's all there is to it.'

Her mouth dropped open. 'What!'

'Look, we'll go to the damn theatre on Wednesday.'

'You know I can't, I've got my photography class. And no, I'm not cancelling it,' she added with relish before he had a chance to tell her how unimportant it was, ''cause I'll sort everything out and then you'll phone me at the last minute and tell me you're in Edinburgh!'

'Fine!' Joe tossed his head in annoyance. 'Let's just not bother going anywhere ever again, shall we?'

'What's the difference? We practically don't anyway.'

They sat in grim silence for several long moments, Emma staring disconsolately at her plate and stabbing at an undercooked sausage. Knowing you'd just been childishly unreasonable didn't make it any easier to admit it. And besides, she told herself, Joe hadn't been much better.

In the end she knew she had to say something conciliatory or her head would explode. 'Want a coffee?'

Joe didn't answer. She looked up at him but he wasn't even looking in her direction, which annoyed her. He seemed to be gazing aimlessly into the middle distance, as though in his mind he was already somewhere completely different. Whatever it was dwelling on, she hoped it wasn't kids. She definitely wasn't ready to have *that* conversation again just yet.

'Do you want a coffee?' she repeated, holding a cup in front of his face.

He started. 'What?'

'Coffee. Do you want one?'

He shook his head. 'I ought to be going.'

'Oh. Fair enough.'

He didn't move. Silence fell again. In the kitchen, somebody dropped a tray of crockery and swore in florid Italian.

'Em?'

'What?'

He cleared his throat awkwardly. 'About what I just said. I didn't mean . . .'

'I know. Neither did I.' Yes I did, thought Emma, but that doesn't matter. Just saying it relieved the crushing weight across her chest.

'I expect things'll settle into a routine once I'm properly into the job.'

'Yeah. Maybe.' Neither of them sounded very convinced.

'I'll call you tonight if I can.' Slowly Joe pushed back his chair and got to his feet. 'Not sure when I'll be back – tomorrow sometime, I guess. Better say that if anybody rings up.'

'Oh yes, I forgot to tell you – I bumped into Rozzer the other day. In the park.'

Almost imperceptibly, Joe stiffened. 'Rozzer? What was he saying?'

'Just something about calling round to see you this week for a "quiet word", he didn't say when. What's that all about, then?'

'Something and nothing I expect, you know Rozzer.' Joe forced himself to look casual. 'Ah well, better hit the road. If I go now I can stop at the motorway services and do some work on the agenda for the meeting.'

'See you then.' She lifted her face to his.

'See you.'

Almost as an afterthought, he bent down and pecked her lightly on the lips; then picked up his briefcase and headed for the door without a backward glance.

'Is this a private sulk, or can anybody join in?' asked Lawrence, hovering beside Emma's table with a tray of cheese salad and Evian.

'Who's sulking?' retorted Emma.

'Well, let's just say I wouldn't want to be that sausage.'

Emma looked down at the dismembered bratwurst. 'Oh that,' she said. 'I'm just not very hungry.'

'Hmm,' grunted Lawrence sceptically. 'Can I sit down or do I have to bugger off and annoy somebody else?'

'Don't mind me. My break's nearly over anyway.'

Lawrence decanted his Evian into a plastic cup as though it were vintage claret. 'Your Joe looks very tasty in that suit, I must say. Charcoal-grey's definitely his colour.'

She sighed. 'Yes.'

'Didn't look too happy with life though – he wants to watch out frowning like that, he'll get premature wrinkles on that pretty face.' Emma was uncomfortably aware of Lawrence's gaze fixing on her like a searchlight. 'You two all right are you?'

'Yes, of course. You're looking perky,' she observed, swiftly changing the subject. 'How's your tangled love life?'

Lawrence nibbled on a fragment of lollo rosso. 'Rather good actually.' He winked. 'Would you believe Duncan's taken to baking cakes, *and* doing the vacuuming *without being told*?'

'Wow,' said Emma. 'What's your secret? I thought you said he was an inconsiderate little slob.'

'He is. He just wants something.'

'What?'

'Me.' Lawrence beamed. 'I'm playing hard to get and loving every minute of it. *Vive l'amour*, that's what I say.' He drank a toast in mineral water.

'I'm pleased for you,' said Emma; and she was.

Lawrence eyed her as he folded lettuce neatly onto his fork. 'So who popped your balloon?' he demanded. 'And don't say "nobody", you look as happy as a wet Tuesday in Scunthorpe.'

'Nobody,' she insisted, pushing away her plate, 'nobody, really. Joe and I just had a bit of a silly argument, that's all. We seem to be having a lot of those lately,' she added ruefully.

'What about?'

'Oh, nothing.' She caught his eye. 'All right, everything. Sometimes we just kind of get up each other's noses.'

'No big surprises there,' said Lawrence. 'The honeymoon's long gone and now you've got to adjust to living together. It just takes time.'

'Well, yes. Maybe.' She looked up and smiled. 'So when did you turn into an agony aunt, then?'

'Darling, you know me: I spend my whole life sorting out other people's little crises. Why do you think I have no time to sort out my own?'

'You don't sound like you have any!'

Lawrence laughed. 'Maybe not right this minute, but you wait. There'll be another one along in a minute, there always is.'

'Isn't there just. Look at my friend Mickey ... I mean she says she's OK, swears she's coping, but how can I tell when she's so far away? And as for Joe, well, Joe just doesn't understand why she matters so much to me.'

Lawrence took another sip of water. 'So what's going on in your life that's *good*? You're making me depressed.'

'Thanks – you're all heart!' She pondered. 'Well there's my photography class I suppose.'

'That's a bit more like it,' declared Lawrence, who liked to spend his spare time painting *trompe l'oeil* cherubs on his rococo bathroom ceiling. 'If you'd only go the whole hog and take up watercolour painting, I might even come along with you.'

'Yes, well, we haven't all got your artistic talents, Lawrence. Getting a tree in focus is enough of a challenge for me.'

'What's the tutor like? Still that rude git you told me about?'

She suppressed a half-smile. 'Oh, he's not that bad. Not when you get to know him a bit. Actually we treated him here in the department a while back – remember those joyriders who smashed up my father-in-law's car?'

'You're being taught photography by a joyrider?'

She swiped him with her paper napkin. 'No, of course not! He's the poor motorcyclist whose bike they totalled. He's taking us all out on a night-time shoot in a few weeks' time, did I tell you? I bet he wouldn't mind if you came along too.'

Lawrence threw back his head and laughed. 'Thanks but no thanks, darling. The last time I went out photographing things at night, I had a misunderstanding with a plain-clothes policeman on Cleeve Common. Don't look at me like that, you foul-minded hussy – it was all completely innocent!' He winked. 'Mind you, he did take an awfully cute Polaroid.'

*

171

If he was going to bump into her anywhere it was in the hospital; but Joe was still startled to turn the corner and walk straight into Zara.

'Hi,' he said. 'Long time no see. How's things?'

'Fine.' Something in her eyes told him that wasn't entirely true, but he let it pass. 'How about you? Matter of fact I was just wondering if you were OK.'

'Yeah, of course. Great. Only visiting.'

'That's good. See you around then.'

'See you.'

It wasn't until he was halfway down the corridor that he turned round and saw she was still standing there, looking at him as if there was something she'd wanted to say but hadn't managed to get it out. Although he was in a hurry, he retraced his steps. 'We really should go out for that drink sometime,' he blurted out.

She smiled, and her face relaxed. 'I'd like that.'

'Me too. I'll call you.'

By the time he drove out onto the A40, he was whistling.

The following afternoon, Emma had just finished a long e-mail chat with Mickey when the doorbell rang.

Much to her relief it wasn't Minette standing on the landing, but Rozzer. Hands thrust deep in the pockets of his sagging trousers, he looked more like an overgrown schoolboy than the assistant manager of a betting shop.

'Hi, Emma,' he said, colouring ever so slightly as she smiled at him. 'Is Joe in?'

'Sorry, Rozzer, he's not back yet.'

'Back from where?'

'York – didn't he tell you? He had to go up there for some kind of big meeting.'

'Nah. Nobody tells me anything,' replied Rozzer without malice. 'Oh well, sorry I bothered you, I guess I'll try again some-time.'

He looked so downcast that Emma called him back. 'Why don't you come in anyway? I was just making a coffee.'

'Oh.' Now he looked like a startled baby owl. 'Well ... OK then. If you're sure you don't mind.'

Rozzer lurked awkwardly in the kitchen doorway while Emma

172

put the kettle on. 'You know, you could sit down,' she pointed out. 'You're making me feel uncomfortable.'

'Sorry.' Rozzer promptly sat on the nearest thing he could find, which happened to be the top of the stainless-steel swing bin. 'Have you any idea when Joe will be back? I just wanted to have a word ... you know, ask his advice.'

You and half the world, thought Emma. Joe Sheridan, the human encyclopaedia. 'Don't suppose I'd be any help would I?' she ventured, handing him a mug of coffee.

It was plain that this hadn't occurred to Rozzer. 'Well, I don't know ... maybe.' The swing bin emitted an ominous cracking sound and Rozzer leapt to his feet. 'Oh no, I've broken it!'

'No I'm sure you haven't, it's fine.' Emma steered him out of harm's way and into the living room, where he headed for the sofa like a grateful homing pigeon. 'So what did you want to ask him about? Or is it private?'

'Well ... no, not really. Between you and me, I've been getting a bit lonely lately, and seeing as my flat's too big for just me, I thought maybe I might consider getting a lodger.'

'Oh, I see! Sounds like a good idea. But what's Joe got to do with it?'

'The thing is, everybody I mention it to says letting's a real minefield, and I'm just the kind of guy who's going to get it all wrong and end up with a psycho in my spare room.'

'And you thought Joe might be able to give you some advice?'

'Yeah. I mean, if Joe doesn't know something it's not worth knowing, right?'

'Hmm,' replied Emma.

'Plus, I thought he might know somebody who's looking for a room. Somebody who works for Unico, maybe. You know, some-body ... normal.'

'I'm sure he'd be happy to help if he could,' said Emma, 'but I think what you need here is some specialist advice.' She glanced at the clock; hours till she had to be on duty. 'Drink up; we're going to see the oracle.'

The Advice Centre occupied the entire first floor above a micro-brewery, at the far end of the Lower High Street. On a warm day you could get drunk on the fumes rising up the stairs, which possibly went some way towards explaining the centre's enduring

173

popularity. Emma had lost count of the number of patients she'd referred there from A&E, to sort out everything from pest control to legal aid.

She opened the door and gently pushed Rozzer through, into the spartan but fragrant interior. 'Go on, she won't bite.'

Rozzer eyed the fearsome, square-jawed woman behind the information desk. 'Are you sure about that?'

'Do you want some proper advice or not?'

While Rozzer was learning the ins and outs of becoming a small-time landlord, Emma wandered around the various displays. Half of the vast room was taken up with an exhibition entitled The Worst of Cheltenham, featuring photographs of potholed roads, a huge traffic jam gumming up the one-way system, and a supermarket trolley festooned with weed, rising up from the depths of Pittville Lake like a budget version of Excalibur.

'I bet the council love this,' she chuckled to herself. 'No wonder they keep trying to close this place down.'

She was so engrossed with finding technical faults in the photos that she didn't notice the small child romping towards her across the blue nylon carpet. In fact the first she knew of it was when something tugged hard at the hem of her jacket.

'My boo-boo's all better now,' piped up a small but confident voice. 'You made my boo-boo all better.'

Emma looked down into a dimpled face surrounded by wispy blonde curls; a tiny, faint scar just discernible below the hairline. 'Hello!' she exclaimed. 'I know you.'

A second figure appeared from behind one of the exhibition screens. 'Sara-Jane, come here and leave the lady alone.'

Bugger, thought Emma. I know you too. I mean, how could I ever forget you? The last time we met, you punched me in the face.

'Oh God,' said Linda Jones. 'It's you.'

Emma had never seen anybody look more mortified.

'Er ... yes,' she said.

'I hit you.'

'Yes thanks, I do remember.'

'Are you ... OK?'

'Well, I had one heck of a black eye, but none of my bits have fallen off yet. How about you?'

Linda was whiter than boil-washed snow. 'I know you're not going to believe this, but I must have stood outside A and E twenty times, meaning to go in and thank you for not pressing charges – especially when I found out that none of it was your fault anyway. But I never had the guts to go inside.' Guilt made her whole body sag. 'You must really hate me.'

Emma could almost hear Joe agreeing with Linda: 'Too bloody right she does!', but that wasn't how she felt at all. 'Actually no. I've been worrying about you and Sara-Jane – especially since I saw that horrible piece in the local paper.'

'Worrying? About us?' Linda's eyes widened in astonishment. She had a pretty face, thought Emma; but her sunken cheeks and the dark circles around her eyes made her look old and tired. 'Why?'

'Why not?' replied Emma. 'Nobody deserves a hard time for doing what they thought was right. So, how are things now? Any better?'

She knew the answer even before Linda sighed and said: 'I wish. If anything, it's got worse on the estate since the last time the police tried to protect us. And the council say they won't prioritise us, so we might as well forget about being rehoused. That's why we're here – I thought maybe they could help us find a safe place to live. Trouble is, everything's so expensive ...'

'Mummy and me are going to live in a fairy castle,' piped up Sara-Jane. 'With a big lake and ponies.'

Linda laughed and ruffled her daughter's hair. 'Maybe one day, sweetheart. Maybe one day.'

Emma glanced across the room to where Rozzer was vanishing under a pile of pamphlets. It must be fate. One person looking for a lodger. One person looking to *be* a lodger. Add in one small person who was just looking for somewhere to be safe and happy, and you had yourself an intriguing equation.

'Excuse me just a minute,' she said, then walked across the room to where he was standing and grabbed him by the arm.

'What's up?' he demanded, promptly dropping an armful of leaflets all over the sticky brown carpet.

'Nothing's up. Just leave those and come with me. There's somebody over here I'd like you to meet.'

Time trundled on, much in the usual way, and the twice-weekly photography class became a beacon in Emma's very ordinary life

– particularly the after-class trip down the pub. But after the next session, everyone – even Terrence and his shoebox – seemed to have somewhere else they'd rather be than down the pub with the course tutor. Well, everyone except Emma.

'So this guy Rozzer actually agreed to it?' Richard helped himself to a peanut out of Emma's bag. 'Just like that?'

'Not exactly,' she admitted. 'Actually, when he realised who Linda was, he said he'd rather let his spare room to Genghis Khan. But that was before Sara-Jane spilled her juice on his trousers.'

Richard frowned. 'And this helped how?'

'While Linda was sponging them down they got talking and Rozzer realised she wasn't mad after all, and that maybe having a kid around the flat might not be as bad as all that.'

'So they're definitely moving into his place then?'

'Fingers crossed. Rozzer's going to have a think about it over the weekend and make his mind up. I think he'll say yes, he's an old softy really.'

Richard raised his glass in a toast. 'You're a devious woman, Mrs Sheridan.'

'Is that meant to be a criticism or a compliment?'

He grinned. 'What do you think?' He picked up Emma's empty glass. 'Get you another?'

She thought about how late it was getting, and then about the empty flat, and concluded what the hell: what have I got to go home for? An empty bed and a mug of Horlicks. 'OK, but just a small one.'

'That kid must have made quite an impression on you.' commented Richard as they sat drinking at their usual corner table.

'Sara-Jane? I suppose I am a bit smitten – she's a real cutie.'

Richard laughed. 'So we can expect the patter of little Sheridans in the near future then?'

He was looking straight into her eyes as he said the words, and a funny kind of intimate shiver ran right down her spine. She could have told him to mind his own business, of course, but she felt such sudden and powerful empathy with him that she had a crazy desire to spill out her heart.

'Only if Joe gets his own way. As far as he's concerned, I should be knitting bootees already. But this is one argument I'm not going to let him win.'

Richard looked taken aback. 'So you don't want children of your own then?'

'Oh yes! For sure I do. Just ... not yet awhile. There's stuff I want to do with my life.'

'Stuff you wouldn't have the freedom to do if you were a mum?'

'Exactly.' Emma realised with a start that she was talking to Richard as though she had known him for years, telling him stuff she wouldn't normally tell anyone but a really close friend. But she had precious few of those in Cheltenham and anyway, he *felt* like a friend, someone who understood her almost scarily well. 'But you try telling Joe that. He just can't see the problem – why on earth would I want to go on working? He earns enough for both of us and after all, I'm *only* a nurse.'

Only a nurse, only a wife, only Emma, she thought. Just married. And maybe that's not enough.

'Surely he can see how talented and intelligent you are,' said Richard softly. 'I can, and I hardly know you.'

Their eyes met.

'In some ways,' murmured Emma, 'I don't think he knows me at all. But then again, I'm not sure I really knew myself until I got married and discovered all the things I wasn't supposed to want to do any more. Funny, isn't it? And yet I don't want to hurt Joe. Sometimes it's so hard to make the right decisions.'

Richard laid a reassuring hand on hers; and she didn't pull away. 'There's only one thing that really matters,' he said. 'The only thing that ever matters. And that's doing what you *feel* is right.'

She looked into his bright blue eyes and, in that fluttering, soaring moment, what she felt was right had nothing at all to do with having children.

21

The Sunday afternoon sunshine beamed down on Pittville Park like a kindly uncle, making all the rabbits in Pets' Corner sit up on their haunches and sniff excitedly at the late-spring air.

'I'm telling you, I couldn't believe it when I saw it,' enthused Joe as they strolled across the grass. 'Only six years old, not a scratch on it. It's a thousand times better than the old heap he had.'

'I know his old car was a bit battered,' conceded Emma, 'but he really loved it. Look at how upset he was when he found out it was a write-off.'

Joe ruffled her hair in the slightly irritating way he did when he was trying to point out that he was older and wiser, and that there were some things she shouldn't worry her pretty little head about. 'Trust me,' he said, 'he'll love this one even more. She's a beast.'

Emma crumbled up another lump of stale cake and scattered it on the grass beside the lake. Another cake baked in an attack of domesticity; another family of moorhens, doomed to be driven to an early grave by a surfeit of home-made chocolate sponge. The trouble was, she might find the time to make the damned things, but Joe never seemed to be around long enough to eat them. Or if he was around, he wasn't hungry any more because he'd necked five Mars Bars on the way down the motorway.

She sighed. Joe looked at her, puzzled. 'Something up, Em?'

'Oh, just thinking.'

'Sounds ominous,' he quipped.

'Don't be silly.' She looked up at him. 'This is nice. It's been ages since we walked down to the park together.'

'Yes, I guess it is.'

'We used to go for walks all the time when I just came to see you at weekends. Why don't we do it any more?'

Joe's brow furrowed. 'We are doing it.'

'You know what I mean.' She scattered the last of the crumbs and wiped her hands on her jeans. In the distance, a teenage couple were chasing each other round the far side of the lake, the girl screeching with laughter as she threatened to throw her boyfriend's hat in the water. Her eyes followed them in their sun-filled happiness, and a small cloud passed across her heart. 'Why have things changed?'

'They haven't.' He followed her gaze. 'Much.'

'Yes they have!'

Joe looked awkward, like a boy whose mother was trying to talk to him about safe sex. 'Well, they're bound to a bit, aren't they? We're married now.' He made it sound like a death sentence.

There was a long and uncomfortable silence, then Joe said: 'Do you want an ice cream?'

And Emma said 'Yes,' because that was easier than telling him that sometimes, in the dark of the night, she could almost feel the weight of the invisible chain that bound her to this man, a man, she now realised she'd only thought she knew. Easier than begging him to hold her, because she needed him to tell her that she was just being silly, and that everything was completely fine.

'Blimey,' whistled Diane. 'He isn't half flash, your Joe. Wish I had a bloke who could shell out on a nearly new Jag without even thinking about it!'

'Hmm,' replied Emma, as the two of them stripped the soiled bedding off the trolleys in the resuscitation room. 'Trouble is, he doesn't think about anything else either.'

Diane scented juicy gossip. 'Oooh, what's this, trouble in the love nest?'

Emma stuck out her tongue. 'Give over. I meant, he doesn't always think about the consequences. His brothers don't earn a fraction of what he does – how are they going to pay their share? And then there's this stupid company weekend ...'

Now Diane was really intrigued. 'I thought you were really looking forward to it.'

'I was,' she replied. 'Till Joe actually bothered to find out what it's all about. Turns out it's a bloody *golf* weekend!'

179

Emma wondered why on earth she was telling Diane any of this; normally she was the last person you'd want to confide in. Maybe she just needed to let off steam and it didn't really matter who got the brunt of it.

'Oh,' said Diane. 'Bummer. Still, you never know, you might enjoy it.'

'Or not.'

'Well ... yeah. But they'll have to do something else as well. They can't play golf all the time, can they?'

'Some of us can't play golf at all. And I don't care what anybody says, I am *not* wearing Rupert the Bear trousers and one of those stupid sun-visors.'

They were giggling like a pair of schoolgirls when a figure appeared in the doorway behind them.

'What's the joke?' demanded Zara suspiciously.

'There isn't one,' replied Emma.

'Good. Then maybe you'll have time to clean up the man in cubicle six. He's just vomited all over himself.'

By the time she got home that night, Emma felt in need of chocolate and sensible conversation. Dirty jobs might be par for the course but dirty looks were a bit much, and she was starting to get distinctly tired of Dr Zara Jeffries and her moods. Pity it wasn't one of her photography nights. She was becoming addicted to her fix of Richard and his caustic sense of humour. His directness was like a breath of fresh air.

Still, a nice long chat to her mum would see her right. Mum had always had a way of putting things in perspective, making her realise that all her mountains were really molehills.

Grabbing the last chunky Kit-Kat from the fridge, Emma kicked off her shoes and flopped gratefully onto the sofa. Lying back on a heap of nice squishy cushions, she dialled up her mum's number and waited to be soothed back to sanity.

'Golden Sands Guest House, can I help you?'

That faux-cultured telephone voice definitely didn't belong to Karen Cox. Karen was a take-me-as-you-find-me person.

'Hello, can I speak to Karen please? It's her daughter.'

'Emma, love!' The vowels slid right back to Salford. 'How're you doing?'

'Auntie Jacqui? What are you doing there?'

'Your mum's a bit off colour, I'm just helping out for a few days.'

'Off colour? Why didn't she call me? What's wrong with her?'

'Oh, nothing much. One of those three-day bugs I expect, they're all over Blackpool at the moment. She's just a bit tired, that's all.'

Maybe she was imagining it, but Emma was sure she caught a note of caginess in her aunt's voice. 'Are you sure she's OK?'

'Tell her I'm right as rain,' came a voice in the background. Her mum's voice. 'And she's not to worry.'

When Jacqui spoke again, the sound was muffled as though she'd put her hand over the receiver. 'You ought to tell her, you know.'

'Shush, don't be silly.'

'Tell me what?' demanded Emma.

Her mother's voice came down the line, breezy and clear. 'Oh nothing important. I've just been thinking about concentrating full-time on the gay market. They're such nice guests, never any trouble.'

'Oh,' said Emma. 'Look, what's all this about a virus?'

'I'm fine! Just a bit tired, like Jacqui said. She offered to come over and lend a hand so I wasn't going to say no, was I?'

'Why didn't you tell me you were ill?' demanded Emma. 'I could've—'

'No you couldn't,' replied her mother calmly. 'You've got a job and a husband to think about. Besides, there was no point in telling you. It's only a bug, I'll be over it before you know.'

'But—'

'Now, hang on a minute while I make myself comfy, and you can tell me all the latest gossip.'

'I'm sure there's something she's not telling me,' Emma repeated, toying with the piece of salmon on her plate.

Joe laid down his knife and fork. He was starting to lose patience. 'Just because you were right about Mickey, doesn't mean your mum's at death's door! Your auntie told you it's just a bug, she's a bit washed out. What more do you want, a medical certificate?'

Emma flicked at a pea and watched it spiral round the edge of her plate like a miniature roulette ball. 'I know, I know, you think

181

I'm being neurotic. But she's my mum, and I'm telling you there's something else.'

He watched her fiddling listlessly with her dinner. 'Are you going to eat that salmon or enter it for the Turner Prize?'

'Oh . . . you have it, I'm not hungry.' She pushed her plate away. 'Mum wasn't herself at the wedding either, she looked exhausted then too. I ought to go up and see her.'

Joe's mouth fell open in mid-chew. 'When?'

'Now.'

'Not this weekend you're not! We've got a date at a country house, remember? An important one.'

She grunted. 'Important for you, maybe.'

'For us! Sir Stanley said only the other day how much he's looking forward to meeting you.'

'To vetting me, more like. This is my mum, Joe, and I'm worried about her.'

'For the last time Emma, there's nothing wrong with your mum! And you're my wife and I need your support.' There was a hard, unyielding line of muscle along the angle of his jaw. 'I *expect* it.'

He couldn't have said a worse thing. Emma's lip curled. 'And what Joe expects, Joe gets, is that it?'

'What is wrong with you tonight? It's like suddenly you don't give a damn about me or my career.'

She squared up to him, feeling curiously cool and detached. 'What – like you don't give a damn about anything except your stupid company image? Well guess what, maybe I've got a life of my own and maybe there are things I care about that don't have anything to do with you.'

'Oh grow up, you sound like a spoilt little girl.'

'Do I? Maybe that's what I am then.' Throwing down her napkin, she stood up. 'Why don't you take your mother on this stupid weekend? I mean, obviously I'm not nearly mature enough for the job.'

'What?'

'I'm sure Minette would make a far better job of brown-nosing Sir Stanley on the golf course,' she sniped. 'And let's face it, she's got exactly the right taste in bloody awful check trousers.'

'Don't you criticise my mum!'

'Why not? She's always criticising me.'

182

'That's not true.'

'Yes it is, she just does it with a smile on her face and calls it "friendly advice". You know damn well she's never thought I was good enough for you. Not like bloody Zara Jeffries,' she added through clenched teeth.

Joe looked momentarily startled. 'I'm going out,' he announced, grabbing his jacket from the back of the chair.

'Where?'

'Just out. Maybe by the time I get back you'll be talking sense again.'

The rest of the week passed in a kind of uneasy truce. And despite all Emma's silent prayers for an asteroid to fall on Great Berkeley Hall, or for time to start running backwards, Friday came round with horrible inevitability.

'You all right?' asked Joe, glancing sideways at Emma as they drove up the huge, tree-lined avenue that led to the Hall.

'Fine.'

'You sure?'

By way of reply, she grabbed his left hand from the steering wheel and plonked it on her forehead. 'See, no temperature, and before you ask, no, I'm not planning on showing you up in front of all the company bigwigs.'

'I never thought you were,' protested Joe, not perhaps entirely convincingly. 'But you've got to admit you've been a bit weird these last few days.'

It took a conscious effort of will not to rise to that one, but Emma was determined not to start another argument so she simply changed the subject. Deep down inside she was aching for everything to be peace, quiet, harmony. She felt so uncomfortable, like she'd thrown away one life and then found the new one she'd bought was too tight for her.

'Wow,' she said with more enthusiasm than she felt, 'that's one hell of a house. And my God – just look at the golf course!'

The Hall stood beside the Severn Estuary, an elegant agglomeration of grey stone turrets and mullioned windows. It was easy to imagine Rapunzel opening one of them and letting down her golden hair; though if she did, there was a fair chance she'd be knocked unconscious by a wild drive from the fourteenth tee. The golf course extended from the house all the way down a gentle green slope to the river's edge, where a heron was staring intently into the depths of the mud-coloured tide, apparently oblivious to the threat of low-flying golf balls.

Joe was already looking. And weighing up his chances of coming out of this with a shred of dignity intact. Tennis he could have handled; five-a-side football he might even have relished; but golf? The last time he'd picked up a putter in anger was at the Crazy Golf in Rhyl, where he'd taken fifty-two shots to get the ball up the ramp and into the little red windmill. Not very impressive, even if he was only eight at the time.

They pulled up outside the front of the house, the Audi's wheels making an impressive scrunching sound on the inches-deep gravel of the driveway.

'You didn't tell me it was fancy dress,' Emma commented drily as a short, round woman in turquoise and pink Gaultier teetered past on needle-thin heels and disappeared up the steps to the main entrance.

'Shh!' hissed Joe. 'That's the marketing director's wife.'

'Is he colour-blind?'

Joe glared at her. 'Are you going to be like this all weekend? Because if you are, you might as well go home right now. This isn't a game, Emma, it's really important to me!'

Emma felt a slight pang of guilt. She knew she'd been irritating all the way here, but somehow she'd felt he deserved it, just for inflicting this on her. Maybe he had a point: it was a bit unreasonable. 'OK, I'm sorry,' she sighed, unclipping her seat belt. 'You know I'll do my best. Now, let's get in there and see the whites of their eyes.'

The turquoise and pink beach-ball woman was enthroned in the marble-pillared entrance hall, holding forth to a gaggle of ladies. 'So naturally I said to Charles, "If Georgina has to go to Millfield then so be it, but you know I've set my heart on the Ladies' College."'

'Of course you have, Dillie,' nodded a motherly-looking woman in expensively shapeless tweed. 'She's your little girl, you're bound to want the best for her.'

'I do! I mean, at the end of the day it's not the education they get, is it? It's the *contacts* they make.' Dillie uncrossed her podgy legs with a zzzzip of overstressed nylon. 'Well *hello*!' she beamed, catching sight of Emma and Joe hovering with their bags, like two underemployed bellhops. 'And what have we here?'

Joe put down his bag and stuck out a hand. 'Joe Sheridan, Midlands and South-West Region.'

'So this must be your lovely new wife Emily ... Well well,' she cooed, 'aren't you gorgeous?'

'It's Emma actually,' she cut in, trying not to feel like a freshly dyed and scented poodle.

'Emma? How lovely.'

'And you're?'

'Dillie Greaves-Ormond, dear.' She aimed little pecks at the air on either side of Emma's ears. 'My Charles is in charge of marketing. And this is Penny Paterson –'

The motherly woman put down *Good Housekeeping* and directed a beatific smile in Emma's direction. 'Pleased to meet you, Emma.'

'Penny's husband's in charge of finance. And that bright young thing over there is Ruth, she's married to Jack Marinello, North-West and Southern Scottish Region.'

'Hiya,' grinned Ruth, her chirpy Lancashire accent somewhat at odds with her black Prada. 'Looking forward to the golf?'

'Er ... no, not really,' admitted Emma, who had decided that honesty was the best policy. 'I don't know one end of a club from the other.'

'Don't you worry about that.' She winked. 'Just wait till you cop an eyeful of the course pro, believe me, golf won't be the first thing on your mind.'

'Ruth!' Penny frowned.

'Well it's true! He's *gorge*. Oh look, here's Alfred come to take you away.'

An elderly man in a red waistcoat arrived, bearing keys. 'Mr and Mrs Sheridan? If you'd like to follow me I'll show you to your suite.'

Joe raised an eyebrow. 'A suite!' he commented to Emma approvingly. 'See? Told you it'd be the lap of luxury.'

'See you later, Emma!' Dillie called after her as they stepped into the magnificent Edwardian lift-cage. 'Don't you worry, Joe, we'll take good care of her for you.'

Emma wished that didn't sound quite so much like a threat.

22

Emma rolled over, squinted in the early sunlight and sat up, brusquely awake. 'What's going on? What time is it?'

Joe was hopping round the room on one foot, trying to get the other into a sock. 'Half-six. Got to get some practice in before breakfast,' he said. 'How's it going to look if they find out I've never played the bloody game before? Oh God, why didn't I take a few private lessons?'

Emma flopped back onto the huge, square, feather pillows. 'You're insane,' she said. 'How much can you learn about golf before breakfast? Come back to bed.'

'Sorry, can't, got a lesson booked with the pro.' Stuffing his foot into a borrowed golf shoe, Joe snatched up his jacket. 'See you downstairs. Oh, and spare a thought for me when you're lounging around in the aromatherapy spa.' He stooped to kiss his wife on the nose. 'Don't be late for breakfast.'

'Yes, all right,' yawned Emma. 'I'll just rest my eyes for ten minutes and then I'll get up.'

The next thing she was aware of was an enthusiastic hammering on her door. 'Emma? Coo-ee Emma, are you ready?'

Emma rubbed the sleep from eyelids that were as gummed together as a hibernating tortoise's. A sudden stab of panic made her heart flutter. Had she forgotten something important? Had she (wishful thinking) slept through the entire weekend and now it was time to go home?

'Ready?' she grunted sleepily. 'What for?'

'For breakfast, dear! Up and at 'em – we've a jolly exciting day to look forward to, you know.'

Penny Paterson's frantic cheerfulness made Emma wince. 'Actually, I thought I might give breakfast a miss.'

This produced a shocked two-second silence. 'Don't be silly, dear! Nobody misses breakfast on one of Sir Stanley's weekends. Besides, Tristram's going to tell us all about the day's programme. Between you and me, I've heard a whisper about an ikebana demonstration.'

Emma tried to swallow a yawn. 'Couldn't you tell me about it ... later?'

'Gosh no, that wouldn't do at all. Lady Iris is dying to meet you. Tell you what, I'll wait here while you get yourself ready. I'm sure you won't be more than a couple of minutes.'

Joe limped into breakfast with the golf pro's words still ringing in his ears. He wasn't sure of their *exact* meaning, seeing as most of them were in Spanish, but the accompanying hand gestures had given him a fair idea.

A heavy hand landed in the middle of his back, almost knocking him flying. 'That's what I like to see, my boy,' boomed Sir Stanley. 'Dedication.' He winked. 'Saw you setting off with your clubs at the crack of dawn.' Joe smiled weakly. 'Now, come and sit down and have some devilled kidneys. Build yourself up for a good hard round, eh?'

Joe was surprised to see no women in the breakfast room; well, none except for Rachael Cummings, and with her sharp teeth, pointed nose and tiny, piercing eyes she looked more like a weasel. His gloom deepened. Obviously this was a managers-only power-breakfast, an opportunity to score points off each other while the spouses swigged Buck's Fizz somewhere cosy and talked about pedicures.

'Hello,' Rachael said coldly. 'Sleep well?'

'Fine. You?'

She sliced a ripe peach in half with sadistic precision. 'Never better.'

Joe grabbed himself a plate and went for the only empty chair that wasn't next to her. Joe had never felt particularly at ease with Rachael, and since he'd been promoted over her head things hadn't got any more comfortable. It didn't help that he knew she was right to be bitter about it. After all, she was five years older, had tons more experience and as far as he could see only had one fault: she was female. Still, he mused as he speared a rubbery kidney, it wasn't his fault if Sir Stanley was a bigoted old dinosaur, was it? All the same, one look at those rodent teeth made him instinctively cross his legs.

David Paterson and Jack Marinelli were locked in hushed conversation over a serving dish of kedgeree.

'If the worst came to the worst,' said Marinelli, 'I'd just falsify my scorecard.'

Paterson raised a sceptical eyebrow. 'Oh, and you'd do that without him noticing, would you?'

'Well, it's a plan of sorts. Face it, Dave, beating the big boss on the golf course isn't exactly the best career move, is it? Unless you're into ritual suicide.'

'Anyway,' said the finance director, forking smoked haddock into his mouth, 'it's not going to be a problem for you or me – I've seen the list.' He turned to Joe and smiled broadly. 'Morning Sheridan. Looking forward to playing the Big Boss?'

'What?'

'Haven't you heard? You're paired with Richard Pike against Sir Stanley and ... now who was it?' He clicked his fingers. 'Oh yes, Rachael Cummings.'

The woman in burnt-orange Kenzo had the bearing of a Parisian grande dame and the voice of a Bridlington whelk-seller.

'Trousers,' she boomed as Emma trundled blearily into the Garden Room, where silver platters of fresh fruit and dishes of muesli had been arranged among the potted plants.

Emma wrinkled her nose. 'Sorry?'

'I said, trousers.' Lady Iris – for it could be none other – pointed her spoon at Emma's genuine black Josephs: the only pair of decent trousers she'd ever owned that hadn't been bought in a sale.

Assuming this was some kind of compliment, Emma glanced down at them. 'Yes,' she said. 'They are nice, aren't they? I like them because they make my legs look longer.'

'Hmmph,' replied Lady Iris, peering imperiously through the top of her gold-rimmed Varifocals. 'Well they're all right for lazing around in I dare say, but I hope you've brought something nice for tonight. Sir Stanley likes a lady to look like a lady.' She laughed. 'I should know, I've been married to the old bugger for thirty-five years.'

Emma blinked. So this was the infamous Lady Iris. The voice

was so at odds with the appearance that it was like watching a badly dubbed film. 'I've brought a dress,' she replied, her cheeks burning with humiliation as all the other wives directed smug little smiles in her direction. 'A blue one.'

'Good, good.' Lady Iris waved an arm around the assembled throng, releasing a waft of something sickly-sweet and expensive that reminded Emma of fly-spray. 'Well, don't just stand there, sit down and eat something. Tristram wants to distribute his hand-outs. And afterwards,' she added, directing Emma to the chair next to her own, 'I want you to tell me *all* about yourself.'

It could be worse, mused Joe, trudging dutifully behind Sir Stanley as they made their way to the next tee. A lot worse in fact. Astoundingly, the gods of golf had smiled on him so far and one of his mis-hits had miraculously landed plum in the middle of the green – the *right* green. Given the fact that Sir Stanley knew his way round a set of golf clubs like a squirrel knew its nuts, and that their opponents weren't trying over-hard, there was even a slight chance he might end up on the winning side.

All the same, he couldn't get rid of the horrible feeling that, sooner or later, something was going to go wrong. And the thin smile on Rachael's face only accentuated his uneasiness.

Sir Stanley placed his ball on the tee with loving care and took a practice swing. 'Pretty girl, your wife. Good choice. Classy.'

'Thank you, sir.'

'Let's hope the kids look like their mother, eh?' Everybody laughed except Joe. 'So, Sheridan. Enjoying the regional job? Not too much for you?'

'Er yes, Sir Stanley. I mean no, Sir Stanley. That is, yes, I'm enjoying it and no, it's not too much for me.' Out of the corner of his eye he could see the word "idiot" silently forming on Rachael Cummings' lips.

'Glad to hear it, lad. And I must say, you've had some good results. Don't think I haven't noticed what you've done with household detergents and processed meat products.'

Joe relaxed a little. 'Thank you, sir.'

Sir Stanley teed off with an effortless swing that sent the ball arcing gracefully down the middle of the fairway. 'Oh good shot sir,' chorused Rachael and Charles Greaves-Ormond. To his credit, Sir Stanley took little notice of his fawning fan club.

'Aye, well, you're doing a good job pushing fancy luncheon meat to the plebs. But there's just one thing that's bothering me,' he went on as Joe waited to take his turn at the tee.

Joe's recovering confidence suffered an abrupt relapse. 'There is? What's wrong?'

'You tell me. My sources tell me there's been a marked fall-off in profits at the HomeWare store in Hereford. The word I heard was that somebody's on the fiddle.'

A small explosive device went off inside Joe's head. The Hereford store? How could he know about that? Joe had done everything in his power to cover it up. He'd lost more sleep than he wanted to think about, fathoming out ways to keep it under wraps until he'd sorted the damn thing out. In fact, the only way Sir Stanley could have found out was if *somebody*, one of the few people in the know …

He turned round, and saw Rachael's smile broaden into something a great white shark would have been proud of. You scheming bitch, thought Joe, with a tinge of reluctant admiration. You've stitched me up good and proper.

'I'm sure it's not a major problem,' he assured Sir Stanley.

'Really? I'd consider a fifteen per cent fall at a flagship store quite major, wouldn't you?'

'I'm … investigating it.'

'Aye, well, I should bloody well hope so. If you ask me, something dodgy's going on in that store. Put somebody on the tills first thing on Monday, undercover. Ex-police or something.'

'As a matter of fact, I was already thinking of—'

'Thinking's no good, Sheridan. Doing's all I'm interested in. I'll send you somebody from head office. And I want this sorted out pronto, got that?'

Joe swallowed hard. 'Loud and clear, Sir Stanley.'

If anybody says 'how nice' to me one more time, thought Emma, I'm going to scream.

'So you're a nurse!' cooed the wife of regional audits as they sat around the conservatory in fluffy robes, recovering from 'Easy Entertaining' and waiting for their turn with the in-house massage therapist. Emma braced herself, and sure enough it came. 'How nice.'

Emma's teeth clenched so hard that her jaw-muscles bulged. Joe, she told him silently, I don't care what you say; if you think

190

you're ever going to get me on another of these company weekends, you've got another think coming. When I next feel like
turning myself into a vegetable, I'll let you know.

'And such a suitable sort of job,' nodded Dillie Greaves-
Ormond.

'Suitable?' Emma thought of steaming bedpans and severed
arteries, and struggled to see what was so suitable about them.

Dillie patted her hand indulgently. 'For a company wife, my
dear. I could tell Lady Iris was impressed with you,' she added,
which if anything made Emma feel even more irritated. She was
beginning to wish she'd turned up in bondage trousers, with a
bone through her nose, whistling the 'Internationale.'

'So many of the young women today are obsessed with their
own careers,' sighed Penny. 'Do you remember that girl ...
Leonie, wasn't it? She was married to Quentin Roberts from
Borders and Grampian.'

'Ah yes,' said Mrs Regional Audits, 'the *lawyer*.' She shook her
head gravely. 'She just couldn't understand that a man in a senior
position needs a wife who's prepared to make sacrifices.'

'Be there for him,' interjected Penny. 'Support him, and understand his needs.'

'What about her needs?' enquired Emma, but nobody was
listening.

'His needs, exactly,' said Dillie. 'You're so right. I mean, one
can't go off trying to forge one's own career in international
human rights, and then expect one's husband to be sitting at home
waiting when one finally turns up. It's just not ... reasonable. Of
course, it ended badly.'

'It was bound to,' agreed Mrs Audits. 'Poor Quentin, it's no
wonder he moved in with his secretary. Now there's a girl who
knows how to look after a man. And *such* delightful children.' She
turned to Emma and beamed her approbation. 'I can tell you're
just exactly what Joe needs. Selfless and kind.'

God, thought Emma. Let me out. She forced a smile. 'Oh yes?'

'Definitely. A proper feminine woman with a caring side.
Someone who knows how important it is to *give*.'

At that moment, the only thing Emma felt like giving was a
resounding raspberry, but she was prevented from disgracing herself by the timely arrival of a manicured young woman in a crisp
white uniform. 'Mrs Sheridan? Time for your colonic irrigation.

191

Would you like the warm garlic and lemon douche, or the coffee and chilli energiser?'

Emma blanched. 'Colonic irrigation? But I thought we were having a massage!'

'Enjoy!' Penny called out as the doors of the therapy suite closed behind her, with an ominous thud.

'Come on, lad,' urged Sir Stanley, jabbing Joe in the ribs with the handle of his sand wedge. 'Are you going to get yourself out of that bloody bunker or what?'

'Sorry, sir.' Joe sweated beneath Sir's withering gaze.

'Honest to God, I don't know what's got into your game the last couple of holes,' Sir Stanley tutted. 'You're all over the damn place. Anybody'd think you'd lost your nerve.'

And anybody would be right, thought Joe, trying not to think about Hereford, or Rachael and her weaselly smirk. He scowled at the ball; a small white blob in a mass of yellow sand. Come on, he told himself; deep breaths. You did it before, just relax and you'll do it again.

'Your stance is all wrong,' advised the marketing director. 'May I?' Without waiting for a reply, he set about bending Joe's limbs as though they were pipe-cleaners. 'That's better: trust me, I've been playing off a four handicap for years. Now, be sure to keep that back straight as you follow through.'

Staring fixedly at the ball, trying to ignore the eyes boring into the back of his head, Joe took a deep breath ... and swung.

'Oh my God, oh my God!' squealed a woman's voice, and high-heeled footsteps clattered through the conservatory.

'Whatever is the matter, Ruth?' demanded Dillie.

'Emma ... where is she? She's got to come right now, Sir Stanley says it's an emergency!'

On the other side of the doors to the therapy suite, Emma lay on her side, buttocks bared to the world, thinking mutinous thoughts. The emergency, whatever it was, couldn't have come at a more climactic moment. Five seconds later, and she'd have been suffering what could only be described as the hot flush to end all hot flushes.

'Sorry,' she announced, nimbly leaping off the couch and into her complimentary towelling mules. 'Sounds like I'm needed outside.'

'But Mrs Sheridan!' The therapist's plastic tubing dangled expectantly from her manicured fingertips.

Emma was already through the doors and in the conservatory. 'What's the emergency?' she enquired, visualising some stressed executive keeling over after a double English breakfast.

'It sounds awful,' exclaimed Ruth, trembling all over. 'Blood everywhere! Hurry up,' she urged, seizing Emma by the sleeve of her robe. 'I heard somebody say it was your Joe!'

It was Joe all right. But not Joe the victim; Joe the perpetrator.

All he could do was stare in dumb horror at the marketing director, who was bleeding profusely into an ice bucket in the breakfast room, his once-aquiline nose now more reminiscent of a horribly misshapen strawberry.

'Oh God,' he whimpered. 'I'm really sorry, I never meant ... you do realise I didn't mean to?'

'Just get him away from me,' mumbled Charles Greaves-Ormond, blowing red bubbles through his mashed-up nose. 'Thundering great prat.'

'You heard,' snapped Sir Stanley, jerking a thumb towards a row of chairs. 'Just sit down ... oh, and give me that, before you do any more damage.' He seized Joe's sand-wedge, and Joe was trudging miserably to a chair when Ruth arrived at a gallop with Emma, still clad in her robe and slippers.

'I found her,' panted Ruth. 'He's not dead, is he?'

The marketing director groaned. Joe sagged. Emma stared at the pair of them, open mouthed. 'What on *earth*?'

All eyes fixed accusingly on Joe.

'It was an accident,' he pleaded. 'How was I to know he was right behind me when I took the swing?'

'Most people keep hold of the bloody club,' replied a nasal Greaves-Ormond, who was rapidly developing two beautiful black eyes. 'Oh God, that idiot's disfigured me for life, hasn't he?'

'It's OK, you'll be fine.' Emma grabbed a couple of damask napkins and soaked them in chilled Perrier water. 'Here, hold these to your nose and try and pinch the bridge, it'll help stop the bleeding. Ruth, go to the changing room and get my bag, my car keys are in it. I'll drive him to the hospital.'

'Em?' ventured Joe.

She turned and glared at him, her fluffy white robe rapidly turning red. 'What? Can't you see I'm busy? Thanks to you.'

'I said I'm sorry,' he repeated, a hint of a sob in his voice. 'What more can I do?'

It was a reasonable question, but there was no answer to it. And for the first time ever, Emma found that the strongest feeling in her heart for Joe Sheridan had little to do with love.

You're being unreasonable, she told herself; it's not his fault he's a klutz with a boss who treats him like a performing monkey. It's not his fault you're having to smile so hard you've got cramp in your ears. But sweet reason had little place in the way she felt right now, because rightly or wrongly it all *felt* like Joe's fault. And all Emma wanted to do was wring his stupid neck.

23

It was late, and Joe was snoring away peacefully; but Emma didn't feel the least bit like sleeping. Or at least, not sleeping in the same bed as Joe. It was just as well that Mickey seldom went to bed before the end of the midnight movie.

Emma keyed in: *You SURE you're OK?*

Yes, told you! came back the reply.

Really?

Stop fussing! The cursor paused then set off again, more slowly now. *Look Em, I'm not pretending the pain's gone, I don't think it ever will. It's part of me now, and so is she. But it's stopped being the only thing in my world.*

She, thought Emma with a pang of sadness. The poor little scrap who hadn't had a chance from the word go. *You're really brave*, she typed.

No! Just getting to know myself better. Beginning to understand my priorities, you know.

Priorities??? Emma was intrigued, shocked even. Mickey's idea of prioritising had always been to throw her dirty socks at the wall and wash the ones that stuck.

It's made me think about what I'm doing and why I'm doing it, why I keep screwing up. And you know what? I think I want some stability in my life.

Coming from Mickey, stability sounded even freakier than priorities. Mickey and stability went together like Domestos and germs. *What do you mean?*

Ordinary stuff. You know, all those boring things people take for granted – a home, and a man in a woolly sweater, and one of those big daft-looking dogs. And I want to be somebody's mum. I

195

didn't know that before, but I do now, I just can't tell you how much.

You've been through an awful lot, Emma pointed out. *Maybe you'll feel different about things in a while.*

Don't think so. OK, maybe the big domestic thing's not going to happen just yet, but I want it to happen. I look at you and Joe, and I think: that's what I want. One day soon.

The killer irony wasn't lost on Emma. She glanced behind her, at the bed where Joe was sleeping the sleep of the innocent, drooling onto his pillow as he cuddled it like a teddy bear. Her empty side of the bed glared back at her accusingly. Why'd anyone want to be like us? she thought, miserably reliving the vicious row they'd had on their return from Great Berkeley Hall. In all the time they'd been together, they'd never before been so vile to each other. Right now, she thought, even *I'm* not sure I want to be me.

You need your head examined, she typed.

Uh-oh. Something tells me you and Joe haven't made up yet.

Emma's fingers were poised over the keys for several seconds before she answered. *Kind of.*

Bloody well hope so. And he's not being sacked?

Amazingly not.

Sued?

Nope. God knows why not. Charmed life.

So you're not going to poison him and collect on the insurance money after all? enquired Mickey, following up with a winking smiley face.

Don't you bloody tempt me, thought Emma, typing a humourless *HAHAHAHAHA.*

At work the following afternoon, the department was unusually quiet. Come to that, so was Dr Zara, which was a refreshing change from her usual snide or snappy comments.

'Obstructive urinary retention in cubicle four,' announced Lawrence as he flitted through the nurses' station in pursuit of a vacant male medical bed. 'Prostate the size of a satsuma. Make him comfortable, poor bloke's not been able to go since yesterday afternoon. Oh, Emma,' he added as she turned away.

'Yes?'

'Come and see me before you go off duty. I'd like a quick word.'

'Oh dear oh dear,' said Janice, tossing Emma a box of male catheters, size ten. 'What've you been up to?'

'Nothing!' she protested, racking her brains for any recent blunders he might have found out about.

'Don't give me that,' scoffed Sunil the agency nurse. '*Everybody*'s up to *something*.' He dipped a hand into his uniform pocket. 'Don't suppose I can interest you in a couple of Cup Final tickets?'

'Sorry mate, no dosh. If you ask me,' said Diane as Emma prepared an instrument trolley for her patient, 'that Zara's got something to do with this. Have you seen the look on her face?'

'Don't be daft, she always looks like that,' retorted Emma.

'Well, when I went into the coffee room just now,' said Sunil, 'she was reading a letter, and the minute she saw me she shoved it in her pocket and walked straight out. Gave me one hell of a dirty look.'

'Hey, it could have been a love letter,' ventured Diane, more in hope than conviction. 'No, you're right; who'd fancy her? Mardy cow.'

Joe might, thought Emma, rapidly banishing the thought as childish. After all, that had been a long, long time in the past, before he'd finally got fed up with Zara and dumped her. 'Well, whatever it was,' she declared, 'I can't see what it could possibly have to do with me. Now, I'd better get on before that poor man explodes all over the department.'

But all through her shift she kept wondering what – if anything – Zara could have found out that was worth grassing her up to Lawrence for. Somehow, the misappropriation of a box of rubber bands from the office didn't quite fit the bill as the crime of the century.

After the evening handover to the night staff, Lawrence beckoned Emma back into the office. 'Word,' he reminded her.

'Is it important? Only I'm knackered and—'

'This won't take long.' Lawrence closed the door behind her, cutting off her escape, and pointed to a chair. 'Si-tt.'

She plonked herself down on it reluctantly and waited for the axe to fall. 'Go on, what have I done?'

'It's what you haven't done that I'm interested in,' replied Lawrence. He opened a desk drawer, took out a sheet of paper and slapped it down in front of her.

'What's this?'

'An advert for a job. A job you haven't applied for.'

Emma frowned. '"Assistant Nurse Coordinator, Trauma and Intensive Care, West Cotswold Health Care Trust"? Why would I want to apply for that? I mean, even supposing it interested me, I wouldn't stand a cat in hell's chance of getting it.'

Lawrence sat down, produced a box of Miniature Heroes, took one and shoved the rest towards her. 'Help yourself, but if you have any of the Double Deckers I'll kill you. Who says you wouldn't stand a chance?'

'How could I?' She unwrapped a chocolate chunk. 'It's a senior post and I'm only a staff nurse!'

'Ah, but you were a junior sister in London and you've got stacks of qualifications and experience. Besides, it's not a senior post, it's a trainee one. They want somebody young who's keen, bright, knowledgeable, articulate and eager to learn. Sound like anybody you know?'

'Yes, you.'

'Darling, I don't need to learn, I know everything already. And sadly, even my own mum wouldn't classify me as young.'

'But why me? I mean, I'm flattered and all that, but why are you so keen for me to apply?'

'Because I've got to work with this person! I want somebody in the job who can *do* the job, not some idiot with ten degrees and no common sense.'

'Or alternatively,' retorted Emma, 'Dr Zara can't stand the sight of me so she wants you to get me kicked upstairs into admin?'

Lawrence looked at her in utter bafflement. 'Zara? What are you on about?'

'She's put you up to this, hasn't she?' She contemplated his aghast expression and her confidence wavered. 'Hasn't she?'

'Yeah, right, so I'm going to let some unstable SHO tell me how to manage my nursing team? Come off it Emma, even Prof. Johnson wouldn't dare tell me how to do my job.' He laughed. 'Well all right, he might, but I'd show him some interesting new uses for a thermometer if he did.'

'So ... she didn't say anything to you then?'

'Read my lips, Paranoid Girl: N–O!'

'Oh.'

Lawrence leaned over the desk, and neatly posted a rectangle of chocolate caramel into her open mouth. 'So – how about it, kid? Will you at least think about it?'

She thought about it all right. In fact Emma was still thinking about it two days later, when she and Joe called a temporary truce and went out for an Indian. 'You're very quiet tonight,' commented Joe, spooning rice onto his plate.

'What? Oh, sorry; I'm a bit tired.'

He didn't look all that convinced. 'You're still angry with me about last weekend, aren't you?'

She could have lied, but why should she? 'Yes,' she admitted. 'I am a bit.'

Joe sighed. 'Look, I know it was bad, but—'

'Bad!' A diner at a neighbouring table turned to look at Emma and she lowered her voice. 'Joe, a weekend in Jurassic Park would've been more fun – and there wouldn't have been half so many dinosaurs.'

'Look on the bright side – I know Unico's a bit, well, *traditional* ... but Sir Stanley really likes you.'

She pulled a face. 'I know he does; he groped my bottom all through the evening buffet.'

'What! You never told me that before.'

'What was the point?' She shrugged. 'I'm never going to get within five miles of the randy old bastard in future, so he won't have a chance to do it again.'

Colour drained from Joe's face. 'Hang on, Em, let's not be hasty. Unico's an old-fashioned family firm.'

'You can say that again.'

'They think these getting-to-know-you things are really important. You being involved in charity events and stuff could make a big difference to my career.'

Emma looked at him without the benefit of the rose-tinted spectacles she'd been wearing since she was a teenager. 'Well thank you very much, Joe, that's really selfless of you, encouraging your wife to get pawed by your boss on a regular basis. After all, it's perfectly OK because it's good for your precious career!'

'It's not like that at all! I'm thinking of us both.'

She snorted. 'Any more golf weekends, and chances are this time next year you won't have a career.'

Joe winced. 'That's below the belt.'

She knew it was, and felt slightly guilty at the buzz of satisfaction it gave her. But not that guilty. 'Tough. You shouldn't go round breaking important people's noses.'

'You make it sound deliberate!'

If it had been deliberate, she thought, I might have a bit more respect for you. 'Your chicken bhuna's going cold,' she said.

They ate in virtual silence for a while, exchanging nothing more than the odd comment on the scratched bhangra CD playing in the background.

'Are your mates coming round this Friday?' asked Emma.

'Don't think so, I may have to work late. Anyhow, you won't be there, will you? You've got your extra photography class.' He made it sound like an accusation.

Emma took a deep breath, determined not to rise to the bait. 'How's Rozzer?' she enquired. 'Heard anything from him lately?'

'Mightily pissed off,' replied Joe. 'That woman you foisted on him never stops talking, and the kid was sick all over his sofa. Poor bastard.' He chewed irritably. 'You know, you've got to stop interfering in people's lives. You can't make people be what you want them to be, just because it suits you.'

It surprised her so much to hear him say that, that she let the dig about her own interfering pass without retaliating. 'You're right,' she said. 'You can't. People have to make their own choices.'

'Exactly.'

She drew a swirly pattern with her fork in her masala sauce. 'You know what you were saying . . . about us having a baby? And I promised I'd think about it?'

All the annoyance vanished from Joe's face. 'You mean you've decided?'

Emma nodded. 'Yeah, I've been thinking about it a lot. And I've decided it's not for me.'

The spoon clattered from Joe's hand. 'What!'

A concerned waiter appeared from nowhere and started dabbing bhuna sauce off Joe's shirt-front. 'Is everything all right, sir? Let me clean that up for you, sir.'

'I'm fine, just leave it.'

'Wouldn't sir like me to—'

'Leave it!'

Alarmed by Joe's tone, the waiter scuttled back into the shadows.

'What do you mean, it's not for you?' demanded Joe.

'I don't mean not for me forever,' said Emma, 'I just mean, not for me as in ... not now. Obviously I'd like to have kids one day, just not right this minute.'

'But ... but you can't just ...' Joe was visibly struggling with the concept that Emma might want something different from what he wanted. 'Why not now? When we got married, we discussed all this and ... I thought kids were the reason we got married!'

'I thought we got married because we loved each other and wanted to be together.' She looked straight into his eyes. 'Was I wrong?'

'Well ... yes. I mean, no. Obviously. But people get married to have a family too; otherwise what's the point?'

'We will have a family. Just not now.'

'But *why* not now?'

She took his hand, willing him to understand. 'I'm only twenty-four, Joe. Twenty-four! That's nothing these days. We could wait fifteen years and it probably still wouldn't be too late. All I want is a few years to ... to do stuff with my life.'

His eyes narrowed. 'Stuff? What stuff?'

She took a deep breath. This had to be said sooner or later, so it might as well be now. 'I've been thinking. About my career. The fact is, I'm not ready yet to drop it and take a back seat; I want to achieve more before I have kids.'

'You've achieved a lot already!'

'Maybe. But it's not enough. I know I've got potential, and I want to find out what I'm capable of. Surely you can understand that?'

Joe's eyes held a glint of steel. 'You've been talking to that Lawrence again, haven't you? He's been filling your head with crap.'

That just did it. 'Joe, I don't let anybody fill my head with anything – and besides, Lawrence never talks crap, he's one of the most sensible people I know. If he thinks I've got what it takes for this new post, then I have to at least consider applying for it.'

'What new post?'

Shit, thought Emma. I never meant it to slip out like that. 'There's a trainee nurse coordinator's post going in Trauma and ICU,' she confessed. 'Lawrence thinks I might be suitable for it, and it does sound interesting. The money's good—'

'We don't need any extra money.'

'—and I think it could be really rewarding.'

He knew her too well to let her get away with only half the story. 'But?' he demanded.

'But, it would mean more training and studying. And since it covers the whole trust, it'd mean travelling so the hours would be irregular.'

'Then that settles it. You can't do it, can you?'

She blinked. 'Why not?'

'You're married! You've got responsibilities.'

'What, like darning socks and dancing attendance on you?'

'Don't be stupid. What I meant was ...'

She challenged him. 'Go on. What?'

'I thought seeing as you're my wife you'd want to be with me, spend time with me.'

'I do!' she protested.

'Yeah, sounds like it.' He folded his arms and sat back in his chair. 'Face it, Emma, what's the point of being married if we're never together?'

She thought of all the nights she'd spent alone in the flat, and stared him right back in the eyes. 'You tell me.'

Thank God I took up photography, thought Emma as she drove into the car park at the Centre. I'd go mad if I didn't have an excuse for getting out of the flat.

It was a pleasant afternoon, sunny and fresh after a rain shower, and squirrels were chasing each other across the lawns as she parked up and retrieved her camera bag from the passenger seat. If I can't be a tree in my next incarnation, she told herself, I'm going to be a squirrel. You never see squirrels arguing about emotional responsibilities.

All art and photography students had access to the Centre's facilities during the day, so that they could work on their creative projects; and Emma had decided that a couple of hours in the darkroom would be the perfect complement to her mood. Besides, once she was locked away in there, there was no danger of being accosted by Terrence and his cardboard box.

As she reached the second-floor landing, her heart sank. The 'engaged' light was on outside the darkroom door. Damn. Somebody had got there before her. She turned and was about to go back downstairs when the light clicked off, the door opened and a figure emerged, carrying a an empty bottle of developer.

'Emma!' Richard smiled and his blue eyes joined in. 'Come to do a bit of work on your portfolio?'

'Well, I thought I might have a go at doing some developing, but,' she nodded towards the darkroom, 'if you're busy ...'

'No problem, just finishing off a few infra-red prints. Tell you what, when I've filled this up why don't you come in and watch and then we can process your negatives too?'

It wasn't what she'd planned, but if she had to spend time with anyone Richard Claybourne would do as well as the next person. Actually, he might do rather better than most.

'OK,' said Richard, twisting the top of the developing tank until it clicked. 'It's light-proof now, so you can turn the safe light back on.'

Emma fumbled in the dark for the light switch and brushed against his cheek. It felt warm and just a little stubbly. 'Sorry.'

'Don't be.'

The light came on, bathing the darkroom in a weird red glow. Emma felt strange. Maybe it was the fumes from the developer, making her light-headed. More likely, it was the fact that she hadn't slept properly for days and it was starting to take its toll. She sat down on one of the stools. 'Go ahead, I'm watching,' she assured him as he poured the developer into the tank.

'Are you OK?'

No, she screamed silently. I'm not OK, I'm so not OK I can hardly remember what OK feels like. 'Yes,' she said.

'Liar.' Richard counted the time off on his watch, shaking the tank every thirty seconds. She watched him dumbly as he poured off the developer and replaced it with plain water, then fixer. Finally he ran the hose from the cold tap into the tank, switched on the negative dryer, and left them both running. 'Right,' he said, grabbing the other stool and sitting down next to Emma. 'While that's washing through you can tell me what's the matter.'

She hadn't meant to tell him. She hadn't meant to talk about it to anyone, probably not even Mickey, who had enough on her plate; but there was something in Richard that reached out to her and made her sure she could confide anything without the fear that it would go further.

He listened carefully as she told him all about the golf weekend, and the rows, and the choice words Minette had come up with when Joe told her. 'I can't believe he went straight to her and told her!' she said. 'And you can imagine what she thought about me going for a better job.'

'Let me guess. You're a bad wife and you ought to be sitting at home washing nappies and making chutney?'

'Something like that. Then she has the cheek to say, "What's the point of being married if you're not prepared to compromise?"! So I said, "That's right, but the compromise is supposed to be on both sides and, as I see it, Joe isn't doing any compromising at all."' She sighed. 'And now I'm feeling guilty, like this whole thing's my fault.'

Richard rubbed his chin thoughtfully. In the background, the warmth and the sound of running water made Emma think of tropical waterfalls and golden beaches. She couldn't help musing that Richard Claybourne would look most appetising on a golden beach ...

'I've no right to advise you or try to tell you what to do,' he said.

She hung her head, embarrassed. 'Sorry, I shouldn't have gone on like that. It's not your problem.'

He slid a finger under her chin and tilted it up. 'I didn't mean that. What I meant was, I have no right and neither does anybody else. And if they're trying to make you feel bad for wanting a life of your own, well, I'd say that's their problem, not yours.'

Emma smiled ruefully. 'You make it sound so easy.'

'Oh, nothing in life's easy, I've lived long enough to know that. But life's a lot less complicated when you realise that nobody understands what's right for you as well as you do yourself.'

'So you think I should take no notice of what they say?'

He laughed. 'You're not listening! I told you, what I think doesn't matter. But I only have one rule in my life, and maybe you'll find it useful too.' His eyes were looking right into hers, and she felt the warmth of his gaze begin to melt her very bones as one hand stroked her hair gently back from her forehead. 'When you can't decide what to do, Emma, follow your heart.'

Richard's words stuck in Emma's mind long after they'd cleared up in the darkroom and shared a cafetière in the cafe-bar downstairs. But more than his words, she was haunted by the look in his eyes, the ways he'd found of standing very close to her; and the excuses she'd found to let her hand brush against his as she reached for another sheet of photographic paper.

It would have been so easy to go further, so very easy ... And she had been so tempted. But that was crazy, and anyway, she'd probably imagined it all. If Richard had any interest in her, it was as a teacher, nothing else.

Or at least, that was what she told herself.

Back home, she found a note stuck to the fridge door: *Came home, you weren't here, gone out. J.* No kisses, no '*love you*', nothing. She screwed it up and threw it away. Well, if Joe was trying to make her feel bad she wasn't going to fall for it – even though she knew she already had.

She got a glass of wine and a handful of dried fruit, put on her comfy slippers and took the phone into the living room. Joe wasn't the only one who could go telling tales to his mum.

'Hello, Golden Sands Guest House, can I help you?'

'Auntie Jacqui? It's Emma. Where's Mum, I thought she was better?'

'Er ... yes,' replied Jacqui. She sounded cagey. 'Well, she was ... but then she got a bit worse again, so I said I'd stay on for a while.'

'Can I have a word with her?'

Jacqui sighed. 'God help her, I told her she should tell you, but would she have it?'

Emma's throat tightened. 'Tell me what?'

'Oh no, it's, "Jacqui, I won't have her worrying for no good reason," and now where's that got us? She's in hospital, love. The Infirmary.'

All the blood in Emma's veins seemed to crystallise and freeze. 'Oh my God! What's the matter with her? What's wrong?'

'It's nothing to worry about, love, really it isn't. They just said she ought to go in for a bit of a rest, that's all.'

'Jacqui,' said Emma firmly, 'don't give me that, I'm a nurse. People don't just go into hospital for a rest! What the hell is wrong with my mum?'

But Jacqui's reply, when it came, was scarcely more informative. 'Why don't you pop up and see her, eh? I'm sure she'd love a visit, and then she can explain it all to you yourself.'

24

Friday night hospital visiting was even more popular than *Take My Husband* on Channel 6. With a 'thank God' of relief, Jacqui squeezed her car into the last empty parking space in the over-stuffed car park. Emma was halfway to the front door before she'd put the handbrake on.

'Hang on,' panted Jacqui, 'wait for me.' And she trotted off in hot pursuit, a plump, red-haired figure with blue nail varnish and a handbag full of Silk Cut.

She caught up with Emma by the lifts in the main foyer. 'Steady on love, it's no use getting yourself all het up like this.'

Emma rounded on her. 'Het up? How would you feel if your mother was in hospital and your auntie refused to tell you what was wrong with her?'

Jacqui's kindly face sagged. 'I'm sorry love, I did try and explain. I mean, it was your mum made me promise. And besides,' she pointed out as they got into the lift with a nun on crutches, 'I'm no doctor, am I? If I tried I'd probably get it all wrong.'

'Hmph.' Emma jabbed the button for the fourth floor. She liked her Auntie Jacqui and knew she shouldn't really take it out on her, but who else was she going to take it out on? 'Well, whatever's going on I'm going to wring it out of Mum, whether she likes it or not.'

'Yes love,' sighed Jacqui, already feeling in need of a cigarette. 'I know you will.'

'Look, I'm just not in the mood, OK?' Rozzer pushed away his plate and got up from the table.

Linda's face fell. 'Is there something wrong with it?'

'No, it's fine.'

'Did I put too much salt in?'

'No.'

'I could make you something else if—'

Rozzer felt the elastic inside his head give way. 'For God's sake give it a rest!' Hearing himself snap, and thinking about Sara-Jane in the next room, turned him red with embarrassment. Rozzer was not a snapping kind of guy. 'Look, I'm sorry,' he said. 'It's just been one of those days and I'm not hungry. I'm going to my room, OK?'

Linda said not a word, just turned her back on him and started scraping the shepherd's pie into the kitchen bin. He felt really bad then. All right, so he hadn't asked her to play house, but how was she to know that today was an especially crap day for him – or the reason why? And it had been a nice thought, cooking him dinner.

He closed his bedroom door and flopped dejectedly onto the edge of the bed, feeling like a sulky teenager who'd made his point and rather wished he hadn't. Sliding open the drawer in his bedside locker, he felt for a crumpled envelope and withdrew an even more crumpled photograph.

Not that he needed the photograph to help him remember. If he closed his eyes he could see them as clear as anything. Maxine and the baby. Little Josie, who would be nine years old today, and was God knows where in the world, asking herself why everybody else had a daddy and she didn't.

Let go of it, he'd told himself a million times. It was your fault Maxine didn't want you in their lives any more and you've just got to live with that. Maybe, if you're really lucky, when she's eighteen Josie'll turn up on your doorstep and curse you to hell for being a crap father. If you're not, you'll probably never see her again.

There was nobody he felt could share this with, not even Joe. Everybody else seemed to want to forget that he'd once had the beginnings of a life, but he never could. And, once a year, it all welled up inside him again and he had to surrender to the numbness of his grief until at last its talons let go of him – until next year.

As he sat there, shoulders slumped, eyes downcast, he didn't notice the bedroom door edge slowly open, or the small, pyjama-clad figure peeping cautiously inside.

In fact he wasn't aware of her until she clambered up onto the bed beside him, jolting him out of his stupor.

'She's a pretty lady,' said Sara-Jane, pointing at the picture of Marie.

'Pretty,' echoed Rozzer. He started. 'Hey, who told you you could come in here? Why aren't you in bed?'

'Not sleepy,' replied the little girl promptly. 'And I heard you pretending to be angry.'

'Pretending?'

'You're no good at let's pretend.' Sara-Jane's large, round eyes fixed him intently. ' Mummy thinks you're angry, but you're not really, you're all sad inside. Like Mummy.'

Rozzer looked at her with interest. 'Your Mummy's sad?'

She nodded vigorously. 'Mummy got sad when the bad people started being horrible to us. Her head hurts bad sometimes, and she cries. But Mr Snuffles knows how to make her all better.'

Rozzer raised an eyebrow. 'Mr Snuffles?'

A loved-to-destruction pink rabbit with advanced alopecia appeared from behind Sara-Jane's back. 'Mummy says he always makes her feel better, so I brought him for you so you'll be better too. But you have to look after him because he's very old and his ear sometimes falls off.'

I know how he feels, thought Rozzer. But in spite of himself a smile broke through his gloom; and he was pretty sure that in the semi-darkness Sara-Jane didn't notice he was crying.

Karen Cox was sitting up in bed in a big pink T-shirt with a penguin on the front. A bowl of fruit and a jug of water sat on the locker, but there were no get-well cards or flowers. It was almost as though Karen had hoped to sneak in and out of hospital without the rest of the world noticing.

Emma had rehearsed some choice words for her mother, but the minute she stepped into the ward bay and saw her mum looking so pale and exhausted, all she could do was rush in and hug the breath out of her. 'Mum! Oh Mum, why didn't you tell me? What's been going on?'

'Emma? Em, what on earth are you doing here?' gasped Karen as her daughter drew back from the embrace. Her eyes flicked across to Jacqui, who was shifting awkwardly from one foot to the other at the end of the bed. 'You didn't. Oh Jacqui, you didn't.'

'I never said anything, Karen! Well, only that you were in hospital. I had to, when she rang up and you weren't there.'

'Is somebody going to tell me what the hell is going on?' demanded Emma. 'Because I have been worrying myself stupid ever since I phoned up Jacqui and she said you were in here. And if you're not going to tell me, I'm going to go and find someone who will.'

She half rose to her feet, but Karen clasped a hand round her arm. 'No need for that, love.'

'So you'll tell me then?'

Karen nodded defeatedly. 'I was only trying to protect you, love. I mean, what's the point of you worrying when nobody can do anything about it? And anyway, it's not as if it's anything really *serious*.'

Jacqui choked on a grape. 'Not serious! I'd call falling down the bloody stairs, pardon my French, pretty serious. Wouldn't you?'

'You fell down the stairs!' Emma stared at her mother, half expecting plaster casts to materialise from nowhere. 'How on earth? Did you trip?'

'Sort of,' hedged her mother.

'Tell her, Karen,' urged Jacqui.

'All right. I didn't trip, not exactly; my legs just sort of gave way. It's something they do once in a while, I have to be a bit careful and this time I wasn't looking where I was going.' She patted Emma's hand. 'No need to worry, though, I'm fine. Just a few bruises. And the steroids will have me right in no time.'

'Hang on a minute,' said Emma. 'What do you mean, your legs give way? Why? And what's all this about steroids?'

There was a short, tense silence. The woman in the bed opposite put away her knitting and put in her hearing aid. It was Jacqui who answered, looking Karen straight in the eye. 'Your mother's not well, love,' she said quietly. 'She's got MS.'

Pants, pants, pants, pants, pants.

That just about summed up the whole of this last week; and Friday evening didn't promise much in the way of improvement. Joe slammed down the phone and aimed a kick at the skirting board. Everything was going to Hell in a hand-basket, and where were your mates when you needed somebody to get totally rat-arsed with?

He wondered what Emma was doing. Not thinking about me, that's for sure, he mused grimly, then felt guilty and reminded himself that Emma hadn't gone to Blackpool to ride the roller-coasters. But that didn't alter the fact that he resented her absence or that he couldn't even find somebody to sit and listen while he moaned into his thirteenth pint. Gary was 'doing a bit of business, know what I mean' in some hard house club in Gloucester; Toby'd got himself a hot date with the Slovakian pole-dancer he'd been leching after for weeks; and even Rozzer, who was *always* on call whenever Joe needed him, claimed he 'wasn't in the mood'.

Thanks very much, thought Joe. I'll remember this the next time one of you needs a shoulder to whinge on.

He toyed with the idea of going round to his mum's, or imposing himself on one of his brothers; but he didn't much fancy being bombarded with questions about where Emma was, and why he hadn't gone with her. He was almost beginning to wish he had. Nevertheless, he restrained himself from calling her on her mobile, and was resigning himself to a solitary evening of canned beer and crisps when the telephone rang.

I knew she'd break first, thought Joe triumphantly. She's phoning to say she's sorry.

But the voice on the line wasn't Emma's. 'Joe? It's me.'

His heart turned a miniature somersault. 'Zara! Hi.'

'Is this a bad time? I could phone some other evening.'

'No! Not bad at all. I'm ... er ... on my own, actually.'

'I know.'

Of course you do, thought Joe, with a flush of discomfort. You work with her. You probably heard her ranting at me on the phone, calling me a heartless git and God knows what else. 'Emma's at her mother's.'

'All weekend?'

'Yes.'

There was the kind of tension-filled silence that throbbed like a ripe pustule.

'I was wondering,' they both said simultaneously, then dissolved into laughter.

'You first,' said Zara.

'No, you. What was it you were wondering?'

'Just ... if you were doing anything this evening. I mean, you've probably got something lined up already, but—'

'No,' cut in Joe. 'No, I haven't got anything lined up actually.'

'Oh. So ... would you maybe like to meet up for a drink somewhere? Say no if you'd rather not.'

'I'd love to,' Joe replied promptly. 'See you in the Jolly Forester, in about half an hour?'

'First one there gets the drinks in?'

'It's a date.'

Joe grabbed his jacket off the back of the sofa, threw the rest of the crisps into the kitchen bin, and walked out of the door whistling. And if his conscience did prick him, he certainly didn't notice.

'I'll leave you two together and go out for a ciggy,' announced Jacqui, slinging her bag on her shoulder. 'You've got a lot to talk about.'

Emma's hands were shaking as she handed her mother a glass of water. 'I don't understand,' she said. 'It's not true.'

Karen stroked the hair off her daughter's face, the way she had done when Emma was four years old and struggling to understand why Daddy wasn't ever coming back. 'Come on,' she urged, 'it's only MS. It's not the end of the world.'

Emma swallowed hard, remembering all the people she'd nursed in her training; blocking out all the ones who'd responded really well to treatment, and recalling only the gaunt-faced, terminal ones lying trembling in their beds, waiting to die. 'Oh Mum,' she whispered, taking her mother's hand and holding it against her cheek. She felt the steady rhythm of the blood pulsing through it, the warmth of the skin, the strength of the fingers. How could this be the hand of someone with multiple sclerosis? 'Tell me it's not true.'

After a little while, a thought struck her. 'How long have you known?'

Her mother took a deep breath. 'Oh, just a few ... years.'

'Years!' The word zapped through Emma like an electric shock. 'How many years?'

'About four ... no, nearer five. Since I had those dizzy spells, do you remember?'

Emma remembered, and wondered how she could have been so stupid, so unobservant. How she could have failed to put the pieces of the jigsaw together. She was supposed to be a nurse, for pity's sake!

'You told me the doctor thought the dizzy spells were just down to low blood pressure!'

'Yes, well, he did. But that was before he referred me to the hospital and they found out it was MS.'

'Why didn't you tell me? Why didn't you tell me straight away?'

'Like I said, love, there didn't seem any point. You'd only have worried and fussed, and I was better again in a couple of weeks, so I practically forgot about it myself.'

'But you're ill, Mum! You need help!'

Karen shook her head firmly. 'No I don't, I've been really well,' she objected. 'Most of the time I'm fine, I just have to be careful not to overdo things. You ask Jacqui.'

'You're not fine now,' pointed out Emma. 'Are you? 'Cause if you were, you wouldn't be in here and Jacqui wouldn't be running the guest house.'

The point had clearly hit home. Karen handed her back the empty glass and flopped back onto the stack of pillows. 'It's just a flare-up. The only reason they brought me in was because I haven't had one this bad before.'

'Then you're definitely not all right, are you? It's getting worse.'

Karen closed her eyes. 'I knew it'd be like this if I told you,' she said quietly. 'That's why I didn't.'

'Didn't you think I had a right to know?'

The eyes opened. 'No,' Karen replied simply.

Emma couldn't believe what she was hearing. 'But—'

Karen took her hand and squeezed it. 'If you're going to go down that road, don't I have a right to live my life with dignity, the way I want to? And anyway, love, it's not about rights. It's about sparing you a load of useless worry at a time when you're just building your own life. You've got a lot going on, you know – building your career, getting married, making a home, thinking about starting a family ...' Her voice tailed off. 'Oh Emma love, is that what's worrying you?'

'What?'

212

'You do realise it's very rare for MS to be passed on in families? You're not pregnant, are you, Emma? Emma love, what is it?'

A tear escaped from Emma's eye and crawled sluggishly down her right cheek. 'Oh Mum, not you too.'

It was Karen's turn not to understand. 'I don't quite see—'

'Why does everybody think I ought to be pregnant?' Emma blurted out. 'Why is it OK for other people to have lots of ambitions, but all I'm supposed to want to do is have babies?'

'Oh Emma, what's brought all this on?'

'Nothing, I—'

The woman with the hearing aid was listening in, goggle-eyed, as a big jolly nurse came into the bay with a kidney bowl and a syringe. 'Ah, Mrs Cox! How are we this evening? Would you like to roll over onto your tummy for me?'

'No,' replied Karen, with unaccustomed coldness; 'I wouldn't. Come back later.'

The nurse stared back at her, slack-jawed with astonishment, then left with a muttered 'Well!'

Karen turned back to her daughter. 'You were about to tell me.'

Emma had taken advantage of the short hiatus to wipe her eyes with her sleeve. 'There's nothing to tell. Anyway, it's not important.' She patted her mother's arm. 'Besides, you don't want to hear about my problems; it's you we should be talking about.'

'Don't give me that, somebody's been saying things to upset you. Was it Minette?'

'No ... well, yes ... not this time, not really. Me and Joe, we had a row.'

Karen smiled. 'Everybody has rows, love.'

'Not like this one, Mum. This was a really big one. You see, there's this job they're advertising at the General; it's a fantastic training opportunity, and I think I could be good at it. I told him I might apply ...'

'And he didn't like the idea?' hazarded Karen.

'He said I was being selfish. Practically accused me of marrying him under false pretences, just because I said I wasn't ready to have a baby yet! Then his mother found out, and started having a go at me. And now ... oh Mum, I don't know anything any more. Maybe ... maybe they're right.'

Karen took her daughter's face in her hands. 'Is that what you *really* feel?'

213

'No,' admitted Emma.

'Then you have to stand up for what *you* feel is right. It's no good doing what other people want you to do if it's not what you want yourself.'

Emma smiled wanly. 'You make it sound so easy.'

'I know it isn't. But this is your body and your life, even if you are sharing it with Joe now. He'll come to accept that – he'll have to.'

'You don't understand, Mum,' whispered Emma. 'All those horrible things I said to Joe – I meant every word. I looked at him and I *hated* him. Surely that can't be right?'

Karen smiled. 'Do you still hate him now?'

'No,' Emma conceded. 'But I don't think I love him either.'

'You're angry, that's all. Let the dust settle; he'll come round and everything will be fine, just you see. Now, come here and give your old mum a hug – and remember: at times like this, there's only one thing you can do. Listen to what your heart is telling you.'

Emma's own heart missed a beat. 'You're the second person to say that to me.'

'Oh. Who else?'

'Just ... a friend,' she replied softly.

When Joe heard the news the next day on the phone from Blackpool, he was utterly gobsmacked.

'MS? Oh my God, people die from that don't they?'

'Thanks Joe, I really needed reminding.'

'Come on, Em, I didn't mean ... well, you know what I meant.' He peered guiltily at his stubbly face in the mirror over the hall table and reflected that maybe, just maybe, he was getting too old for late nights on the piss. Not to mention too old to behave like a sulky child towards Emma. 'It's horrible, your poor mum. How's she managing?'

'At the moment she's not. That's why Auntie Jacqui's practically running the place.' Emma geared up for the big bombshell. 'And that's why we have to think about making some arrangements.'

A distant alarm bell sounded inside Joe's head. 'What do you mean, *arrangements*?'

'For taking care of Mum, in case she gets worse. I mean, we

can't just leave her there to cope on her own, can we? Not now we know what's going on.'

'She's not on her own,' Joe pointed out. 'She's got your Auntie Jacqui.'

'Who's got a family of her own to look after, plus a part-time job and a husband who's hardly ever in work. Anyhow, Mum's already talking about selling the guest house and moving somewhere more manageable.'

'Sounds sensible,' agreed Joe. 'But where do these "arrangements" come in? You think we should help her out with house-hunting or something?'

'Sort of. I think we should invite her to stay with us until she gets on her feet again.'

'What! How long for?'

'How should I know? Until her health stabilises and she finds a flat or a bungalow, I suppose. Does it matter?'

A kind of choking sound came from the other end of the phone. 'She's your mum, Emma.'

'Exactly! And I'm not having her get worse and have to go into a home.'

'We've only been married five minutes! How'd you feel if my mum moved in with us?'

'My mum's nothing like your mum!'

'No. Mine can cook, for a start-off.'

Emma's latent anger bubbled back to the surface. 'What kind of a cheap line is that? She's my mum, she's ill, and she's coming to stay.'

'In *my* flat?'

Her eyes narrowed. 'No, in *our* home. Or have you forgotten all the times you've told me the place belongs to me as much as it does to you? Funny how things change the minute they don't go exactly the way you want them to. Is this some kind of punishment for telling you I don't want a baby yet?'

'Stop talking rubbish.'

'Then stop behaving like a selfish brat.'

This was a red rag to a bull. 'Selfish, me? I'm not the one who wants to move her mother into a two-bedroomed flat. I'm not being selfish, I'm being realistic. I'm trying to protect our marriage.'

It might have been sincere, but it sounded so phoney that Emma

215

almost laughed. 'We've only been married a few months,' she said. 'We're supposed to be wildly in love. Is our marriage really so shaky that it needs protecting?'

'What do you think?' replied Joe curtly, and put the phone down on her.

25

The blood-drenched casualty on the stretcher struggled to sit up. 'Excuse me, miss,' he whispered through blanched lips, 'I'm dead. Can I go home?'

'Certainly not,' replied Zara tartly. 'You can just stay where you are and wait to be processed like everybody else.'

It was one of the Major Incident Training Days, and the field at the back of the Cotswold General was littered with bodies. With the aid of copious quantities of fake blood, stick-on abrasions and gruesome prostheses, the West of England's medical services were acting out their response to a sudden influx of casualties resulting from a huge factory explosion. Most of the 'casualties' came from a group of enthusiastic volunteers who travelled the length and breadth of the country on a regular basis, emulating hideous injuries in their spare time. Well, thought Emma as she helped Lawrence to splint up a 'fractured' femur, it's a hobby of sorts but give me stamp collecting any day.

'So your mum's really selling up then?'

'Eventually, yes. She took a lot of persuading, but in the end the consultant made her see it was the only sensible thing to do.' She sighed. 'It's a shame, though, she loves that guest house.'

'Do you want me to go into shock now?' enquired the lady who owned the femur. 'Or I could have convulsions if you prefer. I'm good at convulsions.'

Lawrence gave the patient's bandaged leg a friendly pat. 'Tell you what, love – one of the doctors'll be along in a minute, why don't you save it for them?'

As they finished the job, Emma half-watched Zara out of the corner of her eye. She was running about all over the place, in the wake of her senior registrar, Sophie Gundersson. Ms Gundersson was everything a Norwegian was supposed to be – athletic, with long, ice-blonde hair and pale skin, and the kind of cool authority that got things done without any visible effort. All with the bonus of a thick Wolverhampton accent. By contrast, Zara looked ragged, breathless, with a kind of fourth-form overeagerness to please. It gave Emma a malicious kick to see her halo slipping in public for once.

'Is your mum staying in Blackpool until she's sold up?' enquired Lawrence as they moved off in search of the less urgent casualties.

Emma shook her head. 'Auntie Jacqui's going to run it for her, bless her heart. Mum's coming down to Cheltenham.' Her lip curled. 'That is, if Joe stops trying to put her off.'

Lawrence raised one neatly plucked eyebrow. 'What's this, squabbles in the love nest? Surely not.'

'Oh ha-ha. It's just Joe being really childish. He knows what a state Mum's in, but will he have her move in with us? Will he hell. And it's not as if we haven't got the room, or—'

'For God's sake,' cut in a voice behind Emma, making her jump, 'why don't you give the poor guy a break?'

Emma swivelled round. Zara was standing there, arms folded, sneering. 'What did you say?'

'I said, give him a break. Hasn't he got enough pressure to cope with, without you forcing your mother on him?'

Emma's jaw dropped. Even the ultra-cool Lawrence looked thunderstruck. 'What the hell has it got to do with you?' Emma demanded when she got her voice back. 'And what do you know about me and Joe, anyway? You've been snooping on us, haven't you?'

Zara shrugged. 'Who needs to snoop? I've got eyes and ears.'

'Don't give me that,' snapped Emma. 'Who've you been talking to? Have you been pestering my husband?'

Zara rolled her eyes. 'You know, I reckon he's right: you are childish. If you really loved the poor bloke, you'd get off his case.'

'What the hell? You lying bitch, Joe would never say ...' She swallowed. 'What's your bloody problem, anyway?'

This was greeted with a grunt. 'From what I hear, love, you're the one with the problem. And by the way,' Zara added, 'why are

218

you standing around chatting when you're supposed to be saving lives?'

It took a massive effort of will not to deck Zara with the nearest defibrillator. Emma indicated Sophie Gundersson, sweeping along a line of stretchers like an avenging angel, minus the fiery sword. 'At least I don't spend all day brown-nosing my boss because I can't do my job properly,' she said sweetly. 'By the way, have you figured out how to give an injection yet?'

She waited for Zara to rise to the bait; but to her astonishment, Zara just turned crimson to the tips of her ears and walked quickly away.

'You promised!' insisted Emma as she and Joe emerged from the cinema that evening. If anybody had asked her right then what film they'd just seen, let alone whether it was any good, she'd have had a tough job answering.

'Oh for God's sake, Em, you're not still going on about that!' Joe barged his way ill-temperedly between the milling cinema-goers, and through the heavy swing doors. 'For the last time, I did not promise anything of the sort!'

Emma hung on tenaciously, like a terrier worrying a rat. 'So you *admit* you've been phoning her then?'

Joe answered through clenched teeth. 'There's nothing to admit! Zara's an old schoolmate, Em; mates do talk on the phone, you know. I mean, they haven't actually made it illegal yet.'

'A mate? Is that what you call somebody you were practically engaged to?' Emma's sniping failed to conceal the deeper vein of hurt. 'How do you think it feels, Joe, being told private stuff about your marriage by your husband's ex-girlfriend? Face it, you've not been discussing the weather with her, have you? God knows what you'd tell her if you were ever actually in the same room!'

Joe looked distinctly uncomfortable at that, but didn't back-track. 'You're overreacting,' he said, striding off ahead.

'Oh am I?' Emma caught up with him, grabbed him by the arm and swung him round. 'Being "childish", am I?'

'If the cap fits.'

'According to bloody Zara it does.' He flinched. 'So what's all this stuff about you being "under a lot of pressure" then? And how come you've told her all about it, but you've never once mentioned it to me?'

219

'I've got a senior job,' parried Joe. 'Pressure's par for the course, everybody knows that.'

'So you're telling me there's nothing in particular worrying you at work? Nothing's going wrong?'

'Nothing.'

'That's not the impression I got off Zara.'

Joe turned aside to hide the look on his face. 'Then she's got the wrong impression, hasn't she? Hardly surprising, seeing as we only talked on the phone for about two minutes.' Joe's expression softened, and he took his wife by the arm. 'Come on Squeaks, let's not fight over a stupid phone call. Let's go home and see if we can still fit both of us into the Jacuzzi.'

'I don't want to fight, you know I don't,' protested Emma as they walked back to the car. 'But you don't know how it feels, having things kept from you, and ... then I start imagining stuff.'

'You've no need to, you know.'

She took a deep breath. 'And then there's all this worry about Mum.'

Joe's hand rested on the handle of the driver's door. 'Oh, I get it. This isn't about Zara, it's about Karen. You're still mad at me because I said your mum couldn't move in with us.'

'Of course I am! This'd all be completely different it if was your mother, wouldn't it!'

Infuriated though he might be, Joe couldn't suppress a small smile. Much as he loved his mother, the thought of ever living under the same roof as her again was hardly enticing. 'No,' he replied, 'it wouldn't. And you know it wouldn't. Like I tried to explain, we've not been married long, we need our private space. The last thing we need is a spare room full of relatives.'

'One relative!' Emma felt her lip tremble. 'She's my *mum*, Joe! She's my mum and what if she's dying? Can you imagine what I felt like when I saw her in that hospital bed? I'm afraid, Joe, really afraid. Why won't you help her?'

'Hey, of course I want to help her! We *are* helping her.' Joe took Emma by the shoulders and forced her to look at him. 'Your mum's not dying,' he said, gently but firmly. 'You know that, you're a nurse. OK, she's not very well at the moment because she had a flare-up, but she's getting better and she's going to be just fine. People can be in remission for years.'

'She needs someone to take care of her, Joe. I need to be able to see that she's all right.'

Joe looked at the tears gathering in Emma's eyes. 'OK. OK, she can come and stay with us.'

'Oh Joe! Really?'

'But just for a while, yeah? Till we sort something else out.'

He slipped an arm around her waist, and said all the things she wanted to hear. But Emma couldn't help wondering if that was how he really felt. And what he'd tell Zara, next time he phoned her up.

Because, though he might brush the idea aside, she knew he would.

On Thursday afternoon, Emma took a half-day's leave and joined the rest of the Creative Camera class on their special 'Wildlife Shoot'.

'We paid for an all-night photographic ramble in the Forest of Dean, complete with woodland buffet,' Mrs Franks had complained as she rattled down the motorway in the Centre's minibus, uncomfortably squeezed between Terrence and Colin. 'Not a day out at the local wildlife park! It's in my course brochure, you know, in black and white.'

'Scrambling through the woods in the dark? Fine, if you don't mind carrying me back when I break the other leg,' replied Richard. 'And as for the buffet, there's a coolbox of sandwiches in the back.'

Mrs Franks brightened a little, until Terrence piped up, 'I made them. Hope everybody likes sardines.'

Once they arrived, they split up into groups. Emma politely declined Roger's invitation to go and film the camels mating, and accompanied Treena and Richard to the hide that overlooked one of the wildfowl lakes.

'It's just like a garden shed with a hole in it,' commented Emma, peering out through the gap in the slats.

'Very calming though,' replied Richard, adjusting the height of his tripod. 'There's something very Zen about gazing out at ducks bobbing about on the water.'

Calm was not the first adjective that sprung to Emma's mind. In fact calm was not something she'd ever really felt in such close proximity to Richard – not that she'd any intention of letting on.

Treena, who had been very quiet for a very long time, got to her feet. 'I shouldn't be here,' she said.

Emma scratched her head. 'Why? What's the matter?'

'I didn't tell Gerald. He'll be furious if I'm not there when he gets home. I should go.'

'Gerald's an idiot,' said Richard, 'and it's about time you told him so.'

Treena made for the door, but Emma followed her. 'Go home?' she said. 'How? We all came in the minibus, remember?'

'I ... I don't know, I'll get a taxi or something.'

'Treena love, it's thirty miles back to Cheltenham.'

'Oh for God's sake,' said Richard tetchily, 'let her go if she wants to. It's high time she made a decision for herself.'

That was all Treena needed. She burst into breathless sobbing, Richard threw his hands up in despair, and Emma had to bundle her patient out of the hide.

Ten minutes later, Emma returned, minus Treena.

Richard looked up sheepishly. 'Is she OK?'

'Just about – no thanks to you.'

'Well, what I said was true. She's married to an idiot and she needs to break free.'

'All the same ...'

'Yeah, I know. In future, keep my big mouth to myself.'

'Never mind, no harm done. She's gone off with Mrs Franks to look at the penguins.' As she closed the door of the hide behind her, Emma became powerfully aware of what a small space it enclosed, and how very close to Richard it obliged her to sit. She lowered herself back onto the rickety folding chair next to his. 'Taken any good shots?'

'Not yet. The light's not quite right, we'll have to wait for the sun to sink just below the tops of those trees.' He set down his camera carefully on the wooden floor. 'You look like crap, by the way.'

She stuck out her tongue. 'Gee thanks. You're really on form today.'

'Sorry, I'm not the best at niceties. I'm starting to get worried about you, Emma.'

'Worried?' She avoided looking at him. 'Why?'

'Don't be like that. I may be thick sometimes, but I can tell when things aren't going well.'

She hung her head. 'Pants, is how things are going.' Swinging her feet so that the muddy soles of her boots scuffed the floor, she added, 'Still, at least Joe finally agreed to let my mum stay.'

'That's good.'

'Temporarily.'

'Not so good. Still,' Richard conceded, 'maybe Joe's right. Sometimes three can be a crowd.'

As he said the words, she could feel his eyes boring into her, and knew he wasn't talking about her, Joe and Karen.

'Sometimes. Maybe.'

He laid a hand lightly on her arm, and she felt his touch zing through her, like the explosive fizz of ice-cold champagne. 'That's not all, is it? You're worried about other stuff besides your mother, I can tell.'

She didn't know why, but she felt a huge compulsion to tell Richard everything, to lay her little wounded heart bare to him. Maybe, subconsciously, it was some kind of payback for Joe's cosy little phone conversations with Zara. Or maybe it was more than that; an attraction that went far beyond revenge. 'It's Joe,' she whispered. 'I... I'm beginning to wonder if he's losing interest in me.'

Richard's face registered a mixture of disbelief and indignation. 'That can't be right. How could anybody go off somebody like you?'

'It's nice of you to say so.'

'No, it's not. I'm never nice, remember.'

'Everything's so muddled ... I used to be so sure about him, about the way he felt for me and the way I felt for him. But now I just don't know any more. And I'm sure there's stuff going on at work that he doesn't tell me about.'

'Maybe it's just stress getting to him, and he doesn't want to worry you.'

'Maybe. But either way, he's stopped sharing things with me. He's started shutting me out.'

Richard contemplated his feet. 'You know, you can never be sure how the future's going to be. Some things don't work out the way you expected them to, then other things turn up just when you least expect them – even better than you'd hoped the first lot would be. The way I see it, if you can stay alive to the new things, then the bad stuff doesn't seem so bad any more.' He laughed. 'Does that make any sense to you?'

'Yes. Funnily enough, it does.' And how, she thought, gazing into those magnificent, undreamed-of blue eyes. 'Richard, can I ask you a question? Why don't you ever talk about yourself? You know, your past.'

He paused. 'Because ... look, the past's kind of like a photograph. You can do things to make it look different, but in the end it's still fixed and dead and you can't change it. Life's about growing and changing. It doesn't matter what you've done or had done to you before now; all that really matters is what you're going to do next. Like Treena, for example. Is she going to tell Gerald where he gets off, or is she just going to lie back down and let him walk all over her until the day she dies?'

Like Treena, thought Emma. Or ... like me.

At that moment, Emma had the strangest feeling; it was like standing on the very edge of a precipice, unable either to step back or to take a running leap into the enticing void.

'I wish I knew what I was going to do next,' she said softly.

'I've been meaning to give you this.' Richard reached into his pocket and produced a business card. 'This is where you can find me. Any time you need me, just call. And I mean any time, OK?'

Joe was monumentally fed up.

His mother-in-law had taken up residence in the spare bedroom, and there were cardboard boxes all over the hall, but that wasn't the reason why; despite what Emma might think, he liked Karen – and besides, it wasn't forever. No, his gloom had a lot more to do with work.

Breaking the marketing director's nose hadn't helped, of course; and with Rachael's dedicated efforts behind it, the story had spread round the company in record time. Joe had long since ceased to be amused by the sniggers he got whenever he entered a store; and there was nothing remotely funny about having Sir Stanley regard you as a cretin.

And now there was this Hereford business. How long had he been trying to figure out the dip in takings? Weeks. And how long had it taken the two security types from head office? Two days. Right under the nose of the dopey store manager Joe himself had appointed, two of the supervisors had been masterminding an ingenious scam. A brother-in-law's dodgy cash and carry had been filling the shelves with dirt-cheap alternatives to some of Unico's own-brand products. The result? A nice fat return for the felons, and a black hole in the store's profits.

How could he not have worked it out for himself? It was so simple. How could he have been so stupid? He was beginning to think Sir Stanley was right, and he really was a cretin. Or at the very least, someone who was learning the hard way that he wasn't half as clever as he'd thought he was.

Joe ran a hand through his dishevelled hair. He badly needed a haircut, but he just couldn't seem to find the time. If only he could share all this with Emma, but it was as if she had stepped through the looking glass into another, quite separate world, leaving a clear, hard barrier between them. Why had she turned so cold towards him? Why was everything he suggested wrong, and everything she suggested right? How could a little thing like marriage have changed her so much?

After all, it wasn't as if he'd changed, had he? He was the same old Joe he'd always been. And he'd sweated blood to make things nice for her: comfortable; safe.

The last time he'd tried to hold her close, he'd felt her whole body tense at his touch, and she'd made some feeble excuse to detach herself and walk away. And despite all this, *he* was the one who felt guilty! As if he had anything to feel guilty about.

For God's sake, he told himself, banishing Zara's comforting face from his thoughts; it was only once! One little meeting, one little drink.

One little lie.

'I'm feeling so much better now,' announced Karen one morning at breakfast. 'See – I can practically manage without the walking stick.' She stood up to illustrate, turned a pirouette and just managed not to lose her balance.

'That's great,' enthused Joe. 'Isn't it, Em? You're doing really well.'

'Great,' Emma echoed. 'But you've still got to be careful, Mum. We don't want you having any more accidents.'

Karen was not impressed. 'I'm not an aged invalid yet, thank goodness, and I'm not planning to spend the rest of my life languishing on a chaise-longue reading poetry!'

'Nobody's saying—' began Emma, instinctively jumping in to protect her mother, the way she had done ever since her father died.

Karen put up her hand. 'I know exactly what you're saying, and I do appreciate that you're only doing it because you care. But I've been a long time on my own, you know; I've grown accustomed to it.'

'Things change, Mum. You can't just ignore—'

'In fact, while we're on the subject I might as well tell you. I've found myself somewhere to live.'

'What – already?' gasped Emma.

'A nice ground-floor flat in Gloucester, handy for the shops and the bus. Wasn't that lucky? Now all I need is a little part-time job to keep me occupied.'

'Gloucester?' Emma glanced at Joe, who wasn't making much of an effort to conceal his delight. 'But you've got somewhere to live! For as long as you need.'

'Now, you've both been very kind letting me stay here, but we all know it was only ever going to be for a little while. After all, I wouldn't want to outstay my welcome and get in the way.'

'How could you ever get in the way?' cut in Joe, and Emma wondered how he could be so two-faced. In his mind's eye he was probably already measuring up the spare room for a nursery.

'It's nice of you to say so,' replied Karen, 'but you two need this place to yourselves. I know what it's like when you're newly married.'

And the knowing look she gave Joe made him think that she probably did.

With Karen out for an evening of non-fat canapés at Minette and Alan's, Emma knew that she and Joe would have the flat to themselves. After all, he had crossed his heart and hoped to die if his last meeting didn't finish dead on the stroke of six thirty. So, although it had been a backbreaking day at work, Emma trailed all the way to the posh new supermarket on her way home, and bought the ingredients for a really nice, romantic meal.

Her mum was right; candles, some nice wine, good food ... they'd soon be talking properly again, the way they always used to.

She prepared the boeuf à la mode and put it in the oven, then decided she had time for a quick aromatherapy bath before she got down to some serious baking. Joe had had a thing about real Sachertorte ever since they went on a weekend trip to Vienna; and if that was the way to his heart, well, she was just going to have to forget that chocolate brought her out in zits.

Emerging from the bathroom all pink and fragrant, she padded into the kitchen in her fluffy slippers. Not quite seven yet – plenty of time to bake a mouth-watering tour-de-force.

Half a tin of Charbonnel et Walker and six eggs later, she wiped the cocoa smears off her face and slid the cake tins into the oven. Sit back, have a drink, chill out, she told herself. It's all going to be worth it in the end, just you wait and see.

As she wandered across the hallway into the living room, she saw the light flashing on the answering machine.

There was no reason to think the message was from Joe; anyone could have phoned while she was in the bath. It was probably Mum, begging her to come and rescue her from Minette. And if it was Joe, most likely he'd just called to say he'd be a few minutes late.

'Hi Em,' said the disembodied voice, over the sound of heated voices. 'The meeting's not over yet, and I've just had a call to go and pick up Dad's car from the other side of Birmingham. Looks like I'm going to be back really late, or I might stop over at Jerry's in Aston. Don't wait up.

'Sorry, 'bye.'

Sorry! Was that all she merited, one miserable little 'sorry'? No 'love you', no 'miss you', no 'I'm going to drop everything and come home because you're more important than stupid supermarkets and stupid cars'? Was she really so low down his list of priorities? OK, he had no way of knowing that she was cooking a special meal for him, but a promise was a promise and he'd broken it. Again. He'd crossed his heart and hoped to die, so why wasn't he dead?

In fury, she stormed into the kitchen, dragged the food out of the oven and tipped the casserole away. As she stood contemplating the forlorn column of steam rising up out of the stainless steel bin, she didn't know whether to burst into tears or just kick the furniture.

Most likely she would have slumped in a corner with the bottle of wine and the Sachertorte, if something hadn't prompted her to

227

look towards the bread bin. There, on the top, next to half a Hovis, sat her car keys.

Without so much as a conscious thought, she picked them up, grabbed her coat and left, slamming the door of the flat behind her with an emphatic crash.

Dead beat, but optimistic for the first time in days, Joe was speeding up the M6 in a taxi. OK, so it was going to cost a bomb to get all the way over there and pick the Jag up, but money wasn't a problem and anyway, Dad was worth it. He was sure Emma would understand. Well, fairly sure.

It was Dad's birthday party in two weeks' time, and, frankly, that was the first bright spot on Joe's horizon in days. He could already picture the look on his dad's face when he stepped out of the front door and saw the gleaming Jag sitting outside, with a giant comedy ribbon tied round it.

His brothers would be impressed, too. OK, so he hadn't actually got round to telling them that the Jag was several decades newer than the old one, or how much it had set him back; but that could wait. They'd just tell Dad it was from all of them, and the others could chip in whatever they could afford. Who could possibly object to that?

He sat back in the taxi's comfortable seat, and relaxed for the first time in days. Yes, Dad was going to be over the moon. At last, he thought, I've got something right.

Richard's cottage stood somewhere between the middle of nowhere and the back of beyond, down a tree-lined lane that meandered off a back road between Bourton and Stow. On this late spring evening, its honey-coloured stone glowed with a sun-soaked inner warmth, as though it were alive and smiling. Bees hummed drowsily in the wisteria, while a blackbird's crystal-clear song rang from the top of a lopsided chimney pot. The world of arguments and supermarket fraud seemed very far away.

Inside, Richard was busy drying off some prints, pegging them to the old-fashioned clothes dryer that hung over the kitchen table. He was surprised and slightly annoyed to hear the doorbell jingle. Five Crows Cottage wasn't really the kind of place you found by accident, and he didn't get many visitors, give or take the odd lost motorist; but curiosity got the better of him and he dried his hands and went to the front door.

When he opened it, he got the surprise of his life. Whatever he'd expected to find on his doorstep, this wasn't it.

'Another cranberry and caper nibble, Karen?' enquired Minette, not so much offering as brandishing the plate.

'Well, I—'

'In your state of health I definitely think you should,' Minette said firmly. 'Think of all those antioxidants.'

For the sake of politeness, Karen took one. 'Thanks,' she said. 'They're really ... different.'

'Of course they are, dear, they're my own special creation. I'll let you have the recipe. Alan.' She snapped her fingers and dragged his eyes away from the football.

'What?'

'Stop watching that rubbish and get Karen a napkin. She's dropping crumbs all down herself. And while you're at it, fetch the Listerine. The dog's got bad breath again.'

Alan left the room, muttering, and Karen stole a surreptitious peek at her watch. Only half past eight! She couldn't possibly make her excuses and leave, not when she knew Emma was planning a romantic night in with Joe.

'So,' she said brightly, 'is Alan looking forward to his sixtieth birthday party?'

By good fortune she'd hit on exactly the right topic of conversation. A huge, smug smile spread over Minette's face.

'It's going to be the social event of the year! We've booked the function at the King's, did I tell you? Naturally, Alan keeps saying he'd rather have just a quiet drink with a few friends, but that's just because he wants to spare me the stress of organising a party, bless him.' She beamed. 'The whole family's invited, you know. And that includes you,' she added, just in case Karen was afraid that she might not qualify for honorary Sheridan status.

'I'm sure it'll be a lovely evening.'

'Yes, dear, so am I.' She swung round as Alan entered the room, napkin in one hand and bottle of mouthwash in the other. 'Not one of the damask ones, Alan! They're for special occasions. One of the paper ones from the drawer in the kitchen.'

'What?'

'For goodness' sake! Put it away, and make sure you fold it up properly.' She turned back to Karen with a heavenward glance as Alan stumped back out of the room. 'I don't know! Men! But where would we be without them, eh?' Then she remembered. 'Well yes, of course, you *are* without them, but—'

'It's OK,' said Karen. 'It's been a long time; I'm used to it.'

'All the same,' said Minette, 'it can't have been easy, all on your own up there. I mean, how on earth did you manage with putting up shelves?'

Karen just managed not to laugh. 'Well, I'm not much good at shelves,' she admitted, 'but I did manage to plumb in the new central heating system last year, and replaster the dining room ceiling.'

Minette gaped at her as though she had just confessed to an interest in occult practices. 'Good Lord,' she said. 'How dreadful for you.' She leaned forward confidentially. 'And of course, now you've got your … er,', she mouthed the word as though it were shameful, '*disability*.'

Alan returned, this time with a paper napkin adorned with pictures of snowmen and holly leaves. 'That's better, Alan. Now, go and find the dog, will you? He's hiding in the airing cupboard again, Lord alone knows why.'

When Alan had left the room, Minette put down her teacup. 'Actually, Karen,' she said, 'I didn't just ask you round this evening for a nice chat.'

'Really?'

'No, I wanted to make you a little proposition. You know how busy we've been with Alan's laptop business lately?'

'Yes, I've heard he's doing well.'

'*We're* doing fantastically. I've really helped him build up the business, you know; given him a bit of *impetus*. But I'm so busy these days, what with my charity work and babysitting my new granddaughter and what have you, that I really don't have the time to do all the administration for him any more. And seeing as you've had experience of running a business …'

Karen blinked in surprise. 'Are you offering me a job?'

'Just a part-time one, of course. And just on a trial basis. I mean, we'd want to be sure we weren't overstretching you in your condition, wouldn't we?'

'I'm not at death's door, you know,' said Karen. 'Now I'm over the flare-up, most days I hardly notice the MS.'

'Yes dear, of course. Positive thinking. You keep telling yourself that and I'm sure it'll help. So, are you interested in the job then?'

'I might well be,' replied Karen. 'Tell me more.'

Minette picked up her cup and settled back in her armchair. 'Oh good.' She beamed. 'I know we've not always seen eye to eye in the past, Karen, but like it or not we're family now. And you can't let your family starve, can you?'

Even if they do intend moving to Gloucester, she added silently, with just the merest wince of disdain.

In Richard's cosy little sitting room, littered with cameras in various states of repair, the marble clock on the mantelpiece chimed half-past. But the two figures on the chintzy thirties' sofa were oblivious to the time.

Richard put a protective arm around Emma's shoulders and offered her a tissue. 'Go on, cry, it's OK,' he said quietly. 'Just let it out.'

Emma snivelled gratefully into the Kleenex and wiped her red and swollen eyes. She'd never felt so unattractive in her life, but somehow it didn't matter. 'H-he promises he'll be home early, and then at the last minute h-he rings up and says he's probably not coming home at all because he's fetching his dad's stupid car. And he doesn't even say he's sorry.' She blew her nose noisily and Richard proffered the wastepaper basket for her to drop the soggy tissue into. 'I thought he loved me,' she said through a veil of tears.

Richard said nothing for a long time. 'I expect he does love you,' he said eventually. 'In his own way.'

'Huh.'

'But that's not enough, is it?'

She met his gaze. 'No,' she said. 'It's not.'

A gentle hand smoothed the wet, tendrils of hair off her hot, damp face. 'Someone special like you deserves a lot better than that,' he whispered. 'More than just an ordinary kind of love.' And then, with the utmost delicacy, he planted a kiss on her cheek.

'Richard, please,' she gasped.

His face fell. 'I'm sorry, I didn't mean to ... I'm sorry.'

He drew back, but Emma seized his hands and held them fast. 'Do it again,' she heard herself say, as if in a dream. 'Please.

Kiss me again, it's just ... I really need to feel as if somebody cares.'

'Oh Emma.' He wrapped his strong arms around her and kissed the nape of her neck again and again, and shivers of excitement juddered through her whole body. 'Of course somebody cares. I care. Haven't you worked that one out for yourself?'

'I thought ... I don't know, I wasn't sure.'

'Yes, you were, Emma. In your heart you've always known.'

Could he be right? she asked herself. Could he really have the power to decipher my heart more completely than I know it myself?

'The question is,' he went on, 'do you care for me?' He held her gently by the shoulders and pushed her far enough away for her to look him in the face. '*Could* you?'

Tears misted her eyes. 'I'm married, Richard.' For the first time, she tasted bitterness in the word. 'Married.'

'I don't give a damn about any of that, and I don't think you do either. Not deep down. Be true to yourself, Emma; for once in your life listen to what your heart's telling you. Do you care for me?'

'I ... don't know.'

'Be honest with me. Please. Even if it's just to say "go to hell".'

She swallowed a sob. 'Yes,' she whispered. 'Yes, I care for you.'

'I knew it.'

They sat there just gazing at each other for what seemed a very long time, their breathing measured by the heavy chunk-chunk-chunk of the clock on the mantelpiece.

'Oh God,' said Emma, struggling to her feet. 'This is all wrong, I have to go.'

But Richard didn't let go of her hand. 'Listen to me first. Please?'

She nodded, and sat back down again.

'You know I'm going to be away for the Thursday class the week after next?'

'Yes, but what's that got to do with me?'

'I'm going up to North Yorkshire for a couple of days, to take some pictures of the moors for a nature magazine. Deserted places, Emma; the sorts of places you can walk for hours and see nothing but the biggest sky in the world. Will you come with me?'

232

At first, his words didn't register. Then, as Emma realised what he had just asked her, icy fingers danced down her spine, making her skin tingle with a feeling that might have been fear, or excitement, or both.

'Come with you?' A laugh died in her throat. 'I can't come with you!'

'Why not? I know you want to.'

'What about Joe? What about work?'

'Take some leave. Tell Joe you're ... I don't know ... going on a course. Nobody needs to know, Emma. Only you and I. Think about it: just the two of us, alone ...'

The blood rushed in her ears, making her dizzy with terror and exhilaration. 'You're crazy!'

He smiled. 'Be crazy with me, Emma. Be brave. For once in your life, follow your heart and don't look back.'

26

'So,' Gary asked with a grin, swinging his big feet up onto Rozzer's coffee table, 'have you shagged the lovely Linda yet then?'

Toby laughed, but Rozzer didn't see the joke at all. 'Don't talk like that!' he hissed, leaping to the living-room door and slamming it shut. 'They're only in the next room!'

'Oh, I get it,' said Toby to Gary. 'She's pug-ugly and he wouldn't touch her with yours.'

'Nah,' disagreed Gary, 'if you ask me he's trying to butter her up with a load of New Man crap. Take it from me Rozzer,' he advised, pointing a finger adorned with a tasteless diamond and platinum signet ring, 'go down that route and you'll get nowhere. She'll just take advantage. If you want to get into her pants, treat her mean. She'll be gagging for it in no time.' Draining his can of lager, he banged it down on the table. 'I'll have another of those if you've got one.'

Rozzer scowled. He was not easily riled, in fact over the years he had carved out quite a niche for himself in the doormat department, but tonight Gary's habitual smirk was making him feel nauseous. 'You've had enough already,' he said; then took a deep breath and added: 'and I don't like you talking like that round here.'

Gary and Toby looked at each other, went 'Oooh – get her!', and fell about laughing.

'Fucking hell, Rozzer,' commented Toby, 'either this lodger of yours is a looker, or you've gone soft in the head; she's turning you into a right wuss.'

'Yeah,' agreed Gary, 'the rate you're going you'll end up worse than Joe.'

'What's that supposed to mean?' demanded Rozzer.

'Nothing, just that he used to be a real laugh and now all he does is drone on about work and babies.'

At least he's not a talking arsehole, thought Rozzer, though he didn't quite dare say it aloud. Besides, he wasn't entirely sure he liked Joe all that much any more, either. His hero's halo had definitely slipped over the last few months.

'Speaking of babies,' said Rozzer, lifting Gary's feet off a copy of *Babar the Elephant*, 'keep the noise down, there's a little girl trying to get some sleep in the next room.'

Gary shook his head. 'I don't know what you thought you were doing, getting one with a kid.'

'One what?'

'Lodger! I mean, I can see why you'd want to let your spare room to a fit-looking bird, but talk about cramping your style. You must have been bloody desperate.'

'Of course he is,' chuckled Toby. 'When's the last time you pulled, Rozzer? Was it BC or AD?'

'For the last time,' hissed Rozzer, 'Linda's a lodger and that's all she is.'

'Yeah, yeah, of course.' Gary leaned forward and peered at something on the carpet. 'Jeez, is that the leg off a doll or something?'

Rozzer stooped and picked it up. 'I was looking for that.' His face turned crimson. 'I sort of said I might try and mend it.'

Gary's expression hovered between amusement and contempt. 'God, you really are pathetic,' he said. 'Look, next time you're desperate for a bit of skirt you give me a call, OK? I'll take you down the club and introduce you to one of Sadie's little friends. thirty-eight-twenty-two-thirty-six and not a brain cell between them.'

Rozzer returned his gaze with a kind of cool fury he'd never experienced before. 'Thanks a lot, Gary,' he said, 'but I'll never be *that* desperate.'

Trust it to be the slowest Friday night ever on A&E. And trust Diane to insist on enlivening it with tales of her friend's hen night.

'You'll never guess what happened next,' she giggled, as Emma slipped into the toilet cubicle next to hers and bolted the door. No, and I don't want to, thought Emma. Just now, ill-advised sexual behaviour was something she was trying hard not to think about.

'Go on, tell us,' urged Sunita, who was standing at one of the sinks, touching up her mascara, 'don't keep us in suspense.'

'Weeell,' began Diane, enjoying the power she had over her audience, 'it turned out that Gilda – you know, the posh one who's married to that bloke who owns the racehorses? – well, she'd only gone and booked a male stripper as well! So of course, he turns up dressed as a policeman just as the other one's down to his fireman's helmet ...'

Sunita giggled. Emma tried to concentrate on going to the loo, but it wasn't easy since, in her mind, the fireman was wearing Richard's face and Joe had just arrived on the scene with a big pair of handcuffs. 'Have you got any paper in there?' she enquired, hoping to divert Diane from her train of thought.

'What? Oh yeah, here you are.' An NHS toilet roll came trundling under the partition from Diane's cubicle. 'Anyway, Katie's standing there, with this aerosol can of cream he's given her, and he whips away his helmet and tells her to squirt it on his you-know-what!'

Sunita yelped. 'Ow! Stop making me laugh, you cow, I've just poked myself in the eye. So what did she do?' she demanded eagerly.

'Well, she's drunk as a skunk so she's game for anything, and the next thing is, she's licking it off. And just as the policeman's about to get his money off Gilda and go home 'cause he's surplus to requirements, Katie—'

Desperate to blot it all out, Emma flushed the loo as noisily as she could. When she emerged from the cubicle, Diane was still in full flow.

'And she says, "Well, I've never done it with anybody but Shay, have I? So this is sort of my last chance to find out what it's like with another bloke."'

'No!' squealed Sunita, dabbing away mascara-streaked tears with a paper towel. 'She didn't *really* ... did she?'

Diane appeared, smoothing down her uniform tunic. 'As I live and breathe. Wakes up the next morning with a policeman on one side and a fireman on the other, and God alone knows what she told Shay when she got home ... you all right, Emma?' she enquired as Emma tried to slink past on her way to the door.

'What? Yes, fine. Why?'

'Oh, nothing. I just thought you didn't quite look yourself. There's nothing on your mind, is there?'

'Only the fact that Lawrence'll slay me for being late back from my break,' retorted Emma, turning aside and leaving before her face could give her away.

Linda stood over Rozzer, surprisingly intimidating in her pink pyjamas. 'Why do you let him talk to you like that?' she demanded.

'Because he's ... my mate,' Rozzer replied lamely.

'Your mate? Some mate he is, the way he treats you.'

Rozzer squirmed in the halogen glare of Linda's honesty. 'He's not that bad,' he protested.

'Yes he is, he's a git.' Linda perched on the arm of the sofa.

'How can you tell? You don't even know him.'

'Take it from me, I know. What are you sitting out here for, anyway? It's past midnight.'

'Dunno really,' admitted Rozzer. 'I didn't feel much like sleeping – you know, stuff going round in my head.'

'Yeah. I know all about that.' Linda smiled. 'Sometimes makes you wish you were a kid again, doesn't it? They go out like a light, the minute their head hits the pillow. Me, I haven't slept right since Eddie died, and what with all the trouble on the estate ...'

He looked up. 'You've had it rough.'

She shrugged. 'I wasn't looking for sympathy.'

'Oh. Well, I didn't mean—'

She laid a finger on his lips. 'Don't you dare say you're sorry. I'm sick of hearing you apologise, especially to prats like Gary.'

Rozzer stared at her. It was all he could do to stop himself apologising for apologising. A rather impressive 'Oh,' was all he came out with in the end.

'"Oh?"' she exploded. 'Is that all you can say? Listen to me, Roswell: OK, you may be a bit of an idiot but you're a decent bloke and you're worth more than a whole barrel-load of Garys and Tobys. So just start believing it, will you?'

She gave him such a look that he didn't dare say no.

'You know,' mused Joe, flipping through his address book the following evening, 'it's ages since we saw Will and Kathy.'

'Hmm,' replied Emma, nervously pushing a boiled potato round her plate.

'We really must make time to see them. I bet Liddy's practically walking by now. I wonder if they'd like to come to Dad's party ...'

Emma made appropriate small noises in the background, but frankly it wouldn't have mattered if she'd donned a gorilla suit and danced the can-can. Joe was into full-on party organising mode, completely oblivious to her and determined that absolutely everybody was going to be there next week to see Alan receive his best birthday present ever.

Everybody, thought Emma, but me. Then instantly dismissed the thought, since frankly any notion of actually taking Richard up on his invitation had to be dismissed because it was clearly deranged. It was flattering to be asked; and maybe for a fleeting moment she'd actually considered going away with him, carried away by the sheer hormonal urge; but when push came to shove she was never actually going to do it, was she?

The food on her plate had lost all its appeal. Her mouth was dry, her heart pounding. Surely Joe must be able to hear it, hurling itself around inside her chest? And even if he couldn't, surely he must have registered the fact that she'd hardly said a word to him since he got home from work, and had scarcely touched a mouthful of her dinner?

But he just kept wittering on about party invitations, more animated than she'd seen him since their wedding day; and didn't even seem to notice when she switched off the television and took herself off to bed, closing the bedroom door behind her.

Over the next couple of days, Joe went on about the party incessantly. If he wasn't phoning his mother about table layouts, he was liaising with his brother-in-law about arranging fireworks in the shape of a giant sixty. It was either very touching or very obsessive, depending on how you looked at it. Emma tried not to look at it at all.

'You will be there early on the night, won't you?' Joe said on Wednesday morning, slice of toast clamped between his teeth as he threw papers into his briefcase and jammed down the lid.

A cold tingle ran down Emma's spine. 'Actually, I—'

He frowned. 'Don't tell me that cretin Lawrence has put you on

238

a late that night! Well you'll just have to tell him to change the rota. Mum needs you and Karen there early to help organise the nibbles.'

Organise the nibbles. There was something quite ludicrous about the idea that a few crisps and stuffed olives actually needed two grown women there to 'organise' them, as opposed to just chucking them into a bowl.

'We're quite short-staffed in the department at the moment,' began Emma. But that didn't cut any ice with Joe.

'Tough. They'll just have to manage without you for once.' He clicked the catch on his briefcase and pecked Emma sexlessly on the cheek. 'See you.'

'Actually . . .' said Emma again, just as he was opening the front door and preparing to walk out.

Something in her tone of voice made him pause and turn round. 'Actually what?'

It was the moment of no going back. At this point, she either smiled and said, 'OK, I'll have a word with Lawrence,' or she exploded the hand grenade she'd been hiding fearfully up her sleeve.

'I have to go away for a couple of days . . . and I might, well, not be back in time for your dad's party.'

She couldn't believe she'd just said that, and neither could Joe. He dropped his briefcase on the ground. 'What do you mean, "away"? Where? You can't go away!'

Something in the petulance of his tone strengthened Emma's reckless determination. 'I'm a grown-up now, thanks,' she said tartly. 'I can go anywhere I want. Besides, it's . . .' she swallowed, 'a course. For work.'

Joe would probably have looked less thunderous if she'd announced that she was jetting off to the Caribbean with David Beckham. The 'W' word was guaranteed to get his back up – unless of course it applied to him. 'You can't . . . What kind of course? Why didn't you tell me this before?'

Emma shuffled her feet and tried not to look too guilty, half convinced that he could see right through her to the adulterous heart of the matter. 'It's to do with the assistant nurse coordinator post I told you about . . . the one I said I might apply for?'

'Not that bloody thing again!' snapped Joe. 'I thought you'd seen sense.'

'I have,' she retorted. 'Which is why I'm definitely applying. And this course'll put me in with a better chance of getting it.'

'You'll just have to tell them you're not going,' said Joe, his narrowed eyes challenging her not to toe the family line. 'This is my dad's sixtieth you know – you can't just not be there! You're my wife, you're supposed to be part of the family!'

Guilt wrestled with spite in Emma's heart and spite won. 'Yeah, part of the family when it suits you and nobody in particular when it doesn't! Half the time you hardly seem to even notice I'm here, and your mother only speaks to me to tell me what I'm doing wrong. Look, this job's a big chance for me, and I'm not throwing away that chance just because you feel like acting the caveman, OK?'

They glared at each other, neither willing to back down.

'Well, if that's how you feel.'

Her chin squared. 'It is.'

'I'll see you when I see you, then.'

'I guess.'

He slammed the door and she listened to his angry footsteps stamping down the stairs. Oh my God, she thought, her heart thumping against the inside of her ribs; what have I said, what have I done? It was the first time she'd ever told Joe a serious lie, and she'd done it so well that she'd almost believed it herself.

It all felt like a dream. Was she *really* contemplating going away with Richard? She could almost hear his voice in her head, repeating the mantra: 'Listen to your heart ... you have a right to a life of your own.' The question was, did she have a right to it at the expense of her marriage and Joe's happiness?

As Emma stood in the hallway, staring blankly at the closed front door, Karen slipped silently back into her room and sat down on the bed in the semi-darkness. Oh Emma, she lamented; it's all going badly wrong, isn't it? And it used to seem so right. Something's driving you two apart, and there's only one thing I can think of that it might be.

Me.

Joe was certain now.

It had started as a suspicion, and grown inexorably as he accumulated all the damning evidence. And then the rumours had started flying around. No matter which of them you believed,

240

there was no point in denying the obvious: all was not well with Unico.

He walked morosely down the stairs from the boardroom, wondering how everything in his life could have gone from great to grim in such a short space of time. Unico's takeover of the German food group Frischli Lebensmittel had brought nothing but problems; Sir Stanley was being more unreasonable than ever about everything; and the pressures on managers to perform had seen more than one of Joe's regional colleagues get the chop in recent weeks.

It wouldn't have been so bad if he could share things with Emma; but he'd started out childishly not wanting to look feeble, and now he'd gone past that stage she didn't seem to want to know any more. In fact, half the time she didn't even seem to want to share the same planet.

He halted for a moment on the landing, and took a deep breath. You do realise you're over-reacting, don't you? he told himself. You're getting good results; nobody's really threatened you with anything (yet); and besides, you know better than to listen to rumours.

As the staircase swung round to the right, he walked slap-bang into a young woman coming the other way, and knocked the leather portfolio out of her hand.

'Hey, watch where you're going.'

'Sorry,' he muttered, picking up the portfolio and handing it back to her.

'Something on your mind?' Rachael enquired sweetly, revealing her spiky teeth. 'Not worrying about work, are you?'

'Why should I be?'

She brushed past him. 'Oh, no reason, except that everybody else seems to be. Apart from me, of course.'

'So what's so special about you?'

She looked back over her shoulder at him and smiled. 'Didn't I tell you? I'm moving to Farmfresh next month, as their new regional marketing manager. I must have forgotten. The MD seems to think I've got a great future with the UK's second largest supermarket chain.

'See you around, Joe.' She grinned. 'Or then again, maybe I won't.'

241

27

The picture from Emma's cheap webcam was a little fuzzy, but it was so good to see Mickey's face again.

'You're looking really well,' said Emma. 'And I love the new haircut.'

'Well? Fat, you mean!' laughed Mickey, continuing before Emma had a chance to deny it. 'But it's OK, I don't mind buying bigger pants. I've decided to stop agonising about my weight and start concentrating on things that actually matter.'

'Good for you.'

'Yeah, that's what I think. Matter of fact, I've made a few other decisions about my life too.'

That sounded ominous, and Emma said so.

'Don't worry, it's nothing silly, I promise,' said Mickey. 'I'm not giving everything away and moving into an ashram. Everything that's happened to me has just made me realise it's time I grew up.'

Emma grimaced. 'Don't! If you grow up, I'll have to grow up too.'

Mickey laughed. 'Come off it, you've been grown-up since . . . forever! Since you met Joe, anyway.'

It was a good thing the webcam picture was so jerky; otherwise, Mickey would surely have picked up on Emma's moment of frozen hesitation. 'I . . . so what are these mysterious changes, then?' she asked hastily.

'Well, to start off with I'm going to start looking after my body, and I've given up smoking once and for all.'

'Again?' said Emma wryly.

'For the last time. Full stop. Second, I've decided if I'm ever

242

going to even think about having kids, I've got to get myself a proper home. I must have been mad, thinking I could bring up a baby in one room. So Rufus and I are moving out of Magenta Street and into our own little flat.'

Emma could hardly believe her ears. 'But ... but you've been there for ...'

'Five years, I know. And it'd be too damned easy to stay. That's why I need to move on now, otherwise I never will. I don't want to be still sharing a bathroom with Phoebe's cannabis plant when I'm sixty.'

'Hang on,' said Emma, 'who's Rufus?'

'My toyboy. He's young, he's obscenely good-looking, and he just loves rolling around on the bed with a piece of string.'

'Huh?'

'He's my new kitten, Em! Didn't I tell you? Hang on a mo ... Rufie, come here, you little tyke.' She bent down and scooped up something that looked like a ball of wool with ears. 'Say hello to Auntie Emma.' A small pink mouth opened in an expanse of fluff, emitting something that sounded like 'Eep.' 'So, what do you reckon to the new man in my life?'

'Definitely an improvement on some you've had. Bigger vocabulary, at any rate.'

'Miaow!'

'Quite.' Emma watched Mickey gently perch the kitten on her shoulder and rub its fluffy head. 'Mickey ...'

'Yes?'

'You are all right, aren't you? All this sudden changing ... you're not just doing it on the spur of the moment?'

'I do appreciate you worrying about me, but I'm OK, Em, truly I am. A lot more OK than I thought I would be. Hey, I even had a civilised conversation with Gavin – you know, the baby's father, and it really helped me think things through.' She smiled as the kitten explored her face with its paws. 'I can't be Mental Mickey forever, even if I might like to be. And I'm not so sure I would, not now. I want to shed my skin and move on with my life. You of all people should understand that.'

Emma felt a tingle of surprise. 'Me?'

'Of course, you! Getting married and all that. Moving your whole life to a new town, doing all kinds of grown-up stuff.'

'Yeah,' said Emma flatly. 'I see what you mean.'

Mickey leaned forward, so that one enormous eye filled Emma's screen. 'You're weird today, Em. I'm starting to wonder if *you're* all right.'

'Don't be daft, I'm always all right. So, what's this new flat like then?'

'Don't change the subject. Is something wrong at work?'

'No, work's fine; I might even be up for a promotion.'

Mickey's eyes narrowed. 'Something's up with you and Joe then?'

'Mickey!'

'You've not been rowing again, have you? Oh Emma, I should come up there and knock your heads together. Don't you realise how lucky you are to have each other?'

'Yes,' replied Emma soberly. 'I do.'

And she did. But it didn't make her feel any better.

Joe couldn't understand it. He'd sent out the party invitations in plenty of time, but he still hadn't had a reply from Will and Kathy. Even repeated phone calls had only got him as far as their answering machine.

There was nothing for it: he'd just have to call round and see them. They were long overdue a visit anyway. So he decided to drop in that night on his way back from work, when he knew Will would be home.

It was still light when Joe drove up to the little pink terraced house, and he couldn't help noticing that there were weeds in the window boxes and a large accumulation of milk bottles on the pavement outside. That was odd; he was sure Will had said they weren't going anywhere.

He rang the bell and waited. Nothing happened, so he rang a second time. Still nothing. Ah well, if nobody came to the door by the time he'd counted to ten, he'd have to assume they were away.

He'd got to eight and a half when the door opened.

'If it's double glazing, you can just fu— . . .Oh! It's you.'

Joe could hardly believe his eyes. Was this ragged-haired, gaunt-faced figure in a stained jumper and leggings really Kathy? 'My God,' he said before he could stop himself, 'what on earth's happened?'

Suddenly conscious that she must look a fright, Kathy raked a hand through her hair. 'Will,' she replied coldly. 'That's what.'

'I don't understand.'

Kathy stood wearily aside. 'I suppose you'd better come in.' The sound of a child crying suddenly filled the tiny house. 'Oh for God's sake, Liddy – all right, all right, I'm coming.'

In a state of shock, Joe followed Kathy into the living room, where a huge pile of dirty baby clothes half filled the settee. 'Aren't you going to ... er ... see to the baby?' he enquired. 'Should I –?'

'What? Oh, yeah, in a minute. I just need one of my pills.' Kathy grabbed her handbag, took out a bottle and shook two blue tablets into her hand. 'For my nerves,' she said. 'It's not been easy since Will went.'

Joe's head was spinning, his entire conception of reality challenged by what he was seeing. This quite simply could not be happening. 'Went? Went where?' he demanded, trailing behind her as she went back into the hallway and started off up the stairs.

Kathy turned and threw him a look of disgust. 'You tell me. "I need some space," he says; and the next thing I know, he's buggered off with a suitcase and all the money from the joint account.' Reaching the baby's bedroom, she stooped over the cot and scooped up her daughter, her face softening as Liddy's cries faded to muted hiccups.

Joe leaned against the wall for fear of falling over. 'This is some kind of sick joke, right? You're having me on. Will wouldn't just walk out.'

'That's what I thought,' retorted Kathy. 'Just shows how wrong you can be, doesn't it?'

'But ... *why*?'

Kathy stroked the baby's golden curls. Liddy, at least, looked warm and well cared for and unaware of the crisis raging around her. 'Well,' she replied drily, 'it happened three weeks ago, the day after I told him I was expecting twins, so what's the betting it had something to do with that?'

Joe struggled to get his head round Kathy's words. 'But I thought you and Will wanted another baby!'

'So did he, till he realised it was actually going to happen. And when he found out it was twins, well, suddenly it's, "I don't think I'm ready for this," and, "How are we going to afford it?". He even had the cheek to accuse me of being "careless", the two-faced git!'

'And he just walked out and left you to manage on your own?'

'I wouldn't call this managing, would you?' Kathy gave Liddy's bottom an expert sniff. 'Oh great, another smelly one. Just lay out that changing mat for me, will you?'

Joe did so mechanically, feeling more than ever as if he'd been hit round the head with a sock full of cement. 'I just don't get it. You've always been the perfect couple, brilliant parents ... I've always wanted to be like you. What on earth got into him?'

Kathy gave a hollow laugh. 'If you find him, you can ask him yourself.'

'You don't even know where he is?'

'I haven't heard a word from him in three weeks, and if it wasn't for the money I wouldn't be bothered if I never saw him again.'

'You don't mean that, surely.'

'Yes I bloody do.' Doing up the tabs on Liddy's nappy, she lifted up the baby and gave her a kiss. 'Daddy's a big fat bastard and we don't need him, do we?' Glancing at the clock on the wall, Kathy turned to Joe. 'Can you babysit Liddy for me for ten minutes? If I run, I can catch the corner shop before it shuts.'

'I ... OK.' In point of fact Joe didn't have a lot of choice, because Kathy had already plonked the child in his unsuspecting arms. 'What do I do?' he asked, as she ran about grabbing her keys and her coat.

'Do? Nothing, just babysit. Back soon, see you.'

At exactly the same moment as the front door closed, Liddy opened her mouth and started crying; and for the first time in ages Joe felt a twinge of panic. Come on, he told himself; it's only a baby, you like babies, what's hard about looking after one for ten minutes anyhow?

At which point Liddy peed abundantly and her nappy fell off, sliding all the way down the front of his new grey suit.

It was the night before Alan's party, and there were a few last-minute preparations to take care of.

'It's not right,' said Matt, following his brothers as they

headed for Joe's lock-up. 'You can't just walk out on your kid like that.'

'Even if sometimes you wish you could,' chipped in Stephen. Joe, Matt and Simon all stared at him. 'Don't look at me like that,' he protested, 'you know I'm right. Sometimes you'd cheerfully strangle the little bleeders.'

'Only sometimes?' enquired Simon.

Joe shook his head. 'Whatever happened to the joys of family life? Listening to you lot, anybody'd think it was some sort of life sentence.' Everybody exchanged looks. 'Oh come on – we had fun when we were kids, didn't we?'

'Yeah,' agreed Stephen. 'I'm not sure Mum and Dad did though. Would *you* have wanted to bring us lot up?'

Joe put an end to the debate by unlocking the door of the lock-up and revealing the treasure inside. 'There she is – what do you reckon?'

The three brothers gaped at the shiny red Jag. 'Strap me,' whistled Simon. 'Will you just take a look at that?'

'Tasty,' agreed Stephen, 'but where's the car we're giving Dad for his birthday?'

'This is it.' Joe stroked the bonnet proudly. 'He's going to be knocked out. Can I spot a good one, or what?'

'Hang on a minute,' said Matt, 'we said we'd club together to buy him a replacement for the old Jag. And unless this is the bargain of the century – no, the millennium – there's no way we can afford it!'

Joe's face relaxed into a benevolent smile. 'Of course we can! Well, I can, and that amounts to the same thing. You three can just—'

'No it doesn't,' cut in Matt.

'Doesn't what?'

'Amount to the same thing. It's not the same thing at all! This is supposed to be a present from all of us, not just from you.'

'And it is!' Joe reasoned. 'What does it matter if I put in a bit more? Dad won't know any different, will he?'

'Yeah, right!' snorted Simon. 'Like, he's not going to realise which one of us is showing off how much money he's got.'

'Nobody's showing off ...'

'Come off it! Who was it that *had* to pay off Mum and Dad's

247

mortgage last year? Who was it that bought those tasteless gold-plated taps for their bathroom?'

'Only because Mum asked for them.'

'Who always seems to think that throwing his money around makes him better than all the rest of us?'

Wounded to the quick, Joe stared at his brother's expression. 'I don't! I've never!'

But nobody was taking his side. 'It's not as if Matt can afford to chip in any extra.' Stephen jabbed a finger in Joe's face. 'Not with the new baby and his landscape gardening business doing so badly.'

'Yeah,' agreed Matt. 'So much for your free business advice, Joe, thanks a bunch. I think I'll pass on it in future.'

This was more than Joe could take. 'I didn't *give* you any business advice!' he protested.

'You said it was a good investment!'

'No I didn't, I said it *seemed* to be, but not to take my word for it because I'm no financial guru.'

'You can say that again,' sniffed Matt. 'Come on lads, who's for a swift half at the Swan? I don't suppose Joe will be joining us,' he added. 'He'll be up all night polishing his halo.'

When Emma arrived home from work the following evening, the flat was deserted. Obviously Joe had left early for the party, and in one respect she was profoundly grateful for that; the thought of having to look him in the eye and then go off to meet another man turned her ice-cold with guilty fear. On the other hand, there was a small part of her that she was unwilling to acknowledge: a part that wished Joe had been home, because then she would have had a good excuse to be cowardly and not go.

Not that there was any question of not going. All the preparations had been made, all the lies told, all her bits and pieces neatly packed into an overnight case, along with a copy of *Jackson's Orthopaedic Trauma Care*, just in case Joe had taken a look inside.

Now all she had to do was drive out to meet Richard.

Her heart raced, the exhilaration of doing wrong cascading through her veins like an icy waterfall. She closed her eyes, and could feel his hands caressing her, doing all the wicked, secret things they had done in her dreams. Was it really so wrong to want

248

to be alive, to want to spend time with someone who thought she was more than just a potential brood mare for his children? Really so unforgivable to want to find out what it felt like with somebody else?

Picking up her overnight case, she walked swiftly down the hallway and didn't dare look back.

28

The King's Regency stood at the very top of the hill in Montpellier, taking advantage of the elevated position to stake its claim as Cheltenham's premier hotel. Flags fluttered from its Palladian columns; almond mini-croissants were served each morning in the tea garden; and it was said that a privy councillor had actually died in one of its four-poster beds.

Minette was in seventh heaven. She and Alan might not be rich but these days they were comfortable, and she'd long harboured ambitions to hold her head up high amid the chandeliers and the haughty waiters. So the Severn Meadows Suite had been the obvious choice for Alan's party – even if Alan had muttered something about the function room at the Swan.

The guests would start arriving soon, and she was buzzing around like a hyperactive wasp, issuing orders and generally getting in everybody's way. Karen followed close behind, calming people down and putting things right. Meanwhile Alan, who was arguably the cause of all this fuss, lurked in a corner with a bag of crisps, talking to one of the waiters about creosote.

'The band, where are they?' demanded Minette. 'If they arrive late—'

'Calm down,' urged Karen, 'they're getting changed in one of the bedrooms.'

'Calm down? I am calm. What about the cake?'

'Two of the waiters are going to wheel it in when you propose the toast. Now, if that's everything I really must go and phone the removal men to check that they've finished unloading.'

Minette softened fractionally. 'Oh yes, I was forgetting you

250

were moving into your new flat today. It's very good of you to come tonight.'

'It's a big event, I wouldn't miss it for anything.' Besides, thought Karen, nobody ignores a summons from Minette.

'Hmm, well, it's a pity your daughter doesn't see things the same way.' Minette dabbed at her itchy eyes with a lace hanky. She might suffer from hay fever, but that wasn't going to stop her having the best floral arrangements in Cheltenham.

'Ah yes, the course. Well, these things happen.'

Minette drew herself up to her full five foot three. 'Not if you don't allow them to,' she retorted. 'If you don't mind my saying so, dear, she's letting us all down.'

The door of the suite opened and a young woman popped her head inside. 'Am I in the right place? Mum and Dad are just parking their car.'

Minette's face blossomed into an adoring smile. 'Zara, darling – come in!' she exclaimed, then turned to Karen with a sniff. 'You remember Zara, don't you, Karen? Now *there's* a girl who wouldn't dream of shirking her family obligations.'

By half past eight, the Severn Meadows Suite was full to bursting and the party was in full swing.

'Not too bad for a crusties' do,' conceded Gary, helping himself to another glass of wine. 'Who's the old crone in the bad wig?'

'Great-Aunt Gladys,' replied Joe, watching her strut her eighty year-old stuff to 'Kung Fu Fighting'. 'And don't let on to her that you know it's a wig, for God's sake.'

'But it's orange,' pointed out Toby. 'She looks like Ronald McDonald's mum, for chrissakes.'

Joe shoved a bite-sized sandwich into Toby's mouth. 'You promised to behave yourselves, remember?'

'Yeah, button it,' agreed Rozzer. 'It's a really nice party, Joe.'

'Thanks.'

Rozzer looked around him. 'Where's Emma though?'

He knew from the look on Joe's face that he'd said the wrong thing. 'On some stupid course for work. Just don't get me started, OK?'

'Er ... right.' Rozzer fiddled nervously with the stem of his wine glass.

'Never mind, eh?' sniggered Toby. 'Isn't that Zara over there? And she's on her own, looks like she could use some company.'

Gary thumped Joe on the back. 'Yeah, while the cat's away, eh mate?' He winked and flashed the bulging inside pocket of his jacket. 'Here, want a little something to soften her up, make the party swing?'

Joe blanched. 'What the fuck do you think you're doing, bringing that stuff in here?'

'Hey, chill out, will you? It's a party, people want to have fun.'

'Not that kind of fun, you cretin. It's not that kind of party! For God's sake get rid of it before somebody sees!'

Gary sighed. 'Pathetic, that's what you are these days. You know that? That girl's turned you into a grade-A wuss. Come on, Tobe, let's go find somebody who knows how to have a good time.'

'Fantastic party, Mum.' Stephen gave his mother a hug and she turned pink with pleasure.

'You don't think the vol au vents are a bit soggy?'

'Don't be daft, everything's great.' Matt put his arm round his wife's waist. 'We're all having a brilliant time, aren't we, Luce? First proper night out we've had since Crystal was born.'

'Are you sure Dad's all right though?' asked Simon, indicating the corner where Alan had been standing for the last half-hour, talking to Uncle Bob and eating his way through the nibbles. 'I haven't seen him smile more than twice all evening.'

'Of course he's all right,' scoffed Minette. 'Probably given himself a dose of indigestion mind you; I've told him crisps don't agree with him, but I might as well talk to the wall. Anyway,' she added, 'I'm sure he'll be smiling when you give him this mysterious birthday present of yours. What is it, by the way?'

The brothers looked at each other, and then at Joe, who was dancing with Zara, a plate of sausage rolls in one hand and a glass in the other.

'Wait and see, Mum,' was all they'd say.

'This takes me back,' reminisced Joe as he bopped along to 'Summer Nights'.

'Me too.' Zara tossed back her dark hair, still as lustrous and silky as it had been all those years ago when she'd played Sandy to Joe's Danny in the school production of *Grease*. 'We got a standing ovation with this one on the last night, do you remember?'

'How could I forget? And no, I haven't forgotten that you dropped an ice cube down the back of my shirt in the encore, either.'

She giggled. It took a good ten years off her. 'You had no trouble hitting the high notes that night.'

He studied her face, recalling very clearly how he had felt about her at seventeen. 'You never really told me, you know,' he said as the song ended.

'Told you what?'

'Why you and me ... Well, all right, you told me but I never totally understood.'

They stood there, in the middle of the dance floor; nose to nose, almost but not quite touching.

'Maybe you didn't want to understand,' she suggested quietly.

Maybe they'd have gone on dancing around the old questions like clubbers round a handbag, if Joe hadn't chanced to glance to one side just as the door to the corridor opened.

And seen Emma walk in.

Emma couldn't pinpoint the precise moment when she'd realised she couldn't go through with it.

It hadn't been a sudden revelation, more of a gradual awakening from a kind of self-inflicted hypnosis. An ugly throb of discomfort that couldn't be disregarded any longer, only got rid of. By the time she reached the turn-off by the Little Chef, she knew what she had to do.

She'd phoned Richard straight away, of course; but naturally he'd switched his mobile phone off – which in a way was a relief. In all honesty, the cowardly parts of her were almost gleeful to have got away with just leaving a voicemail for him to pick up when she didn't arrive at their rendezvous. By the time they spoke again – *if* they spoke again – he'd have got over it and she'd have had time to straighten her head out.

As she drove towards the hotel, she felt the huge weight begin to lift off her shoulders. It wasn't just guilt, it was more than that:

a realisation that sleeping with Richard to get back at Joe wouldn't be revenge, just a stupid mistake. And more: that some things deserved better than to be thrown away in a fit of loneliness and spite.

All the same, the full meaning of it all didn't really hit her until she pushed open the door of the Severn Meadows Suite and saw them: Joe and Zara, dancing together like they were sixteen and in love. Like they used to do when Emma was just some little kid who worshipped Joe from afar, even though he didn't even realise she existed.

It was only then, seeing him almost in the arms of another woman – *the* other woman – that Emma understood. I love him, she thought, as astonished as if she'd just discovered that the world was square. I may hate him, despise him, resent him, but when the chips are down I still love him more than anyone else I've ever loved.

He's never going to be yours, Zara, so you might as well give up now. Joe's mine.

Joe could scarcely believe his eyes. 'What happened? Why aren't you on your course?'

'They . . . cancelled it. At the last minute.'

'What course?' enquired Zara.

Emma flushed slightly. 'Oh, just something to do with trauma management.'

'Really? I don't remember seeing it posted up on the staff notice board. Where was it?'

'Has your dad had his present yet?' asked Emma, swiftly changing the subject.

'No.' He started walking away.

'Where are you going?'

'To get a drink.'

She caught up with him by the drinks table. 'Aren't you pleased to see me? I came here as quickly as I could.'

Joe looked less than bowled over. 'Yes, but you wouldn't have come at all if they hadn't cancelled the course,' he pointed out.

'I know, but all the same—'

Minette cut short the conversation by dragging her reluctant husband out of his corner and proposing a birthday champagne

254

toast. Everything was going brilliantly, exactly as she'd planned it, and she looked positively radiant.

'Now,' she said, clapping her hands for attention, 'our four lovely sons have got a special birthday surprise for their dad. And do you know what? It's such a secret that even I don't know what it is!'

The four sons exchanged looks, and while the others were debating Joe stepped forward. 'Come on, Dad.'

Alan looked mystified. 'Come on where?'

'Outside. We're going for a little walk ...'

The red Jaguar stood outside the front entrance to the King's Regency, zealously guarded by a uniformed commissionaire. An enormous length of gold-coloured sari material had been pressed into service as a bow, and a balloon with "60" on it bobbed above the shiny bonnet.

'Happy birthday, Dad.'

Minette nearly fell off her kitten heels. Everybody waited with breathless anticipation for Alan's rapturous reaction. He walked up to the car, blinked, shook his head and stepped back. 'What the bloody hell is this?'

'It's your present, Dad,' said Joe. 'I – I mean we, the four of us – got it for you to replace the old Jag. We all knew how fond you were of it.'

Alan did something nobody expected. He groaned. 'Bloody hell, lad, doesn't anybody ever listen to a word I say?'

Joe's face fell. Everybody fell silent. 'I don't follow, Dad.'

'Didn't I tell you I wasn't going to replace the old Jag? Didn't I?'

'Well ... yes. But that was because the insurance didn't cover it. Wasn't it?'

Alan sighed. 'Me and your mother discussed it, and we decided we wouldn't get another one because it wouldn't be the same. That old Jag wasn't just any old car, you know! Your brother was conceived on the back seat.'

Somebody giggled. Minette turned white and gasped, 'Alan!'

'Of course, that was in the days before your mother remembered she was a virgin. Anyhow, it's a very nice thought, son, but if it's all the same to you, I'd rather you took it back to the shop.'

'Alan!' exclaimed Minette. 'You could at least be a bit grateful! After all the trouble the boys have been to, not to mention all the money they've spent ...'

'Oh for God's sake put a sock in it, Minette.' She was so stunned at this that she instantly shut up. 'You've had your flash party, and we've all put our best suits on, like you wanted. Now I'm going to have my say. It's supposed to be *my* do, after all.

'Look, everyone, like I said it's a bloody nice car and thanks very much, but it's not for me.' He threw a glance at his youngest son. 'Money can't buy everything, you know, lad. Next time, just get me some slippers eh?'

Joe sat on the front steps of the King's Regency, slamming his heels into the weathered limestone and trying to recall if he'd broken any mirrors lately.

There had to be some reason why everything in his life had suddenly turned to shit. Why did everybody seem to hate him all of a sudden? How had he made the base-jump from golden boy to total idiot in one easy plummet? Sir Stanley was still convinced he was a cretin, his brothers felt patronised, his dad had accused him of thinking that money could buy everything. Even his doting mother had scolded him, saying he ought to have consulted her before he rushed off and wasted his money on a silly new car.

And as for his wife ...

His head sunk lower into his hands. It ached, and the unseasonably chill night air was making it spin after all those glasses of wine. Maybe he'd just sit here until he froze to the spot, and then they'd all be sorry.

'Joe?'

He stiffened.

'Joe, it's me. Are you all right?' Emma sat down on the steps beside him. 'I was worried about you.'

He stood up. 'I'm fine.'

'You don't look it. Tell you what, why don't we make our excuses and go home?'

She got to her feet too, and moved to put an arm round his shoulders; but Joe shrugged her away like an unwanted coat. 'Just leave it, Emma.'

He turned to walk back inside the building and she tagged along behind him. 'Please, Joe. I'm really sorry if I upset you. All I want to do is make you feel better.'

'I don't need your help. I feel fine.'

'Please, Joe, *talk* to me. I know there's something bothering you, and it's not just that business with your Dad's car, is it?'

He swung round and delivered a look that could have turned the sun to ice. 'What the hell do you care?' he retorted. And he walked briskly down the hotel steps and disappeared into the darkness.

29

It was the longest night of Emma's life, every second like a painfully dragging footstep. She spent most of it mechanically working her way through a tin of chocolate shortbread, sitting by the bedroom window and staring down at the empty street below. By the time daylight collapsed, gasping, over Cheltenham, she knew she was in no fit state to go in to work.

It was the first time ever that she'd called in sick, and Lawrence was suspicious from the word go.

'*Ill*? You? You're never ill.'

'Well I am this time, OK?' Her fingers fiddled guiltily with the telephone flex, willing him to just shut up and go away.

'So what's wrong – hangover, is it? From last night?'

'What?'

'Good night was it, the big family party?'

'Er ... yes. I must have drunk too much, stupid I know. But I'll be OK by tomorrow.'

There was a short pause, then: 'You'll have to learn to lie better than that if you're going into nurse management, sweetheart.'

'I'm not lying.'

'What's up, Emma? Tell Uncle Lawrence. Hang on a minute.' His voice muffled briefly. 'Cubicle seven, Janice, not cubicle eight. And make sure that defibrillator's back where it ought to be.' It cleared again. 'Busy for a Sunday morning, not that I'm trying to make you feel guilty or anything.'

'As if you would.'

'Right. Spill the beans and don't spare the lurid details.'

There was something about Lawrence that made people want to tell him stuff. Besides, he deserved an explanation and Emma needed someone to offload her misery onto. 'It's Joe,' she said, a sob rising at the back of her throat. 'He didn't come home last night.'

Lawrence sighed. 'If I had a sequin for every time Duncan's done that, I'd be Shirley Bassey by now. Had a row, did you?'

'Sort of.'

'Meaning?'

Her lip trembled. 'Yes, big time. He said I didn't care about him, and then he just walked off. I've no idea where he is or anything. What if he's left me? One of his mates left his wife a few weeks ago – what if he's decided to do the same?' An even worse thought hit her. 'What if he's been murdered, or run over or something?'

'Well, there's not a sniff of a mangled corpse here, love.'

'Lawrence!'

'Look, don't you worry, he'll be back. They always are, soon as they realise they're hungry and they haven't got any spare underpants. I'll see you tomorrow, OK? And I'm expecting big beaming smiles.'

Fat chance of that, thought Emma, moping around the flat like a bereft Ancient Mariner, with no one to listen to her tale of woe. She could have phoned Mickey, or her mum, but every time she got near the phone she shied away at the last moment, afraid that they knew her too well, that they might guess that a great big dollop of this was her own stupid fault.

As she sat forlornly next to the hall table, wondering what the hell she was going to do, the phone jangled into life. The sudden noise scared her half to death, and she was breathless as she snatched up the receiver.

'Yes?'

'It's me.'

Relief flooded over her like the soothing waters of a tropical lagoon. 'Joe! Where are you, where have you been?'

'I'm at work. Look, I'm sorry if I worried you last night but I checked into a B and B. I needed some space to get my head together.'

His voice sounded so detached, so dispassionate, that all Emma's suppressed tears flooded her eyes. 'Joe, I'm so sorry, I know I haven't been spending enough time with you but I never meant to—'

'Let's not go over this now, eh?' he cut in briskly. 'I've got a meeting in ten minutes.'

That just didn't sound like him at all. 'Joe! Forget the stupid meeting,' she pleaded. 'Tell them you're ill or something. Come home.'

'I can't. There's a lot going on here, and I need more time to think. But I'll see you tonight, OK?'

It wasn't OK, not in the slightest; but it looked like that was the best Emma was going to get.

Round about lunchtime, Emma's heart gave a sudden leap as she heard a key turn in the front door. Unless Joe had been spreading them round the population of Cheltenham, only four people besides herself had keys to that door: Minette, Karen, Rozzer ... and Joe.

She practically threw herself down the hallway as the door opened.

'Hello, love!' exclaimed Karen, struggling in with a couple of pattern books. 'Just brought these round for you to look at.'

Trying not to betray her disappointment, Emma grabbed the pattern books off her mum. 'What are you doing, carrying these things?' she scolded. 'They're much too heavy for you.'

'Rubbish, I'm almost back to my usual self.' Karen followed her daughter down the hallway to the living room. 'Didn't expect you to be here – I thought you were doing an eight-till-five today.'

'I was, only ... I didn't feel too good this morning, so I called in sick.'

'You don't look too good now,' commented Karen. 'In fact I don't think I've ever seen you so pale. Well, not since you were four and you ate all those earwigs.' She laid a hand on Emma's forehead. 'No temperature though. I wonder what's wrong. Should you see a doctor?'

'It's nothing the doctor can help with, Mum. Honest. I'm not ill, I wish it was that simple.'

She had turned her back on her mother and was gazing out of the window, but Karen gently but firmly pivoted her round so that they were facing each other again. 'Emma.'

'Yes?'

'Are you going to explain yourself, or do I have to stand here with my imagination working overtime? Emma? Emma, staring at that grease-stain on the carpet's not going to solve anything.'

Emma knew that tone of voice all too well. It was the same one that had greeted her childhood attempts to redecorate the bathroom in toothpaste, and the out-of-character teenage exploit involving drunken buttock-baring at the agricultural college. No way had Karen Cox ever been the heavy-handed parent; which was why her moments of sudden authority were all the more effective. You didn't run a successful guest house in Blackpool without acquiring a vein of steel.

'This is about last night, isn't it?' Emma didn't deny it, and Karen shook her head and sighed. 'I saw you and Joe arguing at the party – what was it about? Not that silly car?'

Emma shook her head and crumpled onto one of the tub-chairs by the window. 'What's it always about?' she replied bitterly. 'Me and work, him and work, me and him never being in the same place at the same time, me apparently not giving a damn about him any more.'

'This is according to Joe?'

Emma nodded. She looked up, half of her almost hoping her mother would tell her it served her right because it was all her fault, the other half silently pleading for sympathy. 'He didn't come home at all last night.'

Karen sat down in the chair opposite her daughter. 'Oh, Emma.'

'Then he called me from work this morning and wouldn't talk about where he'd been or who he'd been with or anything. Mum, what if he's having an affair?'

This produced a look of wide-eyed disbelief. 'An affair? Joe?'

'He's been phoning that cow Zara, I know he has. What if he's been doing more than that?'

'Emma, love.' Karen laid a hand on her daughter's knee. 'From what you've told me about his work, I wouldn't think he's got *time* to have an affair, even if he wanted to. And I'm sure he doesn't,' she added as Emma's bottom lip started to tremble. 'Besides,' she smiled, 'he completely lost interest in Zara when he fell in love with you.'

'People can fall out of love,' Emma replied gloomily, trying not to think about what had almost happened with Richard.

Karen's brows knitted. 'You're not trying to tell me *you've* gone off *him*, are you?'

261

The suggestion sliced through Emma's heart as savagely as an assassin's knife. 'No!' she exclaimed. 'OK, maybe I did think I had for a while . . .But that was just me being stupid, and Joe being exhausted all the time.' She passed a hand over her brow. 'There's just so much pressure – pressure to do stuff, pressure not to do stuff, pressure to be what you're supposed to be now instead of what you always used to be. All we did was say some words and sign a bit of paper. I had no idea marriage would be like this.'

'Nobody ever does,' replied Karen with a half-smile. 'It's a big readjustment. And with Joe's job being so high-powered, and you doing so well at work too . . .'

'You agree with Minette, don't you? You think I should be a good little wife and not apply for that job.'

She shook her head. 'I don't think anything of the sort. I just think maybe it would have been easier if you two had talked all this stuff through *before* you walked down the aisle. But never mind, you'll just have to work it out now instead, decide what marriage means to both of you and find some kind of compromise. Otherwise you'll still be rowing when you're fifty.'

'If he doesn't leave me.'

'Has he said anything about leaving you?'

'Well . . . no.'

'Then stop jumping to conclusions. Rowing doesn't mean your relationship's on the rocks, it just means there are things you need to get sorted out between you. After all,' she added with humour, 'you don't want to end up like Alan and Minette, arguing all the way home about a car that nobody actually wants.'

'Joe meant well, I know he did.'

'I know that too.'

'They're not still rowing, are they?'

'Between you and me, when I arrived at the office this morning Minette had Alan up against the wall, telling him to pick up the phone and apologise. Of course, Alan being the sort of guy he is—'

As though reminded of its own existence, the phone chose that moment to ring. For some reason that defied logic, Emma felt a strong urge to ignore it.

'Aren't you going to answer it?' enquired her mother after the first three or four rings.

'It won't be anything important.'

This raised an eyebrow. 'Are you sure? It might be Joe.'

'Oh. Yes. I suppose so.'

It might have been, but it wasn't. The moment Emma lifted the receiver and heard the voice on the other end of the line, her heart started galloping like Red Rum in the final furlong of the Grand National.

'Emma, it's me. Richard.'

She swallowed hard, instinctively cupping her hand over the receiver like a schoolchild hiding its work from its neighbour. 'Oh. Hi.'

'Is it Joe?' her mother called from the living room.

'No, Mum,' she called back. 'Just ... just a friend.' She lowered her voice. 'About what happened ... I'm really, really sorry. But I just couldn't ... we both know it's for the best.'

'Can you guess where I am?' Richard's voice was warm and coaxing. 'I'm sitting in my car in the middle of the North York Moors, Emma, watching the sunlight making patterns on the heather. I miss you so much. You know how much I wanted you to be here with me.'

Her mouth was dry, her throat as tense as if a hand were squeezing her windpipe. 'Richard, please don't make this harder.'

'It needn't be hard at all. Not if you—'

Emma cut him short before he could plant any seeds of doubt in her mind. 'I'm sorry, I can't talk now. I'll phone you later,' she added, though in her heart she knew she wouldn't.

'Anything up?' enquired her mother as she came back into the living room.

'Nothing important,' replied Emma, hoping her mother wouldn't notice the muscle beneath her left eye, twitching the way it always did when she was really scared or tense. 'Now, why don't I make us a nice pot of tea, and then you can show me which wallpaper you've chosen for your bedroom.'

It was hard, feeling two kinds of guilt. First the guilt about betraying Joe – OK, so maybe she hadn't actually gone through with anything adulterous, but she very nearly had, and if thinking about a sin was tantamount to committing it, then she was as guilty as hell.

Then there was the other kind: the discomfort she felt about the way she'd treated Richard. Yes, he was a man of the world; yes, he was a free spirit who didn't believe that people should be tied to each other. But he was a man with feelings too: feelings for her. And it was hardly admirable to have let him believe those feelings were reciprocated, only to dump him unceremoniously the moment she remembered she had a conscience.

Well, she told herself; at least it's done, and Richard's the kind of guy to put it behind him and move on. The question is, can Joe and I make things up, or have I left it too late?

It was just after seven when Joe's key turned in the lock and he walked in, looking haggard and crumpled in last night's suit and somebody's borrowed shirt.

He looked so dreadful that Emma's first instinct was to run up and put her arms round him, but she felt so nervous that she hardly dared go near him.

'Are you ... OK?' she asked as he stripped off his tie and threw it onto the hall table. 'You look really tired.'

His eyes met hers. 'Bit of a crap day.'

'I know.' Nervous energy fought the overwhelming guilt. 'Can I get you something? Coffee? A beer?'

'Emma.'

She headed towards the kitchen. 'I bet you haven't eaten anything since—'

'Emma, stop.' He caught her by the shoulders, took her arm and led her into the living room. 'Sit down.'

'But—'

'We need to talk.'

The word slid like an ice cube between her shoulder blades. I don't want to talk, thought Emma in panic. It's what I've wanted to do all day, but now you're actually here I'd rather do anything *but*. 'Oh,' she said. 'Well, can I just go and—'

'No, you can't.' Joe pushed her firmly back into her chair, pushed his up closer and took both her hands. 'Look at me, Em.'

She did, fearfully.

'I know you were worried earlier, and I'm sorry about that, but I didn't want to talk then because I needed to think.'

'About ... what?'

'About us, work, family ... everything.' He took a deep breath. 'Last night, I was so angry I must have walked round Cheltenham ten times before I realised how knackered and cold I was. I thought about coming home, but I couldn't face you. So I ended up bashing on the door of a B and B at three am. Can't say they were too pleased to see me, but it's amazing how helpful people can be when you offer to pay double.

'Anyhow, I couldn't sleep so about five I phoned Rozzer, and he drove over and we talked a bit.'

'You got Rozzer out at five in the morning!'

'He's a good mate. After that I drove into work and phoned you. All day long I've been thinking about you and me, Emma. About the future.'

'So have I, Joe. I—'

He put a finger to her lips. 'Wait a minute, there's something I have to say to you.'

The icy feeling slithered down her spine again, chilling her soul. Whatever this was, she was sure she didn't want to hear it.

'Things have been difficult lately, I know,' he said softly, 'and I've been blaming a lot of it on you. But last night really shook me up, made me realise how much of it is down to me.'

'Joe—'

'Please. Don't stop me, this is hard enough to say as it is.' He held her hands tightly. 'I've been unreasonable, I know that now. Rozzer told me so weeks ago and he was right, damn him. I can't expect you to be sitting at home waiting for me like some lovesick puppy, when half the time I don't make it home at all. It's no life for you.'

Emma felt as if all the blood had drained out of her face, her hands, her feet; leaving her whole body ice-cold save for the smouldering ashes of her heart. Was this the moment when Joe told her he was leaving? 'W-what are you saying?'

'I'm saying I've been really selfish, and you deserve to have a proper career.'

Taken aback, she blinked. 'Sorry?'

'You're doing well at the hospital, you're good at your job. I think you should apply for that nurse coordinator post, and I honestly hope you get it.'

'I'm sorry, I can't quite get my head round this.' She withdrew her clammy hands and sat back in her chair. 'All along, you've been dead against my applying for it. Why change your mind now, all of a sudden?'

'Because reality hit me, that's why. And because I'm proud of you. Besides,' he looked down at his feet, 'one of us ought to have a career that's going somewhere.'

Astonished, Emma felt his words sink in. 'What do you mean? Yours is going plenty of places.' She contemplated his bowed head. 'Isn't it?'

He didn't answer.

Tentatively, she laid a hand on his shoulder and he looked up. 'I'm proud of you too, you know,' she smiled.

Joe shrugged away her touch and got to his feet. 'What's there to be proud of?'

Although Emma asked Joe several times to explain what he'd meant, it was as if he'd never spoken. Most likely, she mused as she shoved bread into the toaster, he'd just been having a moment of self-doubt. The odd thing was, he'd never been prone to them in the past. In fact, until they'd got married, Joe had possessed all the insouciant confidence of a concrete rhinoceros.

'Mail,' he announced, bringing it into the kitchen and tossing it onto the table.

'Anything good?'

'Not unless you like bank statements. Hang on, though.' He peeled off something that the rain had stuck to the back of some junk mail. 'There's a postcard. Who do we know that's on holiday?'

As he held it up and she saw the photo, Emma caught her breath. An expanse of heather-clad moorland, stretching away into an infinity of blue sky and fluffy white clouds. And then the caption.

North. York. Moors.

'Won't you change your mind?' said Joe.

Emma wrinkled her nose. 'What?'

'That's what it says: "Won't you change your mind?". And then it's signed "R". Is it supposed to be a joke or something?'

Emma took the card from him, forcing a merry laugh she definitely did not feel. 'Oh, that'll be Richard,' she said. 'You know, the tutor at my photography class?'

Joe cocked his head on one side. 'What's he mean, "Won't you change your mind?" What about?'

'The course,' Emma smiled and took the card, ripping it in two and throwing it into the kitchen bin. 'I told him I've decided to give it up.'

Joe looked pole-axed. 'But ... why? I thought you were enjoying it. And you said he was really pleased with your work.'

She turned away to rescue the burning toast. 'Oh, not really,' she replied, trying desperately to sound casual. 'It was just a phase. I know now that it's really not for me.'

On the surface at least, everything was fine. Joe was being encouraging, Richard was just a memory, everything was going to be OK.

Except that it didn't feel OK.

It was no good trying to pretend, to keep it all inside. No good at all trying to deny the unspoken things that were gnawing away at her. She had to tell someone. And the next night that Joe was working late, Emma found herself in front of the webcam again.

'Go on,' she said soberly, 'tell me that I'm just getting what I deserve.'

Mickey gave her an odd look. 'Is that what you want me to say?'

'No,' she lied.

'Yes it is! You feel you've done something bad, so you want somebody to punish you. Sorry, kiddo, no can do. And besides, you only *almost* did something.'

'Almost is bad enough,' lamented Emma.

Two small, pointed ears appeared at the bottom of Emma's picture, followed by two paws and two very round eyes. A moment later, the entire screen went blank.

'Rufus, no! Get down Rufie, you can't eat that.' Mickey's face reappeared, accompanied by a wriggling woolly thing with a pink nose. 'Tried to eat the webcam,' she explained. 'He's going through the chewing phase I think, he had the corners off my library books last week.' She gave the top of the kitten's head a kiss and put him down on the floor. 'Em, I know you feel bad, but what's the point? All this agonising is just making you miserable, and even if you did deserve to be miserable – and I'm not saying you do – how does that help Joe?'

'I don't know,' admitted Emma, 'but I just feel as if I have to ...I don't know, *do* something, *say* something. Something to wipe the slate clean.'

A look of alarm crossed Mickey's face. 'Now just you listen to me, madam. The last thing you want to do is *do* something, believe me. Spilling the beans to Joe might make you feel better for about five seconds, but it sure as hell wouldn't do anything for him.'

'Then what do I do?' pleaded Emma. 'I feel so guilty ... and I'm so worried about Joe, he's just not himself.'

'The only thing you can do: the hard thing. You sit tight and you wait for it all to blow over.'

'I can't!'

'Oh yes you can. And you're going to.'

Emma hung her head. 'Oh Mickey,' she whispered, 'I wish you weren't so far away.'

'I'm one phone call away, never any further,' retorted Mickey. 'And you can phone me absolutely any time you want – except during anything with Viggo Mortensen in it,' she added with a wink. 'And anyway, it just so happens that I might be visiting Cheltenham in the not-too-distant future.'

Emma sat up straight. 'Really? When?'

'Well, I've got a few days' leave owing to me, and I thought I might come up there and take my best mate out for lunch. How does that sound?'

'Fantastic!' She peered at the face on the screen. 'Why are you smirking? What's going on?'

'Nothing,' laughed Mickey. 'I just thought I might bring someone with me, that's all. Someone I'd like you to meet.'

30

'Mr Goldsmith,' called the agency nurse from triage. Three people stood up in unison and shuffled sideways towards her, complete with what appeared to be a sawn-off brass handrail from the local theme pub.

'No, *just* Mr Goldsmith please.'

'Sorry miss,' replied the crimson-faced youth at the front, 'you'll have to have us all, we can't get the glue unstuck.'

'Tell her to hurry up, will you?' wailed one of his companions. 'I'm busting for a pee.'

'Ah,' sighed one of the porters, shaking his head with the air of someone who had seen everything and done most of it, 'don't you just love Rag Week?'

Once she was safely shielded by the door of the treatment room, Emma laughed until her ribs ached. It was the first time she'd so much as chuckled in days, and it gave her the most immense feeling of release. At last she was starting to feel better, at least about herself. There was still Joe to worry about, of course, but Richard had obviously got the message, and she was beginning to breathe again. There was no doubt that she'd been an idiot, or that she was going to feel guilty and stupid for a very long time; but like Mickey said, she'd only *almost* done something terrible. And it was the 'almost' that made all the difference.

I'm going to make it up to you, Joe, she told him silently. Everything's going to be all right, just you wait and see.

It was lunchtime, and for once there was actually time to take a break and eat something. In fact for the first time that year, Emma

269

and Lawrence had managed to escape to the park across the road. It was bliss.

'Brie and grape?' enquired Lawrence, proffering his sandwich box.

'Ooh, lovely.' Emma took one of the neat brown triangles. 'Swap you for a cheese and jam?'

'What?' Lawrence peeled open a corner of one of Emma's hastily put-together sandwiches. 'Oh my God, the girl's not joking. Are you sure you're not pregnant?'

'Ha, ha. I'll take that as a no, shall I?' She bit into a sandwich and relaxed contentedly against the back of the park bench. 'You should try it, it's a great combination. Of course it has to be strawberry, or it just doesn't work.'

One corner of Lawrence's mouth curled. 'Well of course it does.'

'If the wind changes you'll stay like that,' remarked Emma through a mouthful of bread. 'And then what will Duncan say?'

Lawrence rolled his eyes. 'Don't talk to me about bloody Duncan.'

Emma settled down for the latest episode of the soap opera that was Lawrence and Duncan's home life. 'Go on, what's he done now?'

'It's not so much what he's done, as what he wants to do. You know a while back he got the idea that he might be bi, and started shagging anything with less than four legs?'

'I thought he'd got that out of his system.'

'Oh he did. Allegedly. But what he didn't do was think about the possible consequences.'

'Such as?'

'Such as, this girl turning up on our doorstep, five months gone and swearing blind it's Duncan's.'

'No!' The sandwich stopped halfway to Emma's mouth. 'You're kidding.'

'Was that supposed to be a pun?'

'Oh, sorry. No, it wasn't.' She looked at Lawrence's face and saw pain and tension behind the archly camp façade. 'You really do love him, don't you?'

He shrugged. 'I must do, mustn't I? Why else would I put up with all this shit?'

A pied wagtail came hopping along the path between the

municipal flowerbeds, its tail wagging up and down like a disapproving finger. Emma crumbled up some cake and watched it dart about, gathering up the crumbs as the breeze chased them away.

'What are you going to do?' she asked.

'God knows. Or rather, Duncan does; he's got all the answers. According to him, the girl's going to move in with us till she drops the sprog, then hand the poor little tyke over to us, and bugger off. Bingo: she gets rid of it and Duncan gets to play instant happy families.'

'Yes, all very convenient for him I daresay, but what about you? What do you want?'

Lawrence paused, mouth half open; and for a moment she thought he was going to say something profound. But before he had a chance to reply, their attention was distracted by the sound of raised voices on the other side of the park, beyond the sunbathers and the foraging squirrels. And they weren't just any voices either.

Shading his eyes against the sun, Lawrence peered at the two figures. 'Isn't that—'

'Linda, yes. And Rozzer.' Emma couldn't hear what they were arguing about, but the body language said it all: Linda tossing her head and gesticulating, Rozzer looking more and more like a wilted gorilla, arms dangling limply at his sides. 'Oh dear, I thought they were getting on better.'

'Look on the bright side – if he turns up unconscious in A and E, we'll know who to blame.'

As they watched, Linda turned and stalked off, disappearing from view where the path ran behind a mass of rhododendron bushes. For a few moments Rozzer stood gazing after her; then readjusted his work tie, and plodded off in her direction.

That'll teach you to try and sort out other people's lives, Emma told herself sternly as the pair vanished from sight. From now on, you're going to concentrate on sorting out your own.

'Come back,' pleaded Rozzer as he rounded the corner by the rhododendrons. 'You're being silly.'

Linda stopped and turned round, hands on hips. 'No I'm not. Factory work's all I'm good for, I might as well just accept that and get on with it.'

271

'That's rubbish,' retorted Rozzer. 'You're worth far more than that. All you need is a bit of confidence.'

'Confidence!' Linda laughed. 'Hark who's talking: Mr "I'm-only-working-in-this-betting-shop-because-nobody-else-will-have-me".'

Rozzer thrust his hands deep into the pockets of his navy-blue polyester work trousers, and looked uncomfortable. 'But it's true! Who else would want somebody like me?'

'Lots of people.'

'Like who?'

For a moment, they stood staring defiantly at each other as a squirrel scampered between them, the remains of a sausage roll in its mouth. Then:

'Like me,' said Linda quietly.

Rozzer didn't know what drove him to it, and he sure as heck wasn't the impetuous type; but the next thing he knew, he'd marched right across the gravel path, grabbed Linda by the shoulders and planted a kiss right on her lips.

A moment later, he was so overcome with the enormity of what he'd done that he turned right round and fled.

It was mid-afternoon, and Joe was taking advantage of a rare opportunity to work from home when the doorbell rang. To his surprise, when he opened the door he found his parents standing on the doorstep.

'Your father's got something to say to you,' announced Minette, giving Alan a meaningful prod in the back.

'Oh,' said Joe, somewhat taken aback. An unscheduled visit from his mother was always a distinct possibility, but his father's social round tended to consist of regimental reunions and wakes. 'Come in,' he added, rather superfluously as Minette had already nudged his father halfway to the living room.

'Get on with it, then,' said Minette.

'Get on with what?' asked Joe.

'I'll go and make us some coffee,' replied Minette. 'Your father'll tell you. Won't you, Alan?' she added, with a look that brooked no disagreement.

When she was safely out of the way, Alan lowered himself onto Joe's settee with an exhausted 'oof'. 'She's a good woman, your mother,' he remarked, 'but a little goes a long way.'

272

Joe sat down opposite his father. 'What's all this about having something to tell me?'

Alan grimaced. 'Your mother put me up to it. I know she's right but that doesn't make it easy.' He coughed. 'I've come to apologise for the other night. You know, at the party.'

'You've no need,' Joe assured him. 'In fact, I was going to apologise to you, for being such a bonehead. You were right, I've been throwing my money around like it makes me better than everybody else, and it doesn't.'

'Maybe,' conceded Alan, 'but you meant well. And I shouldn't have been so bloody rude. It's a damned nice car,' he added, with a hint of wistfulness.

'Oh.' Joe perked up. 'Does that mean you're keeping it, then?'

Alan laughed and shook his head. 'Not bloody likely. Have you any idea what the insurance is on something like that? Besides, I meant what I said; it's not for me. I did have an idea though.'

'What sort of an idea?'

'Well, Matt and Lucy are going through a bit of a rough patch at the moment. How's about we sell the Jag, and invest some of the money in Matt's gardening business? That way, he won't feel like it's charity but it'll help them out.'

'Sounds good,' nodded Joe. 'You're a born diplomat, Dad.'

Alan sat back comfortably, knees apart, arms spread along the back of the settee. 'Speaking of rough patches, did I hear you and Emma having a bit of a barney at the party? Nothing seriously wrong I hope?'

'Of course not,' cut in Minette, appearing like magic in the doorway with a tray of coffee cups. 'Is it, Joe?'

Joe wished he could be so sure.

All things considered it had been a good day at work, and Emma wasn't even that tired when she came off duty. A young couple had thanked her for helping to save their baby after a choking fit, nobody had died, and the vending machine had been restocked with KitKats. Best of all, Joe had phoned her at work – something he hadn't done for ages – to tell her that he and his dad had made up.

It was even still warm and sunny as she emerged from A&E; so sunny in fact that at first she was dazzled by the brightness, and when someone stepped in front of her she saw only a dark shadow.

273

'Emma, thank God. I've been worried sick about you.'

Hot though it was, Emma suddenly felt as though she had been deluged with ice-water. She didn't need to be able to see the speaker clearly to know that it was Richard.

Blinking away the last of the dazzle, Emma instinctively stepped away, maintaining the distance between them. 'Richard, what are you doing here?'

He looked at her and shook his head, a half-smile on his lips. 'What am I doing here? I've just got back from North Yorkshire, and I've driven straight over here because I wanted to see you. Needed to see you. God, I've missed you, Emma.'

Richard reached out to touch her but again she backed away. What was going on? It was as if he hadn't heard a word of what she'd said to him before. 'Richard, don't. And not here, people might see.'

He looked wounded. 'Why not here?'

'Not just here, not anywhere, don't you understand? There can't ever be anything between us, Richard. It wouldn't work and it's not right. I told you already, that's it, finito.' She began walking across to her car in the thankfully deserted car park. 'You're a great bloke, and I really like you, but I've already got a great bloke and I'm married to him and it would be a terrible mistake getting involved with you. I'm so sorry if I've hurt you or led you on in any way.'

The smile on Richard's lips did not fade but his eyes weren't smiling any more. 'Don't play games with me, Emma. I know you love me, just as much as I love you.'

'*Love* you!' Every alarm bell in Emma's body jangled at full volume. 'What the hell ...?' She swung round to confront him, suddenly shocked to the core. 'Hold on a minute, Richard, we're talking about sexual attraction here – love's got nothing to do with this.'

'You can deny it all you want, but I know the truth about how you feel,' he replied, with a quiet confidence that chilled her to the bone. 'The two of us are meant to be together.' My God, she thought; this guy's not just wrong for me, he's not *normal*. What on earth have I got myself into?

'You're imagining things, Richard. It was just a . . . a minor flirtation that got out of hand.'

He shook his head. 'It's a lot more than that, Emma, you know it is.'

For the first time, her body shrank from him in horror as he reached out and stroked her bare arm. 'And I won't let you throw your life away on a man who treats you like you're just an outgrowth of his own personality!'

Snatching her arm away, she grabbed her car keys and unlocked the driver's door with trembling fingers. 'Let me go, Richard.'

'I can't. You don't want me to.'

'I said, let me go!' Furious, she practically threw his hand off her shoulder. 'Don't you dare do this, don't you dare!'

She was shaking all over as Richard caught her hand and carried it to his lips. 'Don't ask me to do the impossible, Emma.' It sounded more like a command than a plea.

Her mind was working overtime, frantic to find a way of resolving this horrible situation. 'Please stop this,' she implored him, changing tack. 'I'm *begging* you to.' She wrestled the door out of his hands, slid into the driver's seat and slammed the door shut. 'If what you say is true and you really do have ... feelings for me—'

'You know I do.'

'Then please, just turn round and go home and forget all about me. Because, I swear, there can never be anything between us.'

31

'Nurse Sheridan?' enquired the receptionist as Emma was walking past the main hospital reception desk.

Surprised, she stopped and turned round. 'Yes?'

The girl's pink cheeks dimpled. 'Oh good, I thought I recognised you.' Reaching down under the desk, she produced the most enormous bouquet of red roses Emma had ever seen. 'These were just delivered. Haven't you got a romantic husband, you lucky thing!'

Emma gasped in amazement. Joe hadn't made a grand romantic gesture since their first Christmas together, and even then it had only been two dozen freesias. 'Wow, I don't believe this . . . it isn't even my birthday!'

Colouring up with pleasure, she reached in among the thornless stems and extracted the little white envelope with the card.

'What does he say?' asked the receptionist eagerly.

Emma didn't reply. She could hardly tell her that it read: To the most beautiful woman in the world, Richard xxx.

Basically, it was a clash of cultures.

In twenty years of running a busy guest house, Karen had had to learn to be organised, tidy, and clean. Perhaps that was why, when the shackles were off, she loved nothing more than a nice bit of mess. Nothing too sty-like, of course; no half-eaten pizzas in the bed or piles of fluff swept under the corners of the rugs. Just the odd overflowing ironing basket, or a jumble of magazines all over the sitting-room floor. A nice, comfortable kind of mess.

Minette, on the other hand, had lived her entire life on a cleanliness crusade. No dog's bottom had ever sparkled like Pepe the poodle's; no other toilet bowl had been so ruthlessly scrubbed that the glaze had started to come off the inside. Minette's lemon-fresh world was one in which socks were always ironed, cakes always home-baked, and biological stains unthinkable.

She nearly had the vapours when Karen answered the door dressed in a pair of paint-spattered dungarees, with a faint waft of boiled cabbage in the background. Smells seldom made it more than a couple of inches into Minette's house before chemical death rained down upon them.

Karen's eyes widened. 'Oh, gosh, Minette!' Surprise just about masked the dismay in her voice.

'I brought you some flowers,' said Minette, thrusting the freesias in Karen's direction. 'I thought they might help cheer up your new flat.'

'Thanks, that's really kind. But you didn't have to trail all the way out to Gloucester, you could have given them to me at work tomorrow.'

'Well, seeing as I'm here . . .' hinted Minette.

'Ah . . . yes, of course. Come in, can I get you a cup of tea or something?'

'Earl Grey please, no sugar, and just a sliver of lemon.' She took in the look in Karen's eye and the open box of PG Tips on the kitchen table. 'Whatever you're having will be lovely, dear. Anyway, I didn't come here to drink tea.'

No, thought Karen with amusement as Minette wandered off into the next room; you came to have a good old nose at my bits and bobs. Not that I mind; I just wish you'd come out and say so.

'Heavens,' exclaimed Minette at the sight of all the tea chests in the spare bedroom, 'haven't you got round to unpacking yet?'

'Oh, I like to take my time,'

'If you're having trouble managing, I could send Alan round to help,' Minette ventured hopefully.

'No, no, I'm fine. After all, what's the hurry?'

'Er . . . yes. I suppose you're right.' Minette swallowed and smiled weakly, but couldn't restrain herself from straightening up a crooked watercolour as she passed.

'Anyway,' Karen went on, emptying a packet of biscuits onto a plate, 'I'm far too busy replastering the bathroom ceiling to unpack boxes.'

277

Minette clutched the door-frame for support. 'Replastering? In your condition?'

Karen laughed out loud. 'You make it sound as if I'm pregnant or something!'

'It's not a laughing matter, Karen,' scolded Minette. 'You're not a well woman.'

'Nonsense, now the flare-up's died down I'm as right as rain. I'm not an invalid, you know.'

But she stumbled slightly as she picked up the tea tray, and Minette whisked it out of her hands. 'Nobody's saying you are, dear, but you don't want tea stains all over this white rug, do you? Now, come and drink your tea and then you can tell me where to start with my squeegee.'

Emma's first instinct was to dump the bouquet in one of the giant hospital bins; but it was so huge and lovely that she had second thoughts and donated it to the geriatric unit instead. Somebody might as well derive some pleasure from it, and it certainly wasn't going to be her.

She agonised long and hard about what to do – if she phoned Richard, or wrote to him, wouldn't that just be encouraging him? In the end she didn't do anything; and as the next few days produced nothing untoward, it looked as though that had been the right decision.

'Do you want some paracetamol, love?' enquired a kindly cleaner as Emma searched the hospital computer system for a patient's notes.

She glanced up, puzzled. 'Why? I'm not in pain.'

'Oh, sorry, love. You look so pale, I thought you must be having your period.'

The cleaner went off humming 'Oh What a Beautiful Morning'. Emma contemplated her reflection in the window of Lawrence's office. You've done this to yourself, you idiot, she reminded herself. If you feel like crap it's no more than you deserve.

Hot chocolate, that was what she needed. It was barely half past seven in the morning and there wasn't a single patient in the department. Nobody would mind if she nipped out to the vending machine for a moment. She rifled through her uniform pockets for change, dumping the results on Lawrence's desk. Tissues, crumpled envelope she kept forgetting to throw away, chewing gum, scissors, scrunchie, sticky tape ... God, what a mess, she'd have to sort it out later. Aha, fifty pence.

Leaving the little pile of bits on the desk, she dashed out. 'Just going to the drinks machine,' she called to the very pregnant Janice. 'Back in a mo.'

'Make mine a triple vodka!' She joked.

If she hadn't remembered on the way back that she'd left her watch in her handbag, Emma wouldn't have stopped off at the changing room. And if she hadn't stopped off there, she wouldn't have discovered until much later that the padlock on her locker door was mysteriously missing ...

Or found the little gift-wrapped package sitting inside.

Her stomach turned over. She didn't need to read the tag to know who it was from, didn't need to unwrap it to guess that this was another missile from Richard's love-arsenal.

Struggling not to hyperventilate, she slammed the locker door shut and ran back to the department, not even bothering to take her drink with her.

Lawrence was back in his office, going through some routine paperwork. He looked up as Emma barged straight in. 'Good God, woman, what's got into you?'

'Somebody broke into my locker,' she snapped.

'Shit, I thought we'd stamped that out. What did they take?'

'Nothing.' She plonked the package on the desk in front of him. 'They left this.'

Lawrence scratched his head. 'A thief who leaves presents? Well, it's different. What is it?'

'I don't know, and I don't want to.' Emma picked it up and threw it straight in the waste bin. It was only then that she noticed the pile of old tissues already in there. 'Oh.'

'Oh what?'

'I left some stuff on your desk for a minute while I nipped out. You didn't get rid of it, did you?'

'Oh, that.' Lawrence opened up his desk drawer and produced Emma's scissors, chewing gum, sticky tape and scrunchie. 'I slung out the tissues, somehow I didn't figure you were that attached to them.'

This was like one of those memory tests, with items laid out on a tray. Emma could have sworn there was something missing. All at once she realised what it was. 'There was an envelope,' she said. 'A long brown one.'

'The one addressed to Personnel? I figured that must be your application for the nurse coordinator post.'

The colour drained from Emma's face. 'You threw it away, right? Please tell me you threw it away.'

'Would I do that? No, Janice was on her way to Pathology, so I got her to hand it in at Personnel on her way there.'

When Matt arrived home for his lunch, dirty and exhausted from a morning's paving, he had a pleasant surprise for his wife. In fact, he had two.

'Oh Matt, what a lovely present!' exclaimed Lucy, tearing off the paper and opening up the box. Inside was a pair of silver earrings, set with peridots. 'But it's not my birthday or anything.'

Matt sat down beside her and slipped an arm round her shoulders. 'Can't I buy my wife a present just because I want to?'

'Of course you can.' She kissed the end of his grimy nose. 'But can we afford it?'

'As a matter of fact,' replied Matt, tickling the soles of Crystal's feet and making her giggle, 'we can.' Sticking a hand in his shirt pocket, he took out a cheque. 'Dad gave me this, this morning. He and Joe want to invest in the business.'

Lucy was so startled by the amount, she nearly dropped the baby. 'I don't believe this . . . you're having me on.' Matt shook his head. 'Hang on, though, didn't you say you wouldn't have Joe's money if he went down on bended knees?'

'That was when he was flinging it around like he was Lord Muck. I talked to Dad and this is a proper investment; if the business picks up, they'll get a share of the profits.'

'Not if, *when*,' said Lucy firmly.

'That's my girl. I love you, you know.'

'Love you too.'

And the little family snuggled contentedly together and reflected on how good life was.

Never in her entire life had Emma felt this much stress. As if it wasn't bad enough being pursued by a man who couldn't take no for an answer, Lawrence had gone and submitted her job application just when she was on the point of persuading herself that the whole thing was a thoroughly bad idea.

Whatever Joe might have said to the contrary, she knew he

didn't really want her to take the job; and besides, at the moment you couldn't take anything he said at face value because Joe definitely wasn't himself. And that was something she was determined to get to the bottom of.

It took some persuading to get Joe out of the house, but at last Emma managed it. 'It's Friday night and for once you're not working late,' she pointed out. 'Let's do something nice.'

'Do we have to?'

'You used to love Friday nights with the lads,' she reminded him. The way things were, she'd have been almost glad to hear that Gary, Toby and Rozzer were coming round to spill beer everywhere and fart into the white leather settee. But – apart from that brief glimpse of Rozzer and Linda in the park – she hadn't seen anything of them in weeks.

'I'm not in the mood,' complained Joe. 'Why don't you phone up one of your mates from the photography class, or something?'

Anything but that, thought Emma with a shudder. Why the hell did I ever sign up for that bloody course? 'I told you, I'm not in touch with them any more,' she replied briskly. 'Besides, I'd much rather be with you. Come on, get your coat on, we're going out for a meal.'

They didn't have far to go. The Queen's Gambit was only two streets away; its cool, blue and white chessboard interior secreted away behind a narrow Georgian facade and a tiny painted sign. They didn't bother much with advertising. Frankly, with truffles flown in from Tuscany and a Michelin star in the offing, they didn't need to.

'This is on me,' Emma whispered to Joe as they scanned the menu.

He raised an eyebrow. 'Go on, tell me; it's a special occasion and I've forgotten all about it.'

'It's special to me,' she replied, and she meant it. 'We're spending time together and we haven't done an awful lot of that lately. Have we?'

He sighed. 'True.' He looked around him. 'Are you sure you want to eat here? It's incredibly expensive.'

'You're worth it.'

'Yeah, right.' He sounded so dejected that Emma could hardly believe this was the same young man who was going to change the face of supermarket retailing, single-handed.

'Hey, c'mon, this isn't you. Where's the wonder-boy who can do anything with one hand tied behind his back?' She stroked his cheek. He caught her hand and held it fast, then let it go and pulled away.

'I don't know. Maybe somebody tied both his hands and he realised he wasn't so wonderful after all.'

'Ready to order sir, madam?' enquired the waiter, pencil poised above his pad.

'Actually, I'm not very hungry,' said Joe, pushing back his chair and tossing his napkin on the table. 'I'm sorry Em, I'm just really tired. Come on, let's go home and microwave a pizza or something.'

Open-mouthed, Emma and the waiter stared at him crossing the restaurant; then Emma mumbled an apology, dropped a five-pound note on the table and ran after him.

If she'd thought the evening had got as bad as it could get, she was in for a nasty surprise. Because, as she grabbed her coat from the row of hooks by the front desk, she half turned and saw a face reflected in the mirror tiles. Heart in mouth, she swung round and saw him sitting there at a corner table, drinking red wine.

She turned away instantly, hoping he hadn't noticed her. But as she fled, she saw Richard out of the corner of her eye, blowing her a kiss.

Little by little, she was beginning to understand the lesson he was trying to teach her: there was simply no escape.

How it had happened, Rozzer couldn't begin to imagine; but somehow, his flat had shrunk to about half its normal size. It didn't help, of course, that three people's stuff was now taking up the space previously occupied by one. But even so, the flat had seemed to have perfectly normal dimensions until last week's incident in the park. Suddenly Linda was wherever he turned; and wherever she went, Rozzer was. All they seemed to do was get in each other's way, while desperately trying not to; flattening themselves against the wallpaper whenever they passed each other in the hall or both went to get something out of the fridge at the same time. It was like two landmines trying not to step on each other.

Neither of them had mentioned that one, astonishing kiss in the park. A hundred times Rozzer had tried to broach the subject, but chickened out every time. Occasionally he'd had the feeling that she wanted to say something too, but whatever it was had petered out in some excuse about Sara-Jane's unfinished schoolwork, or having to get ready for work at the pie factory.

On the face of it, things had not been going too well. And yet, there was a new energy in Rozzer's life that he'd never experienced before, not even back in the days when he was sixteen and thought he was invincible. He found himself whistling for no apparent reason; more than once he caught himself scanning the Situations Vacant column in the evening paper; and at work his boss had asked him to stop smiling because it was scaring the punters away.

He took off his horrible uniform and changed into his comfy old jeans. It was Friday night; he had an open invitation to go out on the piss with Toby and Gary, but that prospect had long since lost its appeal. There was something that smelt suspiciously like a lavender sachet in his sock drawer, a home-made pie was baking in the oven, and a certain little girl had challenged him to a return match of Pass the Pigs.

Tonight, he told himself, I'm going to have that talk with you, Linda Jones. And this time neither of us is chickening out.

Ever since the incident at the Queen's Gambit, two nights ago, Emma had felt as though she were holding her breath, waiting with a kind of ghastly calm for the inevitable confrontation.

But it didn't come. Everything pottered on normally, or as normally as it could when your husband would hardly say two words to you and your ex-almost-lover kept turning up like Banquo's ghost, constantly reminding you of your horrible guilty secret.

It was probably guilt-fuelled paranoia that was making her feel that way, but she had the distinct impression that her life had been reduced to a tiny little box; and that the six walls of that box were continually pressing in until, eventually, they would all meet in the middle and squash her to nothing. Which, in the circumstances, might actually come as a relief.

She took refuge in work, because that was the one thing she excelled in even when everything else turned to crap. The busier it was in the department, the less stressed out she felt. Consequently she was already feeling edgy by break-time on Monday afternoon, when absolutely nobody in the whole of Gloucestershire seemed to have anything wrong with them.

'Emma!' called Lawrence.

'Yes?'

'Got something for you. Knife wound in seven, no nerve damage. Just needs cleaning up and suturing. Now, Kevin ...'

Grateful for this distraction from her own thoughts, Emma got together a trolley and treatment packs, trundled into the cubicle area and pushed aside the curtain of number seven.

'Oh my ... God.'

Richard was sitting up on the examination couch, his left hand loosely wrapped with a gauze pad and a bandage. 'Hello, Emma.'

'What are you doing here?'

He raised his hand and gave a wry smile. 'I was trimming prints. My hand slipped and the knife went right through. Clumsy me.'

Reluctantly she peeled off the bandage. There was a small, clean-edged wound in the middle of the palm, running right through the thickness of the hand from one side to the other. Whatever else it might be, it didn't look like the sort of cut you'd get if your hand slipped with a trimming knife.

Light dawned. 'Did you do this deliberately? You did, didn't you?' Richard shrugged. 'You're crazy.'

'I'd do worse to myself if it was the only way I could get to see you.'

'Keep your voice down!' hissed Emma. Thank goodness there was nobody else in the cubicles, no other nurse hanging around to hear Richard proclaiming her shame all over the hospital.

'But Emma, I love you. You know I do. Just listen to me, please—'

'No, Richard. I said no, and I meant no.' She could bear no more. Tears sprang to her eyes; tears not just of anger and frustration, but of fear too. 'You're destroying me, Richard. Is that what you want – revenge?'

He followed her as she stepped out into the aisle that ran between the treatment cubicles. '*Destroying* you?' He stared at her in incomprehension. 'It's not me that wants to destroy you, Emma, it's *him*. Don't you see?'

Richard reached out his arms to hold her, and the bloody palm of his left hand brushed her shoulder, leaving a dark red stain. The contact was brief, for she stepped away, but it felt like five thousand volts, jolting murderously through every artery and nerve.

'For the last time, leave me alone,' she said, struggling not to hyperventilate, gathering up all her strength and all her failing courage to defy him. 'Stop following me around, stop sending me things, just leave. Me. Alone.'

'But Emma, I told you, I love—'

'No buts. Now stay here, I'm going to get another nurse to treat you.'

That might have been the end of it, had she not turned round to discover that they were not entirely alone in the treatment area. At the far end of the aisle, by the door to the Resuscitation Room, stood Zara.

Well that's it, thought Emma: the end. She'll run off and tell Joe what she's seen, and he'll put two and two together and it'll serve me damn well right.

What the hell am I going to do now?

32

The following morning, Emma could hardly wait for Joe to get out of the flat. It seemed like an eternity before she was able to lean over the balcony and force a cheery smile as she waved him off to work.

Two seconds later, she was on the phone to Mickey, spilling her heart out.

Mickey was horrified. 'What, right there – in the middle of the department?'

'Right in the middle, bold as brass, declaring undying love. And that's not all. He broke into my locker last week and left a present for me.'

'My God, that's scary. Did you tell anybody?'

'How could I?' pointed out Emma. 'The last thing I want is people asking awkward questions. Oh, Mickey,' she agonised, 'what have I done? What am I going to do?'

'Well, I suppose you could always tell Joe there's this loopy ex-patient who's developed a fixation on you.'

'Yeah, right ! And then he'll tell his mum and she'll insist on bringing the police into it, and the next thing you know, Richard'll be telling his story on page three of the *Courant*! No thanks, I think I'd rather take my chances with Zara.' She swallowed down a tear. 'I just know she's going to tell Joe, and then that'll be the end of everything, and it's all my fault.'

'Whoa, steady on,' urged Mickey. 'Let's not jump to conclusions. You don't *know* she's going to tell him.'

'Mickey, she's never got over Joe dumping her for me. From what I've heard she's barely looked at a man since. I bet she can't wait to tell him what a terrible mistake he made marrying me, and then offer to help him get over it.'

'Hmm,' said Mickey, 'if she's really as bitter and twisted as you say she is...'

'Oh, she is.'

'Then you're stuffed. On the other hand, you might just be wrong ... and there'd be nothing to lose by it, would there?'

Emma frowned. 'Mickey, what on earth are you on about?'

'Going to see her,' replied Mickey.

'What!'

'Sorry, Em, but what else can you do? You're just going to have to go round to see Zara, get down on your knees, and beg.'

It was a beautiful morning, hot and sunny, and a gentle breeze was playing in the treetops, making a sound like waves on a beach.

Not that Joe could hear them. He was stuck in a hot car on a hot A-road, with the tarmac already melting beneath his tyres and a whole day of bad-tempered meetings to look forward to.

He tapped his fingers impatiently on the steering wheel as he sat in traffic, engine idling and brain-numbing mush playing on the radio. He was going to be late, there would be a stack of phone messages on his desk, and his inbox would be stuffed with e-mails about Jerusalem artichokes. And when he finally got into the first meeting, all his ideas would be shot down in flames. Yes, he ought to be getting steamed up about the horrible day to come, but the only thing that was really rattling his cage right now was the sheer pointlessness of sitting in a fug of exhaust fumes. On a day like this, anyone with even half a brain ought to be stretched out on a beach with a bottle of wine and someone he loved more than anything else in the world ...

Maybe it was the BMW cutting him up at the roundabout that was the final straw, or maybe he just ran out of patience. But suddenly Joe reached out for his mobile, switched it off, and tossed it onto the back seat.

The next turning he came to, he took. He had no idea where it led, but frankly he didn't much care.

There really was no good reason to put it off any longer. Emma kept trying to come up with excuses, but there just weren't any. She wasn't on duty until lunchtime, and she knew it was Zara's day off; what better time to catch her at home? True, Mickey's plan didn't offer much hope of success, but what was the alternative – sit around in agony until Zara chose the right moment to pull the plug on her?

The staff residences were situated in a new accommodation block, overlooking school playing fields. The view was nice enough, thought Emma, but she'd seen inside before, and the flats weren't much bigger than the study bedroom she'd had at college. Typical of Zara to want to live in a rabbit-hutch, two minutes from work. What was the point of having a nice home to invite your friends to, if nobody actually liked you?

Meow.

She showed her staff ID to the porter, and took the lift to the fourth floor. A dead-straight corridor of identical blue doors stretched away into seeming infinity, everything else was painted porridge-grey, and a flickering fluorescent light made the whole thing reminiscent of a scene from a low-budget horror flick.

This was it: Flat 64. The butterflies in Emma's stomach took flight. Her raised hand hesitated for a moment, and then knocked.

The door swung open of its own accord.

'Zara?' She stuck her head round the door. 'Hello?'

Nobody answered. Her instinct was to turn tail and run away, but that wasn't an option so she stepped into the flat and pushed the door shut behind her. She was standing in a tiny living room with a television, a few bits of modern furniture, a couple of goldfish in a tank and a shelf full of medical books. So this was it: the sum total of Zara Jeffries' existence.

'Zara, are you there?' she called. 'It's Emma Sheridan.' This time, there was an answer; not words, but the barely audible sounds of sobbing, filtering through the wall from the bedroom. She took a couple of steps towards the bedroom door. 'Are you OK?'

If Zara had called out, 'I'm fine, go away,' then Emma would probably have done precisely that. But she didn't. And something – whether curiosity or genuine concern she wasn't sure – made her walk right in.

Dr Zara Jeffries was flat on her belly on the bed, sobbing her heart out. She didn't even look up as Emma sat down on the edge and laid a hand on her shoulder. 'What's wrong? Has something happened to you?'

The answer, when it came, was muffled by the duvet. 'It doesn't matter, none of it does any more.'

'What doesn't? Do you want to tell me about it? Hey, surely it can't be that bad.'

'Want to bet?' Zara rolled over onto her back. She looked a complete mess – eyes swollen and bloodshot, nose like a cherry tomato – not like Little Miss Perfect at all. Emma was vaguely aware that a nice dose of *schadenfreude* ought to be kicking in right now, but you couldn't look at distress like that and not feel concern.

Zara's fingers uncurled. She was holding a screwed-up piece of paper. 'Here, read it – you might as well know I'm a failure, everybody will soon enough.'

It was a letter, from the Royal College of Surgeons. 'Oh Zara, I'm sorry,' said Emma. 'But hey, lots of people fail their registrar's exams.'

'Twice?'

'Yes. Yes, I'm sure they do. You can take them again.'

Zara wiped the back of her hand across her eyes. 'You don't understand, do you? I've spent all these years training for my job, and I'm useless at it. Do you know what happened last night?'

'Tell me.'

'It was nothing special. Just another RTA, I can't even remember her name. But I couldn't ease her pain, and when she died in my arms, I went to pieces. Cried my heart out.'

'It happens to everyone sometimes,' said Emma.

'I bet it never happens to you.'

'Then you bet wrong. I can't tell you how many times I've run off to the loo and flushed the chain so nobody could hear me crying.'

'But you don't make mistakes like I do. Everybody talks about you like you're some kind of saint. Have you any idea how it makes me feel, having you looking over my shoulder all the time, waiting for me to balls something up?'

'I've never done that deliberately,' said Emma. 'OK, maybe just once or twice. And I'm always getting far too involved with the patients. Caring doesn't make you bad at your job,' she added. 'It just means you're human.'

Zara threw her a sideways look. 'Hey, me? Human? Are you sure you meant to say that?'

Good God, Emma thought, bringing herself up with a start.

She's right, I did say that. Maybe I don't know everything about her after all.

Rozzer was taking a bet on the two twenty at Lampeter when Sharron called him from the back office. 'Phone call.'

'OK, I'll be right there.'

Pushing across the betting slip, he put the cash in the till and went to answer the phone. A minute later, he was tapping the manager on the shoulder.

'Ken.'

'What?'

'Got a bit of a crisis to sort out. I'm taking half a day's leave, OK?'

Ken's moustache bristled. 'Oh no you're not. There's punters out there want serving.'

'Well you serve them, then.' Ordinarily, Rozzer would have muttered something about slave-drivers and slunk back to work, but this time the worm turned. 'I haven't had a day off in six months, Ken. And who was it covered for you when the area manager got wind of you and Sharron?'

Ken's florid complexion deepened to a nasty shade of aubergine. 'If you're not back by—'

But the door was already jangling shut, and Rozzer had gone.

Emma handed Zara the cup of tea. 'Go on, have some; it'll make you feel better.'

Zara's hands were shaking as she raised the cup to her lips. 'This is good of you.'

I know it is, thought Emma; I must be soft in the head. But try as she might, she couldn't feel any hostility towards someone so abjectly unhappy. 'That's OK,' she said. 'It's crap being miserable on your own.'

A tear dripped down Zara's nose and plopped into her tea. 'You're so lucky to have Joe,' she said softly.

That felt too deliberate; too personal. Emma's hackles rose instinctively. 'Yes,' she said. 'I know I am.'

Go on, say it, urged a little voice inside her head. She had completely forgotten why she had come here, but that didn't seem to matter. Come on, Emma, you have to say it now, or you never will. Tell her you've got her number.

'You're still in love with him, aren't you?' she challenged. 'You'd try and take him off me if you could.'

The question hung in the air between them for several immense seconds; big and threatening and grey. Why did I say that? thought Emma. If I hadn't put it into words, it might not be true. The question might have gone on hanging there indefinitely, if Zara's lip hadn't started to tremble.

First her lip, and then the rest of her face, and then her entire body began to shake. With a shock, Emma realised: Zara was *laughing*. And that hurt.

'I get it, you think I'm pathetic. All this time you've been laughing at me behind my back.'

'No!' Zara grabbed her by the shoulder. 'I'm not laughing at you, I'm laughing because ... because I thought you knew and you obviously don't.'

'Knew what?'

'Lawrence knows – he saw me down at the club one night. I thought he must have told you, seeing as you're thick as thieves.'

'Lawrence hasn't said a word about anything; what's this all about?'

'I couldn't bear the two of you watching, wondering what you were saying about me and who you were going to tell ...'

'Tell *what*?'

Zara closed her eyes and tilted her head back. She took a deep breath. 'Joe's a great guy, Emma. But he's really not my type.'

Emma ran a hand through her hair, raking it off her forehead. 'I don't get it. I mean he must be, you went out with him for nearly four years until he ditched you.'

'Is that what he told you?' Zara smiled ruefully. 'Please listen, Emma, this is really difficult for me. Joe's not my type; *men* aren't my type. Now, do you get what I'm saying?'

The penny dropped with an almighty clang. Suddenly an awful lot of things started to make better sense. The apparent lack of a social life; the secrecy; the total lack of boyfriends ... 'Oh! You don't mean you're a—'

'Yes. Exactly.'

'How long have you known?'

'Always. Only when I was younger I didn't want to admit it to myself. Nowadays I've just about managed to accept what I am but telling anybody else, well ... that's a different kettle of fish.

Especially the one person I really want to tell.' She hung her head. 'The one I'm in love with.'

'And ... that's not Joe, then?'

Zara half laughed. 'No, Emma, it's not Joe. Besides, how could I tell Joe what I really am? Despite everything we had some happy times, and it'd really hurt him, I know it would. I was terrified you and Lawrence would spill the beans.'

'Maybe it would be better if everybody knew?' hazarded Emma.

'I wish.' Zara wound a strand of hair around her index finger. 'But if your mum and dad were elders at the local Pentecostal Chapel, preaching everlasting damnation, would you tell them you were gay?'

'Well ...'

'And if the woman you were in love with was happily married with two kids, and was someone you had to work with every day, would you tell her?'

It wasn't hard to guess. 'It's Dr Gundersson, isn't it?' said Emma.

'Does that matter?'

'It does if you love her ... and if there's a chance that she loves you. If she knew—'

'No, Emma, she's never going to know. She *mustn't* ever know. Oh God.' she drew up her knees and laid her aching head upon them. 'I shouldn't have told you, I should have kept my big mouth shut.'

Emma thought of all the times they'd fought, all the times Zara had put her down, all the times she'd yearned to get her own back. Funny; all she felt now was compassion.

'Look, I won't say anything if you don't,' she promised. 'Lawrence isn't the only one who knows how to keep a secret.'

'Th-thanks.' Zara wiped a hand across her eyes and looked up wonderingly. 'Why did you come here now? How did you know I was feeling like this?'

It hardly seemed the moment to admit that she hadn't come here for Zara's benefit at all. Or to ask her to keep schtum about her and Richard. Emma just gave her arm a friendly squeeze. 'Oh, I don't know,' she said. 'Call it woman's intuition.'

Rozzer slammed the car door, producing a small shower of rust flakes. 'You're going to be in one big load of trouble, Joe my man,' he commented as he picked his way across the scrubby grass, avoiding the broken glass and dog turds. 'Come to that, so am I; but I don't care.'

Joe looked up from his seat: an upturned plastic milk crate on the riverbank. 'Neither do I,' he replied. 'Unico can manage without me for one day.'

'What's all this about?' asked Rozzer, commandeering the only other thing he could find to sit on – the remains of a pile of soggy old mattresses. 'And why here of all places?'

A fly-tipping site by the side of the bore-inspiring River Chelt was scarcely the ultimate in scenic rendezvous, but Joe had his reasons. 'Don't you remember, when we were kids? We used to skive off double French on a Friday afternoon and come down here and catch sticklebacks.'

Rozzer peered over the edge into the majestic waters, fully six inches deep and clogged with old tin cans. 'More likely to catch tetanus these days,' he remarked.

'Things change,' Joe nodded sadly. 'Don't you ever wish they didn't?'

Rozzer scratched his head. 'No,' he said after a few moments' thought; 'actually I don't. It's crap being a kid; people are always kicking your head in or making you wash behind your ears.'

'But we had some good times, didn't we?'

'Some,' conceded Rozzer.

'Like the time Gary tried to make fireworks and blew the side off the sixth-form common room.'

'Yeah', murmured Rozzer darkly. 'He was into chemistry even back then.'

'And the school plays. *West Side Story, Grease, Oliver* ...'

'Yes, they were great if you were playing the lead,' agreed Rozzer, 'but playing Second Oyster in *Alice in Wonderland* isn't all it's cracked up to be.' He looked at his friend sharply. 'What's with all this sudden nostalgia anyway? Why this sudden urge to bunk off work and go native?'

Joe picked up a stick and threw it into the water. It disappeared with a muddy plop.

'Things aren't going so great, Rozzer,' sighed Joe. 'Sometimes I wonder what's the point of trying any more.'

'I used to think like that,' replied Rozzer.

'What did you do?'

'I stopped trying. And things got even worse. You don't want to go down that road, man, it's crap.'

'So what do I do?'

'I dunno. Decide what you want out of life, I guess. Think about all the other people who depend on you.'

'OK then,' announced Joe, standing up, 'what I really want out of life right now is a game of one-a-side football with this empty Coke can. You can be Arsenal,' he added by way of incentive.

'OK, but give me your mobile first.'

'Why?'

'I'm going to phone work for you, explain why you're not coming in.'

Joe waved the offer aside. 'That's pointless.'

'No it's not. Keep your options open, make sure you've got a job to go back to.' Joe threw him the mobile and he caught it and dialled. 'Right, Mr Sheridan, what's it to be: domestic crisis, dead granny or mystery stomach bug?'

'They're not that bad, are they?' asked Emma. 'Your mum and dad. They seemed really nice at the party.'

'They *are* nice, that's half the trouble,' replied Zara.

'And they're really proud of you.'

'That's the other half.'

'How do you mean?'

Zara picked up her comb and started easing some of the tangles out of her hair. 'It feels like … they're only proud of me when I'm doing something they can boast about, like coming top in my exams, or getting some really great job. And those things … well, it took me a long, long time to realise just how much I'd been doing to please Mum and Dad, and how little to please myself.'

'We all do stuff to please other people,' pointed out Emma. 'I took a part in the school play just to try and make Joe notice me.'

Zara smiled. 'And did it work?'

'Like hell it did. I was sick every night with stage fright, and the make-up brought me out in acne.'

'There you go then. See what happens when you try to be some-body you're not.'

'But it's not as if you—'

'Isn't it?' Zara drew the comb right through the length of her hair. 'Do you want to know the truth? I'm only training to be a surgeon because that's what Dad always wanted me to do – the job he wanted and never quite got. It'd have broken his heart if I'd told him I wasn't interested.'

Emma was appalled. 'That's terrible. You can't do a job like that for somebody's sake; you have to want to do it for yourself.'

Zara stopped combing. 'I know. That's what I've come to realise.'

Their eyes met in the dressing-table mirror. 'Then maybe it's time you started thinking about what you want to do, instead of what everybody else wants.'

'It's been so long, I'm not sure I even know any more.' Zara's gaze held Emma's fast. 'What about you? Are you doing what you want? Is married life the way you thought it would be?'

Fleetingly, Emma thought Zara was going to say something about what she'd seen the day before; then the moment was gone.

'No,' admitted Emma; 'it's not what I thought it would be; but I'm going to try hard to make it something better than that.'

'Hi, Em.' That evening, Joe came in through the door just after nine, a little earlier than Emma had expected. 'Good day?' he enquired, peeling off his suit jacket.

'Oh, you know . . .' She banished her conversation with Zara to the back of her mind. 'Cuts, bruises, little boys with saucepans stuck on their heads. How was yours?'

'Oh, nothing special. Stuck indoors, usual boring meetings. Supper ready yet?'

She popped her head out of the kitchen. ''Bout half an hour or so.'

'Right-ho, I'll go and get changed then.'

And off he went into the bedroom, jacket slung over one shoulder. It was only then that Emma noticed he had grass stains all down the back of his shirt.

33

The next few days felt weird. It was as if Emma and Joe were tiptoeing around, each making such a conscious effort not to annoy the other that they hardly managed to say anything at all. Joe's story about slipping on wet grass at the Leamington store didn't really ring true, but Emma couldn't bring herself to say so. If there was something else he wasn't telling her, something terrible – well, frankly, she didn't want to know. She had enough to worry about already.

Emma awoke on Sunday morning with a massive tension headache. The whole room seemed to lurch with pain as she levered herself gingerly out of bed and eased her body upright.

Still half-asleep, Joe rolled over and found empty space. 'Where you going?' he slurred.

'Nowhere. I just need some paracetamol for my head. Some in the kitchen cupboard, isn't there?'

'Think so,' he yawned. 'Put the kettle on?' he added hopefully.

'Yeah, all right. In a minute.'

Emma shuffled her feet into her slippers and headed for the kitchen. She so rarely ever had a headache that she wasn't even quite sure where she'd put the painkillers. But she had a hunch they were somewhere in the wall cupboard above the dishwasher.

Stifling a yawn, she dragged over the step-stool and opened the cupboard door. Instant coffee, expired oregano, four packets of Angel Delight ... good grief, how long was it since this cupboard had been emptied? Two half-empty tubes of indigestion pills, a rusty bottle-opener ... aha, was that a packet of headache pills right at the back, behind the tin of own-brand butter beans?

'Hang on,' called Joe, leaping out of bed with a sudden thought.

'I wouldn't bother looking in there,' he said, appearing like a genie in the kitchen doorway. 'I think I moved them to the ... oh.'

Too late. Emma was standing there with his guilty secret in her hand, mouth open, looking like she'd seen a ghost. 'What the hell ...?' she murmured.

Joe's overwhelming feeling was relief. Relief that he'd finally had the good sense to chuck Gary's remaining little 'present' down the loo a week ago, and that all Emma had found behind the butter beans was a sheaf of job ads, clipped from the trade press. 'Just a few job vacancies,' he said with a shrug, trying to look as if everybody had a kitchen cupboard full of them. 'No harm in looking, is there?'

Karen got on the phone to Minette straight after breakfast. 'Do you still want me to come in and do those invoices today?'

'Of course!' Minette scrutinised the alarming symmetry of her coiffure in the living-room mirror, on the alert for any rebellious hairs. 'There isn't a problem, is there?'

'No, no, Sundays are just like any other day for me. It's just that I thought I'd pop over to Emma and Joe's first and pick up a few things I left behind. I shouldn't be long.'

Minette's brow furrowed. Covering the receiver with her hand, she informed Alan in a stage whisper: 'She says she's going to be late.' Alan shrugged. 'How long? Only I have to be there to open up for you, you know.'

'Yes, I do realise. Don't worry, it won't take me ten minutes to put the stuff in my car and drive round to you. See you by half past at the latest.'

'Yes dear, well, mind you do.' As Minette put the phone down and turned back to her husband, Pepe the apricot poodle let out a thunderous fart. 'Alan,' she said sternly, 'have you been feeding your Grape Nuts to the dog again?'

'Yes, but *why* are you looking?' repeated Emma, throwing the newspaper clippings on to the kitchen table. 'You're supposed to be blissfully happy with the job you've got, remember?'

Joe remembered. Remembered all the times he'd smiled and said everything was fine when all he'd really wanted to do was admit that it was anything but. 'Well all right, maybe I haven't been *entirely* straight with you.'

'You mean, you've been lying to me.'

'Not lying, as such,' he protested. 'It's not that there's anything really *wrong*, I'm just not enjoying the job as much as I thought I would. And I'm not exactly flavour of the month with Sir Stanley at the moment. I didn't want you to worry.'

Emma flopped onto a chair. 'For God's sake, Joe, I'm your wife, it's my job to worry!' It hurts to know he's deceived me, she thought; hurts more than you'd think it would. But how much more would he hurt if I told him all that I've been keeping from him? 'I suppose you told Zara all of this ages ago.'

The delay in his reply gave her her answer. 'I just wanted a bit of impartial advice. And like I said, I couldn't bear to worry you ...'

'Great. What else haven't you been telling me?' she asked dully.

'Nothing!'

She grunted.

Maybe it was something in the tone of Emma's voice, but a kind of angry desperation flared in Joe's eyes. 'OK, I should have told you, I admit it. But for pity's sake, Emma, I'm only me, I fuck things up. Big time. Not everybody's bloody perfect like you.'

She stared at him, stunned and all at once ridden with guilt. 'Oh Joe, I'm sorry. I didn't mean to go on like that, it's just that I felt hurt. I'm not even slightly perfect, I make mistakes all the time, if you only knew.'

Joe humphed, as if to say, 'Pull the other one'.

'I do.'

'Such as?'

'Such as ...' For a brief moment, she almost told him everything. It would have been such a release to empty her soul, unburden the load that had been building up inside her over Richard. But that would have been totally selfish, for her own benefit, not Joe's. And besides, at the last moment she bottled out. 'Such as, I ended up applying for that nurse coordinator job.'

Joe frowned. 'And that's supposed to be a mistake?'

'Oh yes. I was about to throw the form away, then Lawrence found it and handed it in to Personnel.'

'But you didn't throw it away, did you?'

'No,' she admitted.

'And you haven't phoned up Personnel and withdrawn your application?'

'Well ... not yet.'

'Doesn't sound like much of a mistake to me. Sounds like it's what you wanted to happen.'

His voice sounded toneless and flat. 'Joe, I don't know. I really don't know what I want. Except that I want to make you happy, and do what you want me to do, and right now I can't even begin to understand what that is. Why have you stopped talking to me, Joe? Why are you shutting me out?'

Joe flicked a crumb across the table top, his eyes firmly fixed on some invisible point in the distance. 'I just thought it would be better that way,' he said finally. 'Better if you didn't know, better if I shielded you from it all.'

He took her hand. 'If I'm honest, Em, things are going really badly at work. Sir Stanley's stopped listening to my ideas, and most of the rest of them don't give a shit anyway because they know there's a hefty takeover bid on the table.'

'Somebody wants to take over Unico?'

'Oh yes. Somebody big. And if it happens, an awful lot of people are set to lose their jobs. Me included.' He swallowed. 'I couldn't see the point – still can't – of dumping all that stress on you before it's even happened. I wanted to protect you, isn't that what husbands are supposed to do?'

'Joe? Joe, you *idiot.* I don't need protecting from anything!'

'But if I lose this job, I won't be able to provide for you. I'll just be another faceless failure on the dole ...'

Emma snorted, relieved beyond belief that this was all it amounted to. 'This is the twenty-first century! Don't be such a bloody caveman! Have you never heard of share and share alike? Right,' she announced, 'I'm going to have a shower. When I come back I want you dressed, got that?'

'I'm taking you out for the biggest brunch in Cheltenham.'

Karen hummed to herself as she slowly climbed the stairs to Emma and Joe's flat. If she took her time it wasn't too hard, and it was much better for her than taking the lift. People had to realise that she fit and capable, and not yet ready to be a burden on anyone, thank you very much.

When nobody answered her knock, she realised she ought to have phoned up first. But Emma and Joe were always in on a Sunday morning, it was the one time you could guarantee finding them together. Ah well, never mind; she had a key. And she could quite easily collect her few bits and pieces without having to bother them about it.

The cardboard box with her knick-knacks in was still there, on top of the wardrobe in the spare bedroom. If Joe had been there he could probably have fetched it down just by standing on tiptoe, but Karen was going to have to be a bit more creative. A step-stool would have been useful, but still, no problem. That folding chair in the corner would do just fine.

It did, until the moment when, standing on one leg to get a firm grip on the box, she stumbled; and the lightweight chair fell sideways, snapping shut beneath her. It wasn't that far to fall, but as Karen hit the floor she twisted, and there was a sharp cracking sound that wasn't cheap plywood.

It hurt so much that she screamed. But nobody heard her cries.

34

'Well, honestly,' sniffed Minette. 'You give some people an inch and they take a mile.'

Alan lowered his Sunday paper a few inches. 'She's not *that* late. And she did tell you she was calling in at Joe and Emma's on the way.'

'Yes, briefly!' Minette brandished her watch under her husband's nose. 'Fifty-seven minutes, I don't call that "a little bit late", do you?'

Alan and the dog exchanged looks. Maybe this was a good time to go out for a walk, which might coincidentally take them past the pub and keep them out of the way for an hour or two.

Alan levered himself halfway out of his armchair. 'It's a nice day out there, I think I might just go and—'

'Oh no you don't, you're not going anywhere.' Minette pushed him firmly back into his seat. 'You're going to stay right here while I go out and find Karen.' She slipped on her jacket and grabbed the keys to her Micra. 'If she turns up here while I'm over at Joe's, don't you dare let her get away, got that?' She lowered her glasses and peered at her husband's neck. 'Is that a flea-bite? Perhaps I'd better get the spray.'

At the words 'flea' and 'spray', the poodle vanished underneath the sideboard.

'Don't worry, love, I'll spray him while you're out,' promised Alan.

The minute Minette was out of the house, Pepe's head reappeared.

'OK, dog, it's safe to come out now,' Alan promised him. 'I had my fingers crossed behind my back. Now, who's for a nice greasy fry-up?'

*

Minette had long since accepted that if she wanted something done properly, she had to do it herself. All the same, it was disappointing to have helped Emma's mother out, only to be let down. Harsh words were going to be said once she located Karen.

Not that there would be much locating to do. It was obvious that Karen had decided a cosy morning with her daughter and son-in-law was much more fun than a morning of invoice-checking in a converted garage. Some people simply had no concept of duty. They seemed to have the dangerous idea that life was about doing things you enjoyed. And if everybody went down that road, well, where would the world be?

Reaching the door of the apartment, she gave the bell her usual three sharp rings – the second one in case they hadn't heard the first, and the third so that they would know it was her. She waited. And then she waited a bit longer. But half a minute's ringing and hammering produced no response.

Puzzled that she could have been so mistaken, she was about to leave when she heard a faint sound. Not just a sound: a voice. Pressing her ear to the thick wooden door, she listened and it came again. This time, there was no mistaking what it was saying:

'Please ... help me.'

'You know, this is really nice,' remarked Emma as she and Joe lingered over lattes in Sleepers, the town's newest café-bar. 'I can't remember the last time we did this.'

The remnants of a humungous brunch lay strewn across the wooden refectory table, warm sunshine was pouring in through the open window, and Emma had had to undo the top button on her trousers. For a Sunday morning that had begun so disastrously, it really wasn't shaping up too badly at all.

'Great,' agreed Joe. 'But I should really be in Birmingham, I was planning to catch up on some paperwork.'

Emma looked at him sternly. 'What did you promise me?'

'Not to think about work, I know. But I did sort of say I'd be there ...'

'Look.' Emma put down her coffee cup. 'If you're going to be out of a job soon anyway, what's the point of knocking yourself out?'

'Whoa, don't jump the gun. This takeover thing's still only at

302

the discussion stage, you know. And Unico's Sir Stanley's baby. What's to say he won't refuse to sell on principle?'

'I guess. All the same, you're not happy there, are you?'

Joe fiddled with his spoon. 'It's just a difficult phase, things'll work out. Probably.'

He looked like a hapless fourteen-year-old, and Emma reached out and ruffled his hair. 'Not probably, definitely.'

'If you say so.'

'Which I do.'

He sighed. 'I'm really sorry about ... you know, keeping those job ads from you. I was hoping I could maybe find a new job before I had to tell you what was going on at Unico.'

'It doesn't matter, just promise me you won't do it again. And next time you're feeling low and I'm pissing you off, will you do something for me?'

'What?'

'Just talk to me.'

He opened his mouth, but at that moment his mobile rang. 'Oh fuck, that'll be work.'

Emma grabbed the phone. 'Don't answer it.'

'Emma ...'

'Please.'

'Sorry, Em, I've got to, it might be important.'

'More important than us talking like this?'

Joe didn't answer. He reached out and reluctantly she handed over the phone. 'Oh. It's not work, it's Mum on her mobile. I wonder what she wants.'

Emma pulled a face. 'Let me see ... to get you to divorce me and marry someone more suitable?'

'Shh, don't be silly. Mum? What's up?'

As he listened, his face fell.

'Is something wrong?' whispered Emma.

A few seconds later, Joe said, 'OK, we'll be there as fast as we can.' Then he turned to Emma. 'It's your mum, Em. She's in hospital.'

It was not a good day to injure yourself if you lived in Cheltenham. The waiting time in A&E was four hours, and the department was thronged with green-faced people looking for things to be sick in.

'How dreadful,' commented Minette. 'You'd think they could keep the food poisoning people away from the others. What if you catch something off them?'

'I'll be fine. But I'm sure they could let me go home,' said Karen hopefully, as she lay on a trolley in the corridor. 'It's only a broken ankle.'

'Excuse me, madam,' Minette corrected her, 'it's a triple spiral fracture of the ankle and the doctor said you're not going anywhere. So you'd better lie still and get used to it.'

'Yes, Matron.' Karen shifted uncomfortably.

'Are you in pain? Do you want the nurse?'

'No, I'm fine.' Karen lowered her voice to a whisper. 'I just need a wee, only I don't like to bother them when they're so busy.'

Minette rolled her eyes. 'So you'd rather lie there until you wet the bed? Right, I'll fetch a wheelchair and take you myself.'

'Is that OK? Won't they mind?'

'How else are you going to get there, Karen? Hop?' Heedless of Karen's protestations, Minette launched herself in the direction of the most helpless-looking person ... who just happened to be Lawrence. 'Mrs Cox needs to go to the lavatory. If you let me have a wheelchair, I'll take her.'

Lawrence raised an eyebrow. 'And you'd be?'

'Mrs Sheridan, why?'

'Emma's mother-in-law?'

'While we're standing here making polite conversation, Emma's mother is in extreme discomfort,' Minette reminded him sternly. 'So just tell me where I can find a wheelchair.'

'Well, Mrs Sheridan, until she's plastered up I think it's probably best if she either has a bedpan, or someone qualified takes her to the toilet. We don't want any more accidents, do we?'

With Minette fulminating in his wake about her first-aid certificate, Lawrence grabbed a chair and trundled it towards Karen's trolley.

'Karen, this man wants to take you to the lavatory,' said Minette in grave tones. 'And I really don't think you should put up with it.'

Karen laughed. 'That's not a man, that's Lawrence.'

'Gee, thanks!' commented Lawrence.

'I'm sorry, I didn't mean it to come out like that. What I mean is, this is Emma's boss – you know, that nice charge nurse she's always talking about? Emma introduced me to him a while back.'

'Oh,' said Minette, her composure somewhat rattled. 'I didn't realise.'

'Let's get you into this chair, shall we?' Lawrence helped to ease Karen onto her one good leg, then skilfully swivelled her round until her bottom was over the seat of the chair. 'There we go. Lovely girl, your Emma,' he commented as he took the brake off. 'Pity we can't keep her here in the department, but it'd be a waste; that girl's got a real future ahead of her.'

'A future?' echoed Minette.

'Definitely. But I'm sure I don't need to tell you that – after all, she's your daughter-in-law.'

Emma was out of the car before Joe had even put the handbrake on; running full-pelt across the car park towards the double doors of the A&E department.

How many times had she passed through those doors in the last few months, on her way to and from work? How many injuries and illnesses had entered and left through them? Suddenly none of that mattered: it was as if this was the very first time Emma had ever really seen the doors. Certainly it was the first time she'd really understood what it meant to have a loved one on the other side of them. When her father had died, she'd been too young to comprehend how someone could be there one minute and gone forever the next.

She punched open the door and ran towards the desk, almost colliding with a girl in full bridal finery, retching into a waste-paper bin.

'Where's my mum?' gasped Emma.

'Your mum?' enquired Sunita.

'Mrs Cox,' cut in Joe, arriving on the scene. 'And what on earth's going on in here? It's chaos.'

'Bridal party – seems they all went out for a dodgy Chinese last night. Groom got as far as "with this ring", then passed out in a pool of sick.' Sunita pressed a button. 'Oh, there she is – Mrs Cox, cubicle five. I don't know, all you want is a lovely quiet Sunday wedding, and—'

Emma didn't wait to hear any more. She launched herself towards the cubicles, slaloming her way round chairs, trolleys and people's legs.

'Mum!' she exclaimed, wrenching open the curtain. On the

other side of it, Karen was lying propped up on pillows, talking to Minette. Her left ankle was so swollen that it looked as if she'd grown an extra head. 'Oh Mum, just look at you ...'

Karen looked up in delight. 'Emma, how lovely!'

'They're going to take your mother to theatre soon and pin the bones together,' said Minette.

'But ... what on earth did you do?' demanded Joe, drawing the curtain behind him. 'Why didn't you tell us you were coming round?'

'Oh, I didn't want to bother you, just for a few of my bits and bobs. All I had to do was get them off the top of the wardrobe.'

'Only you didn't, did you?' said Minette meaningfully. 'You just fell off the chair and crocked yourself. Lucky I came along when I did.'

Karen patted Minette's hand. 'Your mum's been wonderful, Joe, a real tower of strength.'

Minette looked pleased but embarrassed. 'Now, now, I wasn't fishing for compliments, Karen, I'm just annoyed about you not taking proper care of yourself.' She turned to Emma. 'You do realise her bones are thinning?'

'Mum?' demanded Emma.

Karen slid a couple of inches down the pillows. 'It's not that bad, they said it's probably just because of all the steroids I've had over the years. A bit more calcium and I'll be fine. No need to worry her, Minette, I'm right as rain.'

'If you're right as rain,' retorted Minette, 'get off that trolley and run round the hospital grounds.'

Everybody fell silent. 'If only we hadn't gone out,' lamented Emma.

'Don't be silly, you can't stay in twenty-four hours a day just in case I turn up,' her mother chided. 'And it's only a broken ankle.'

'Karen,' said Minette sternly.

'All right, a triple spiral fracture then. But it's still only a broken bone. Once I've got the plaster on and they send me home, I'll be able to manage just fine with crutches.'

The mere thought of her mother hobbling around her flat on crutches, utterly alone, chilled Emma to the core. What if her mother had fallen at a different angle, and broken her back, or her neck? 'You're not going home,' she declared. 'Either you move in with us again, or I move in with you until the plaster comes off.'

Joe's mouth dropped open.

She threw him a meaningful look. 'That's right, isn't it, Joe?'

'Er ... yes.'

'Hmm,' said Minette. 'Why don't we all talk about it later? Look, Karen, the porter's coming to fetch you.'

Suddenly feeling all adrift on an alien ocean, Emma sat forlornly on the nearest chair. 'I guess I'll ... wait here then.'

'Don't be silly, dear,' scoffed Minette. 'I'll stay around and see that your mother's all right.'

'What about Dad?' enquired Joe.

'Alan,' replied Minette with a casualness that made jaws drop, 'will just have to get his own tea for once. Anyway, Emma, you'll be no use to anyone, moping around and getting in everybody's way. Why don't you get your apron on and give that nice Mr Lawrence a hand?' She surveyed the evil-smelling mess that was the waiting room. 'It certainly looks as if he could do with one.'

'You've done enough,' said Lawrence as Emma returned from taking yet another sample. 'More than enough. It's supposed to be your day off!'

Emma shrugged. 'I can't go home, not with Mum, you know ...'

'Hmm.' Hands in the pockets of his uniform tunic, Lawrence gave her one of his hard stares. 'You mean, you're on a guilt trip because your mum fell over when you were out having a nice time.'

'That's a bit unfair—'

'And you think cleaning the bottoms of the mean and lowly might make you feel better.' He shook his head pityingly. 'Sad, I call it. Go on.' He jerked his thumb upwards.

'Go on where?'

'Fanthorpe Ward. They just rang down to say your mum's wide awake and demanding toast.'

Although she knew her mother was all right, Emma's heart was still in her mouth as she walked onto Fanthorpe Ward.

Karen was lying in bed in Bay C, a huge bed cradle over her plastered leg. To Emma's surprise, Minette was still by her side.

'Hello, sweetheart,' Karen smiled.

Emma kissed her on the forehead. 'How are you feeling, Mum?'

'Apparently I'm "comfortable",' she replied wryly, 'but that's not quite the word I'd use. Minette's been keeping me entertained though – it's amazing how many bad jokes she knows.'

'You tell *jokes*?' marvelled Emma. Never mind seeing an elephant fly, she mused, now I really have seen it all.

Minette turned slightly pink. 'Well, when you've got four young sons to keep busy on long car journeys, you get through a lot of joke books.'

'Thanks, Minette,' said Emma, sitting gingerly on the edge of the bed. 'I really appreciate what you've done for Mum today.' Minette waved away her thanks. 'But I'm back now, Mum, and Joe and I have had a chat, and we're not taking no for an answer. As soon as they discharge you, you're coming back to stay with us.'

Minette and Karen looked at each other. 'Actually,' said Karen, 'Minette and I have been having a little chat too.'

'And your mum's coming to stay with me and Alan.'

Emma could hardly believe her ears. Mum and Minette? Two women so different in outlook that they made chalk and cheese look like clones? Mum and Minette, under the same roof? 'Mum, you can't!'

'Yes, I can,' declared Karen, 'and I'm going to. The last thing you and Joe need is me hanging around, day in day out. You haven't the room, for one thing. And you've got your own lives to lead.'

'And Alan and I have the annexe where Joe's granny used to stay,' chimed in Minette. 'So that's settled. Actually,' she added, 'I'm quite looking forward to having another woman in the house. Alan's never quite understood the sexual chemistry of Alan Titchmarsh.'

35

On the way back down from Fanthorpe Ward, Emma was surprised to hear footsteps on the stairs behind her. Turning to look over her shoulder, she saw that it was Minette.

'I hope you won't mind, but I just feel I have to say something,' she began.

Oh no, thought Emma; not now, Minette, please. I've said my thank-yous to you for being so good and looking after Mum, and you've made me feel guilty for not being there when she needed me. Now is not a good time to tell me my eyebrows need tweezing, or that I'm not wearing the right colour mascara. 'It's been a long day,' she pleaded, 'can't it wait?'

'Not really,' replied Minette, slightly out of breath. She indicated a bench beside a picture window on the next landing down. 'Can we sit for a minute?'

Reluctantly, Emma followed her down the remaining stairs, cleared a space among the back issues of *Hello*! and sat down on the hard wooden bench. 'What's this all about?'

To her surprise, her mother-in-law didn't launch into her usual breezy explanation of the world according to Minette. In fact she looked down and started fiddling with the buttons on her Jaeger jacket. 'I . . . er . . . this is harder than I expected.' She looked up. 'I think I may have got a few things wrong about you, and I want to say I'm sorry.'

It was all Emma could do not to topple off the end of the bench. 'Sorry?'

'That nice man Lawrence thinks the world of you, you know. He tells me you're a wonderful nurse, and could really go far.'

Emma thought back to the last time Lawrence had carpeted her for mislaying a patient's false teeth. 'He does?'

'I think I always knew you were good at your job,' Minette went on, 'I just didn't quite want to admit it to myself. You see ... I was brought up to think that men have careers and women stay at home.'

'Times have changed,' Emma pointed out.

'I know. Did you ever wonder why Joe had no grandma on my side of the family?'

'I don't know. I suppose I've always assumed she died a long time ago.'

Minette shook her head. 'Mum left us when I was twelve; found another man and ran off. We never saw her again.'

'No!' exclaimed Emma. 'What happened?'

'There were five of us children, and I was the eldest, so either I became a substitute mother or the family was broken up, and I couldn't let that happen, could I?'

'But you were only a child! What about school?'

'I left at fifteen. It was a pity really, I was quite clever at maths; but you can't have everything, can you? Family comes first, that's what I've always believed.'

'That's so sad,' said Emma. 'What about your dad, why didn't he get a housekeeper or something?'

Minette sighed. 'Poor Dad. He meant well, but he was hopeless, especially with money; I expect that was why Mum left him. She must've got fed up of holding him together and getting none of the credit. Once Mum was gone, that became my job. That, and a couple of days a week in the local dry cleaner's. Then, when I was eighteen, I met Alan.'

'And you fell in love.'

That provoked a smile. 'I suppose I did. Nice handsome young soldier, paying me lots of compliments, how could I resist? Plus, he desperately needed somebody to organise him, you know, make something of him.'

'Well, you certainly succeeded there,' said Emma. 'Alan's business seems to be doing really well.'

'And I've brought up four decent sons, so I suppose you could say I've not been a complete failure. All the same, if things had been different ...'

'You'd have liked a career of your own?'

Minette's look of discomfort returned. 'I think maybe I would. And that's why I've not been fair to you. I know things have changed; I just didn't want to admit they could have been different for me, too.' She patted Emma's hand. 'You should take your chances while you still have them, dear.'

'I'm not sure I understand.'

'Yes, you do. I'm talking about this job you've applied for. If you really want it you should go for it; the babies can wait till later.'

'I ... can't quite believe you just said that,' admitted Emma.

'Even dragons don't breathe fire *all* the time. By the way, just one other thing.'

'Yes?'

'You must let me take you shopping again some time soon. That navy-blue mascara doesn't suit you at all.'

It was a time for revelations, upheavals, for having your world turned upside down and inside out. At least, that was how it seemed to Emma.

Mum and her illness; Joe and the threat to his job; Minette and her astonishing change of heart: these were big, disorienting things to get used to. And still in the background lurked the grim spectre of Richard Claybourne.

Not that that was the first thought on Emma's mind when Mickey phoned her on Monday night. 'You still got a day off on Wednesday?'

'Yes, why?'

''Cause I'm a-hittin' those mean streets of Cheltenham, that's why. Better raid your piggy bank, Em, we're going to do some serious lunch.'

Heads turned as they walked into the pizzeria.

They certainly made an interesting couple. She bought most of her clothes from Gap Kids, while he was so tall that Emma had to crane her neck back just to look him in the face. But there was no denying the fact that they looked happy. So uncomplicatedly happy that, despite the deep sense of friendship she felt towards Mickey, Emma experienced a twinge of jealousy. If only Joe and she could start again, she thought; go back to this lovey-dovey stage where faults just don't exist, and this time be sure not to make the same mistakes again.

'Hi,' beamed the curly-haired giant, 'you must be Emma. Mickey talks about you all the time.'

'That's nice,' said Emma. 'I think.'

'Don't worry,' Mickey told her with a wink as they ordered drinks and enough garlic bread to build a Coliseum, 'I haven't told him about the time you got your toe stuck in the plughole and you had to lie in the bath till the fire brigade turned up – oh damn, I just did!'

'Ha ha, just you wait till I tell him about when you and Feebs ate all that laxative chocolate.'

The giant coughed politely. 'Shall we start again?' He proffered a paw the size of a jumbo pizza. 'Hi, the name's Midget. Mental Midget. Though some people know me as Gavin.'

Mickey giggled in embarrassment and punched him on the arm. 'Gavin!'

'It's OK,' he assured her amiably, 'I quite like it. And nobody's ever accused me of being smart, have they?'

Emma saw the giant with new eyes. 'What – not *the* Mental Midget?'

Mickey's expression grew serious. 'The baby's father, yes,' she said quietly. She reached across the table, and Gavin took her hand with surprising gentleness. 'You know I said I wasn't going to tell him about the baby or anything?'

Emma nodded. 'I tried to persuade you, but you weren't having any of it.'

'You were right. I changed my mind and went round to see him, didn't I, Gavin?' He nodded. 'And after that, we started to talk – I mean properly – for the first time. The weird thing is, I realised I was actually getting lonely when he wasn't around. And you know what I'm like with men – five minutes and I'm on to the next one.'

Emma raised her glass in a toast. 'Congratulations – I think you're officially smitten.'

'I hope so,' remarked Gavin, 'otherwise I don't know what I'm going to do with myself for the next fifty-odd years.'

Several pizzas and a lot of red wine later, Gavin headed for the men's room.

'He seems really nice,' said Emma.

'He is. Nicest guy I ever met.'

'I'm really glad it's working out for you.'

Mickey heaved a sigh of relief. 'Thank God for that. I had this nightmare last night that you took one look at him and called the police. And when I turned round to ask why, he'd turned into a ten-foot gorilla.'

'Well, he's certainly big enough,' commented Emma.

'It helps when you play prop forward for London Welsh. And you should see how scary he looks when he takes his front teeth out.'

'Er ... I think I'll pass on that, thanks.'

Mickey drained the last of the wine into her and Emma's glasses. 'You still haven't told me how you and Joe are getting on,' she said pointedly, 'and that makes me worry.'

Emma wilted slightly. 'Better, I think,' she said. 'But not that great. Joe thinks he might get made redundant, and you remember a certain person I told you about, who wouldn't take no for an answer?'

'Don't tell me he's still hanging around? I thought you made it clear it was all over.'

'I did, believe me. But I'm starting to think the man's seriously sick in the head. Last week, he actually injured himself just to get into A and E.'

'You're having me on.'

'I wish I was. And then he came on to me, and Zara saw us. I don't think she'll say anything, but – oh hell, Mickey, what am I going to do if he does something *really* stupid? Should I tell Joe everything before Richard does it for me?'

'You haven't heard a word from him in ages,' pointed out Mickey. 'Perhaps he's got the message at last.'

'Perhaps.' Emma gazed dubiously into the bottom of her wine glass. 'But I still keep wondering if I ought to tell Joe everything.'

Mickey thought for a moment. 'Hang on,' she said, 'has Richard ever met Joe?'

Emma frowned. 'No, why?'

'I've just had an idea.' Gavin was striding back towards their table, juggling a handful of Mint Imperials. 'Hey, Gav – you're game for anything, aren't you?'

'As long as I don't have to put a dress on.'

'Excellent.' Mickey caught one of the mints and popped it into her mouth. 'Right, just you phone me if that guy gives you any more trouble, you hear?'

'But what can you—'

Mickey interrupted her firmly. 'I mean it. I've got a little contingency plan in mind, something to slap that bastard down if he tries to slime his way back into your life. One word from him and I want you to phone me, any time of the day or night. Nobody messes with my best mate and gets away with it. Now.' She drained her glass with a ferocious smile. 'Here's what I've got in mind ...'

By early evening Mickey and Gavin were on the road again, heading back to London, leaving Emma feeling as though a very localised whirlwind had just passed through her part of Cheltenham. It was a dizzy sensation, but for the first time in ages she felt as though the outside world had broken through the wall surrounding her new life, reminding her that not everything revolved around her or her own domestic dramas.

She might not be living in Hackney any more, but that didn't mean she felt any less connected to Mickey. Joe was wrong about that: real friendship couldn't be consigned to 'the past'; it was something that could weather any separation, something that could remake itself over and over again, fitting into whatever space you could spare it.

Joe had gone to a meeting in Nottingham, and wouldn't be back until late. Even after she'd paid her mum a visit in hospital, that left Emma with the best part of an evening to fill and nothing remotely decent on TV. She'd almost resigned herself to the horrors of the ironing basket when the doorbell rang.

Steeling herself to expect the man from the residents' association and his eternal petition, she was surprised to find Rozzer standing outside, wearing an embarrassed expression.

'Hello, Emma. Can I come in?'

'Of course you can ... but Joe's not here. He won't be back for hours.'

Rozzer sloughed off his jacket and followed her into the living room. 'That's OK, I came to see you. I ... er ... are you any good at application forms? It's not really my thing. Or Linda's for that matter.'

That was a turn-up for the books and no mistake. 'You're never applying for another job!'

Rozzer looked worried. 'Why, don't you think I'm up to it?'

'No, no, it's great. I'm just surprised, that's all. I mean, how long is it you've been with Parrott's now? Ten years?'

'Twelve and a half,' Rozzer replied soberly. 'And how far have I got? Assistant manager. Exactly one step higher up the chain than I was when I started. Not exactly spectacular, is it?'

'I never really saw you as being into spectacular,' admitted Emma. 'Not that you're not capable of it,' she added clumsily, 'if you wanted to be.'

'Hmm, nice of you to say so, but to be honest all I'm after is a bit of respect, and I can't see me getting that taking bets on who's going to win "Rear of the Year".'

'What's brought this on?' wondered Emma.

He coloured slightly. 'Something somebody said made me think, that's all. That's why I've decided to have a go for this.' He produced a crumpled copy of the previous Wednesday's *Courant*, folded open at the Situations Vacant. 'There you go, that one there.'

Emma followed his pointing finger. '"Wanted, busty barmaid for private club, must look good in red suspenders"?'

'Not that one! The one underneath. "Trainee Environmental Health Inspectors, uniform and full training provided. Excellent prospects for the right candidate".'

'Blimey,' said Emma. 'Well, it's certainly ... different.'

Rozzer shrugged. 'I know, I know, crawling around rat-infested drains isn't my idea of glamorous either, but it's good enough for me. Plus it's steady,' he added, 'and you've got to think about things like that when you've got ... responsibilities.'

'What responsibilities?' Emma was intrigued. 'The mortgage on your flat, you mean?'

'Among other things.'

She rather hoped he might expand on this, but Rozzer went on looking enigmatic and produced a ballpoint pen. 'Right then, Emma – are you going to help me with this application form, or what?'

36

The following afternoon after work, Emma was unlocking her car door when her mobile rang. She glanced at the screen but didn't recognise the number.

'Hello?'

'Is that you, Emma? It's Treena here.'

Good grief, Treena. That voice took Emma instantly back to a period of her life that she'd rather forget; but it wasn't Treena's fault that Emma had got herself embroiled with Richard, and, after all, it was nice of her to call.

'Treena! How are you? Have you sorted Gerald out yet?'

This produced an embarrassed laugh. 'Emma, you are a scream. Nobody can sort out Gerald, least of all me! I don't honestly know how he puts up with me half the time.'

Give me strength, thought Emma. 'He sounds like a bully to me,' she replied, 'and you shouldn't let him make you unhappy.'

'Oh, he doesn't! Not really. And when he's shouting at me,' she reasoned, 'at least I know he cares. Anyway, I didn't call to chat about me, I came to find out when you're coming back to Creative Camera.'

'Actually I'm not,' replied Emma. 'I withdrew, didn't anybody tell you?'

'But why?' Treena sounded utterly bewildered. 'You were so good at everything, and anybody could see you were Richard's star pupil.'

Don't remind me, thought Emma, cheeks burning with shame. 'I just wasn't enjoying it any more,' she said, 'and I wanted to spend more time with my husband.'

'Ah, well, I can see why you'd want to do that,' agreed Treena, 'but if I can find a couple of spare hours a week, I'm sure you can too. Besides, Richard was only saying the other day how much he missed having you in the class, and how much he wished you'd change your mind.'

A lead weight switched places with Emma's stomach. 'He did, did he? Well, I'm sure he was just being polite.'

'Oh no, I don't think so,' insisted Treena, 'I mean, politeness isn't really Mr Claybourne's thing, is it?'

A thought occurred to Emma. 'Hang on, did he put you up to this? To phoning me up?'

'Well ... he did sort of mention that I might have more luck in persuading you than he had, but we all thought it was a good idea. In fact it was Richard who gave me your mobile number.'

Now there's a surprise, thought Emma darkly. 'Treena, it's lovely to talk to you, but I really have to go now. And I'm afraid I'm much too busy to come back to camera class.'

'But Emma, won't you change your mind?' pleaded Treena.

'Sorry, no,' replied Emma. Not in a million years, she thought to herself, switching off her phone with a shaking hand.

'You know, I'd never have thought it,' declared Minette, 'but I actually think you may be right!'

Karen restrained herself from saying something sarcastic. If truth were told, she was actually quite enjoying herself, which was something she'd never expected to do in Minette's company.

They were sitting together in Minette's front room, watching a regional documentary about young fashion designers in the Midlands. Alan had escaped to his workshop, to tinker with microprocessors and listen to Shakin' Stevens on his knackered old Walkman.

'It's a really flattering style,' said Karen encouragingly, 'and you've definitely got the legs for a shorter skirt.'

Minette lifted up the hem of her crisp linen dress and contemplated her knees. 'You don't think they're rather ... bony?'

'Gosh no, you've got fabulous legs! I wish I had,' added Karen. 'Mind you, right now I'd settle for both of them working properly.' She shifted her bottom to get more comfortable, but it was no good; she felt all wriggly and full of surplus energy. 'Shall I make us a coffee or something?'

She grabbed her crutches but Minette was already on her feet.

'Stay where you are, Karen, I'm not having you overexerting yourself.'

'But I only—'

Minette shook her head. 'If you want a coffee I'll make one.'

'Actually,' admitted Karen, 'I don't really; I'm just looking for something to do. I'm not used to doing nothing.'

'You're not doing nothing, you're keeping me company,' pointed out Minette. They sat and watched catwalk models flouncing up and down a runway in Stoke-on-Trent. 'What would you call that colour – fresh grape, gentian, soft violet?'

'Er ... purple,' replied Karen, with her usual simplicity.

'And you really think it would suit me?'

'Definitely. When you've been around as many gay men as I have, you get to learn a thing or two about colour coordination.' Karen sighed nostalgically. 'I know selling up was the right thing to do, but sometimes I do miss my boys ...'

'What boys?' puzzled Minette.

Karen laughed. 'From the guest house. The pink economy's huge up there, you know; once word got around, we almost always had a house full, even in the off-season. They used to come back year after year. And they were such good company.'

Minette nodded in empathy. 'Yes, it's funny how you complain when you have a house full of noisy young men, dropping their dirty laundry all over the place and eating you out of house and home. And then suddenly they're gone.'

'And you wish they weren't.'

'Exactly.'

'Well,' pointed out Karen, 'there's not much point in sitting here moping, is there? Why don't we get out there and have a bit of fun?'

'Out where?'

'On the town! You've got dozens of nightclubs and restaurants and trendy bars here, why don't we go out and sample a few?'

Minette was aghast. 'You can't go out, you've got a broken leg!'

'That's what the crutches are for.'

'What if something happens?'

'That's what I'm hoping! If I don't do something soon, I'm going to go potty.'

'But I've never been to a nightclub in my life!'

318

'Then it's high time you did,' declared Karen. 'Why don't you go and get your glad rags on, and I'll phone for a taxi?'

Minette wrangled forlornly, but there was a vein of steel in Karen that she hadn't encountered before. And two minutes later, she was heading upstairs in search of some black devoré trousers she'd let Alan persuade her to buy in a moment of weakness.

She'd only got as far as the third step when Karen called her back. 'Minette, come and look at this!'

Minette reappeared in the doorway. 'What, dear?'

'On the local news, look – the young chap they're pushing into that police van. Isn't he that boy Joe went to school with?'

Gary was in an excellent mood. He'd just been promoted, he had half a dozen hot babes fighting over him, and tonight he was going to make a fortune at the Phat Phandango Club.

All he had to do was nip over to the Meadows Estate and pick up his order from Trevor.

He whistled as he strolled past the terraced council houses, with their identical concrete porches, and headed for Soweto House. The estate was a much better place now the troublemakers had been 'encouraged' to move on, and Gary was proud to have played a small part in that.

You couldn't let people go telling tales to the police, getting in the way of a man and his livelihood; but a brick or two through the window or a lighted rag through the letter box always made them see sense in the end. Yes, it was a much better place now. Unless, of course, you had to live here; but that wasn't a problem Gary would ever have to face.

Turning in through the front door of Soweto House, he climbed the stairs to the first floor and banged on the door of Flat 10. 'Trevor? It's me, Gaz.'

Bolts scraped back, chains jangled and a moment later the door opened. Trevor was a pallid, wobbly-arsed man with tattoos and a BO problem, but he was one hundred per cent reliable and that was all that mattered to Gary. 'Got the money?'

Gary patted his jacket pocket. 'Show me the stuff first.'

Trevor disappeared and returned with a plastic carrier bag. 'Five grand's worth.' He opened the bag to reveal the contents. 'Best quality, like we agreed.'

'Better be.' Gary was just reaching into his inside pocket for the cash when all hell was let loose. It happened so fast that at first his brain couldn't quite adjust to events– people running along the landing, other people shouting, doors slamming and – oh fuck – a whole lot of police uniforms.

It wasn't until his face was slammed into the wall and his arms almost wrenched out of their sockets that he realised this wasn't some kind of drug-induced trip. There really was a gun in his ribs, Trevor really was face-down on his own doormat, and somebody really was intoning: 'I am arresting you for possession of Class A drugs, with intent to supply.'

'I can't believe it.' Rozzer shook his head slowly and switched off the TV. 'I mean, I always knew he was stupid enough to take the stuff, but getting himself arrested for drug dealing . . .'

Linda hugged her cardigan to her thin shoulders. 'I told you he was bad news,' she reminded him.

He looked up. 'You knew, didn't you? You must have seen him around the estate . . . why didn't you say?'

She shrugged. 'He was your mate, I thought you might throw us out. Besides, telling tales on people had got me and Sara-Jane into enough trouble already. What was the point?'

'I wouldn't throw you out. Surely you know that.'

She leaned against the doorpost. 'That's not what you said when Sara-Jane was sick on your sofa,' she reminded him.

'That was two days after you moved in! I was a bit shell-shocked.'

'Well,' said Linda, 'now the police have raided the estate and arrested all the dealers, I guess it's going to be safe for us to think about moving back.'

Linda's words hit Rozzer like five thousand volts of ball lightning. 'Go back? You can't go back!'

She cocked her head on one side. 'Why not?'

'Because . . .' His mouth turned instantly to sandpaper, the way it did every time he tried to tell Linda anything of the way he felt. 'Because I don't want you to, that's why.'

She came towards him and lowered herself slowly into the armchair beside his. 'And why would you not want us to go? You'd have your flat to yourself again and everything.'

It was now or never. Rozzer grabbed the nearest source of relief he could find - a vase of carnations - and took a massive swig.

320

'Because ... I love you,' he blurted out as rivulets of foul-tasting water ran down his chin. Linda said nothing. 'It's OK, I've finished,' he added helpfully. 'You can laugh in my face now.'

And she could. But she didn't.

Minette directed a stern gaze at Karen in the rear-view mirror. 'You know what you are, don't you?'

Karen settled herself comfortably on the back seat. 'Go on, tell me.'

'You're a bad influence! I don't know *what* Alan must have thought of me the other night, coming home at one in the morning smelling of drink.'

'I don't suppose he thought anything much, he was asleep.'

'All the same, I *know* he must have smelled it on my breath the next morning. Whatever was I thinking of?'

'Did you enjoy yourself?'

'That's not the point, Karen.'

'Yes it is. Did you enjoy yourself?'

'Well ... yes,' admitted Minette. 'But I'm a middle-aged married woman! I can't just go gadding about enjoying myself willy-nilly!'

'Why not? I don't remember anything in the marriage vows about being bored rigid for the rest of your life.'

Minette flailed about for some sort of self-justification. 'It's different for you, you're not on the church flower rota!'

Karen mimed banging her head in frustration. 'For goodness' sake, Minette, you didn't do anybody any harm, did you? I don't think they excommunicate you for two port and lemons and a couple of dances round your handbag.'

'*Anyway,*' said Minette with an emphasis clearly intended to bring the topic to a close, 'we're here. Are you coming in or staying in the car with the dog?'

'Oh, coming in, definitely. Come on, Pepe, we're going to see Emma and Joe.'

'I was going to leave him here.' The woolly pooch slobbered over Karen's face enthusiastically, releasing a cloud of evil-smelling breath into the car. 'Ugh, I wouldn't let him do that, if I were you. Dogs have germs.'

'That's OK, so have I,' replied Karen brightly. 'And you can't leave him in the car in this heat. Besides, he's so sweet.'

'Sweet?' Minette contemplated the dog's vacuous, drooling face in the mirror. 'You're as daft as Alan.'

'Cool plaster cast, Mrs C,' remarked Joe approvingly as his mother-in-law stumped into the living room on her crutches.

Karen beamed. 'I had some yellow emulsion left over from doing the kitchen. And the spots are some Day-glo stickers I found at the back of a cupboard. At least it's a conversation piece.'

'Emma, your mother is incorrigible,' declared Minette. 'She has the mind of a hyperactive thirteen-year-old.'

'See?' Karen flopped, panting, onto the white settee. 'I told you she likes me. Do we get a cup of tea? I swear that staircase gets longer.'

'You should take the lift, Mum,' scolded Emma.

'Tell me about it,' retorted Minette. 'It's in one ear and out the other. She wants to try sky-diving, you know.'

'Is that wise?' asked Joe in concern.

Karen laughed. 'Would it be any fun if it was?'

'Anyway. 'Minette sat down next to Karen, smoothing her skirt neatly over her knees, 'I've come for my hat. You know, the grey feathered one I lent you for the country-house weekend. You don't still need it, do you?'

Emma suppressed an urge to punch the air and shout, 'At last.'

'No, no, that's absolutely fine. I got it out and gave it a brush as soon as I knew you were coming – it's on the dressing table in the bedroom.'

'Good. I've sort of promised it to my friend from the Ladies' Luncheon Circle, for the Mayor's summer barbecue. She was telling me about this pearl-grey cocktail dress she has, and I was thinking if she . . .' Minette's voice tailed off. 'What in the name of heaven has that dog done!'

'Oh my God.' Emma saw the smirk developing on Joe's face, and clapped a hand over his mouth.

In the doorway stood an apricot-coloured woolly thing, with what looked like grey streamers trailing from its drooling jaws. Around its neck, arranged in the manner of a decrepit horse-collar, were the remains of what might once have been a rather expensive hat.

But only Minette was looking at Pepe the poodle. Everybody else was looking at Minette, waiting for the inevitable explosion.

And sure enough, it came. White as a sheet, pencilled eyebrows vanishing under her bristling hairline, Minette opened her mouth wide and ...

Laughed.

It was such an unexpected sound that Pepe immediately took fright, legged it to the bathroom and hid behind the shower curtain. Emma was so startled that she very nearly joined him.

The next day, Joe left early for a course and Emma wasn't on duty till lunchtime, so she indulged herself in a nice lie-in. She was luxuriating in the bath when her mobile rang, and left a trail of curses and bubbles across the hall as she lunged for her handbag before the ringing stopped.

'Yes?'

'Emma. You haven't called me in such a long time.'

Her blood froze and the phone felt like ice in her hand. 'Richard, I told you not to contact me any more.'

'Yes, I know. And I understand why.'

His voice was soothing, reasonable even. 'You do?'

'Of course. It's because you're afraid of your husband, of what he'll do if you tell him about us.'

'For the last time, there is no us!'

'Now you know that's not true, and so do I. You want me as much as I want you, but he's just got to be told, Emma, there's no way round it.'

She felt sick to the pit of her stomach. 'Go away Richard, go away, you're crazy!'

He carried on as if she hadn't said a word. 'So I thought, why don't I give you another week or so, and if you haven't told him by then, perhaps I'll take a trip up to Birmingham and have a little chat with Joe? How does that sound?'

'Don't you dare, don't you bloody dare!'

Ice-cold and dripping water, she switched off the phone and hurled it against the bedroom wall. Richard was crazy, un-stoppable. What the hell was she going to do?

37

'Emma. Emma, what on earth's got into you?'

A hand fell on Emma's shoulder and she started as if someone had drenched her in ice water. 'Nothing's got into me,' she snapped, 'what do you mean?'

Zara persisted. 'That wasn't normal saline you were putting up, that was glucose,' she said, lowering her voice and thrusting the bag under Emma's nose. 'Are you trying to kill somebody?'

A wave of horror washed over Emma. 'Oh God, I didn't ... did I?'

'It's OK, I took it down, no harm done. But I think you and I need to have a little talk, don't you?' Without waiting for an answer, she announced to anyone who might be interested that 'Nurse Sheridan is coming to help me with a patient in the plaster room.'

If the closed door offered relative security, it also cut off Emma's escape route. 'I'll be all right,' she pleaded. 'Maybe I should go home sick, I've just got something on my mind.'

She looked up at Zara hopefully, but that hope was misplaced. 'If you think I'm taking that for an answer, you must really think I'm a prat,' Zara commented. 'I'm the one who makes mistakes around here, not you! Look, I don't want to pry, I'm just trying to help.'

'Why would you want to help me?'

'You helped me when I was down,' Zara reminded her. 'Doesn't one good turn deserve another?'

The quiet friendliness in Zara's voice was just too much to bear. It started as a single tear, forcing its way between Emma's eyelids, then the storm broke and suddenly there were salty rivers running down her cheeks. 'I've done something terrible,' she sobbed as she sat in the treatment chair, 'and now I'm going to get what I deserve.'

Zara was on her haunches beside the chair, her chin resting on the arm. 'Hey, it sounds to me like you're being a little harsh on yourself.'

'You don't know what I've done.'

'So tell me.'

And, to her own immense surprise, Emma did. In every excruciating, shameful detail. 'You see, it's all my own fault and now there's nothing I can do about it and everything's ruined and I love him so much ...'

'Here.' Zara grabbed a handful of wipes from a box on the nearest shelf. 'Big blow, you'll feel better.'

'Why are you being nice to me? Why aren't you slagging me off?'

Zara stood up, looked round for something to sit on and opted for an abandoned wheelchair in the corner. 'Let me tell you something. A story. About me.'

'What's this got to do with my problem?'

'Just listen. A long time ago, when Joe and I were going out together, everybody thought we were the perfect couple, didn't they?' Emma nodded. 'And we weren't, and you know why. But do you know why we split up?'

'Joe ended it ... he said you'd drifted apart or something.'

Zara smiled. 'Actually, it wasn't quite like that. I got drunk at a party and two-timed him, and then I felt so guilty I told him about it. The only thing I didn't tell him was that I cheated on him with another girl. I really don't think Joe could have coped with that.

'Anyhow, he wanted us to carry on seeing each other but I said no, it's run its course, let's just be friends. He accepted that; he didn't need to know the rest. And I guess, in a way, it's made him better to see me on my own, like I've never met another man who matched up to him.'

Emma smiled through her tears. 'That's definitely what Minette thinks. She's still half convinced Joe's going to admit he's made a horrible mistake and run off with you instead. But what's this got to do with me and Joe?'

'Everything.' Zara picked at a bit of chipped nail varnish.

'Honesty's a great thing, Emma, but not all the time. Sometimes telling people everything is the worst thing you can do.'

'But if I don't tell him, Richard says he will!'

'He might be bluffing. Or Joe might not believe him.'

'And the moon might be made of green cheese.'

'Then there's only one thing you can do: stop Richard telling him.'

'How on earth do I do that?' demanded Emma.

Zara sighed and stood up. 'That's for you to decide – sorry if that sounds like a cop-out, but it's true. But for the record, I won't say a word about any of this to anyone else. You're not the only one around here who knows how to keep their mouth shut.'

That night, Emma huddled in a miserable ball on the sofa and waited for Armageddon to arrive. It didn't, but Rozzer did – bearing a copy of the evening paper.

'Hey, have you seen page six of the *Courant*?'

'Gary's not in again, is he? Joe's still really cut up about the drug dealing thing.'

'Not him, no.' Rozzer pointed to a smallish headline: CHELT MAN FOUND. Look, it's about Will Carter – isn't he the one Joe knows, who walked out on his wife and kid?'

'Oh, him. Yes.' Deep down, Emma felt a kind of dulled sympathy for Kathy and Will, but overlaying everything like a big black oil slick was the horrible fear of what Richard was going to do. 'What about him?'

'Apparently the police found him in Southend, working as a bingo-caller. Had some kind of breakdown, so they say. 'Course, the really sad thing is, he wants to go home but she won't have him back and …' Rozzer stopped talking and waved a hand in front of Emma's unseeing eyes. 'Anybody at home?'

'What? Sorry, what were you saying?'

'Nothing that important, I'll leave the article for you to read.' Rozzer laid the paper down on the hall table. 'Really I stopped by to tell you I got the job – they're starting me in a month's time.'

'Great,' said Emma. 'I'm really pleased for you.'

'Thanks for your help, you know, with the application form and that.'

'No problem.'

'I'll be on my first infestation in no time.'

'Yeah. Whatever.'

By now, Rozzer was thoroughly spooked. He'd never seen Emma like this before. He'd once seen her blind drunk, doing handstands at a party in a zebra-print thong, but never anything like this. This was not Emma at all.

'Are you all right?' he asked.

'Yes, of course I am.' She smiled. 'Why wouldn't I be?'

'Good question, Em, you tell me.'

She avoided his full-on gaze. 'Oh you know, Joe and I have had a few teething problems, we're both working hard ...'

'I'm worried about you, Emma. I'm worried about Joe too, but I'm really worried about you. If you've got any dragons you want fighting, you know where to come, don't you?'

'I do.' She couldn't help smiling at his earnest face. 'Linda's struck lucky with you.'

Rozzer shuffled his feet embarrassedly. 'We're supposed to be talking about you, remember?'

'There's absolutely no need to worry, honestly,' she assured him with the last of her energy.

Rozzer made to leave, but at the last minute turned back. 'Whatever it is you're doing, Emma, you need to stop it right away. Because it's making you unhappy, and I can't bear to see that.'

'Oh Rozzer ...'

'And if Joe loves you half as much as he ought to, he won't be able to bear it either.'

For a few minutes after Rozzer had left, Emma stood staring at the door, his words echoing round and round inside her head. And something in those words stealthily tripped a switch, short-circuiting the paralysis of fear.

It's no good just standing here, waiting for the inevitable to happen, she told herself. That's exactly what he expects me to do; do that, and he's controlling you. Is that what you want?

She supplied her own answer. Picking up the phone, she punched in a familiar number. 'Mickey? It's me. Did you mean what you said about coming up here and sorting out Richard? Great. Well, whatever you've got planned, it'd better bloody work.

'Fast.'

38

Emma stood in the bedroom of the B&B where Mickey and Gavin were staying, shaking from head to foot. 'I don't know if I can go through with this.'

'Of course you can,' Mickey replied sternly. 'I haven't come all this way to have you chicken out on me. What do you reckon to the suit?' She pirouetted to give Emma the full benefit.

'Very ... grey.'

'Good. And the specs?' She balanced them on the end of her nose.

'No, lose the specs, you look like Buddy Holly.'

Gavin emerged from the tiny bathroom like a very large moth from a cocoon several sizes too small. 'Will I do like this?'

Squeezed into the black suit he had been given the last time he played in a cup final at the Cardiff Millennium Stadium, Gavin looked more monumental than ever: a kind of curly-haired mausoleum on legs, crossed with a lowland gorilla.

'Perfect,' declared Mickey. 'Every inch the successful businessman.'

'Mickey,' protested Emma, 'he looks like he ought to be running a dodgy debt collection agency.'

'And would you find such a person ... intimidating?'

'Of course I would!'

'Then I rest my case. Come on, Emma – and remember he's not Gavin, he's Joe. But I want him back afterwards, OK?'

'Fine. The question is, will Joe want me?'

As a rule, the lane outside Richard's rented cottage was one of the most peaceful spots in Gloucestershire. Birds twittered, butterflies played kiss-chase among the hollyhocks, the occasional cow lowed prettily in the distance.

But not today. Today, a strident blonde in high heels was broadcasting Richard Claybourne's shortcomings to everybody within a five-mile radius.

'Just you get out here, you spineless little shit!' She hammered on the door then went to the front window and pressed her face up against the glass. 'It's no good hiding in there, I can stay here all day if I have to.'

After a few seconds, the front door opened a few inches. 'For God's sake, Corinne, what do you want from me?'

This was possibly not the right thing to say. The blonde hurled herself at the door, pushed it open and practically dragged Richard out into the daylight. No longer Mr Self-Assured, he looked more like a hunted weasel, run to ground.

'What do I want? *What do I want!* What the hell do you think I want, Richard? Well, for a start-off I want what's owing to me.'

'I'd love to help you out, you know I would, but what with the bad leg there's not much money coming in and—'

'Don't give me that crap! It took me three months to track you down to Cheltenham, and OK, when I did you were in hospital, so maybe you couldn't afford to pay up. But you've got work now, good teaching work – yes, Richard, I've been asking around – and I've had enough of your pathetic excuses.'

He tried backing away, but made the mistake of letting her trap him between the drainpipe and the wall. 'Corinne, listen ...'

'No, *you* listen. Let's get this straight, you sick fuck, this money isn't for me, it's for your daughter.' She brandished a handful of photographs under his nose. 'Yes, the daughter you've never seen because you're still trying to make out she isn't yours. My God, you've got a nerve. You pursue me, you break up my marriage, you get me pregnant, you bugger off and leave me ... and when the chickens come home to roost, you haven't even got the dignity to pay your way.' She snarled in his face. 'I should've listened to your ex – at least she had the sense to throw you out on the street.'

'Don't do this, Corinne. You know how much you still mean to me, maybe we could try again ...?'

'Nice try, scumbag.' He flinched as she threw the photos in his face. 'I'll be back next week. With the man from the CSA.'

*

Sitting just round the corner, in the car, Emma, Gavin and Mickey had been listening with a kind of horrified fascination.

'Oh my God,' breathed Emma, 'did you hear what she said?' Emma watched as the blonde stalked off and drove away in her car, certain that she recognised her from somewhere but unable to think where.

'I could hardly avoid it,' replied Mickey drily. 'Sounds like seducing married women's a favourite hobby of his.' She saw Emma wince. 'Sorry, Em, I didn't mean it to sound like that, but face it, this guy's slime from a particularly smelly pond.'

Gavin leaned forward into the gap between the front seats. 'Enough of this idle chit-chat,' he said, cracking his knuckles with relish, 'when do I get to rearrange his face?'

Richard could hardly believe his eyes. He'd only just escaped from the ghost of liaisons past when a second car drew up in front of the cottage. It all happened so swiftly that he didn't have time to dodge back inside and slam the door.

'Good morning,' said Mickey, walking up the front path. 'Michaela Jones, solicitor for Mrs Emma Sheridan.' She flashed a printed card before his eyes. 'Stalking, harassment, blackmail ... these are serious matters, Mr Claybourne.'

Richard froze. 'What do you mean? I haven't done anything.'

'Indeed? My client sees things rather differently, and of course she has kept recordings of all your voicemails. We shall have to see what a jury makes of them.'

Emma watched from the car, her stomach churning. How could I ever have fancied that man? she asked herself. I thought he was so cool, so clever, so bohemian – and he's nothing. Nothing at all.

A look of real panic crossed Richard's face. 'Hey, hang on ... I'm sure there's been some misunderstanding, I never meant to ...' He swallowed. 'Can't we come to some arrangement?'

'I don't know about that,' replied Emma, getting out of the car. 'You'll have to ask Joe.'

It was almost worth the fear and shame she'd been through, just to see the look of utter terror on Richard's face as Gavin emerged from the back seat, slowly unfolding to his full six foot six of solid, bone-crunching muscle.

'That's ... your *husband*?'

Emma slipped her arm lovingly through Gavin's. 'I knew how

much you wanted to meet Joe, and I think Joe's got a few things he wants to say to you, haven't you, Joe?'

Gavin smiled grimly, revealing a row of missing teeth. 'Let's go inside,' he suggested, 'I'd hate to get blood all over these nice begonias.'

'Are you all right? You look like you've seen a ghost,' said Mickey.

'I have,' replied Emma. 'That blonde woman . . . I knew I recognised her. She visited Richard when he was in hospital, he told me he did freelance work for her!'

'Yes, well, he'd tell you anything, that much is clear. I think I'd better drive us back. Be a good girl and get in for Auntie Mickey.'

Emma didn't protest. She let herself be pushed into the passenger seat and just sat there like a dollop of steamed pudding, too shaken to do anything, too overwhelmed even to think straight.

They were halfway back to town before she felt even slightly normal. 'I can't believe it,' she whispered. 'I can't believe I ever felt anything but contempt for a man like that. How could I have nearly . . .?' She hung her head.

'Stop punishing yourself,' said Mickey. 'The man's an expert at getting women to fall at his feet. And anyway, it wasn't all your fault, Joe was neglecting you.'

'Well, maybe . . . but that's no excuse, is it?'

Gavin peeled off his suit jacket and threw it onto the seat beside him. 'I'm just sorry I didn't get to hit him. God knows, he deserved it.'

'You didn't need to,' pointed out Mickey. 'He was that scared he'd have cut his own head off if you'd told him to.'

They arrived outside the guest house where Mickey and Gavin were staying.

'Thank you,' said Emma. 'Both of you. For everything.'

'No probs,' Gavin answered her with a grin.

'It's all over now, you can put it behind you.' Mickey smiled. 'And Joe need never know anything about it.'

Unless I tell him, thought Emma; and her conscience was telling her that maybe she ought.

The following evening, as Emma was preparing dinner, the phone rang. It was Mickey.

'He's gone,' she announced.

Emma dropped the potato peeler. 'What?'

'Slimeball, he's upped sticks and legged it. Gavin ... er ... popped round to the cottage to have another quiet little word with him, before we drove back to London, and the bugger has vanished.'

'No!'

'Honest to God. The place is deserted, and there's a "To Let" sign outside. Looks like the CSA are going to have another hunt on their hands.'

For quite a long time after Mickey had rung off, Emma sat on a stool in the middle of the kitchen, just gazing into space and trying to get used to the idea of a life that didn't have Richard Claybourne in it; a life without shadows. But, gone or not, she had a feeling she was going to be looking back over her shoulder for a long time to come.

Later, as Joe washed and changed and the sauce was reheating in the microwave, Emma placed the last dish on the dining-room table.

It was a beautiful table, with the best china and a crisp white cloth; a setting for the kind of spectacular meal she'd cooked in the days when they only saw each other every other weekend, and every moment together was something precious, to be savoured. Tonight felt like one of those times, fragile and laden with significance.

I can't do it, she told herself as Joe came back into the room. I can't tell him, and yet I have to. How can I get rid of this guilt if I don't tell Joe what happened with Richard? Don't be an idiot, snapped the devil on her other shoulder; why did you go through that pantomime with Mickey and Gavin if you're going to turn round and ruin everything for yourself?

Oh God, what do I do? What do I do?

'This is amazing,' said Joe, lifting the lid on Emma's confit of duck with white truffles. 'Must have cost a fortune – are we celebrating something?'

'Er ... no.' Come on, come on, she told herself. Say something if you're going to.

'More wine?'

Dutch courage. 'Yes please.'

Joe topped up his own glass and took a long drink. 'Actually,' they both said simultaneously. Joe laughed, but sounded tense. 'You first.'

'No, you. It's nothing important.'

'OK then. Actually, I've got something to tell you. It'll be on the news tomorrow anyway.' He looked down at the tablecloth. 'The takeover's going through. Sir Stanley's selling out to First Quality Foods.'

'That big Australian company?' Joe nodded. 'And what does that mean ... for you?'

He reached across the table and took her hand. 'We've all lost our jobs – all the senior and regional managers. Emma, I'm so sorry; I never meant to let you down like this.'

She saw the misery in his eyes and knew she couldn't add to it, not just for the satisfaction of easing her own guilty conscience. If she had to keep some things to herself forever, well, maybe that was her punishment.

'You haven't let me down,' she assured him. 'It's not your fault. And besides, I'm really proud of you!'

'You are?'

'Of course I am. Anyway, there are lots of other companies out there who'd jump at the chance to employ someone as talented as you.'

Joe fiddled with his napkin. 'As a matter of fact,' he began, 'one company has made me an offer.'

Emma beamed. 'There you are! Who is it – one of the other big UK supermarket chains?'

'Kind of. First Quality Foods are looking for a young manager to help set up and run a chain of mini-markets. It's a great opportunity, lots of autonomy and scope for creative thinking.'

'Sounds good.' She nodded. 'So what's the catch?'

'The job's in Australia.'

39

For Emma, the next two days at work were like sleepwalking. She managed to do her job without harming anybody, but the greater part of her brain was endlessly mulling over what Joe had said.

'Australia? Wow.' Lawrence offered her a chocolate biscuit from the tin marked 'bandages' in his desk drawer. 'Golden bodies on Bondi Beach, I wouldn't mind a bit of that.'

'I don't know about Bondi Beach,' replied Emma. 'From what Joe says, it's more about dusty little outback towns. He seems to think I can just jump up and say, "let's go," but I can't get my head round it . . .'

'So what do your parents think? Ah,' said Lawrence, 'you haven't told them, have you?'

'Parents, that's another thing,' sighed Emma. 'My mum's ill, and she'll be moving back into her own flat soon – I can't just jet off to the other side of the world and leave her to fend for herself, can I? It's not as if I've even got any brothers or sisters to help keep an eye on her.'

'Well, darling,' said Lawrence, 'it's none of my business but won't you feel better once you've made a decision, whatever that decision turns out to be?'

'Not if it's the wrong one.'

'I'm not so sure there's such a thing as a wrong decision. At any rate, being in limbo is the worst thing of all. Listen to Uncle Lawrence, darling, 'cause believe me I should know.'

Emma helped herself to another biscuit. 'Has something happened with Duncan?'

'No, something has happened *without* Duncan. He is out of my

334

life, deleted, abolished, officially defunct. He packed his bags and left last week, and he's not coming back.'

'Oh Lawrence, I'm so sorry.'

'Don't be. I was the one who told him not to. I've had enough of him shagging his way through Cheltenham while muggins stays in and irons his Calvin Kleins.'

'So you're on your own now, then? Isn't that lonely?'

'Not exactly.' He winked. 'Actually, I'm shacked up with a rather attractive pregnant young woman.' Emma's mouth fell open. 'And before you start a rumour, sorry but it's not mine. It's Duncan's, not that he's got any interest in its well-being.'

'The mother of Duncan's baby's living with you? But I thought you said—'

'Emma, love, I could hardly see her out on the street, could I? And she's got nobody now, you know. After all that crap about us adopting the baby, Duncan turned round and practically told the girl to get rid of it.'

'That's awful!'

'Tell me about it. God knows, it's bad enough having to admit you've had Duncan as a boyfriend. Having his baby must be the last straw. Besides, she's a nice girl and it's somebody to watch *Family Affairs* with.'

Lawrence's exotic home life had always had the power to distract Emma from her own woes, and it hadn't let her down this time. 'So how long are you going to let her stay? Till the baby's born?'

He shrugged. 'Who knows? She's going to need some support, and well, I always did fancy myself as a kind of prodigal uncle. We'll just play it by ear, I guess. But enough of me, what are we going to do with you, young lady?'

Emma pulled a face. 'Write me off as a hopeless case?'

'No hopeless cases in *my* department, Nurse Sheridan. But you've certainly got some tough decisions to make, and guess what, I'm about to make them tougher.'

'How?' she puzzled.

'I had a phone call from Personnel this morning. They want to interview you for the nurse coordinator post next Tuesday – and between you and me, I've heard on the grapevine that it's a short-list of one.'

*

Zara stopped her as she was coming out of Lawrence's office. 'Is it true?'

'Is what true?'

'About you and Joe emigrating to Australia.'

Emma could scarcely believe her ears. All you had to do in this department was *think* about something, and five minutes later everybody knew all about it. 'No, it isn't,' she replied. 'Well, not yet, anyway; it's just a possibility. Who told you?' she added.

'One of the theatre porters. Graham, I think he's called. Didn't you tell him then?'

'I didn't think I'd told anybody!' Emma felt distinctly rattled. It was just about possible to cope with this crazy situation as long as she could keep it to herself, mull it over in the privacy of her own thoughts; but if everybody else knew, it was tantamount to having an audience of thousands, constantly demanding to know if she'd made her decision. 'Anyway, I've just found out I've got an interview for the nurse coordinator post next week, so that's given me something extra to think about.

'Talking of telling people things,' she added, 'have you...?'

Zara shook her head. 'I just can't do it. I look at her and I can sense she's not happy with the way she's living, that all this "happy families" stuff is just playing a part; but what if I'm imagining it because that's what I want to see?'

'That's the chance you take, I guess.'

'But I'm not going to take it. I'm not going to risk ruining her life – and it's not just hers or her husband's either, it's her kids'. But on the other hand I can't just do nothing, either. That's why I'm leaving.'

This is a day of surprises, thought Emma. And the biggest surprise of all is that I'm sad to hear she's going. 'Leaving? But what about your training?'

'What's the point of training for something you're not really any good at?' pointed out Zara. 'Mum and Dad will just have to cope with not having a surgeon for a daughter. If I stayed here,' she laughed, 'I'd probably cut the wrong bit off some poor patient and end up getting sued!'

They walked together as far as the reception desk. 'I'm going to do some locum work for a while, then think about what I want to do next. The great thing is, it'll be what *I* want to do, not what anybody else wants for me. You should think about that,' she added with a sober look at Emma. 'Don't do anything if it's going to make you unhappy – you won't be doing Joe any favours.'

Sunita came bustling up and nipped behind the desk. 'Emma, just the person I've been looking for! These arrived for you.' Stooping down, when she straightened up her arms were filled with a gigantic bouquet of dark-red damask roses. 'Who's got a secret admirer then?'

Emma blanched. Her heart lurched in her chest. Please God no, not again. This isn't supposed to happen any more. Afraid even to touch the flowers, she took a step back.

Sunita winked. 'Come on, don't be shy. Let's have a read of the card!'

Emma looked at Zara, who seemed to understand. 'I'll get it.' She reached in among the flowers for the little white envelope, and tore it open.

'What does it say?' demanded Emma, hardly able to breathe.

'It says, "Australia's not important, but you are. Say the word and we'll stay. With all my love for always ... Joe."'

'Goodness me,' said Karen, running her finger along the top of her kitchen work surface. 'I don't think I've ever seen so much dust in my life – and for me that's saying something!'

It was the first time she'd gone back to her flat in Gloucester since the accident. Even now her ankle was still too weak for her to drive, and Alan had had to bring her over. 'Ah well, I'm sure with a bit of elbow grease it won't take too long to smarten everything up again. I can't put it off forever.'

Minette dug Alan in the ribs. 'Yes, you can. Can't she, Alan?'

'All right, Minette, give me a chance.' Alan cleared his throat. 'What Minette's trying to say is, you don't have to clean this place at all if you don't want.'

'You mean, you'll help me?' Karen beamed. 'Oh, that's really kind of you, I must admit I'd appreciate a hand with some of the heavy stuff, and—'

Alan cut her off. 'No, not that. She means if you want to, you can move in with us.'

Karen looked at Alan, then at Minette. 'You mean ... permanently?' They nodded. 'No, I couldn't! I've already imposed on you for far too long, you must be sick to the back teeth of me already.'

337

'Karen –'

'I mean, getting under your feet and cluttering up the annexe and everything.'

Minette raised her voice to the one she used on the Johnson twins at Sunday School. 'For goodness' sake Karen, will you stop babbling and listen?' Karen's mouth closed in surprise. 'It just so happens that having you around is the most interesting thing that's happened to me in years.'

'It is? Good grief.'

'Yes, I know, pathetic, isn't it. Anyhow, it's obvious that neither of us wants to put any more stress on Joe and Emma. And seeing as we were thinking of renting out the annexe come the autumn, why don't we keep it in the family?'

'Go on Karen, say yes,' urged Alan with a wink. 'Nobody else feeds us chocolate eclairs when Minette's back's turned. Do they, dog?'

Pepe gazed pleadingly into Karen's eyes, and licked her hand.

Joe was waiting for Emma in the drizzly car park when she came out of work that evening, her arms laden with roses.

'What on earth are you doing here?' she exclaimed. 'Aren't you supposed to be in Stoke-on-Trent?'

'As if I give a stuff about that! Sir Stanley lost any right to order me about the day he sold out. Anyhow, my loyalty's not to him, it's to you.' He slid his arms about her waist. 'Like it says on the card, you're the only thing that truly matters to me. God, I was a complete idiot not to realise that before. Can you forgive me, Squeaky?'

'Oh Joe, there's nothing to forgive.' She melted into his kiss, her heart touched more deeply by his tenderness than he could ever know. For she had come so close to losing him, to throwing all of this away. And now she began to glimpse a new Joe emerging out of the dark mist of dejection that had surrounded him for too long. A Joe who had, quite simply, grown up. She prayed that she had grown up too.

'Can we start again?' she asked him. 'Pretend it's our wedding day all over again, and this time get it right?'

He laughed softly, and all the raindrops on his eyelashes quivered. 'From now on, every day's going to be a new beginning. Just you wait and see. And I meant what I said about Australia, I don't care if it is a good job, I shouldn't act like your career means nothing.' He stroked her hair back from her forehead. 'Zara told me about your interview. Go for it, kid, I'm so proud of you.'

She caught his hand and carried it to her lips. 'When are we going?' she asked.

'Going where?'

'Australia, of course!' She smiled at the look on Joe's face. 'I turned the job down, Joe.'

'But—'

'You know what I just realised? Deep down I didn't want to do the job, I just wanted to see if I could get them to give it to me. That's hardly a valid reason to hold you back, is it, and besides,' she squinted up at the leaden sky, 'when's the last time we had a decent English summer?'

'What about your career?' Joe protested.

'They have sick people in Australia, don't they?' She slipped her arm through his. 'Come on, Joe, let's go home. I could do with an early night.'

'It's only half past eight!'

Their eyes met and they both burst out laughing. 'Actually,' she confided, 'I wasn't thinking about sleeping. Come on, tiger, let's see if I can still make you growl.'

Epilogue: three years later . . .

A lofty sun burned down on the dusty, baking airstrip, from out of a topaz-blue sky. As Joe stood beside the single-storey air terminal, the twin-engined plane landed lightly on the runway and taxied to a halt, its propellers gradually slowing to a standstill. The words 'Royal Flying Doctor Service' shone out from the plane's flank, through a shimmering heat haze.

After a couple of minutes, steps were pushed up against the door and the patient was brought out on a stretcher: a young girl with huge, surprised eyes, cradling the possible cause of that surprise - a tiny swaddled baby.

'Emma!' He waved to her as she came down the steps, tanned and healthy from the Australian sunshine, natural blonde streaks in her hair, her short-sleeved uniform shirt open at the neck.

As she saw him her mouth curved into a huge smile, and she said goodbye to the rest of the crew and came running across the tarmac to him. 'Joe! I thought you were going to be away until Wednesday.'

He swung her up in his arms. 'I was, but Craig's really pleased with what I've been doing at the Woomera store, and he said I wasn't taking enough holiday.'

Emma laughed. 'Can't imagine Sir Stanley ever saying that!'

'Too damn right, this is a whole different world. I can't believe how much more I've enjoyed working for Craig. Anyhow I thought, hey, if there's holiday on offer let's spend some quality time with my lovely wife and son. So I picked Kieran up from the nursery, and here we are!'

'Hello, Kieran.' Emma crouched down and gently lifted the

plump little child out of his pushchair. 'Have you been a good boy for Daddy?'

The baby gurgled. 'Of course he has,' laughed Joe. 'He's a Sheridan.'

'No he's not, he's *half* a Sheridan!'

'Yes, the good half! Just look at that noble nose.'

'And those dribbly lips and that fat little tummy ... hmm, yes, maybe you're right. He does take after your side of the family.' Emma settled him back in his chair and adjusted the parasol to keep the sun off his face. 'Do you think he'll ever forgive us?' she wondered as they strolled back towards the terminal building.

'What for?'

'Well, Roswell is an unusual middle name.'

'Roswell's an unusual bloke,' retorted Joe. 'Not many people can say they've won the National Vermin Control Award two years running. Or have a wife who's a kick-boxing teacher in her spare time.' He sighed nostalgically. 'I do miss him, you know.'

Emma nodded. 'Me too.'

'I even miss Gary sometimes.'

'Well I wouldn't go that far. Even if he is out of prison now. It's having family around that I really miss - a once-a-year visit's just not enough.'

'Oh, I don't know,' mused Joe with amusement. 'I should think a once-a-year dose of my mum would be enough for anybody.' He chuckled. 'What did you reckon to those photos Lawrence sent? Proud surrogate father or what?'

'Well, it's an unconventional family he's got there, but heck, it seems to work. Naomi's blooming and I've never seen a happier-looking kid in my life. It'd be nice to see them in the flesh some-time ...'

As they reached the building, they turned and gazed out across the ochre-coloured emptiness.

'Maybe we will,' said Joe.

Emma looked at him. 'Invite them over to stay, you mean?'

'Or go back and see them.' He took in a deep breath and let it out slowly.

'You know, these last three years in Australia have been fantastic.' He took Emma's hand and smiled at her with the same openness they'd shared when she was a kid of seventeen. 'Heck but I love you, Mrs Sheridan.'

341

They kissed, and in the distance somebody wolf-whistled. 'I love you too,' murmured Emma, and the hot Australian sun seemed to shine right into her heart.

'By the way,' Joe went on, 'Craig said they'll happily give me a permanent contract here if I want it.' They looked into each other's eyes. 'Do I want it, Em? Or do I want to take you and chubby-chops here back to damp, grey, cold old Blighty? It won't be so glam, but there's some kind of job back there if I want it.'

'If we don't go back home soon,' replied Emma, 'Kieran'll be wearing corks round his hat by the next time he sees his two grannies.'

'Besides,' said Joe, 'your mum says mine is threatening to take up paragliding, and that is something I *definitely* can't miss.'

'Will we regret it, do you think? Going back?'

Joe shook his head. 'You're my wife, Em, my home's wherever you are. It doesn't matter where we are, just that we're together. How could I ever regret anything as long as I'm doing it with you?'